# 9 LORDS
# OF NIGHT

## A NOVEL BY CESAR TORRES

FIRST EDITION

*Paperback design by Cesar Torres*

*Front cover illustration by Trevor Fraley*

ISBN: 1-7326953-0-X
ISBN-13: 978-1-7326953-0-6

*To Crispin. Cowabunga, today and always.*

# INTRODUCTION

A curious thing has happened to me in the past four years. I find myself being swept downward in a circular kind of motion, into a place that is both strange but familiar at the same time. It's a dizzying ride, thrilling and light, as if I were riding on the back of giant birds. I know the place where we are headed. It's a place at the end of a deep spiral. That place is called The Coil.

But the Coil has a much older name. The Aztec empire called it Mictlán, a place the Aztecs (also known as the Mexica) considered just as real as you and I consider the Eiffel Tower today. To the Aztec culture and mind, this was the underworld, a place of darkness where souls traveled on their journey after physical death. Mictlán, or The Coil, is a place I created in my debut novel *13 Secret Cities*, which published in 2014. In this vast canyon the size of millions of galaxies dwell gigantic snakes, pyramids made of talking flowers, and if you know how to get there, the dwelling place of the god and goddess of death.

Today you hold in your hands the sequel to *13 Secret Cities*, titled *9 Lords of Night*. And I am proud to inform you that this is officially now a series that will follow this story across several novels and other artistic works. It is for this reason that I have officially named this series The Coil.

Now that I have you here, at the precipice, I want you to follow me. Relax, you'll get used to the darkness. Your eyes will adjust. I am not sure if you may like the people and creatures you encounter, but they for sure will not want to let *you* go.

Cesar Torres
Chicago, August 2018

## ACKNOWLEDGMENTS

This book would not have been possible without the love and support of what has now become the team behind Solar Six Books and my novels.

First, I want to thank my parents, for believing in me when no one else could, or would. They know the path I have chosen as an artist, and I wish all parents could let their children fly free the way they have. I also want to thank the following Patreon subscribers who have stuck with me over time: Gregory Meyers, who gets his name used as a new character in *9 Lords of Night* because of his level of sponsorship. Additional thanks to sponsors Norma Carmona, Angelica Carmona, Beth Saba, Darrick Jackson, Todd Fleming, and Matthew Saba.

I also want to thank all my first readers, starting with Rob Tolar, Eyre Price and Matt Saba, who have been there to witness the evolution of my work over the years, and who have provided key feedback throughout. A story has to move, yo. My conversations with Julie Callahan were also invaluable in developing this novel. She is a true inspiration. Huge thanks also to readers Tom Malinowski, Deborah Douglas, Carla Eboh and Melissa Bright.

# CONTENTS

# DAY 1
## MONDAY OCTOBER 20, 2025

## MANHATTAN
### 3:59 AM ET

Marlene Grue drifted in a dreamless dark, until a shriek woke her up. Night greeted her.

The muscular body lying next to her changed shape, bulging and twisting beneath the sheets. It elongated with a violent thrust of a leg, then it shrank, and after a moment, it stopped moving. Its breathing rumbled, then whispered. Marlene patted the head through the white sheet.

And then the shriek returned, filling the high ceilings of her bedroom.

"Ignore it, baby. It's just my wife calling," Bryan croaked from under the sheet.

This bed was a sacred place for Marlene and Bryan. Under these linen sheets, she was no longer his manager at the law firm, and he was not her subordinate. Here they were equals, partners, inseparable.

Marlene kicked off the sheets and stood up. The breath of the central air conditioning made her skin break out in gooseflesh.

Phone calls at this time of night could only mean one thing: someone had died. She thought about her mother in Florida (Old Nessa as everyone called her), and how she stashed fifty-dollar bills

1

inside coffee cans in her house so she could keep up her cigarette habit without using credit cards. Maybe tonight, that shriek was the phone ringing, announcing Old Nessa's second stroke. This could be the fatal one, the final chapter in a long, complicated story of a woman who would never be satisfied with her husband, her daughters, or life itself.

*Could be.*

Or perhaps it was a call from Marlene's sister, Lilith. Maybe when Marlene picked up the line, Lilith would announce that her daughter Paris had been in a bad road accident. Paris would have slammed shots at a bar with friends, with no designated driver. Dead a twisted heap of metal at the bottom of a sharp turn in her college town. Paris would be slumped over the wheel of a Honda Civic, forever youthful. Marlene's favorite niece.

*Maybe.*

Or maybe the call was from Thaddeus's housekeeper, letting Marlene know that her ex-husband was finally dead from complications from diabetes. Of course, the real cause was *beneath* the diabetes: Thaddeus's never-ending relationship with Maker's Mark. If she picked up the line, she would learn that Thaddeus was dead, fat, and even in death, forever attached to Marlene's life like a shadow or a parasite.

She felt around the top of the dresser for her smartphone. She found the flat object and clicked the nonexistent button on its side. The device shifted and unfolded like a flower, revealing a tiny screen in its center. No messages, no calls. The ringer was turned off, and the phone was set to Do Not Disturb mode. The shriek was not coming from the device.

And next to her phone, Bryan's iPhone, also dark.

A third shriek cut through the silence.

"Where the hell is that coming from?" she said to herself.

Marlene stepped in front of the full-length mirror in her room, and she appreciated the way the night gave her black skin a bluish hue, like ink. Her legs were a little thicker in the thighs than they were ten years earlier, but they remained strong and elegant. Her flat stomach gave her a youthful veneer, but the truth was that she didn't feel as energetic as she did in her twenties. She shook hear her head in the black mirror and made her way back toward the bed.

Another shriek cut through the night. This time, the sharp

sound seemed to be coming from outside rather than inside the bedroom.

Marlene yanked the blinds at the center window. The cord fought her. She tugged a second time, and the blinds rose.

Light flooded her bedroom. Columbus Square sparkled in the distance, and the green canopy of Central Park spread out before her. The park's orange lights washed away the shadows in the room, and she waited in the silence, peering down at the winding taxicabs in the streets. The roar of the city, the car horns, the rip of wheels on asphalt — those sounds massaged her ears. She looked down, gasped and recoiled from the windowsill.

"Oh hell no," Marlene spat.

A bird perched on the ledge of the building, looking right up at Marlene, staring right *at her. Into her.*

The bird was easily the size of a turkey, or maybe even a vulture, and its plumage shimmered like jewels. Its head feathers sparkled with blue and gold, and its belly and back shone in a deep metallic scarlet, like red garland on the tree at Rockefeller Center. Even under the bluish LED lights of the city, it was clear this animal was no pigeon, sparrow, starling, or any city bird that she knew of. Its beak rounded over its face into a razor-sharp point, and she was grasping for the word, for the name to describe this creature, because she had seen an animal like this before — yes, a macaw! It was a fucking macaw!—and its eyes—its curious, uncanny eyes—glittered like pools of water under the moonlight.

But something was wrong with those eyes. Very wrong. It had two of them on each side of its head. And they looked wrong, corrupted, not of this world. Birds weren't supposed to have four eyes.

The creature opened its beak, shrieked, emitting the infernal ringtone that had woken Marlene up.

She tried batting the bird away with a hand, but it was much too large to be frightened off.

"Get the hell out of here," she said.

The bird craned its neck, widened its four eyes, and croaked a single word, silky and elongated:

"Marlene."

She stifled a scream as her blood ran cold.

## 4:17 AM ET

The bird's four eyes cascaded with pinpoints of light, like galaxies, solar systems, stars and asteroids. Marlene had never seen any animal in any zoo, or anywhere in the world, really, with eyes like these.

For a moment Marlene forgot who she was. She forgot *where* and *when* she was.

The animal smelled of pine needles and incense. Suddenly, Marlene genuflected. She did it reflectively, out of pure muscle memory, just like she had learned to do in her days in St. Vincent's School.

The bird cocked its head up toward Marlene and screamed its ringtone song. She could see that its mouth was not like the mouth of any macaw she had ever seen. Silvery barbs on the bird's tongue stood on end, as if it was lined with sewing needles of the shiniest metal. The needles bristled and squeaked like a rusty wheel.

"Marlene. Get your ass back to bed," Bryan shouted from inside the bedroom.

Something rough scraped Marlene's knee, and she lost her balance. She stared down at her hand and gasped when she saw what she had been doing.

Marlene was on hands and knees on the cement lip of the building. When had she crawled on her hands and knees along the ledge?

Her hair hung over the vast heights of her high-rise apartment, pointing down toward the sidewalk. If she lost her center of balance right now, she would topple twenty five stories to her death.

Below her, New York City spun like a roulette wheel, and nausea strummed inside her belly. The bird took a few slow steps toward her. Now that she was closer to it, she could see deep slits in its breast, like the gills on a shark. They opened and closed, as if it were breathing through them.

Marlene crawled backward toward the window and into her apartment. She genuflected once again, dazed.

"What do you want?" she said.

It only stared at her now, silent, as if her question had angered it.

She shut the window immediately and scurried back to the bed, and burrowed herself beneath the covers. After a few moments in which she tried to calm herself down, she peeked out from the blankets. The animal was still there at the window, staring at her through the glass.

Marlene's hands fumbled on Bryan's body. They found his shoulders, then his elbows, and she slid onto him to gave him a bear hug. His heartbeat was strong, slow, calm. She felt a little better.

"Bryan, you awake?"

"Now I am," he said. He rolled his athletic body onto hers.

"I need to make sure I'm not dreaming."

"Boo, you're not dreaming."

"Did you hear the phone ring earlier?"

"Yep yep. Told you, just ignore her."

"No it wasn't your wife. Your phone never rang."

Bryan grumbled. He kissed her once on the mouth, and he slid out of the bed. He stood naked, facing the windows. His erect posture and the way in which he pointed his feet straight out reminded her of divers at the Olympics. He had snapped fully awake. He turned on the light switch on the wall and drew back the curtains to let more of the city lights into the room.

"I do see something out there. Want me to take a look?"

"I told you. Should we call the super?"

"Honey, it's the middle of the night. And besides, look."

The bird had wandered into the center of the windows, as if it needed the people inside the apartment to view it. It turned around and looked out into Central Park. It spread its wings, and they unfurled to an impossible length, more than six feet from end to end. For a moment, Bryan and Marlene drank in the colors of ruby, jade, obsidian, sapphire, and other precious stones with no name. The wings shook, and then the bird flew off into the sky. As it tore into the air, it left behind a streak of red and orange sparks, like fireworks.

"Gorgeous," Bryan said.

Marlene was shaking.

"Did you see that crazy shit?" she said. "The sparks?"

"I just saw a tropical bird. Probably an escaped parrot from Central Park Zoo. What did you see?"

He stroked her hair, but she pushed his hand away.

"That was not normal, Bryan."

"Shhh" he said. "See? No bad dreams, and no calls from my wife. Just you and I, losing precious sleep before a long day at the office. A *big* day."

He took her in his arms, and his kisses made her forget for a few moments.

*You still have time to undo this mess. You can still cancel his promotion,* she thought. *Pull the plug.*

Bryan's stone-hard profile, the jut of his brow, his full lips, and the softness of his eyes intoxicated her thinking.

"I owe you so much," he said. "You're my mentor, and someone just so special, so—"

Her mind went to a place she didn't like, to a dark thought. She pushed him away at the pec, using just her fingertips.

"You should stay at your own apartment tonight," Marlene said.

*Come on, girl, take control. Send the boy home, cancel his promotion, defer it, whatever it takes. Let him climb his way up the ladder on another side of the house, not on your front porch.*

Bryan clicked his tongue, reached over to the wall to turn the lights off, and shook his head at her.

"No, I'm staying with you, Marlene."

"You said she monitors everything you do."

"But our time as a married couple is up, baby. I've been telling you that for a long time. Soon, I won't have to worry about her and I can only worry about…us."

Here they were, like clockwork, the promises from a married man. Marlene didn't want any of them. She had seen enough of her girlfriends and female relatives fall for the trap.

"I like how things are between us right now. You have your place, I have mine, and tonight, you take a car back to sleep on your own."

"You can't be serious. I want us to have something big, something special. I want us to make a life together."

"I don't want a marriage or 'a life'. I already attempted to make a 'marriage' with Thaddeus, and look how things turned out there."

Bryan slid his hands under her breasts, and he kissed her mouth as the sheets flowed back over their bodies. She relished the wetness of his lips, the ghost of pomade on his short hair.

Bryan nuzzled Marlene's arms, her neck, and she in turn explored his body in the dark, high up above in this tower in the Upper West Side. Time moved much too fast when he pleasured her with his mouth, and she wished she could slow down, let it pass more carefully through her, but the electricity he gave her came on suddenly, like a flash, and she moaned, while grabbing his hair.

Bryan squeezed her back with his hands, and Marlene caught a glimpse of the bedroom windows. He had forgotten to pull the blinds down, and the window reflected part of their image back like a mirror — a tangle of pillows, sheets, arms and breasts — in silver and blue. She didn't like what she saw. She twisted her hips in the bed so she could turn away from the windows.

He pressed his hard-on up to her body, but before she could let him continue, she pulled away.

"The blinds," she said, ungluing herself from Bryan, and walked over to the windows. She was afraid to get too close, afraid to see the alien-like bird with the galaxy eyes, but the sill and ledge were empty. It was gone. Nevertheless, she pulled the shades down.

Marlene tiptoed back to the bed, and she got lost in their combined breathing, the tangle of her own hair in her mouth, the shape of his penis on the tip of her lips, and his hands that never stopped exploring her curves. He switched roles and took over her with his tongue, exploring every available portion of skin, pressing his face onto her pelvis, never leaving the pleasures of her sex.

Her breathing sped up and heat rose to the top of her head. As time raced and she approached climax, she felt a touch of regret, the same regret she had about promoting the man she was sleeping with, and regret about a chain of decisions she had made in life that had left her successful, wealthy, and utterly lonely. The swell of tingling and anticipation in her body soon blotted out those thoughts, and for a few brief seconds, she was free of the aches inside her, free of a longing and suffering, and free from thoughts about monsters at her window. As she climaxed for a second orgasm, she remembered what had happened at the ledge, and she broke out in gooseflesh.

The bird had spoken her name as if it knew everything about her.

**7:31 AM ET**

"I have to Facebook my old Morehouse crew," Bryan said, "to let them know what a big day this is."

7

He was feigning surprise in front of all his peers at the firm, but genuinely happy, thrilled. Marlene understood that Bryan had to go through these motions. A long time before, she had done this too, citing NYU's black alumni network, at her alma mater, to prove a point, to assert herself, to make herself be seen. Bryan's Morehouse statement was mostly directed just at Marlene, the only other black person in the room. She could not imagine what Morehouse College meant to the rest of the partners at Morton & Morton, nor did she care.

"Another coup for your alumni," Marlene said. She did her best to fill her words with a congratulatory tone, but this morning, there was a flatness in her voice she could not suppress.

Marlene sat on at the farthest end of the board room, strategically as far away from her lover as she could, in order to not draw any attention to them as a pair. Between her and Bryan sat three more partners, Albert Morton, Quentin Morton, his father, and Scott Waite, who had become partner just a year ago. Marlene had worked as an associate twenty years before making partner in 2010.

"Today, Bryan Berger joins our ranks," Quentin said. "His promotion to partner arrives early in his career, just barely three years after his arrival here in our Midtown office."

"Your drive, tenacity, and ability to articulate complex legal matters into simple language for major clients have paid off," said Quentin Morton through his white mustache.

"It's truly an honor," Bryan said.

*And one of the hungriest.* Indeed, Bryan hungered for prominence, influence, and there was so much of herself, her younger self from twenty years before, that Marlene saw reflected in his ambitions.

Of course, that similarity ended in other ways. Bryan was not a woman, and he hadn't known the shitty things the men at this firm had said to her over the years, or the sideways glances she had gotten from other female attorneys and staff, nor the endless battle for salary that came with the ownership of ovaries and female hormones. No, Bryan had no idea.

He did understand Marlene in some significant ways. He perhaps could see why the color of skin seemed to matter so much to most people, and the ways it could distort and warp a career. Being black meant that every conversation with a white colleague would always teeter on the edge of some unspoken truth, a hidden set of words that lurked beneath the surface, and every politically correct statement would sting at least one of the parties involved.

In fact, Marlene was just waiting for one of the other partners — probably Albert, the youngest Morton — to make some awkward comment about diversity this morning, to drive the point home that there was, after all, a progressive and thoughtful point to be made about the color of a person's skin.

Only one of Bryan's parents was black, but most people he came into contact always thought he was just plainly black, one hundred percent black. At least that was how Bryan put it to her when they shared dinner and wine on nights they got together. But there was another truth to what he said: his lighter skin, creamy like coffee and cream, was palatable to many people, including the men in this firm. If he were much blacker, she wondered how well these stuffy white men would get along with him.

*If we read as too black, we scare people away,* Marlene thought. After a silent pause in her line of thought, another thought arrived, hard, and fast: *Fuck all these people.*

Now Morton & Morton had its diversity, a woman of color and a man of color. Sure, lots of other puzzle pieces were missing, but her peers had enough to brag to the professional associations for a good half-decade with this promotion.

The irony was that Marlene respected these attorneys she worked with, and she thoroughly enjoyed working with them. But that didn't take away the fact that they had hurt her many times, and reminded her of her days as a girl, when she had first started to understand how her kinky hair and dark skin were vectors in American society, vectors that sent her careening into directions she could not control.

She had learned this in the early 80's, when Marlene rode in a car with her father, the air conditioner blasting icy air on high, and headed toward Atlanta to visit relatives. Those were the days when the cops pulled the family over on road trips along I-75 and shone a light into her eight-year-old face as evening started to set, and she first heard the phrase *you people.*

Nothing was perfect, and no one was perfect, and Marlene knew that. But it seemed nowadays like no one was trying to improve relations in any significant way. *What the fuck do I even bother for?* she thought.

Albert Morton leaned forward in his chair. "You've always had the best nose for new hires, Marlene."

"Thanks."

The younger Morton was hard to read. Marlene often wondered if his remarks were small digs at her.

"I envy your life. You know that?"

"My life isn't all that rosy, trust me," she said. She began to dig her nails into the thigh of her business suit. The pain that bloomed on her skin felt good.

"Come on. You're in a great position here at the firm, you have that kickass co-op — please have another dinner party soon, please — and I'm sure you have a long list of men waiting to have dinner with you."

"Albert," Quentin said, reprimanding his son with a single word.

"No, it's okay, Quentin," Marlene said. "I can respond to that. Being on the dating market in Manhattan as a woman in her fifties is not the paradise you'd expect. It's the opposite, in fact."

"You're serious about that statement, eh?" Albert said.

"Plus, I'm black."

Awkward silence seeped into the room. She was so fucking tired of it, but it had to be said.

"Let's get on with our day, shall we?" Quentin said. "We can talk more over dinner to celebrate."

They filed out of the conference room, and she kept a distance of at least six feet from Bryan as she moved past the threshold. Inside, she felt dead, wooden.

Today was one of those days when Manhattan felt more like a prison than anything else.

**8:03 AM ET**

The men stood up and filed out of the conference room. Bryan's eyes stopped for a moment at the swell of Marlene's breasts through her blouse. Bryan was so careless, playing games, flirting with disaster. She walked through the threshold before it got any worse, and raced into her office.

She skimmed the subject lines of her email, and she felt her body grow thin and tiny — a black Alice in Wonderland inside a forty-story building that housed Morton & Morton. She could't answer a single email without feeling a knot in her gut.

She stepped out of her office and into the tiny hall in the back row of executive offices and slid her key into the bathroom. She put her head down into the porcelain sink and waited for vomit that never came. She sprinkled cold water on the back of her wrists and touched up her makeup. As she re-set the powder on her face, she fell into a memory that she hadn't visited in a long time.

More than thirty years earlier, her father had taken her to a haunted house in the suburbs of Atlanta, when she used to visit him around holidays while she was an undergrad at NYU. It was just her and him, both of them always suspicious of one another, but friends nonetheless.

She had just turned nineteen the week before, and they drove to Sandy Grove, an abandoned campground that featured a haunted house for the month of October. Marlene didn't like haunted houses, but he had insisted. The attraction was run by a black family, and this was a good thing, he said to her. *We need more businesses like this,* he had said, snorting quick bursts of laughter as he drove off the highway and onto side roads. *Think of what this could mean for the unsuspecting white folk who come through here. They'll get the scare of their life from black folks, and this time, they'll pay them cash to top it all off.*

As they drove through the gates of the old estate and parked their car a hundred feet away from the campground, Marlene could smell the liquor on her father's breath. He always drove drunk.

About half of the teens and families that parked in the lot had been white, and the other half black. They waited in line to pay the twenty-five dollar fee to enter. Her father squeezed her hand as they climbed rickety stairs that still smelled of sawdust and wood glue. As they rose, they visited rooms where the undead rose from a morgue, a church where a demon slithered from under the altar to swipe at their ankles, and a mock motel room led them into a a white bathroom where an old shower ran with real running water and a figure waited around the corner to yank the curtain and stab them.

Marlene clawed at her father's forearms with her nails, and she screamed each time the demon scarecrows and zombies lunged at them. Halfway through the haunted house, they had to walk across a field from the farmhouse to the grain mill, and the flat piece of land had been decorated like a graveyard. As Marlene's sneakers stepped into the muddy ground, she realized she was having a lot of fun, and her father's problems with gambling debts and his unwillingness to back off from alcohol didn't seem to matter much, at least for a few moments.

They walked through the doors of the grain silo, and her father led the way with confidence, and no matter how suddenly a specter or a masked killer jumped out at them, he never screamed or flinched. In fact, he hummed along as they traveled through the silo, delighted by Marlene's screams. They walked through a dark room in which they could hear a snake hiss. From up above, the creature's eyes lit up in bright blue light, and spit from its flickering tongue showered them as she screamed. In the upper floors, a skinny werewolf, bare except for a loincloth but wearing a giant dog's head, lunged at them so he could snatch them into the world of the dead.

Toward the end of the ride, they tiptoed through a hallway filled with the sounds and projected images of birds. They descended once more along creaking wooden stairs, and the sounds of the birds grew loud enough to drown out the world. As they neared the exit, an invisible trapdoor popped open, and a flock of pigeons burst into the room. Marlene felt feathers, thousands of feathers around her and screamed, and she grabbed her father by the arm, leading him straight for the door marked EXIT. They ran out into the field, and she was still screaming, imagining the birds had cut her face, her lips, tangled their talons in her hair, and that they had done the same to her father.

As the cool night kissed their foreheads outside the haunted house, Marlene realized she was safe, intact, and so was her father.

He laughed, and he hugged her. Afterward, he bought cheeseburgers, fries, and a bag of boiled peanuts for each of them, and they ate in his car while Marlene played one of her CDs in the car's stereo. *I had a good time*, she said, and the Fugees blasted the Toyota Corolla with melancholy and rhythm.

He turned to her and laughed.

*You know, the people that get scared the most are the ones that have the most guilt in their heart. You do know that, right baby girl?* He nodded toward the wide patches of farmland behind Sandy Grove. It was those fields where slaves had done labor for the white owners of the farms.

*You saying I should feel guilty about something?* she spat.

She tossed the rest of her meal in a trash bin in the empty

parking lot and picked at her nails the rest of the way home. The silence between them grew tense, arid.

She heard his words over and over.

*You know, the people that get scared the most are the ones that have the most guilt in their heart. You know that, right baby girl?*

But now, years later, in this luxury corporate bathroom, she realized she had been wrong about what her father said.

That night in Atlanta, he had not been talking about the guilt of white people, or *her* guilt. He was talking about *his* guilt.

She reapplied powder to her face and avoided looking at her eyes in the mirror, and then she walked back to her office.

She read an email subject line from the HR director titled *Can you do a keynote on diversity and hiring practices this November? You would be perfect for this, Marlene!*

Marlene's cursor hovered over the reply button.

"Fuck this," she said to herself and shut down her email app.

### 8:40 AM ET

*Maybe I should end the affair,* Marlene told herself as she walked around in circles in her office.

The idea sat there in her mind, and it spread, like a virus, growing, replicating itself.

She and Bryan had been sleeping together on and off for a full year now, and they had always been more than careful. If anyone ever found out, Marlene would lose her job. She was a senior partner, true, and she knew that the Morton family would provide her a solid level of protection from a scandal, but they could not perform miracles of God, either. Marlene had been the person to lobby for Bryan's promotions, his best spokesperson, his advocate.

She knew better than anyone else that allegations of sexual harassment against her would grind her career to a halt. And she would know better than anyone else. It was her own fucking specialty. In the past decade, she had handled sexual harassment suits against Airbnb, Uber, Microsoft, and executives at Monsanto. Hell, she had worked on the Harold Weinberg case, leveled against one of the best-known Hollywood producers of the twenty first century, and won.

She didn't think Bryan would ever betray her, but if there was anything she had learned in her twenty-five years of experience is that when it came to sex and adultery, betrayal is *always* possible, and more than likely. Most people had a burning need to confess, to have a release valve for their secret transgressions. And if Bryan opened his mouth about their clandestine game after hours, it would be all over for her.

She swiped inside her desk for Pepto-Bismol but only found a pack of gum. She couldn't exit the endless loop of ideas, the threats of a future that would be so bleak, so miserable. Her career was the only solid structure she really had, and here she was, putting it all on the line.

"I can't stay here," she said out loud to herself.

She flipped up the lid of her laptop and made sure the screen was left on, with her email inbox proudly displaying its brimming contents. This would give the appearance that everything was moving along as usual. She took her handbag with her and left her coat draped on her chair.

Suddenly, ending the affair made the most sense, and it ran in circles inside her mind. She couldn't let it go.

Inside the elevator, she glanced at her reflection in the chrome. Her business suit, her armor, as she called it, was custom-made, folding over her athletic body and accentuating her curves, and her makeup Chanel. But her eyes looked hollow, sullen. Flat.

"You look like corruption, darling," she said.

She glanced at her watch. Only 8:45 AM.

She stepped out onto 42nd Street and its cacophony. She had no idea where she was going to go, but her feet never stopped moving. Growing up, her father had told her there's only one direction to go in: forward.

The vulgar consumerism of the LED walls of advertisements and chain stores bombarded Marlene's eyes. Ads the size of buildings flashed before her. She took in the preview of *The Gold Apocalypse,* a new TV series on HBO dripping with the sexuality of men's semi-naked bodies in superhero costumes. Beneath that screen, women in submissive poses got fondled by a horde of men in Abercrombie jeans. On the next block, an expensive AI coffeemaker provided a man and wife the most orgasmic cup of coffee ever, defining and validating their lives in one sip.

All the Gulliverian ads centered on the sale of youth, unattainable youth, to sell cosmetics, cars, and perfume, the seduction of children's souls with ads for movies and fast food—

and this blanket of products and illusion became her perfect cover.

She ducked into CVS and purchased six half-bottles of chardonnay. She opened one right in the store, not giving a shit, and slammed its contents in just a few swigs. The rest she jammed into the bottom of her shoulder bag. She exited the pharmacy and continued to walk west on 42nd Street. She let the wine guide her.

## 8:44 AM ET

At the intersection of 7th avenue and 42nd Street, military police performed routine bag checks. Men and women formed two neat but separate lines, and opened their purses, backpacks and shopping bags for the uniformed police.

Marlene no longer thought that these security checks were a big deal now that drones floated above every single intersection scanning biometric IDs. Had she given up on some ideal by accepting these checkpoints, by allowing her pockets and purse to be fair game for any officer of the law? If so, she had given up in a collective, alongside millions of Americans who also felt that as long as they got to experience the Disney-like magic of Times Square, this was a concession they could make.

She recalled the bird with the galaxy eyes in her bedroom the night before. Its eyes had twinkled like the LED billboards that lit up the streets before her now. In all her life, Marlene had never cared for birds. They were awful creatures, whose eyes stared out into the world from the sides of their heads. And yet, the eyes she had seen had felt different, foreign.

"Hey."

The wiry cop standing before her slid his sunglasses down on his nose to take a look at her. His blue eyes bore into her.

"Hold it there," he said. "You're in quite a hurry."

Suddenly, she felt scared, as if she would be found out for sleeping with the man she just promoted at her firm.

"Yes, I didn't intend to take so long at my doctor's appointment," she said. "I almost had an accident last night from sleepiness."

"Open your bag, please."

She parted the leather lips of her designer handbag, and his hand reached in touching some of the items without shuffling them about. He glanced at the wine bottles just as she was trying to close the designer bag up.

"You dash through Times Square like this often, miss? You know, you can't skip the line for bag checks. Everyone has to comply."

"Did I break any laws?" she said, her eyes firm and defiant, like her mother's.

"No, can't say you have."

"Then I'm free to go."

"And nothing is wrong, then?"

"Of course not. Am I acting like I broke a law?"

"May I see your ID?" He waved to two other police and asked them to take the overflow of people waiting to go through the checkpoint.

"Excuse me? I don't see you asking for white people's IDs *before they line up for security checks.*"

She handed over her New York State driver's license. She knew she couldn't win in a situation like this one. He flipped his sunglasses back on his face and inspected the card. She kept her lips pressed tight and her face stern, unmoving, yet her heart was racing.

He handed the ID back to her without saying a word.

After she tucked it back into her wallet, she didn't walk; she ran away from the checkpoint.

### 8:46 AM ET

Hands pushed Marlene from behind. "Sorry!" someone said, then laughter. A second shove. A pack of teens marched, pushing her aside, and she lost her balance for a moment. Her ankle folded, and she stumbled toward the building on her left. They walked in a trio, wearing chunky heels and flipping their long hair in waves of teal, gold, and purple. They laughed seemingly at nothing, their hands glued to their phones, and their teeth white as snow. Who the hell were these little bitches?

The girls pushed forward, snapping photos on their phones and oblivious to the middle-aged woman in the power suit they had almost knocked over. Marlene reached out toward the wall for support, and she stumbled onto a wall of LEDs. She regained her footing and looked up.

Movie titles and showtimes formed a grid of black text on

bright white.

Of course. Why didn't she think of it before?

She read through the titles.

*The Three-Body Problem*
*Transformers 10: Return to Unicron*
*The Hateful Fiction*
*Lament Configuration: Hellscape*
*Frederick Cody and the Pupa*
*The Godfather 2025*
*We Share Our Mother's Health*
*The Internet's Best Cat Videos*
*ØIE*

All she needed was a proper start time. She hated missing the beginning of a movie.

Her phone's notification system was already blowing up. She flipped the screen and saw messages from her secretary and Bryan, looking for her. She should return the messages, but instead, she tucked the phone back into her purse.

Only in New York could she get into a movie theater this early. *Thank you, Manhattan, for keeping me comfortable.*

At the very end of the grid, she found a showtime for 9:10 AM, for a movie called *ØIE*.

*That's the one.*

### 8:57 AM ET

Marlene walked into the lobby and bowed before the vending machine in the front.

"One for *ØIE*," she said out loud, and slid twenty-five dollars through the glass slot. The printed ticket slid toward her through the slot and a prerecorded female voice thanked her for her purchase as a faint smile projected itselfonto the glass, like the Cheshire Cat. The theater, like most theaters in America, no longer employed ticket staff.

The theater's vast lobby displayed nothing more than movie posters, and two escalators led up into the heavens, promising popcorn, soda, hot dogs, and some of the best projection screens the city could offer.

Marlene took the escalators up into the second level of the multiplex. She bought a bottle of water at the concession stand, which was staffed by a human, this time a young black woman no older than twenty.

"Love your manicure, girl," the attendant said. Her hair was braided and tied back. Marlene looked down at the pearly sheen of the young woman's lacquered nails.

"Thank you."

"Keep my claws pretty as blue hummingbirds."

"Huh?" Marlene said. What a strange thing to say.

"*Keep my claws pretty as hummingbirds.* It's a line from an old Beyoncé song."

"Strange, I never heard of it." Marlene had heard the young woman say *blue hummingbirds* the first time. She had omitted it the second time. This attention to how people spoke had made Marlene very good at her job. But today, in this vast and lonely cinema, the expression gave her a queasy feeling.

Marlene smiled back and made eye contact as their hands exchanged cash and the plastic bottle. Marlene glanced at her ticket and took two more sets of escalators up to the top of the building. The escalators hummed as she rose into the building, catching glimpses of 42nd Street pouring into Times Square, throbbing like a desperate and overworked artery in a chambered heart.

As she rose higher in the building, Marlene caught a stiff but pleasant smell. Artificial and familiar. Swedish Fish. She should have bought a box at the concession stand, dammit.

*Stop losing yourself in make-believe bullshit,* Marlene's father had commented once as she scanned the newspaper listings for movie times during a holiday in her junior year in high school. He was already drunk, and it was barely 1 PM. He snatched his car keys from the table, tucked the newspaper under his arm, and walked out into the driveway. His red Chrysler peeled off down the street. The comment had stung, but her mother had handed Marlene her jean jacket, and they drove down to the Plaza Theater. That day, she had taken Marlene to see *Field of Dreams*. During those high school years, they watched anything they both wanted at the Plaza Theater in Atlanta. She and Old Nessa favored movies like *You've Got Mail* and *Pretty Woman*, as well as the yearly showing of religious epics like *Ben-Hur*. It was inside the walls of the movie theater, with its smell of stale grease and Swedish Fish, that Marlene found the only neutral ground with her mother.

She reached the fourth floor and walked toward theater number thirteen. A man in a hoodie crossed in front of her, headed from the bathroom into one of the screening rooms.

Marlene traced her hand along the wide windows that looked out onto the city. Gray, time-worn Midtown, with its veneer of newness, courtesy of Starbucks and H&M. Fake tits, flawless clothes, and endless youth. What was her life going to be like in ten years when she was sixty two? Why had she pushed herself so hard to become Marlene Grue, attorney for Morton & Morton, leader of multiple teams, winner of litigations, champion of severance packages, mother of none? She sighed.

Marlene paused in front of the framed poster for the film she was about to see. *SAMUEL KAHAN'S ØIE*, read the lettering. A man's silhouette raced through a long hallway. He was framed in shadow, nothing but a cutout. Above him, mosaic tiles created a vast archway bathed in gold and royal blue. It was unmistakably a mosque, yet the style of the hand-drawn illustration was nothing but science fiction. The mosaic tiles doubled as lights on a control board, or pixels on a computer screen.

"I have to get out too, brother," Marlene said, and tapped the glass on the poster frame with a manicured nail. She pushed through the doors, and the darkness of the cinema embraced her, swaddled her, took her in without judgement. It welcomed her back.

She took a seat in the middle of the theater. The previews started. While the fiercest American brands showered her with their advertisements, she took a sip of her water and unscrewed the second bottle of chardonnay. She welcomed the swoon she was already feeling from the first bottle she had drunk at CVS. She smacked her lips. By the time the previews were done, she had already finished the second bottle and started on the third.

From deep inside her bag she pulled a white prescription bottle. She popped a Norco to give the wine a nice smooth edge.

### 9:09 AM ET

Marlene knew that it wouldn't be long before someone at Morton & Morton would be looking for her. She tapped on her email app and set up her out-of-office message. *I'll be back in the office at midday, October 26.* Let them assume she had a client meeting.

She put the empty container into her purse and started working on the third bottle.

Marlene turned her phone off and tucked it into the deepest corner of her bag.

"Keep searching, darlings," she said into the empty theater. The chardonnay was sweet as candy. It was so basic-bitch and yet so delicious. And all hers.

As the movie titles glided downward on the screen, beams of light from the right side cut through the darkness. A wiry man took a seat a few rows directly in front of Marlene.

A vast ocean spread out on the screen, and classical music swelled in the digital speakers. The title cards flickered on in their usual sequence: cast, editor, director of photography and so on, until the last card. DIRECTOR, SAMUEL KAHAN.

Marlene had always enjoyed Kahan's movies, and she generally stayed up to date on the latest titles that floated in dinner conversations with friends on the weekend, and yet she had no idea that Samuel Kahan had released another film. In fact, she thought he had died a few years back. He was in his seventies now at the very least, wasn't he?

ØIE wove two women's stories together across a time span of twenty days, the narrator announced. The younger woman, a seamstress in a Baghdad clothing factory, brash, on the verge of nineteen years of age, clashed with her mentor, a woman in her early seventies who compromised nothing. Within the first thirty minutes of the film, a suicide bomb tore open the street where their factory was located. The women were physically unharmed, but for those twenty days, they left their jobs behind to help the rescue operations on their street. They were to deliver buckets of water to victims in the areas of the blast, as well as for the rescue workers. Men pushed them aside, shouting at them to let the men do it, but the two women, both nameless, continued to carry their buckets, even while soldiers threatened them with their rifles to stop.

And then, as the young woman delivered a plastic jug of water to a rescue crew, the camera dove into the site of the wreckage, which was nothing short of a horror.

Marlene reached the bottom of her bag for the fourth bottle of chardonnay. Days passed in the movie, and on day fourteen, the two women began to rebuild their lives after the tragedy as they traded stories about a ghost they both had spotted in the burning rubble on the day of the explosion. The women sat inside a stall that served freshly baked flatbread and tea, and they stared off into the torn Baghdad skyline as they talked. The older woman had seen him when she delivered water one late night. The medical workers were on break, and she walked a little deeper into the rubble this time, noticing that a man was crouched on top of the debris. He sat on his haunches and stared past the older woman. His eyes were red as fire, glowing like embers, and he sang a song under his breath, like a nursery rhyme. The woman grabbed the jugs of water she carried and left the site.

And then the younger woman said she saw the ghost too. And he too had eyes the color of fire.

The women had started to dream about him.

The man reappeared to each of the women in their dreams, in crowded buses, and in the faces of the other people in Baghdad who survived the suicide bombing.

Marlene fell deep into the film. Her happy place. This was the silence she had needed most. Inside the womb of the movie theater, she lived through the two women inside ØIE, and she was no longer part of Morton & Morton, she was not a co-op owner with a mortgage that was a bit more than she could handle, she was not a person that had some serious scares with mammograms every couple of years, she was not Marlene.

Halfway through the run time, hard noises in front of her snapped her out of ØIE. The man a few rows ahead was mumbling to himself, and making cracking sounds, as if he were chewing sunflower seeds by the mouthful. He nodded as if he were having a conversation with someone, but clearly the seat next to him was empty.

### 11:11 AM ET

Marlene cracked open the sixth bottle and drank in its syrupy goods.

She fished in her bag for her smartphone. Maybe it was better to break up with Bryan Berger via text. *Cut the cord. Stop the bleeding. Mix the metaphor and be done with it.*

She didn't care any more—she just wanted to be done. Her

fingers tapped relentlessly on the glass. She hoped the man seated in front of her wouldn't notice the glow of the device in her hands.

She had bitched out teenagers many times in other Manhattan movie theaters when they were texting inside the theater, and now, here she was, composing messages to the man she was having an affair with.

*We have to finish this,* she texted. She cupped her hands over the screen and dimmed the brightness. Bryan was quick to reply.

*Why?*

*It just isn't right. Your promotion complicates things.*

*Why are you texting me about this now? This is very strange, boo.*

*Not strange at all.*

*I'm coming to your office right now.*

*No, don't do that. We've already drawn too much attention to ourselves. Stay in your office.*

*You can't end this, Marlene. You can't do this to me.*

Her throat tightened up, and tears began to well in her eyes. She fought them. She was not going to cry over this. She was too old to let this affair trip her up.

*It has to be over.*

*And you're texting me to tell me? What the hell is wrong with you?*

*This isn't a negotiation, Bryan.*

His end of the chat went silent, though the bubble icon simmered, showing her that he was typing something on his other end. It stayed that way for a long time, almost three minutes by her count.

*Fucking bitch, I told you that you can't do this to me.*

She re-read the message in the blue bubble. Did he really just call her a bitch? Her stomach tightened with fear. She had seen so many domestic violence cases start with language like this.

*You don't get to talk to me like that.*

*Oh I can't? I'll do what I fucking want. You can't take this away from me, Marlene. I am nothing without you.*

*What else do you want? You made partner today.*

*You don't understand. You're supposed to be with me.*

Bryan texted Marlene the only photo they had ever taken together. It was a selfie in Bryant Park, taken in a hurry and blurred at the edges. She looked genuinely happy in that photo. She had only ever felt that kind of contentment twice in her life. Once with Thaddeus, and the second with Bryan. The photo self-destructed in the chat app in both of their phones after thirty seconds, a safety precaution that gave Marlene a lot of relief.

*Told you to delete that image from your camera roll, Bryan.*

*You can't do this to me.*

*Stop.*

*You can't do this to me.* If he was repeating himself, she knew he was very upset.

*It's over. End of discussion.*

She was glad she hadn't ever let Bryan keep a single toiletry at her apartment. Even just a toothbrush would make this a bigger mess than it already was. The only physical evidence of their affair was the memory of his stubble on her skin, the way he pumped her thighs with his veined forearms, the ghosts of his arousal inside her body, and the way she had penetrated his body with her mouth, her fingers, how he had moaned when she put her middle finger inside his ass when he felt very submissive.

But there was also that single photo, the selfie they *never* should have taken together.

*Uptight bitch,* he texted. Bryan's anger was not new to her, but it still stung to hear him act so surprised.

She pressed her hand to her forehead and hoped the Norco would soon dissolve the headache behind her eyes. She jammed the phone back into the bottom of her bag.

∅IE continued before her, and the younger of the two women rolled out dough to make flatbread in the older woman's kitchen. The young woman wore a head scarf, and she stared into a small magnetized mirror on her refrigerator. The mirror was dark, like obsidian, and she lifted the black linen of her scarf carefully, as if she wanted to show it to an unknown presence inside the mirror, to reveal herself to whatever thing lived on the other side. Electronic music blended with notes from an orchestra, swelling, swooning, lurking. A slice of the young woman's chin was visible now, and the music grew quiet. She was so close to showing herself to the other side of the mirror.

But a knock at the door interrupted her. She let out a scream and flipped over the hot griddle with the flat bread on the stove. She burned her arm doing so.

Someone growled in the theater, then hollow laughter boomed from the rows in front. Marlene didn't think the scene in the film was funny at all, but the person cackled and howled some more.

The man in front stretched his arms out toward his sides. He stopped his laughter and shook his head from side to side.

He chanted a long string of syllables up into the darkness, and their wet clicking sounds reminded Marlene of drumbeats. He turned his palms toward the ceiling, and *How odd*, Marlene thought, *it's as if he's praying, asking for the grace of God.* He held his arms back out at his sides again, and they seemed much too long, like puppet arms. Then the man tucked them back onto his lap. The chants sped up, and then it became clear that it was not chanting. It was a prayer.

His shoulders and arms shook, and she wondered if he was jerking off in his seat, harkening backs to the days of a Times Square that no longer existed.

## 11:11 AM ET

The film flashed in shades of indigo and cornflower blue, and Marlene felt it then, an anger, a loneliness packed up into one neat little nugget that festered in her chest. She was not paying attention anymore to the plot of the movie. Instead, her anger was calling out to her to do something about this Jesus-loving perv in the screening room.

"Hey you shit, knock it off!" she shouted into the darkness.

"Shipay tow-tek," the man shouted. It was a tenor voice, deep, but also a little ragged at the edges. "Shipay tow-tek" he repeated.

"I'm calling the police—"

She stood up from her seat, swiping in the bag in search of her smartphone.

A public indecency charge was insignificant, but she wanted to feel right, to get the last word in. She wanted to scare this asshole.

He stood up, and the light projected from the back of the room turned him into a figure of dark blue, gray, and green, contoured by shadow. Marlene couldn't see his face but she could see his wiry outline.

"Shipay tow-tek" the man shouted again, extending the puppet arms again at his side. They still seemed way too long, frail, almost like those of a rag doll.

Marlene was not afraid. She was angry. Her mouth and arms tingled. She wanted to show this asshole what it looks like to behave in a movie theater.

The man hooked his arms over the back of the seat and, with a single stride, thrust one leg over the row of chairs. His other leg followed. The extremities cleared the cinema chairs with the agility of a praying mantis clambering over a branch. As he hopped over the row, Marlene could see his face was pockmarked, like the aftermath of many bouts of teenage acne.

"Shipay tow-tek."

He was just one row away from her. She stood up.

"What the hell are you doing?"

"Shipay tow-tek."

He climbed over one more row and loomed over her. She clenched her fist, ready to clock him if needed.

"I'm not playing games with you."

He was much shorter up close than she had imagined, shorter than her, maybe 5'6". But she could still not make out his face, despite the fact that the light from movie projection should have lit his features up. *ØIE* went dark as the two women ascended into an abandoned bombed-out apartment building, and the lack of lighting in the film put the man into a deeper shadow.

"Shipay tow-tek."

Just a moment before, he had been clothed in some sort of short-sleeve shirt, but now up close she could see his bare skin was exposed, or what was left of it. In the murk, she saw horrible things, flaps of skin and wounds and cuts that should not be possible except in a butcher shop. The man opened his mouth, but he did not smile. The mouth was toothless, like that of a very old person. His gums were wet, black, runny.

The man held a long, sharp object in his hand, and it glinted silver in the theater. She had seen something like it before, but she couldn't recall when or where. The man fondled the weapon with tenderness.

The film continued, and the dialogue of the Iraqi women spattered through the speakers. The man stared right into Marlene's eyes, and now that he was up close, his chest and belly no longer looked like hamburger meat, and he was no longer naked. He was clothed in the T-shirt and jeans, but the sharp objects was still there, at his side. His shoulder muscles bunched up as he gathered energy and stood before her, just two feet away.

"Shipay tow-tek."

"Oh God."

She turned on the balls of her feet to pivot away from the man and run down the aisle, but she was too late. He swiped at her with the sharp object, once, twice, and she felt stings across her breasts and in her chest. The movie projector flashed like a strobe, and the blade in front of her sliced.

Wetness spread across her torso, and she put her hands up, remembering the boxing stance she had learned from her personal trainer, but soon the man lunged right at her, and she could see right into his face. One of his wiry arms pinned her shoulders while the other hand swiped and sliced. Did she smell something like freshly cut flowers? She shouted as the sharp objects cut through the air sideways, up and down, and her neck snapped back. She lost consciousness, and the darkness of the movie theater shrouded her vision.

## 2:28 PM ET

Detective Nestor Buñuel pushed with two hands on the doors of the megaplex screening room to join the rest of the police on site. Some heads turned, and others, used to his presence, went back to the work at hand.

All the lights in the cinema were turned on, and the screen — a gigantic screen at that — stared at the police like the milky eye of a dissected animal. Nestor had never been in this theater, and he noticed that the decor was a blend of contemporary and art deco design. The seats were upholstered in blue fabric, and the aisles carpeted in a dull gray with tiny flecks of yellow like sprinkles on an ice cream cone.

Detective Buñuel walked on the balls of his feet, barely making a noise as he moved deeper into the cinema. The victim had chosen the best seats in the whole house to watch the movie: Right in the middle aisles, and centered right before the gigantic screen. He caught a glimpse of her now, reclined—no, cascaded was more like it—over the back of one of the seats. Hair trailing downward. Hands open, pointed up toward the black ceiling. A ragged hole in her chest.

Her face, even in death, radiated beauty. The cheekbones were strong, the chin sharp, the skin dark and supple. Marlene Grue, fifty two years of age, bore a striking resemblance to the former first lady Michelle Obama, yet Grue was perhaps even more beautiful. Michelle Obama invoked memories of a different time in the United States—a time of sweet imperfection and good intentions, before everything went into the shithole. Before they literally rounded up black people in the streets like cattle, and the country crawled toward a new civil war.

Nestor kept his observation tucked away in his mind and focused on the scene at hand.

"Gentlemen, step over this way," Captain Aiden Smith said. He found a position in the aisle, about fifteen feet away from the body and closer to the silver screen so he could talk to his officers.

The group of police investigators was made up of four men as well as one woman, Delia Douglas, but the captain made no excuse for his faux pas in addressing the group.

One of the detectives helped Smith slip his hands into nitrile gloves, as if assisting a surgeon in an operating room.

"At 11:32 AM today, we received a 911 call from one of the managers at this theater. He reported finding a body in one of the aisles. Officers arrived at 11:41 and discovered the body of a black female, age fifty two. There were six employees on duty in today's morning shift. They are all accounted for, and waiting downstairs for any further questioning."

"And patrons?" someone asked.

"Officers counted five in total, including the victim, distributed throughout the eighteen screening rooms. All were in the theater for the first showings of the day, which generally start at 9 AM. Officers have interviewed them already and released them."

Smith glanced at the corpse of the victim, curled his lip, removed his gloves, swept lint off his three piece suit and nodded at Delia Douglas.

"Possible cause of death is massive hemorrhage," Delia said, "due to the damage to the thoracic cavity. The victim's torso has been punctured and lacerated—"

*Stabbed,* Nestor thought. *Can't candy-coat the words. She's been stabbed, cut, sliced.*

"—approximately twenty six times. The heart has been removed from the rib cage. The shredded clothing indicates a struggle, and we are still working to determine the particulars and where and when death actually occurred, especially if the victim bled for an extended period of time."

"Any signs of sexual assault?" Nestor said.

"None. Her undergarments are untouched, no sign of tampering, though we will look for fibers and DNA, certainly."

"The team has found blood spatters as far down as eight rows already," Captain Smith said, "so I advise you to not walk through the aisles unless you are with the crime scene unit or you have been cleared for access. We have no suspect at this time."

"And what do we know about the victim?" Nestor said.

"Grue, Marlene. Partner in a law firm just down the street," Smith said. "Made a name for herself in corporate law. Quite a looker."

A couple of investigators giggled. Delia Douglas turned her facial expression into stone. Angry or disenfranchised — Nestor couldn't tell, though he could make a very good guess.

*When you've been murdered,* Nestor thought, *it would be fucking nice to get some respect and not have your investigator focus on your face and tits.* But there was little he could do about Smith's comment. Over the years, Nestor had to figure out when it was wise to go to battle, and this was not one of those times.

"Any domestic-abuse leads?" Nestor said. "Maybe she was followed here."

"None. She's divorced and her ex-husband's alibi is already set. He works at NBC News and is accounted for."

"Any boyfriends? Lovers?"

"We're just beginning the investigations, but she was single and not dating anyone, as far as anyone knows."

Nestor made a note in his notepad to go deeper into the lawyer's personal life once he finished up at the scene.

Marlene Grue had been laid face up over the back of the seat, and her eyes had rolled back in her head, showing only the whites. Nestor ran some calculations on the length and width of the theater, and he was ready to start surveying the scene himself.

"And the projectionist?" Nestor said.

"Oh, that's nothing but a memory of the old days," Smith said. "There are no projectionists in movie theaters anymore."

"Let me guess," Nestor said. "Robots."

"Pretty much."

Nestor glanced up into the back of the room and noticed the lights were out in the projection room. He made another note to himself.

"We have a manager on duty. He's your guy." Smith continued.

"He's on site for further questioning."

Nestor caught a whiff of wetness in the air. It reminded him of the mangroves in Florida from his summer vacations with his mom and dad in elementary school, digging in the wet clay with his father, looking for god knows what. It was an earthy, sweet smell. There was no breeze in this theater, and with the fall weather nice and cool outside, that meant that neither the furnace nor the air conditioner was running inside the theater. The clay smell vanished, but Nestor jotted down one more note in his horrendous handwriting, which resembled nothing but Velcro hooks.

"And the staff member who found the body?" Nestor said.

"An usher. He dialed 911 after he walked into this screening room at approximately 11:15 AM. The 911 call came in at 11:32," Smith said.

"So seventeen minutes pass before he dials for help. Do we know what he did during that time?" Nestor asked.

"The usher said he ran out of the screening room to alert his manager," Delia said. "He and the manager came back to he screening room at around 11:23 AM. The usher said he was afraid to get near the body."

"Do we know why?"

"You'll need to chat with him later today, but he said that every time he tried to get near to the victim, loud noises frightened him away."

The detectives murmured among themselves.

Plainclothes officer Devin Jordan spoke up with a question. "Captain, can you unpack that? Was the employee high?"

"We don't yet know that, but it doesn't seem likely. My guess is that the movie was still playing, and the usher was in a panic, overwhelmed by the sound coming from the soundtrack. Detectives, the employee was walking through the very corridor outside that you just walked through, and he said he heard something unusual coming from this theater. He said he heard growls, voices, and—"

"—And?" Nestor prompted Smith.

"The manager heard the distinct sound of thunder and rain coming from inside."

Smith's mouth twisted, and Nestor knew that his captain was saving one last bit of information to toss out to the team. This was done for dramatic effect, but also to inspire his detectives to dig further. Nestor disapproved of such theatrics, and he was not in the mood for the suspense.

"But there was something else, right? Another sound."

"Correct, detective. The manager reported three sounds coming from the screening room. Thunder, rain—and the sounds of *birds*."

## 2:54 PM ET

Smith pulled Nestor aside so they could huddle by the emergency exit.

"It's good to see you, Nestor."

"Same here. This thing with the sounds is very unusual."

"Not so much. It was probably the soundtrack for the movie."

"Smith, have you actually seen the movie?" Nestor said.

"No, I haven't."

"Well, we can't assume, then. *ØIE* opened just two weeks ago."

"Are you saying the killer brought in his own portable speaker to commit the crime?"

"No. What I'm saying is you don't know what the soundtrack of the film is, and you can't say for certain whether it contains the sounds of thunder, rain, and birds, or not."

"You're just always so…"

"Yeah, I know, I can't help it."

"I can see you want to get started. Walkthrough is over," Smith said. "Buñuel, debrief me by end of day."

"Yes, sir."

Smith tucked his chin into his phone and returned to shouting into the speaker. Nestor flipped up a fresh sheet on his notepad. He walked down to the foot of the projection screen so he could begin his work.

The forensics team, made up of two specialists in organic fibers and metals, worked in concentric circles around the body, inspecting every aisle and every inch of the floor until they would eventually reach the mutilated body of Marlene Grue.

Nestor carried his own LED flashlight, because in all his years working up cases, he had never had too much light on a crime scene. He focused on his breathing, letting his shoulders drop and softening his belly. Without mental focus, he wouldn't be able to do his job. He took in the scene with eyes, nose, and even skin.

Nestor withdrew a Sony RX500 III point-and-shoot camera

from his jeans pocket and powered it on. The innocuous camera took better 10K video than the DSLRs the department provided, and the low-light images were better than any he had ever seen. More importantly, since he was the owner of the gear, Nestor had disabled Bluetooth and Wi-Fi on the camera permanently to add an extra layer of security for his data.

Nestor took four steps back in order to frame the murder scene as widely as the aisle would let him. He needed a landscape view. He glanced up above and saw the gray eye of the projection screen tower above him. The theater before him seated roughly 350 people.

It was important to not begin to inspect a scene visually with the smaller details first, because the first view, the macro view, needed to be understood first.

Before him, the screening room extended upward and out, like a coliseum of red upholstery and black plastic. Up in the middle of the seats, slightly toward the left, the forensics team hovered over the victim.

The layout of the theater was typical of a big chain: a main aisle in the center, and narrow aisles flanking the sides. No stadium seating, at least not in this screening room. The theater itself was as vulgar as could be: part of a major corporate chain of theaters, and it looked and smelled exactly the same in the twenty continental states they operated in. A McCinema. This was yet another great contribution to the monoculture of the planet that was making so much of the culture so bland. Nestor pressed the shutter button multiple times, and the flash crackled with harsh light.

The forensics team took a few steps away from their work, giving Nestor a view of who he had come there to see. Floating a vast ocean of cinema seats, the victim lay face up.

Nestor took a couple more deep breaths and analyzed the body, the pose, the colors, and the silhouettes. This was Marlene Grue.

She faced the ceiling, and her half-naked torso, bathed in blood, bent outward in a crescent shape. From this angle, Nestor couldn't see her eyes, but instead just a long, elegant neck and her lips. Between her breasts, the hole where her heart had been. Ragged bits of flesh glimmered wetly under the lights from the sconces and the ceiling lights. Her breasts were full, bathed in blood, the nipples the color of rust. The position of the body, the hands at the sides with the palms facing up, and the smooth lines of the neck that curled back over the seat, was actually very serene, as if something very important had just happened in this room.

Nestor snapped more shots, took a few steps closer to the body, and snapped a few dozen more. The camera clicked and whirred, like an extension of his hands, eyes, and brain.

Nestor breathed in deep, and instead of trying to brush aside the stench of copper from his nostrils, he allowed himself to really smell it, to open up his nose to all the notes of the room. Beneath its sharp tang, there was also the smell of Almond Joy, nachos, carpet cleaner, and even stale urine. Women's perfume, and expensive soap. And another smell, like swamp, or dirt after the rain. Somewhat pleasant, but unusual. And suddenly, he also detected that mangrove smell he had caught earlier when he entered the room.

He took five more steps so he could get as close to the body as he could without stepping into the aisle. When he saw her up close, his throat cinched up.

Nestor had seen many bodies at murder scenes before, but never one whose heart was missing. As he leaned in closer to the wound, he did not look away.

**3:10 PM ET**

Nestor ran the penlight along the edges of the wound. He spotted small cuts radiating out, even more precise than the main wound. These were shallower incisions, just like paper cuts. They covered the perimeter of the main wound, and Nestor could not make out their meaning. The cuts formed some sort of glyph, but none that Nestor could recognize.

A vertical incision, not unlike a cut for heart surgery, split the center of the chest open.

Nestor caught a shape in his peripheral vision. Officer Devin Jordan.

"I don't mean to tell you how to do your job Detective, but you may want to look underneath the body if you can, get a shot of the lat muscles, right in the back beneath the shoulder blades—"

"I know what the lats are, Devin."

"Ah of course you, how would. Your bodybuilding and all that. Of course you would know."

"I'm not a bodybuilder, Devin."

Nestor felt sorry for Devin. He had the potential to be a great investigator, but his passivity, his craving to please and not show any kind of dissent to anyone, was a huge setback for the man.

"Help me out, will ya, Devin?"

"Of course."

"Just grab my camera and shoot while I shine my flashlight on the wound. It's a good suggestion you made."

There, beneath the straps of the bra beneath the shoulders and just an inch or two below the armpit, Nestor spotted a couple more symbols, carved just deep enough into the skin to draw blood.

"Follow me," Nestor said.

Together, they walked out through the back of the theater, crossed the hallway to reach to the other door, and walked over to the body from the right aisle. By doing so, they could avoid walking in front of the screen, which was no longer accessible, as the crime scene investigation unit worked on blood that had dripped down beneath the seats toward the front of the room.

Nestor scribbled more notes in his notepad, while Devin tapped notes into his phone.

"We're going to miss you, Detective," Devin said.

"I'll miss everyone too. Well, *almost* everyone."

"I know what you mean," Devin said. "But despite that, almost everyone in the department is pretty nice. It's a good place to work."

"I suppose."

This was exactly Devin's problem. He sugarcoated, he hid what he really felt. In fact, Nestor had been there for many conversations where other officers and staff referred to Devin as a fag—even to his face—but Devin had carried on, smiling, taking all the abuse without actually responding to what was being said to him.

"So, you think you can close this case in just one month before you're out of here?"

Nestor ignored Devin's question.

Nestor clicked his penlight off and tucked the notepad into his jacket. He pressed his lips together turned to Devin. The officer was in his early forties, and he supported two adopted children with his partner. He always worked extra hours. Devin had joined the force in his late thirties, which was much too late, but Nestor couldn't judge any man on that account. A journey was a journey, and it wasn't up to him to tell other people how or when to navigate their trips.

"I bet you'll be glad to just do what you really want to do, just write your books and forget the problems of this department."

Nestor checked his phone for messages and snapped off his nitrile gloves. He patted Devin on the shoulder.

"Writing doesn't help the problems I've got," he said, and walked out of the cinema and into the hallway.

## 3:13 PM ET

One of the uniformed police was waiting for Nestor in the hall. He talked to a thin man with a mustache in a shirt and tie. The officer gave Nestor a look up and down, squinted, and turned to the thin man next to him.

"Nestor, this is David Avila. He manages the theater."

Avila's handshake was firm but also nervous, jittery.

"You can call me Nestor."

"Detective, I already called corporate," David said. "We'll be shutting down the theater for the rest of the day."

"That's wise. None of the teams will be done anytime soon. What else did corporate tell you?"

"To not answer any media questions, to let corporate PR make any statements."

"Walk with me back toward the doors of the screening room. We won't be going back inside for now, but I want you to help me retrace some steps."

Avila frowned for a moment, as if he had been asked something he didn't want to answer, but then he nodded. The officer peeled off and walked back into the screening room.

"My men tell me there are no projectionists here," Nestor said. He set the pace for their walk: slow, measured, even, creating a sense of privacy between them to make Avila feel safer and more willing to trust Nestor.

"That's correct. We manage all the projecting using a computer. The server programs the showtimes of the main feature, plus the trailers."

"Maybe times have moved faster than I ever imagined. I should have guessed everything's automated now."

"We employ very few people anymore. Even the cleaning crews

are being replaced with automated cleaning robots."

"Does that mean the projection room was empty during the showing where the murder took place?"

"Technically yes. Managers or select employees can enter the projection rooms, but they generally run by themselves. We only go in there in case we have to reboot hardware."

"And there are no cameras inside the actual screening room?"

"None. You could say there's only one eye in the cinema, and that's the eye of the projector, which is just a robot."

"But you have cameras everywhere else."

"Correct. We monitor every hallway, bathroom, the concession stands, and space inside the theater, but we don't actually have cameras in the screening rooms."

"Yet."

"Detective, how do you know that?"

"Well, surveillance is everywhere."

"Corporate announced that infrared cameras are coming, but that's a year away."

They reached the doors of the screening room. Nestor eclipsed the theater manager with his girth, and he stepped away from the overhead lights to diminish himself and seem less harsh under the lights, to build even more trust.

"Who on your staff discovered the body?"

"John Dean. He was on duty on this floor at that time. He heard noises."

"Tell me about that."

David Avila hesitated. The bags under his eyes were gray, and his body language spoke of a discomfort and perhaps a certain kind of loss, but the man was energetic nonetheless.

"This is the thirteenth and final movie by Samuel Kahan, and any chances I get to see the film, to hear the film, I'll take them. There is no director like him, and there never will be."

"Can you be more specific about what you mean?"

"As you may already know, part of Kahan's genius comes from his use of music. He always picks the right music for each and every one of his films. He used Beethoven in *Kino Ludovico*. Johann Strauss' Blue Danube Waltz and John Coltrane in *Xenogenesis*. Simply masterful."

"So tell me about the music in *ØIE*."

"I've seen the film three times since it premiered two weeks ago, and I am just blown away, blown away, detective. How did Kahan do it? How could he infuse such magic into a single movie?"

"You tell me."

"Kahan based *ØIE* on the novel by David Saba, do you know the book?"

"I don't."

Nestor shook his head. When he had started publishing his novels in his early thirties, he had stopped reading fiction altogether. Nowadays, he only read science journals, military histories, and biographies of Colombian novelists.

"It's about two women who join a rescue mission after a suicide bomb tears apart a whole city block in Baghdad. Why do these two women survive, and why do they keep seeing ghosts in the rubble?"

"Seems very different from Kahan's movies about outer space and aliens, or correctional techniques for criminals."

"Ah, but that's the magic of Kahan. Each of his movies is as different as can be from the others, detective. Just look at *The Marsten House*. It's Kahan's foray into the horror genre, and it was unlike any others he had directed up until that point. And he never made a movie like *The Marsten House* again. He was a true original."

"So, about the music in *ØIE*—"

"Mind-blowing. Kahan used the music of the Swedish synthrock group Arkangel, and juxtaposed it with Béla Bartók's *Bluebeard's Castle*. Just thinking about it sends chills up my spine. We have lost one of the true greats of film, is all I can say."

"I didn't know he died."

"A year ago, in his house in upstate New York. The end of an era."

Avila put his hands together, close to his lips, as in prayer. His eyes watered, and he looked very afraid.

"If you wander down the hall when the movie is playing, you can hear its music. It's very hypnotic. And this morning, I could hear it from where I was, one floor below."

"You must be bullshitting me. The sound carries that far?"

"In some spots, the flooring is very thin. Today, I heard something *different,* but even as I noticed it, I decided not to make a big deal about it."

"Different how?"

"I heard thunder. Loud cracks, like the end of the world. I thought it was raining outside. But raining wrongly."

"Wrongly how?"

"Ever been to the jungle or to the woods?"

"Yes."

"Like that. The kind of rain where the trees and the earth are part of the sound. Like a titan is shaking the world."

"And what happened next, David?"

"John Dean came running toward me, babbling, telling me we had a medical emergency on our hands." Avila cleared his throat. "He was very spooked, and he didn't want to go back into the theater by himself."

"So you went together."

"Well, only up to the main doors. I walked in, and at first, I thought the room was empty. But as I went down the aisle, I saw her, just like you found her."

"Is it possible for someone to enter the theater from the emergency exits near the screen?"

"Yes, of course, but we are notified in an app if those doors are opened. They set off an internal alarm. No such thing happened today."

"Whoever did this would have had to be in the room with her."

Avila bit his lip and turned his head, and his eyes welled with tears.

"Do you need a minute?"

In all his time as a detective, Nestor had always been able to spot this type of moment. It was as if the source had something lodged in his or her throat and needed to spit it out.

"You need to know something."

"What's that?"

"I knew immediately from the way the killer left the body that I was looking at something special. Come with me, please."

Nestor followed Avila out into the lobby, away from the teams of investigators. Once they were out of earshot, Avila leaned in with spearmint-gum breath.

"Detective, that body, the way the killer sliced open the chest, the way it just...lay there, I saw that before. Did you ever see Kahan's movie *9 Lords of Night*?"

"Never."

"I have seen it at least thirty times. I own a copy of it on

LaserDisc, if you remember what those were. She was cut up and positioned just like one of the murders committed in that movie."

"What is *9 Lords of Night* about, David?"

"It's a mystery unlike any you could ever imagine."

**3:31 PM ET**

Avila pushed the tablet right beneath Nestor's face. Google Images showed him a distorted image, fuzzy and grainy, a mirage in VHS.

"That's a still from *9 Lords of Night*."

"But what is it I am looking at? Help me out."

A human figure had been draped over a wooden bench, arms splayed at the sides. The gender was impossible to determine, because the figure was dressed in long robes. Sunlight from a courtyard or maybe a skylight washed out their features. The robes had been ripped open at the chest, and a hole had been carved out.

Superimposed on the image was a shape, something vaguely humanoid inside a wide black sky. Objects hung from the figure's neck, wrist, waist and ankles. Nestor didn't know that much about film, but it looked ghostly, overexposed.

"Do you see a tentacled monster up in the ceiling?"

Nestor squinted. He shook his head.

"Funny, that's the one most people see. I see it. A squid-like thing, bristling with eyes, horrible looking."

"Just ceiling."

"And in lower right corner of the frame, Detective, what do you see?"

"The shape of a man, or a woman, not sure. Grayish white."

"You don't see dots and loops, or the eye of an eagle?" David Avila bit his lip.

"No, not at all."

"That's the strangeness of the film, Detective. Some people see the figures. Some see the squid monster. And a few like you, see a white figure."

Nestor had dealt with copycat murders in the past, but this was a fucking stretch. He took a second look at Avila, to search for clues. A harmless eccentric, most likely. But a determined one.

"What other things do people see in the film's images?"

"Some see a beautiful pair of twins. Other people have reported seeing the face of Jesus Christ."

Nestor noticed how quiet and still these carpeted hallways were, even now, with a dozen officers milling about. The elevator doors loomed at the very end of the hallway, with massive red doors beneath fan-shaped art-deco dials. Every inch of space silent as a cave. Nestor snapped out of his distraction and turned back to David Avila.

"What's the movie about?"

"We would need a couple of hours to really unpack that. You see, Samuel Kahan's films worked on so many levels."

"I've heard that. What kind of levels?"

"Many people think that *The Marsten House* was commentary on a cover-up by the US government about the AIDS crisis."

"You're kidding me, right? The vampire movie?"

"There's symbolism in every frame, clues that Kahan inserted."

"And let me guess: *Xenogenesis* has subliminal messages too?"

"Of course. They say that the moon landing in 1968 was a hoax and that Kahan's mastery of cameras and special effects in *Xenogenesis* was shared with NASA—"

"Get the hell out of here."

"—And Kahan left clues inside the movie *Xenogenesis*."

"People really spend this much time picking apart his films?"

"Come on Detective, it's Kahan! He was nominated for the Academy Awards *thirteen times!*"

"Okay, relax, Avila. And how many did he win?"

"Just one, for visual special effects on *Xenogenesis*."

Nestor had to admit, this man's passion was infectious. But he had a big day ahead, no time to waste.

"So what is the movie *9 Lords of Night* about?"

"About a man and a woman who conspire together to commit the perfect murder in order to avenge their people. You see, they have been sold out, and they want justice."

Nestor took a deep breath.

"Don't get angry, Detective."

"I'm not."

"I just thought you looked like the kind of person who might appreciate this esoteric bit of film history."

"What makes you think I look that way?"

Avila blushed, and broke eye contact.

"I don't know. Sorry I brought it up."

"No, humor me. What is it about me?"

"You're not like other people," Avila said. "I can sense it. You are *different*."

The air conditioning system kicked in and filled the air with a robotic hum. Nestor's stomach cramped for a moment.

## 3:45 PM ET

Nestor took a seat in the manager's office and squeezed the water from the teabag into the trash can. The decor was generic, and it housed a couple of computer workstations, several phones, and filing cabinets. The walls were lined with inspirational quotes in photo frames.

*You can't start the next chapter of your life if you keep rereading the last one*

*Doubt kills more dreams than failure ever will*

*Nothing is permanent in this wicked world, even your troubles*

*Leadership is about making others better as a result of your presence and making sure that impact lasts in your absence*

"Jesus fucking Christ," Nestor said under his breath. This was the stuff Captain Smith lived for. Self-help garbage, nothing but a jargony opioid to forget the brutal realities of what office environments were actually like.

Nestor took the first sip off the Lipton black tea just as David Avila came into the room with John Dean.

Dean was a short, stocky man of about twenty-four years of age, with a baby face and a pencil-thin mustache from the Clark Gable era. His face was drained of any joy, but he stared at Nestor intensely as he pulled up a seat with his boss across the table.

Dean extended his hand first. "Detective," he said. The handshake was hard and unrelenting.

"John Dean," Avila said.

"Detective Nestor Buñuel. Good to meet you," Nestor said. "John, can you describe what happened this morning?"

Dean smiled, cleared his throat.

"I do routine checks throughout the theater, and if I may say so, I'm damn good at it, aren't I, David?"

David nodded just as he let out a short sigh. "I've taught you well."

"I had checked theaters six through twelve this morning

already, and thirteen was the last one on that floor."

"Tell me what the checks were like in the other theaters," Nestor said.

"Routine. Just a handful of patrons in the building, mostly parents bringing children to see Pixar movies."

"What are the steps when you perform the check in each theater?"

"I check the main doors, make sure they open and close properly, I check the corridor to make sure there's no trash or obstructions. I make sure the fire exit signs are working, and as I do all of this, I check for any potential terrorist threats."

"You specifically look for terrorist threats?"

"Yes, of course, it's how they train us."

"They?"

"Corporate."

"And what makes for a possible terrorist threat?" Nestor said.

"Unusual bags, parcels left in the aisles, and, of course, people that look like they don't belong there."

"What does such a person look like?"

"You're kidding me, right Mr. Buñuel?"

"No, I'm not. Tell me."

"Well, nowadays it's a little more complicated, but, you know, I look for certain kinds of ethnic people."

"Go on."

"Dunno," Dean continued. "It's something you just have a feel for. A knack. Because it's not just Arabs and Muslims anymore."

"I see."

"You've seen what's happening in Chicago and the South, right? Vigilantes is what they call them, but I call it as I see it. Terrorism. I mean…some of these maniacs want us all dead."

"So tell me why their race matters, John."

The young man pursed his lips and blushed. He fidgeted in his seat and glanced sideways at his boss.

"You know, I am thinking of going into the police academy myself. I think I can do this better than other people."

Dean drew air into his belly and cupped his hands together, doing his best effort to impress the two men in the room.

"Why is that, John?" Nestor said. Dean had ignored his question about race, but he let it drop. Better to just let him talk.

"Because I know what's wrong and what's right. That's really what's needed in a cop nowadays in such a complicated world."

"And someday, you want to be a uniformed officer or a detective?"

"Neither. I want to go all the way to the top. FBI. CIA."

Nestor clenched his teeth, smiled at the young man. This kid had been too scared to go back into the screening room by himself. *If you are afraid of dead bodies, you will never cut it in this job, John Dean.*

But instead of negating Dean's words, Nestor would feed his ego so he would reveal himself further.

"If you're headed to the FBI, you're in the wrong line of work, running a movie theater, then."

"I realize Detective. All things in due time."

"And today, did you spot anyone who gave off any signs of being a terrorist?"

"Can't say I did. Most people in here were white. Except for, you know, her."

"*Her* who?"

"The dead lady."

"So walk me through what happened when you checked theater thirteen."

### 3:59 PM ET

"I thought it was rain at first. Maybe a storm had rolled in and I was hearing the rain spattering on the ceiling. But, no, the sound was much closer than that. It was inside the theater."

Nestor took a sip of his tea, and the room shrank as Dean's words filled the tiny office.

"It's as if the sound was not just around me, but *in* me. Like at a rock concert. It just fills you up."

"And like I told you Detective," Avila interjected, "the movie doesn't have any rain sounds in its soundtrack."

"Noted," Nestor said. "Please let John finish."

"Thank you Detective. Under the rain, I heard a new sound."

Dean bit his lip, and his face turned very pale.

"The sound of wings. So many beating wings that it sounded like machinery. I walked down the corridor, and I could see the front seats from around the corner. The movie was playing, and there that sound tore through me—like the screech of a gull. Squishy and ridiculous, like a kid's toy. Then other sounds, like sparrows or robins, I don't know the names of birds, but sounds birds make in the morning."

Dean drew circles on the table, unaware that he was doing so.

"Then louder screeches, so loud, like bombs, and they sounded crazy, like jungle birds, just screeching, holy shit, so bad."

The young man scowled, and he shifted in his seat.

"What do you think caused those sounds?"

"Not sure."

"Do you ever drink on the job? Smoke or eat marijuana before work?"

"I certainly do not."

"Can't get into the academy with habits like that," Nestor said.

"Exactly, exactly. I stay clean as—"

"Yes, I get it," Nestor said. He smiled at Dean. The kid wanted so badly to be a cop, no doubt about that. But sometimes, it was heartbreaking to get a hunch about how wrong the vocation was for some people.

"I really heard the birds, Detective," Avila said. "You must believe me."

"I know you said you did."

"We live in an age of technology," Dean said, "and I know there's always a scientific explanation for things. I have come up with a theory, just like you, Detective."

"Mr. Dean, policemen don't come up with 'theories.' We are not academics. We collect evidence and present that evidence against specific crimes."

Dean ignored this statement and kept on talking, gesturing with his hands.

"So here's the deal. It's more than possible that someone hacked the projection in the room. If they did so, they could hijack the THX sound system. Maybe they pumped in the bird sounds just toward the speakers near where I stood. So I could hear the birds."

"So *you* could hear them?"

Nestor wanted to laugh, but he contained himself.

"And what would be the purpose of targeting you, Mr. Dean?"

"To distract me while the killer got away."

"I see. This must be some hacker."

"These are crazy times we live in. Hell, they hacked Social Security and Chase Bank last week, didn't they?"

"Good point. And so, your heard the birds. What then?"

"I took a few steps toward the screen, down the left aisle, to get a closer look. Maybe it was some high school kid, or maybe a bum who snuck in from off the street."

The ventilation system shut off in the office, and silence prevailed.

"I was about ten feet away, and then I could see — I could just see it — all the blood all over the woman's chest. And then the sound of wings was louder, so loud, like handclaps, no longer like rain."

"And then?"

"I ran the fuck out of there. Not because I was scared, but because I needed to contain the situation, you know, take charge, like a man."

"Do you need a glass of water?" Nestor said. The question snapped Dean out of his tale of heroics. He turned very pale and broke into a sweat.

"No, I'm fine. I just…"

"What is it, John?"

"Why did no one ever tell me how sickening blood can smell like in the dark? It's like pennies, or like the taste of liver and onions."

"But the room wasn't in pure darkness," Nestor said. "The projector lit the room partially, didn't it?"

Dean had a lot to learn about minding the details.

"I hear what you're saying, but if you had been there, you would have *felt* it all as darkness, Detective Buñuel. The worst darkness there is."

**4:20 PM ET**

Kelela Abebe tapped her fingernails along the wall as she leaned onto it for support.

"Can I go now?" she said to Avila.

"But you haven't told us anything at all, Kelela."

She shrugged her shoulders.

"I need a few minutes with Kelela," Nestor said. "I'll come find you later."

Avila looked disappointed in his dismissal, but he complied and took off down the hallway.

Nestor took out a notepad. Sometimes, certain witnesses responded positively to the physical act of scribbling in a notepad. As he jotted the day's date, he could feel the young woman's gaze.

"She had liquor on her breath," Abebe said.

"What kind?"

"Don't know. Something sweet. Rosé. Muscato. Maybe."

"She stood that close to you?"

"I have a good sense of smell. I could smell her perfume, the alcohol, even her perm."

"Did she act like she was drunk?"

"Not at all. But yeah, man, she was crunk. It was all over her breath. And it wasn't even ten in the morning." Abebe laughed and shook her head. "Fucking hell."

"Anything else you recall about the victim?" Nestor said.

"She was pretty. Her clothes were expensive. Like she had made it. Can I go now?"

"I would like to keep talking. It's important"

"Uh-uh," she said. "I know my rights, and I am done here if I want to stop talking." She said this without rage, just as a matter of fact.

"You're right. But yet you are still here, sharing your anecdote with me. Something tells me you actually want to share what you saw."

A trace of a smile crossed her lips.

"I sold her some bottled water, and she took off like she had better things to do."

"And you saw no one else in the corridors?" Nestor said.

Kelela frowned.

"It's the only concession I sold all that morning."

"But you saw no one else in the escalators or coming out of the elevators besides her?"

"You think I don't know that this theater has cameras in every room, every bathroom, every stairway? Why don't you go look at the footage and tell me who got in here to ice that lady? Cameras are going to do a better job than me, shit."

She made a good point. Nestor had already reviewed all the footage with Avila. All the people on the video files were accounted for.

"You need to check up on the woman's drama, though," Abebe said.

45

"Check what exactly?" Nestor said.

"Wasn't sure if it was just me, but the lady looked like she was in the middle of a fight. I could see it in her face."

"What kind of fight?"

"The kind of fight when a nigga steps up to you. When you know you are pissed off as hell, or maybe scared as hell, or both. and you just trying to do one thing. You just trying to tell his ass to be real or go home. When you trying to tell the whole world to back the fuck up."

"Can you elaborate on that?"

"You didn't meet my boss just five minutes ago? *I can't stand him.* Like that."

"Did the victim say anything to you about her having a problem with another person?"

"Ain't you listening, man? It's called a *feeling.*"

"Fair enough. Did you hear any unusual sounds coming from theater thirteen, Miss Abebe?"

"It's Kelela."

"Kelela."

"That's better. I heard nothing. My workstation was quiet as a grave."

"That will be all, Kelela."

"You gonna ask me who I think did it?"

"Don't know, am I?" Nestor said, smiling.

She cracked a smile back. There it was, a touch of softness beneath her sandpaper exterior.

"You ask me, it was some sort of serial killer. You know those motherfuckers is always white, right?"

"I can't say this is a serial killing, so I can't say."

"They always white."

**4:30 PM ET**

The body of Marlene Grue waited on a gurney in the center of the small supply office next to the mortuary at the New York Police Department Office of Chief Medical Examiner. Smith unzipped her bag with his latexed fingers, exposing the body from forehead to chin.

She had been beautiful indeed.

There was that scent again, an expensive perfume that only

women or gays would recognize. Smith only unzipped the bag only as far as the neck, because he didn't want to see her butchered chest.

"Anyone found the heart yet?" Smith said. No one answered, but he felt a shift in the air, as if someone had flung a door open.

He turned around. He was sure that Max, the coroner, had been standing just behind him, but there was no one behind Smith. Just shelves of cleaning supplies and latex gloves.

Smith zipped up the body bag, and he put his index and middle finger on the spot where the woman's heart should have been. He pressed down on the plastic to see how deep his fingers would go into the hole in her chest, like a child playing with clay for the first time. Before he touched the bottom of the carved chest, he pulled his hand out.

Ripping noises burst into the tiny supply room. Smith walked out into the cool air of the mortuary.

"There you are, Miriam," he said.

Miriam McGuire moved right past Smith and hauled Marlene Grue's body into the room, along the refrigerator compartments that faced each other along the length of the room.

"We finally got a vacancy," she said. "Are you just going to stand there? I need your help."

Miriam McGuire didn't give one shit about Smith's rank. He followed her orders and helped her lift the body onto one of the stainless steel drawers. He liked this about her. Reminded her of his mother back in the suburbs of Chicago.

"We are never to leave bodies in a place like the supply room," she said. "Capisce?"

"I hear what you're saying, but you were the one who said we're at capacity. Where else are the bodies to go?"

"Don't know. You're the one making the big bucks to create budget. But I'll tell you what: we don't keep them in a supply closet. This isn't a freakin' crate of papers."

"And why the overflow of bodies today?"

"Here, I'll come and show you."

He liked Miriam very much. She was one of the best assistant coroners he had ever worked with. However, she never stopped playing the woman card.

She flicked on a monitor at her work station.

"Murder rate is actually pretty steady, and as you know, lower now than it was in 2020," she said. "But you should know that already, shouldn't you?"

"Just humor me, Miriam."

"This week, we have more than a few accidental gun shootings. People who mishandled the firearm in the home. And the other bucket of bodies — that's neither the gang murders, nor the car accidents, nor the crimes of passion. These are *other* deaths."

"I know about those."

"The Laments."

"Yes, The Laments."

The Twitter personality that had come up with that label for the dead still hadn't come forward to this day. He simply went by the name Ricky Collazzi, but he had been the first person to analyze the data from NYPD from the department's API to label the unusually high number of suicides that had started at the beginning the twenty-first century and only kept on growing. Nowadays, everyone inside the department called these cases the Laments. They were all suicides, and they grew each year. Chicago, New York, San Francisco, and LA had the highest number of Laments in the world. 97 percent were men, mostly white, but lately, many more blacks, Asians and Hispanics.

"So, you're telling me we have new Laments this week?"

"Nine arrived in four days."

"And all of them were tied to criminal activity?"

"Yes. More than a handful of them owned illegal handguns in the home, so we have to keep them here until that is cleared. Two others could be linked to opioid trafficking. One was married to a former felon and had a record. You can read the list yourself."

She waved a tablet near his face. Smith shook his head.

"No, I don't have time right now."

"This body, Marlene Grue, is no Lament," McGuire said. "Just another crime against a woman that won't get equal treatment."

"What makes you say that?" Smith said.

"If you have to ask me why, you've got some real problems," Miriam said.

*This is why you're never going to get promoted, you fucking pest,* Smith thought.

A message floated in a small flag at the top of McGuire's computer terminal. It was a message from the front desk.

"The victim's family is here."

**4:35 PM ET**

Lilith Grue tried to vaporize the police captain with her eyes.

"I demand to see my sister's body," Lilith said.

"We do need you to identify it," Captain Smith said.

"I have been checking Twitter and CNN nonstop today. The murder of my sister is nowhere to be seen. How can that be?"

"There are details about this case that are too sensitive. We don't want to draw attention to them until we can investigate further."

"But she wasn't just some fool off the street. You know where she worked, yeah?"

"I am aware."

"We got all this attention going to the vigilantes and Antifa, but when it comes to the killing of an upstanding black person, crickets."

Lilith took a half-step closer to the policeman. Her cheeks felt hot as lava, and for some reason, the shiny texture of his hair pomade bothered her. She wanted to punch a wall, to punch herself. To just grind her teeth to powder.

"Can you at least tell me, was this random—or—"

"We don't know yet. We still haven't determined what Marlene was doing in the movie theater this morning."

"In a theater?"

What the hell was he talking about?

"Over on 42nd Street, near 8th Avenue."

"I thought this happened to her in the street. A mugging."

"Incorrect. It was inside a movie theater."

*Can't trust any of these motherfuckers.*

And yet she wanted to trust Smith. She needed to. She had no other choice, if he was leading up the investigation. He was high up on the chain.

"Did your sister go to the movies much?"

Lilith nodded.

Back in 1991 in Atlanta, when Lilith had only been fifteen and Marlene eighteen, a phone call had come in the middle of the night as rain pelted the house. The news from relatives: Philip and Brett, two cousins in Chicago, both shot to death simply by being in the crossfire of gang warfare in Englewood. The next day, Lilith's mother had taken a flight to O'Hare to attend the funeral, and it was their father who had called the high school to let them know both Lilith and Marlene would be taking a sick day. After they ate sandwiches in the kitchen, he filled three hip flasks in the kitchen with whiskey and drove them to the movies. That day, they saw three movies in a row, skipping around from theater to theater. They had started with *The Addams Family*, saw most of *Beauty and the Beast*, and finished with *Fried Green Tomatoes*. Occasionally their father got up to go to the bathroom and check the messages on their answering machine at home to see if their mother had any updates.

Lilith had sat between her father and Marlene.

Marlene had doubled over with laughter during *The Addams Family* and bitten her nails during *Beauty and the Beast*. She rolled her braids between her fingers, and she leaned over occasionally to whisper commentary into Lilith's ears.

Marlene watched the screen with intensity as always. She had brought her notebook with her, and from time to time, she jotted down notes about what she was seeing. No one except Lilith knew that her sister did this secret note-taking at movie theaters.

*What you writing in there?* Lilith had said.

*Dialogue. Marking the plot twists. Trying to understand why things turn out a certain way in the story. I want to know why the characters do what they do.*

The theater offered free refills on popcorn and soda, and Lilith volunteered to refresh the cups and the tub every hour or so. Each time she returned to the seat, she could see the glassy stare of her father intensify as the perfume of the whiskey interlaced with that of the salty butter. She had liked *Fried Green Tomatoes* the most. As the credits rolled, she had leaned in and asked her father, "What did you think?"

Roderick Grue, clean-shaven to perfection, clicked his tongue at Lilith.

"Bullshit fantasy for white people to romanticize black folks and forget what reality lies beneath. Don't make me watch trash like this again."

"But you were the one who brought us here."

"You want me to smack your fucking face? Just shut up."

Lilith had felt tears well fast, but Marlene had gripped her hand. "It's all right," she whispered to Lilith, and then she turned her voice back over to her father.

"She's not being disrespectful. You should watch your language and not disrespect her."

Roderick Grue's neck swelled with rage, and his eyes spat out fire as the theater lights came on.

"Who are you talking to like that, Marlene?"

Lilith remembered how Marlene had sat upright, stiff as a steel rod, never backing down.

"You. And you're not driving home. Not in the state you're in. Give me your keys."

Marlene had stared into her father's rheumy eyes in the twilight of the movie theater for what seemed like hours. He handed over the keys, and they slipped out of his hand. Marlene had fumbled in the dark on her hands and knees. She re-emerged with the keys in her hand, standing tall, lit in green and gold by the hues from the theater lights.

Roderick let out a big breath, and clicked his tongue.

For the first time since they were little girls, their father did not spit venom back. He sulked and sat in silence on the ride back to their house. When they got there, he stripped his shirt off and landed face down on his bed. And despite what happened, the memory of sitting in the theater with Marlene, who loved the silver light of the projector on the screen, and her father, who liked to sip throughout the movie, became one of Lilith's favorite memories of her sister.

And now Marlene was gone. It still didn't feel real. Since receiving the news, Lilith hadn't been able to cry a single tear. Instead, she only felt a rage. Who knew; maybe she would cry when they showed her the body. Tears were not helpful to her right now. Only justice was.

Captain Smith motioned to a long hallway. "Lilith, if you're ready, you can help me identify the body down this way."

"Is that normal?" Lilith said, pointing to the large windows that faced First Avenue.

In the building across the street, a long shape stood motionless but blinking its large eyes. It was as large as a German Sheperd, or at least it seemed so from this far away. Perhaps it was even bigger than that, she couldn't be sure.

Captain Smith turned too. He looked puzzled, but he ignored her question. The bird on the ledge shook its muscled body and widened its eyes, as Lilith shuddered.

Lilith checked her messages from Paris. She had been pulled over the night before after leaving a bar with friends. No ticket, but a good scare. Lilith assured her she'd be home by dinnertime.

When Lilith looked up, she noticed the bird had flown from across the street over to the windowsill. The wings were a dark greenish color, like tarnished copper. The animal looked dirty, smudged. Sort of oily. No, *oily* was the wrong word. It looked sooty, as if it were covered in ash or black smoke. Its eyes peered at her, never blinking. She recognized it then as something that resembled a great horned owl.

She had never in her life seen an owl this close up. Weren't they supposed to be nocturnal?

She didn't know they could stare into your eyes like that.

Like they knew you.

As if it knew *her*.

## 5:15 PM ET

There was a ramen place Nestor liked up on 52nd Street, a tiny shack below street level, where he could gather his thoughts and write notes, to begin piecing together the evidence, the various threads of information that were swirling in his head. If he grabbed a seat now, he could beat the rush of tourists that would flood the place later in the evening.

Nestor tucked his briefcase under the stall and ordered a large bowl. While he waited, he unfolded his smartphone. The credit-card-sized device opened up its flat panels outward, like an origami flower, and propped itself on the table, creating a perfectly angled tablet screen. Nestor plucked a Bluetooth keyboard from his pocket and began to draft up an email to Smith. However, Smith was online, according to the green dot next to his name, so Nestor chose to chat with him instead.

*How did the family take it?* Nestor typed.

*That doesn't really matter. They were of no help,* Smith replied.

How so?

*Sister came in from Baltimore, ID'd the body. She may give us problems.*

?

*She said this murder isn't going to be treated the same way as that of a white male attorney.*

Nestor slid his fingers along the space bar of this soft keyboard, once, twice, thrice. Then he stopped and repeated the operation. He slid the fingertip in the exact same motion, over and over.

"Fuck," he said, and slammed the keyboard shut, cutting off communication with Captain Smith. Then he reopened it, saw that Smith was still there.

There was so much he wanted to say, to protest, and he wanted to drill common sense into Smith's head. But instead, Nestor just slid his fingers along the glassy bezel of his mobile. You have to pick some battles, Nestor thought. He switched the subject.

*Just let me know if anything else pops up around my retirement package, ok?*

*I got your back, don't worry. Just take care of this case for me. Get us a suspect.*

*Sure, as long as I get a pension lol*

*HR is working on it, buddy, relax.*

Nestor cut off the chat.

He knew he had obsessive-compulsive tendencies from time to time, and checking in on his retirement package seemed to take up a lot of his attention lately. But with good reason. If he didn't, he had no idea how he would get to the next decade of his life in the city. Even with a multi-book contract, the royalties from his Mutant Chronicles book series wouldn't get him into his mid-sixties.

The screen dimmed, ready to be used. He ran a search for images of Samuel Kahan, ignoring his biographies and news articles for the moment. The engine returned hundreds of images.

Nestor clicked on the younger versions of Kahan. In his twenties, Kahan had worn a crop top and his clean shaven-looks gave him a bookish look. As the director entered his forties and fifties, he took on a harder appearance, wearing a ragged beard and letting his hair grow into a nimbus around his head as his hairline receded. He wore wool jackets with a black pencil tucked into the lapel pocket. His eyes peered out through his glasses as sullen orbs.

In several photos, Kahan stood side by side with his wife, the renowned painter Marina Torres. She radiated beauty with her dark good looks and stylish pixie haircut. They had married in Mexico City, where they met while he was working on pre-production for *9 Lords of Night*, according to the *New York Times* article in which the photo ran. Together, Samuel Kahan and Marina Torres looked like the unlikeliest pair. She glamorous and aloof, he boy-faced but awkward, and more than a little bit toad-faced.

The engine suggested that Nestor watch a video clip of Kahan on the BBC, in one of the few video interviews he ever granted in his lifetime. The interviewer asked how he selected his film projects. Kahan looked into the camera and said, "I'm just a Jew who discovered he had a bigger interest, and a bigger life, in worlds beyond those of the United States."

Back to the noodles. Oily, salty, flavored like animal bones and seaweed. The smallest sip of water was glorious contrast against the savory wash on his tongue.

Nestor tucked the phone into his pocket so he could eat, but just two minutes after he had done so, his fingers itched. This happened all too often, and he was too weak to fight it.

There was something he wanted to Google, something he really should not revisit, but it was something that seemed like it needed attention, now that a woman had been carved to death in Times Square. But it was a bad idea to go back down to the past, a very bad idea.

And yet his fingers pulled up the search box.

*Don't do it*, he told himself.

Nestor typed *Bowery murders* and hit the search button.

**5:20 PM ET**

The smartphone screen showed several news articles from the year 1999 in the *New York Times* and *Washington Post* archives. *Bodies found in Manhattan tied to Human Trafficking. NYPD Busts Smuggling Ring, Discovers Massacre.* Nestor did not open any of the links. He didn't' have to, because his memories relived the case over and over, like a video player on repeat.

The Bowery Murders case had brought Nestor fame and a reputation. This was the case that pigeonholed him forever, the case that brought him attention he did not want.

Back in 1996, Nestor had been assigned to investigating transnational crimes in Lower Manhattan. It was mostly a paper-trail kind of assignment, looking for irregularities in the importation of goods in order to catch illegal trade. Nestor had been fairly proficient at following the dollars and money orders back to criminal families in Chinatown and Brooklyn. He was not a genius, but he was good at what he did, because he was a workhorse, and he was thorough. At that time, Nestor was glad not be working the streets in a uniform. He needed a break from street crime and when he was working transnational crime, he didn't bring this kind of work home with him.

Back then, there were still many sweatshops operating in Manhattan, and warehouses were often used in conjunction for illegal activity. Nestor followed a lead on a sunny Wednesday morning in June of 1999 to investigate a warehouse at 242 Bowery Street. For months, Nestor and his unit had been tracking the Bowery warehouse, an informal port where illegal and black-market items, mostly electronics and pharmaceuticals, were stored temporarily on their way in or out of the country. All the invoices and tax records the Nestor had gathered pointed to the same place: 242 Bowery.

Nestor should have gone to the warehouse with his partner Lino that day, but even now, he still didn't know why he hadn't. He had parked outside and forced the door when no one answered. Nestor had expected to find boxes of Percocet, Valium, and computer parts in the warehouse, and though he did not know why, it didn't occur to him to call for backup at the time. Instead, he worked the lock on the door on his own, and stepped inside.

He had a warrant in hand, and the bitter aftertaste of coffee in the back of his throat.

*You were green, boy, you were green.*

The warehouse was in bad shape, full of boxes, and sure enough, some of the illegal goods he sought, were there, stacked along the walls. Nestor worked his way up the eight flights of stairs. The upper floors were mostly empty, and they smelled of piss and cum and sweat. Squatters or drug addicts had used this building, but today, the building was empty, and bright yellow sunlight filtered in through the filthy windows.

He finished his inspection of the seventh floor, and even then, it didn't occur to him that there might be people in the building.

When he reached the upper floor, the sounds of the street faded away. He had found one last door, and it was closed. It was seafoam green, with a red marking shaped like a birdcage right in its center. Years later, when it was much too late to undo the past, Nestor had discovered the symbol was part of the Chinese word for blood.

Nestor pushed the door open.

Inside, he had found the bodies of eleven young men, mutilated, burned, and partially chewed. The decapitated heads, flaccid penises, livers, and brains stank of rot, but they formed an image that demanded attention at all costs. Whoever had done this to these young men arranged the organs so that they radiated out from the center of the room in a perfect spiral shape. That murderer was Michael P. Ace, though at the time, Nestor had never heard of his name.

Ace had been lurking in the corner of the room, still as a rock, as Nestor walked into the spiral, holding his hand up to his nose to quench the smell of rot. He was in a praying position in a kneeler one would find in a Catholic church. The skinny man in the corner looked up and snarled.

Ace shot at Nestor once, missing him, screeching unintelligible words. He was panicked, his eyes wide and his mouth full of teeth. By the time Nestor fired again, Ace had done something unexpected: shot himself in the face. His head exploded as he howled. However, Ace did not fall over. He had tied himself to the church kneeler for his final act, and in fact, he had been interrupted in prayer when Nestor had walked in on him.

Michael P. Ace had worked as a hired hitman for the Ukranian and Chinese mobs, and his job had simply been to collect money from undocumented workers, all of them male and around 18 years of age. Ace had not properly been identified in as a suspect in the investigation, because he was never paid on the books, though he had been doing this work for the mob for ten years at least.

When debts were too high, or when the undocumented workers caused problems, the mob asked Ace to take out the young men. With little access to resources and often a lack of English speaking skills, those workers were easy to make them disappear.

But Ace took his job much further, way beyond what his employers had asked of him. Ace had raped, burned, and tortured his victims, often disposing of them in the incinerator in the warehouse but keeping an organ or two as a trophy. It was this collection of trophies that became his spiral of human flesh in the upper floor of the warehouse.

Ace had killed once or twice this way in the mid '90's, but he had sped up his own timeline in 1999. That year, he had killed eleven people in just twenty days. Some of the organs Nestor saw on the floor were still fresh from a killing just the day before.

And that was the story of the Bowery case. A shadow that Nestor would never lose.

The search engine suggested images from the Bowery search, and Nestor clicked on the first result. Suddenly, he was back at 242 Bowery again.

The photo was simple, and deceptive. It showed walls the color of seafoam, streaked with grime, and in the center was a large metal door, with the bird-cage-like Chinese symbol. The door was ajar, and through the opening, a figure kneeled by the large windows.

Nestor remembered that when the photo had leaked onto the Internet (back then it was a much more innocent kind of Internet), detractors had claimed it had been doctored to include shapes that weren't there: shadows of insect faces and long wings, silhouettes of towering figures. The photo lived on in infamy, propagating as a meme through the engines and providing fodder for teenagers who wanted to spook each other with tales of the a serial killer in the attic and the ghosts of his victims. The Internet had nicknamed the killer the Mantis, because of the position of his hands in the photo after he killed himself. Nowadays, it was easy to find variations of the tale alongside Slenderman, Polybius, and the Smiley-Faced Killers.

"Holy shit," Nestor said, and he swiped away all the images away from the screen of his smartphone, snapping away from his memories and back to the ramen shop.

*Not again. Just stop it. Stop going back to the past.*

He was about to clear all his web searches from his browser when Google's engine suggested a new link to Nestor in the sidebar. It was a single news story from *Rolling Stone* magazine from 1987.

"What the hell? What's this got to do with that?"

But there was no simple answer as to why the engine's neural network suggested related links and media anymore. This was what was called now the Machine-Learning effect, by the Oxford Dictionary. According to the engine, this was only one of three interviews Samuel Kahan ever granted in his life. Nestor tapped the link.

## 5:27 PM ET

*The Rolling Stone Interview: Samuel Kahan in 1987*
*An afternoon with the auteur and his controversial new film*
*August 27, 1987*
*By Tom Rogers*

I am trying to find Samuel Kahan in the Algonquin Hotel, and I am seemingly lost. The hallways go on forever, turning, bending, and after twenty minutes wandering, I can't find his room. I get distracted by the hexagonal crochet patterns on the carpeting, and the distant sound of rain, presumably coming from outside. Finally, I get to the suite and let myself in, as Kahan has instructed. The alarm clock in the room reads 2:37 PM. I wander inside, greeted by the smell of orange peels and vintage wallpaper that seems like it has a life all its own. I still can't find him.

Of course, I already know that Samuel Kahan, 59, hates all kinds of interviews, and he's quick to evade journalists. I call out his name, and it echoes back from the vaulted ceilings. There's a cluster of birds outside the window, flitting from rooftop to rooftop, and I am reminded of a scene in *9 Lords of Night*. The movie is Kahan's tenth feature film, which was shown to the press earlier this year in spring, and which has been postponed for release for almost a year. Warner Brothers will finally release the movie in December nationwide.

In *9 Lords of Night*, the birds perch on the shoulders of two Aztec citizens of New Spain as they plan out a murder in the hopes of preventing their own colonization and genocide. Their home, the city of Tenochtitlán, floats on water, like a dream, and yet, the film unfolds with savagery and the persistent horrors of history. The film is stranger and scarier than audiences could ever expect.

As I drift into this daydream, I realize that Samuel Kahan has been sitting in the room all along. He coughs and I jump in my seat. He scribbles in a notebook, seated in a small armchair, cloaked in the shadows of a rainy summer day in Manhattan. He beams at me and motions toward the tea laid out on the table. His big glasses engulf his face, and his full beard pulls focus away from his bald pate. The eyes smolder. He cocks his head and winks at me.

This is the type of odd behavior that Kahan is known for. He is one of the most demanding directors in Hollywood, but also one of the most sought-after. The director of both *Kino Ludovico* and the Academy-Award-nominated *Xenogenesis* takes no vacations and no breaks, choosing instead to work throughout the year from his estate in upstate New York whenever he is not on set shooting in the UK.

This is the only interview Kahan has granted in more than eight years. Ever since he battled with author Octavia Butler on the adaptation of her *Xenogenesis* book series, the director deflects phone calls and requests, yet today, he seems eager to sit next to me, to peer into my eyes.

Earlier this year, the movie studio suspended the release of *9 Lords of Night*, citing issues related to the marketing of the film, as well as fears that it may be banned in the UK, just like his last two films were banned. When *Kino Ludovico* generated copycat crimes in the UK in 1984, Kahan absolved himself from any blame. In the end, three rapes, four robberies, and a fatal beating in London and Manchester were all linked back to *Kino Ludovico*. In each crime, the perpetrators cited their preference for "a bit of the ultraviolence."

When Kahan released his stunning science fiction space epic *Xenogenesis* in 1984, protesters in a Los Angeles movie theater clashed with police, citing racial insensitivity in his film, in which a black woman decides the fate of the human race as nightmare-inducing aliens colonize what's left of humanity. But even at those protests, it was unclear if the activists were denouncing themes in the film or the unusual amount of white armed police forces that showed up to the screening, which was attended mostly by black moviegoers.

And now, *9 Lords of Night* seems headed for the same fate of controversy. None of the executives currently at Warner Brothers were willing to talk to me for this article, but Scott Andrews, 89, former executive producer for the studio, said that all movie studios feel uneasy about Kahan's film right now. Andrews saw an early cut with me this year.

"It's an artistic marvel, that picture," Andrews said. "But *9 Lords* is going to inspire all kinds of violence. If you thought the civil rights riots of 1968 were bad, just you wait."

What is it exactly about the film that can generate such emotions, and why does Hollywood think that this feature by Kahan (who is neither black, Mexican, nor Hispanic) will spark such racial chaos?

Eager cinephiles who worship Kahan's oeuvre gathered this week at Warner Brothers executive offices in Los Angeles to protest the delay of Kahan's film. These are the obsessive fans that have remained loyal to him throughout his career, from films like his adaptation of Nabokov's *Lepidoptera* to the nuclear-political satire *Momma Do You Think They'll Break My Balls?*

Kahan nods my way. Without saying a word, he indicates that he is ready for me by setting his notebook and pen face down next to his seat.

**SK:** You're not going to ask me about growing up in the Bronx, are you?

**RS:** I prefer asking questions about the now rather than the before.

**SK:** I just hate questions about the past.

**RS:** So, tell me about why you chose to tackle a project as demanding and difficult as *9 Lords of Night*.

**SK:** I don't like low-hanging fruit. It's better to go after the most difficult projects.

**RS:** Four years ago, you had already begun development on an adaptation of *The Luck of Barry Lyndon* by William Thackeray, and you abandoned the project.

**SK:** I did start pre-production on it, and yes, I chose *9 Lords* over that picture. *9* became more relevant on many levels, and I convinced Warner Brothers to let me jettison the Barry Lyndon picture in favor of this one.

**RS:** Some would say you have a lot of pull in Hollywood.

**SK:** More tea? It's really good Ceylon.

**RS:** Is it true you learned the ancient Nahuatl language in order to direct?

**SK:** Was that reported in a newspaper or magazine?

**RS**: Yes.

**SK:** Then be skeptical.

**RS:** I understand that you used 5,000 extras and your team designed and sewed 2,300 costumes for *9 Lords of Night*. You also created stunning sets recreating the original architecture of the Aztec city of Tenochtitlán, pushing you beyond the limits of previous Hollywood epics like *Ben Hur* and *Cleopatra*.

**SK:** Journalists always ask me about these small details. Yes, those things are true, but I prefer to talk about the act of experiencing a movie in a cinema. That's meatier stuff.

**RS:** You've been described as cagey by most journalists.

**SK:** Nothing could be further from the truth. I am free as a bird.

**RS**: So what are you trying to say with *9 Lords*? That murder can be justified for political causes?

**SK:** I don't discuss the meaning of my films. It's up to the viewer to enter each one and take away what he wants.

**RS:** Or what she wants.

**SK:** Of course. *9 Lords of Night* is a story that I felt passionate about telling, mostly because I discovered the richness of Mexico through the loving guidance of my wife and her family. She showed me mysteries there that are deeper and stronger than the building you and I are sitting in.

**RS:** Is it true you invented new camera lenses for this movie?

**SK:** I tinker, and I am grateful that Kodak is willing to work with me. The new lenses I designed allowed us to shoot by candlelight in our night shots.

**RS:** Describe the story of *9 Lords of Night* in your own words.

**SK:** In my historical drama, my husband-and-wife team seek vengeance on a true-life historical figure named La Malinche for selling out their people to the Spaniards, their colonizers. Many people think that Malintzlin, or La Malinche, as most Mexicans call her, was the turncoat that allowed Hernán Cortés to defeat the Aztec Empire. She was Cortés' translator, lover, and even the mother of his child. I simply took the script to its logical conclusions.

**RS:** These two Indians—

**SK:** Do not call them Indians, you understand? They are Aztecs, or Mexica.

**RS:** These two Aztecs invoke dark magic and offer to murder La Malinche as a tribute to bring back fertility and strength to the Aztecs.

**SK:** And that's not how it turned out. They worked tirelessly on a quest that they would eventually fail. They were decimated.

**RS:** Do you think La Malinche was a traitor?

**KS:** I don't know. La Malinche was all at once very Aztec and in other ways not Aztec enough. My own wife Marina struggles with this notion living here with me in the United States. Is she Mexican enough, she asks me, when she feels like she can't fulfill every cultural and political expectation that American culture imposes on her? I do not have answers. I just make the films that pose the questions.

**RS:** The cinematography in the film is stunning. It's as if the whole city of the Aztecs radiates with light. The colors of buildings and the pyramids bleed in shades of red, green and pink, like neon.

**SK:** The metropolis of Tenochtitlán had light. It also had dark.

But you know that already, don't you?

**RS:** I don't. Many of your fans believe that you have inserted hidden cryptic messages into your films, especially *Xenogenesis*.

**SK:** I told you I won't discuss past films.

**RS:** You portray La Malinche, as well as the murdering husband and wife, as very sympathetic characters. So, who's the real monster inside *9 Lords of Night*?

**SK:** Well that's easy. There's two. The first one is described in vivid detail, as a myth, invoked in myths by the elders of the Aztecs to their children, He is present in the movie but always off screen. He's red as an apple, with eyes that stare out at you like this. [Kahan makes a gesture with his hands to mimic a mask].

**RS**: You're spooking me, Samuel.

**SK:** [Laughs deep in his belly]. But I mean it. That's our monster. He's a powerful god, more savage than Dracula or the boogeyman. He is the Lord of Sacrifice and Renewal. They call him *The Night Drinker*.

**RS:** Yes, the Night Drinker. How did you come up with a creature so horrible for your film?

**SK:** I didn't. He is simply a deity in the Aztec religion. As real as Jesus Christ or the Buddha, really.

**RS:** And the second monster in the film?

**SK:** Well, that's man. The most terrifying and corrupt monster of them all.

**RS:** The Mexican writer Carlos Fuentes lamented that it took American money to make this film about such a sensitive topic in Mexican history. He said the picture should have been made by a Mexican director. That it's a story that belongs to Mexicans.

**SK:** Octavia Butler voiced a similar complaint when we worked together on the adaptation of her book *Dawn* into what became *Xenogenesis*. She lamented the lack of any prominent black directors, producers or directors to champion her novel, and its adaptation.

**RS:** Do you think you've appropriated *9 Lords of Night* from the Mexican people?

**SK:** Look, Fuentes is a great writer and a smart man. His skin is thick enough to take it. More tea?

**RS:** For this project, you adapted the seventeenth-century novel *Los Nueve Señores de la Noche* by Friar Maximiliano Carmona.

**SK:** I'm a voracious — hell, rapacious — reader. Back in 1968, I was browsing one of the bookstores near the historical center of Mexico City when a tiny man with a gold tooth placed a paperback in my hands. It was one of only a hundred copies of an edition that contained the original Spanish and an English translation of *Los Nueve Señores de la Noche*. The cover showed an red-and-blue owl, made of smoke, set into a mandala of gold. When I went to the register to pay for the threadbare paperback, the man had disappeared, so I couldn't thank him. I read the whole book that afternoon, and the next day, I knew the project had found me. Acquiring the rights took years, but well, here we are.

**RS:** *9 Lords* kept me awake for many nights, and I don't know why. The only two movies that made me feel that were Friedkin's *The Exorcist* and Wes Craven's *Nightmare on Elm Street*. I think it's fitting to ask you, then — what do you think is the nature of evil?

**SK:** I don't mean to speak in riddles, but take a good listen at the stories people tell you about their past, the way grandparents unravel a tale for their grandchildren. Those stories are full of human pain, suffering, theft, rape, and murder. Take a deep listen. Like this. With your belly soft, breathing in, and tuning in. Open your heart. Put your hand up to your ear if it makes it easier to catch every single word. From those stories shapes emerge, like colossal shadows, malevolent creatures out of time. Never stop listening to those stories, my friend.

"You sound like a real asshole, Kahan," Nestor said.

Nestor tapped on a link at the end of the article. It was a short update in 1990 by Tom Rogers, the journalist who wrote the piece:

*Just days after the piece was published, Warner Brothers canceled the release of the film. The expensive production 9 Lords of Night was never shown in cinemas and remains virtually inaccessible. It was released on LaserDisc in 1991, but only 1,000 copies were made at the time.*

"Can you believe we're supposed to get a nor'easter?" said the waitress as she cleared Nestor's plates. The noodles roiled in his gut.

"Huh?" he said. One of her eyes drooped, staring out into space at an odd angle, as if she had suffered a stroke.

"Well, it's warm now, but yeah, freak storm system is coming over the next day or so," she said.

"Global warming."

"No, probably much worse," she said.

Nestor left a tip and headed out of the restaurant. He still had enough time to walk from 52nd Street to 35th to get to the police department.

## 5:59 PM ET

Nestor scurried past the crowds outside the AMC Patriot theater, which was still cordoned off. He crossed 8th Avenue, headed west on 42nd Street, toward the Midtown South Precinct located at 357 W. 35th Street, where he had served the police all his adult life.

A black woman in the blond wig standing outside the 42nd Street subway station wielded a backpack like a war flag. Her long legs shimmered, exposed by the short shorts she wore. She was probably no older than twenty one, though her watery eyes looked like she had lived for two hundred years of hardship and meth abuse.

"But this shit ain't right," she said. "Y'all gonna let those cops take away a black person just like that? No one's going to call that shit out?"

People exited the subway station, emerging onto the ground. Almost all of them ignored her.

"Do you not SEE what the fuck is happening down there?" she screamed, eyes wide as saucers. "It's hell down there!"

Nestor sidled up to the subway stairs and placed his right hand on the railing.

"What happened?"

"Nigga arrested, taken away in cuffs. Beat the side of his head with the baton, too."

"Do you know him?"

"No, but I know what the police were after. Man was probably an illegal. African. They walked up to him in a pack, like jackals, went through his bag, and just like that hauled his ass away. What the fuck ever happened to reading a person their Miranda rights?"

"Calm down, okay?" Nestor said. "Police can't really do that." But he knew better. Police in NYCPD *could* haul someone's ass away, and fast. It was not a possibility; it was present reality. She was right.

"What these motherfuckers want is to sink New York into some sinister shit, like those vigilantes and curfews in Chicago. We're next, man." Nestor kept his mouth shut, though his thoughts blazed. *New York doesn't have to wait for that. We're already living it.*

The woman cocked her weight onto one hip. She flipped her hair back. She shook her head and got ready to walk off.

"Hold on, just a sec," Nestor said. "Tell me what you know about the vigilantes."

"Excuse me?"

"Yeah, I'm just curious."

She wrinkled her nose and stepped back.

"Aw, nah, you're not police, is ya?" Her eyes scanned the space around his armpits, and she spotted his firearm. She waved him away with elegant hands tipped with long pink nails.

"Fuck that. Not telling you shit."

"Hey! I just asked a question."

"Just look at you, you little *bitch*," she said. "All dressed up like one of *them*, trying to pass for something you're *not*. Don't you know we trans people in the crosshairs of the police?"

Chills ran down Nestor's spine.

"That's right motherfucker. Trans girls, and trans boys, too."

"Listen, you don't fucking know me," he said. He could arrest her, but he didn't want to confirm her suspicions that he was police. In fact, he wanted to just walk away from this awkward moment. A couple of passers-by glanced at the exchange, but most moved on, too busy to care.

The woman narrowed her eyes and studied Nestor even closer. She looked him up and down, his face, his clothes, his thick body. She clicked her tongue, and her eyes widened.

"Oh, this is fucking rich. So, you really *are* police."

"And so what?" Nestor said.

"Well you're not *just* police, are you, sir? You one of *us*."

"Fuck off," he said.

"Oh, I just clocked you, bitch," she said, and laughed, tossing her head back.

"Excuse me?"

"You no longer a brick. You can be out here and pass as a biological man, and so now you think you somebody."

"You don't know me."

"You ain't shit. Cooning and selling us out."

Nestor couldn't remember the last time he had been clocked in the street. During his mid-thirties, it had been a very big deal for him to walk in the city as he was thinking about transitioning, and he supposed it was back then, in bars or restaurants or the subway, when he had felt most vulnerable. When he started wearing more men's clothes and taking hormones, the stares had become almost unbearable, even though there was a certain thrill, subtle and almost sexual, in the way in which strangers appraised his face, and his body with their eyes. Awkward glances, people unsure if they should call him *sir* or *ma'am*, and sometimes, the sting of words.

But now, this woman was shouting to the world what he knew, and what she also knew.

Nowadays, he didn't actually care as much about his face, his facial hair, or whether his body looked "authentically masculine." He knew that he was privileged to pass as male in most situations, but after 52 years in his body, he was starting to no longer care so much about its exteriors. And yet, somehow, this woman had managed to drill deep into some unnamed, shadowy emotion inside him.

"Fuck off," he said.

"Oh, I clocked you, bitch," the woman said. "Clocked! You just keep on betraying all of us — and there's going to be a special toilet in hell for *your* kind to eat shit from."

The woman flicked trash from her purse at Nestor, and it struck his face, fluttering all over the place. The woman turned on her high heels and stormed off toward Hell's Kitchen. Nestor plucked the used tissues and makeup sponges at his feet. He walked them to the trash.

## 8:09 PM ET

The dinner hour tended to clear out the station, and Nestor liked it that way. When he was done writing a narrative version of the notes about Marlene Grue's murder, he went back into the editing screen. It was in the editing process of these reports where time flew away from him, and he rewrote each sentence carefully, with as much time as the night would allow.

A half-eaten salad wilted on his desk, and he took a swig of iced tea. Hunger was the least of his worries right now. The murder of the attorney Marlene Grue was slowly consuming him, the way kindling picks up speed and heat in a campfire. He was onto something, and he retraced his steps, reread his notes, and flipped through the camera roll on his point-and-shoot camera.

Smith slipped into his suit jacket in front of Nestor's desk. Nestor noticed him from the corner of his eye.

"Heading out for the night," Smith said. "Any updates?"

"Crime lab is running toxicology, the works. Thanks for expediting those resources."

"Toxicology won't move any faster than they usually do, but I was able to bump up this case in their queue. I have more than a few people breathing down my neck to move things along."

"Grue's firm?"

"Yes, they pulled some strings with the mayor. And they want as tight a lid on this as possible. She's somewhat high-profile."

"Reporters were buzzing around the movie theater after I left."

"We're doing our best to keep her identity out of the news. I'll make a statement tomorrow morning, but keep it vague. Gum?"

Smith opened the packet of gum and displayed the interior like a deck of cards. Individually wrapped pieces of spearmint gum, white and pristine, in white paper, tissue-paper thin.

"No, thanks."

"Oh, and one more thing—"

"Sure, what is it?"

"I'm testifying tomorrow. On the Valadez suit."

"I know that."

"And hopefully, that tidies everything up for you before you're out for retirement."

"Your confidence in neat and happy endings is baffling," Nestor said, "but this time, I'll take it."

Nestor and Smith had been friends for twenty-five years; they had vacationed in Florida together, attended funerals together, even shared Thanksgiving dinner with each other's families. And yet, there were times when Nestor couldn't figure Smith out. The man liked to promise lots of things, including closure. Smith was obsessed with his image and politics. Even though Smith could be pretty grounded, his need for power turned him into a complicated figure in Nestor's life. The man loved to overpromise. Nestor knew nothing was ever as neat or simple as what Smith promised.

And the Valadez lawsuit still kept Nestor up at night. Not because of fear but because of worry. Worry over three million dollars.

Back in 2014, Nestor had been working narcotics. He had been part of a stakeout in Sunset Park on a rainy day in June. The target was Julio Valadez, a man who had been in their crosshairs for months. He was a well-known drug lord, hitman and embezzler, and he had ties to the drug cartels via Mexico and Colombia.

After a warrant was served for Valadez's arrest, a team of eight officers, including Nestor, approached the ramshackle apartment building, which overlooked Green-Wood Cemetery. Five officers walked up to the front of the house, while Nestor and two other officers waited in the back of the apartment building, to make sure Valadez didn't have an escape route while the warrant was served.

Nestor had never really expected for Valadez to do anything but answer his front door. But instead, he burst out into the backyard. The tattooed man screamed like a jackal. He waved a knife in one hand and a small firearm in the other. And he ran toward the police.

Nestor had shot Valadez in the shoulder, groin, and stomach. Tiny flaps of fabric flew in the air like moths, and Valadez widened his eyes and bared his teeth. Despite the gunshot wounds, Valadez tackled Nestor. They crashed on the concrete steps of the apartment building.

Valadez, a strong man of 250 pounds of muscle, fought back even as he lost copious amounts of blood. Nestor wrestled him to the ground, aided by the two other officers, but it was Nestor who pinned him down by sitting on top of the man.

Nestor had let his fists fly, striking Valadez over and over. Valadez let go of the knife and gun, and he put his hands up to his face, to no avail. Something hot, like lava, came alive inside Nestor as he struck the man in the face and throat. It tasted good, and he wanted more of it.

Nestor's fists struck many times. He heard the cheekbones crack, and a soft thud when he punched the man right in the Adam's apple, once, twice, ten times. An eye burst into pulp. He lost track of time, and he pummeled, unaware of the pain in his own knuckles.

Nestor didn't want to stop. His teammates, stunned, and also aroused by the rage that poured forth, didn't stop him.

Valadez rolled over and kicked out at Nestor, striking him in the knees and knocking him off his feet. But Nestor slithered to get the upper hand so he could choke and punch Valadez further. After almost fifteen minutes of struggling, Valadez died, face up on the grass.

Men, especially large, strong men, don't die instantaneously from gun wounds, Nestor thought. That's just Hollywood trickery. In real life, they can last for a long time, in agony, in desperation, and sometimes, in an ocean of pure rage.

And if it hadn't been for that long struggle under Nestor's thirst for blood, Valadez would have probably lived.

Nestor's teammates had to peel him off the body, because he was still punching it even after Valadez had stopped breathing.

The officers on the scene had backed Nestor's story up. The suspect had resisted arrest, he said, and with knife and firearm in hand, Valadez had posed a lethal threat. None of other officers who were part of that raid ever contradicted the story. They had remained loyal even if more than two of them had called him a tranny and faggot cunt many years later.

To this day, Nestor could not understand why, on that day, his rage became so unstoppable. In all his years on the force, Nestor had never treated a suspect in such a savage way, but the brotherhood of that unit was willing to turn a blind eye to what actually happened on the ground.

But what police didn't foresee in the timeline of the case was Valadez's wife, his brother, and his sister-in-law, who had witnessed the scuffle right from inside the apartment building, capturing the scene on their mobile phones from various angles. They posted the footage to YouTube and Facebook, before it was taken down. Nevertheless, several thousand people got to see it.

That fall, Valadez's family sued the police for the sum of three million dollars in damages, and thanks to the incredible amounts of pressure they exerted through protests they organized on Facebook and in the streets, an internal affairs investigation began in full in early 2015. Nestor had been down this road before, but not for such a long time. And looking back on it now felt like a dream. Interview upon interview, threats, questions from investigators and lawyers.

The IA investigators cleared Nestor's name, even though the smartphone footage showed his lack of compassion—and common sense. If it hadn't been for Valadez's own history as a criminal and killer all his own, things would have been much different.

Some media outlets had covered the case, but it soon faded in favor of stories about the latest iPhone and the effects of the economic crisis on jobs.

It was the civil case which turned out to have a life all its own, and where Nestor had lost the most sleep.

The civil suit had continued through 2016, but due to the criminal's wife's battle with cancer, it had been put on hold. Years passed. Now, with remission on her side, and newly gained time, Valadez's wife was back, and she wanted three million for damages.

The last person to provide a new deposition in the lawsuit on the use of excessive force would be Smith, and that was scheduled for tomorrow.

The judge would probably ask Smith lots of questions about what it was like to work with Nestor, and how he managed him. This would include a description of his working style, Nestor's habits, and Nestor's temper. Hopefully, they would not conflate Nestor's transition ten years earlier with a character flaw, but Nestor knew better than to expect the best from people. What's worse, they would possibly ask if all the testosterone he took would make his aggressive tendencies worse. Because, after all, Nestor had already transitioned by the time they served that warrant on Valadez.

"I don't expect you to attend, but if you do, I'll see you there," Smith said.

"I'm putting my cases to bed, including this Grue murder. I don't think you'll see me at the Valadez case until the judge makes a decision or my attorney needs me there. Don't save me a seat."

"I'm getting a lot of pressure from above to make this Grue murder a neat one. You think you can do that for me?"

"Depends on what I find."

"All I am saying is, do your best work here. Show us what you're made of before you leave the force."

"Are you busting my balls, Smith?"

Smith's ample smile loomed over Nestor. His dusty blonde hair was fading at the crown, but he was a handsome man, regardless of age.

"Trust me, you'll be nicely rewarded."

Another promise.

Smith tapped the edge of Nestor's desk with the first and second knuckles of his right hand, and headed out of the station. Nestor shrugged and shoved a forkful of salad into his mouth.

A cluster of uniformed officers entered the station, and one of them peeled away from the pack, headed straight for Nestor's desk. He recognized him from earlier in the day. Devin.

"I just ran into Captain Smith, sir. What an honor."

"Good to see you, Devin."

"Evening, Detective Buñuel."

"Captain Smith's good at what he does."

"As are you. You two make quite a pair."

"We were friends before we ever worked together. The 90's were very different times. We lived at night, partied hard."

"Why did you become a detective, Nestor? Just curious."

*There he goes with all his questions. Why don't you just ask me what you really want?* Nestor thought. With Devin, there was always a question lurking beneath the surface. He could sense that Devin harbored some doubt, some feeling about Nestor that he couldn't pin down.

"Devin, let me give you a piece of advice about this job."

"Shoot, detective."

"Never eat everything they give you, never drink everything they pour for you, never believe everything they tell you, and don't ever tell them everything you know."

Devin smiled.

"Mind if I write that one down, use it someday?"

"Not at all."

Devin actually produced a notepad and scribbled the quote with a red pen. Nestor remembered how many times the other officers had given this man shit, and watching him scribble with his tongue sticking out of the mouth like a schoolboy only brought Nestor sorrow for the man.

"Just don't take shit from people, okay?" Nestor said.

Devin winked back at him, but Nestor looked away, knowing that Devin wasn't likely to ever change.

Nestor slipped on his jacket and headed out of the station. The clock read 9:00 PM, and that meant that he could still make it to Soho. It had been a long day, but there was one more place he needed to visit to finish up the day's work on the murder of Marlene Grue.

## 9:08 PM ET

Nestor found a table inside Bleecker Street Bar, as far from the speakers as he could. Coldplay was blaring throughout the place, but it was a small price to pay in exchange for a cold beer in his hand and a place where he could think. Bleecker Street Bar barely fit into the definition of a dive bar, but in this part of Manhattan, it was the last of its kind. The restaurants and cafes in this part of Soho catered to the tourist, to the wine drinker who had something to prove, to the woman or man on the go who just needed a quick cold-pressed juice for the meager price of seventeen dollars.

Nestor's ex-wife Alexa slid into the seat across the booth, slinking out of her jean jacket and adjusting her hair into a ponytail at the same time. She was older than him, already nearing sixty, but age didn't seem to affect her in any negative way. Deep crow's feet had sprung in the corners of her eyes and lines had appeared around her mouth, but her red hair and its white streaks shimmered in good health, as Nestor always remembered.

"We've been doing this a long time, you know that?" he said.

"It will be fifteen years next month," she said. She reached across the booth and kissed him on the lips. "But soon you'll run out of places downtown to have a decent beer."

Her peck was light as a feather, platonic.

"How's the gang?" he said.

"Complicated. With lots of new drama. Many are paralyzed by

the political climate, but others are not. And yes, lots of interpersonal problems, as usual. But not much new there. Lee, Arianna, and Maryam say hi, by the way. They miss you."

Three names Nestor hadn't heard in a long time. Lee was the queerest of the bunch. She was a high school teacher in Brooklyn, married to a lesbian accountant. He had heard that Lee was dating men in a newly negotiated open relationship, but Nestor shut his mouth.

Arianna, an old friend who Nestor had met once on a lesbian cruise, lived in upstate New York with her baby, close to family and as far away from Nestor as she could get. The day Nestor had announced his transition, Arianna had brought him a stack of novels that she had borrowed from him over the years. *I don't need these*, she had said. She refused to talk about the transition, but why would she? She had published a whole book pointing out the contamination of true feminism now that women were transitioning to men. Since the book's release, she had become a subtle enemy and detractor all at once. Nestor was not sure if he thought of Arianna anymore as a friend.

Maryam was a former lover of Nestor's from his early days in the university, an administrator for a public health clinic and overworked to the brink of breast cancer, which was currently in remission. All three of these people felt like human postcards, faded and dog-eared. The five of them had once been a close-knit group of women, there for each other at the drop of a hat.

"Tell those three I miss them, too."

"Are you mad at them, Nestor?"

"Not at all." He loved the group of friends he had cultivated in Manhattan and Brooklyn thanks to Alexa. Dykes, fags, queers, they had been the reason he had such a good time in his thirties, and the reason he survived his forties. The group morphed, grew, and shrank over the years, and Nestor had been at the center of it all, the organizer of parties, trips to the sex play spaces for queer and trans women in Park Slope, keeper of the bar when he hosted parties at his apartment, and organizer of their yearly trip to Puerto Vallarta. He wished he could get excited about seeing the gang again, but his mental focus was somewhere else, and he needed to know less, rather than more, about Maryam, Arianna, and Lee. Alexa was the exception. She still got him, no matter what he looked like or what path he chose. He, in fact, should make an effort to spend more time with her. He made a mental note to text or video call her more often.

"Time passes, you know that? And, well, some of us drift off."

"But why, Nestor? Is it something *they* did? Something I did?"

"Not at all. I just do better on my own."

"But you're *retiring*. You need to socialize."

"I'm leaving the police, but my writing—that's just beginning."

"Yeah, your writing. Always that." Alexa took a long sip from her beer. He didn't like the judgement in her eyes. His first published book, *Eden's Mutation*, had led to their divorce, and Alexa was never going to let him forget it. His books were the wedge forever between them.

"Alexa, I need a favor."

"Something's wrong, isn't it, Nestor?"

How did she always know? There wasn't a thing he could hide from her.

"Remember the Bowery Murders?"

"How couldn't I? It's something I never want to live through again. Those were eighteen months of pure hell."

"During those years, how would you describe the way I looked and...felt?"

"What an odd question, Nestor."

"I'm an odd man."

"You are just so cerebral, you have such an annoying way of framing your emotions. But, this is not a therapists' office. The best way I can put it is that you were...hollowed out."

"Oh, jeez."

"Like a jack o' lantern. As if something was eating you from inside. Every day, I wanted you to just quit that case. You would walk the dogs for hours down by the river and never answer calls on your cell. Do you remember that?"

"Yes." The two beagles were a sore point between them. "While I walked them, I was working out details in the case, ways to put it all together."

"You were killing yourself slowly through your work, is what you were doing."

"You're the best person to ask for perspective on the Bowery murders."

"I wish you could compartmentalize the horror of that case in your heart," Alexa said. "Keep it under lock and key."

"I started a new investigation today," Nestor said. "Female black attorney. Sliced up in a movie theater." He could count on Alexa to keep his confidentiality. In the twenty-five years he had known her, she had never betrayed his discussions about his cases.

Alexa shivered.

"We had fifty-two murders of black people by police this year already. This murder is not going to go over well in the city."

"And it *shouldn't* go over well. Murder is not okay," he said. "But I don't know yet if this was racially motivated."

"Was it sex?"

"Not that, either."

"The way this was done — it's something I have never seen before, something out of a movie—"

"Nestor, look at me." She stepped out of the booth and slid in next to him. Coldplay was gone, and U2 took over. "Is this case—"

"Yes, it is."

"But how so?"

"It's too early to tell, but the way the murderer staged the killing, it's making me think about what you said about being hollowed out. The killer took a sharp instrument and carved into her —"

"Stop."

"Huh?"

"You're doing it again. You'll talk my ear off with lurid details of your crime ledger, lose sleep, and forget to eat for weeks. Nestor, you're retiring. Why are you even working on this case?"

"Because I have to find justice for the victim, and you, you always have the best ideas. Because you—"

"This is why I made you sign divorce papers," she said. She slid her smartphone, which was lying face down on the table, toward herself like a casino playing card. She tucked it into her jean jacket. This meant she was done with the conversation.

"But I have a favor to ask, legitimately, Alexa."

She was already standing up, ready to leave. She looked down at him with pity. That strength was what he had fallen in love with. And lost.

"Go ahead, ask."

"I need to find an expert in film who can help me out with the history of Samuel Kahan."

Alexa, a producer of television for Showtime, was his best and only source. She knew the brightest minds in film and television. And although he had used Alexa as a sounding board for decades, he had never called in a favor like this.

Nestor sipped his beer. He felt small, like a child, beneath her gaze, and seconds ticked off, heightening his discomfort.

"Why Samuel Kahan?"

"You said you didn't want to know the details of this murder."

"Good point, Angela Lansbury. Here, take this name down. Shazeb Umrani. Here's his number too."

"Thank you, this means a lot to me."

Alexa placed the pads of her five fingers on the wooden table, her back erect, and her eyes lovingly cold, and boring into Nestor's.

"You still single?" she said. There was no anger in her voice, just true concern.

"Of course."

"But look at you. Any woman or man would drop their panties for you in a second."

"Dating life in New York isn't simple."

"What's wrong with dating someone, with sharing your life with them?"

"It led to divorce once, and I would never want to go through that again."

"Nestor, you keep going this way, and the only person you will be able to divorce will be *yourself*. And that's even too grim a metaphor for someone like you."

She kissed the top of his forehead and smacked his cheek, with a lot of love, then left Nestor sipping his beer. He nodded to himself and considered a second beer. Instead, he left the bar. He had research to do on Shazeb Umrani tonight, so he could call him first thing in the morning.

## CHICAGO
## 11:35 PM ET

Felix Calvo slipped a deck of cards from his pocket and slid his thumb under the lid to free the pack from its cardboard box. On the speakers, Beth Ditto and The Gossip screamed about climbing to the top of the world, and his riffle forced the cards to dance on the oak bar.

It was strange for Big Chicks to be so empty, even on a

weeknight. He expected to see more than a few regulars, including bears, some otters, neighborhood twinks and the occasional out-of-town visitor.

He slid his last ten-dollar bill across the bar. "Can I get another rum-and-Coke and a shot of tequila?"

The bartender, whose beard and body were sculpted to perfection, but whose eyes were flat and dead from the boredom of the job, pushed the ten back to Felix.

"That cocktail was your last one. Last call passed."

"You kidding me?"

"City's on a curfew. All drunks have to drink at home after 12."

"When did this new curfew go into effect?"

"It's the third one this year. Come on, now, bud."

"One for the road," Felix said, but the bartender ignored him and wiped down the mirror behind the bar.

Felix put his arm around his half-empty cocktail and full shot that he had been saving.

The only other person there besides the bartender, a woman seated in the corner of the bar, nodded his way, as if to acknowledge the injustice of such an early last call.

"Why is the back door locked?" she said. "I had to walk all the way around the block when I parked."

"The bar had a break-in last week," the bartender said. "Burglary. Some neighborhood cops like to come in here for a drink from time to time. So, naturally, the pieces of shit that broke in through the back wanted to send a message to us about what they think about friends of police."

The bartender went back into the Facebook hole into which he was descending.

"Have you ever seen the vigilantes?" Felix asked the woman.

"Of course I have, and you have too."

"Really?"

"They have a dress code. Subtle, but they have one."

"A dress code makes no sense. It would be a dead giveaway for the police," Felix said.

"I don't think these men give a damn anymore about what the police think. That's the whole point."

"Maybe it was the vigilantes that broke into this bar," Felix said.

"Maybe. Maybe not. Only the ghosts of this place would know."

On the speakers, Peaches lamented about pain and how to get rid of it. She faded out and the Pixies told a story about the risks in a town full of strangers.

"I'm gonna tell you something, but I gotta keep my voice down, because the bartender's a white dude, and he's not ready for this type of download," she said.

*I'm half-white,* Felix thought, but she carried on.

"Look," she said. "Last month, CPD officer Michael Doppler, a white man, was shot six times in the head, execution-style, by vigilantes, and the grieving is not stopping anytime soon."

"I heard. And they wore masks."

"I am no fortune-teller, but those vigilantes are going to shoot more police officers. Soon. The city will retaliate. They'll use drones to get into Englewood, the West Side, and this part of Uptown. And when the drones aren't sufficient, they'll go in and 'terminate' standoffs using the SWAT teams and their robots. We will soon have a mini civil war. And through and through, we'd still like to say that Black Lives Matter. But I don't know *what* matters anymore."

"Yeah, but surely, there's some better way to arrive at answers."

"Oh, you really think so? You tell that to our fucking dead," she said.

Felix shuffled the deck, cut, shuffled, cut. He pulled cards, set them back in the deck. Finally, he pulled out a new one, the ace of clubs. He set it face down by his drink.

"Oh, you trying to play with me?" the woman said.

"This?"

"Yes, the ace of clubs. That ace of clubs. Didn't you ever see *The Marsten House?*"

"I'm not into movies."

"But you live in Chicago, right?"

"I do."

"Then you would—or you should—know that a key scene of the movie *The Marsten House* was shot in this very bar. And that corner you're sitting in, that's where a very young Benicio Del Toro flips up a single card from a deck just like yours. *That very same card.*"

"The ace of clubs?" Felix said. The woman nodded, and Felix felt around inside his coat pocket for the Glock 19 he had loaded earlier today. He fingered it, eager to discover what the firearm would accomplish.

## QUEENS
**11:41 PM**

Nestor slid the key inside the lock, and the door creaked, a long feline howl that filled the silence. He slung his coat off and tossed it over his sofa. He had decorated his place with relics from his days with his mother and father in Colombia, faded photographs dotting the walls, woven tapestries in the hallway, photos of vacations in Bogotá on a mantel. Those colorful objects kept him company, providing some comfort exactly at these times, when he walked in late at night. Nestor had painted the one-bedroom apartment in a soft ivory color, and infused the decor with red and green furniture, which reminded him of his childhood far away from New York.

He snapped off his shoulder holster and walked with his gun back through the rail-car hallway, into his bedroom. He slung the weapon over a wooden rocking chair next to his bed. His grandmother had used it for a lifetime, and he had inherited it when she passed away.

He brushed the taste of beer out of his mouth and flossed. He made a pot of herbal tea, and when it was steaming, he placed it on his nightstand. He sat in the wooden chair, with the gun swinging by his shoulder.

He fished a Chromebook from his dresser. He searched for a torrent for ØIE, and when he was satisfied with the quality of the potential download, he began to pull the movie down into his computer. He used this computer only for this type of illegal operation, and it was separate from his police laptop or the iMac he used for writing his novels.

Nestor stripped down to his briefs and ran his hands down his hard stomach. He felt hunger, but it was much too late to eat. He would need to wake around 7 AM. He laid out his clothes for the next morning — a freshly laundered set of his usual designer jeans and black tee. He inspected his weapon, and when he was done, he checked on the progress of the download. Only 5 percent.

He should sleep, but instead, he walked over to the desk at the end of the room. Photographs of his mother, father, sisters, and even Alexa filled the wall in a wide arc, and down in the left-hand corner, images of the Virgin of Guadalupe and St. Paul glittered in gold leaf. There were two votive candles beneath each icon. He lit them. He said a small prayer for his mother, his father, his nieces and nephews, his dead grandmother Paloma, and for himself. He genuflected.

He pressed the on switch on his iMac, his writing computer, and the darkness of the room receded as the blue glow of the screen bloomed. Nestor opened the file labeled *Mutant Tactical: The Inquisition,* and began to write.

If he grabbed just two hours of sleep later tonight, he'd be all right. When he was inside the world of his mutants, teen freaks who fought against a fascist regime in a dimension filled with alien colonies and intergalactic wars, he felt alive, and no longer himself. It was then that writing made his sense of self vanish into thin air. For that span of time, he forgot about Marlene Grue.

## CHICAGO
## 11:50 PM ET

"Exactly. Benicio holds the ace of clubs up in front of the camera—kind of like you just did— thinking that it's going to be his talisman against the vampires. And that's when the undead arrive. They get his ass *quick.* The vampires drink his blood and laugh at him. Everyone dies."

The woman laughed much too hard at her own joke. Felix shrugged his shoulders. He let go of the Glock and put his hands back on the bar. Sour sweat soaked his T-shirt.

"Why would vampires attack in a bar?" he said, still feeling the urge to remain polite, interested.

"You sure are weird. Of course vampires attack bars. They attack any place that has people."

"I think of vampires as dull, sluggish. Like sad zombies."

"Not if you ever saw *The Marsten House.* They move like jungle cats in that movie. The mansion where the main vampire, Kurt Barlow, lived—it's not too far from here. You just walk down Clarendon until you reach Hutchinson. 803 West Hutchinson. Same number in real life as in the movie."

"Never heard of *The Marsten House,* honestly."

"Stop shitting me. Of course you have. That's why you pulled out your deck of cards there."

"When did it come out?"

"1993."

"I was born in 1993."

"Well, while you were sliding out of the love canal, waiting to fulfill your destiny one day as a—"

"A packaging associate at an Amazon warehouse."

"Straight up? That's your actual job?"

"I pack stuff that the robots can't handle. Yet."

"They say those warehouses work people to death."

"It's one of the few places hiring. No benefits, but pays the rent."

Felix didn't want to say he was an anthropologist, because the fact was, he didn't have a job as one, even though he had finished his Ph D at University of Chicago. He had struggled for three years on the job market looking for teaching jobs, and instead, he was packing dildos, Snuggies and unicorn T-shirts on the graveyard shift. And still hoping to get a full-time teaching job.

"Stephen King himself came out to stay at the Somerset Hotel across the street from Big Chicks when they were shooting the movie here around 1991 and 1992. He wanted to see what changes they would make to his novel *Salem's Lot* when Kahan decided to rename the project as *The Marsten House*. That's how they grew to hate each other. A bestselling author from Maine, and a control-freak director from New York, united in Chicago, surrounded by the angry black, brown and yellow people of Uptown, whom they probably just ignored anyway. This was the city that split Kahan and King apart forever."

"Well, you learn something new every day."

Felix didn't want the pop culture lesson. He wanted time to stew and to evaluate his plan. The woman's nose was full of burst capillaries, and up close, her skin had a waxy look. Alcoholism was literally taking away her youth. *We're both kind of the same,* he thought.

"What's your name?"

"Felix Andersen Calvo."

"A pretty name. Where you from?"

"Minnesota."

"No, I mean, are you Latin?"

"I'm nothing," he said.

"No one is nothing," she said, miffed. "Everyone is

something."

"I grew up in Minneapolis. My dad married my mom, who is Mexican. That's all."

Felix slipped the ace of clubs back into the deck, and he popped the cards into their sleeve. He should have tipped seven dollars, one for every shot and rum-and-Coke he had consumed in the two hours he had sat in Big Chicks, but he only left two.

The muscular bartender looked up from his mopping duties. Felix headed out into Sheridan Road, and the wind whipped his long hair over his eyes.

"You should call an Uber, you know?" said the bartender.

"Why?"

"These aren't safe nights anymore. Why do you think we closed down the back entrance? Come on, I'll call a taxi for you."

"No, thanks."

"Come on, now."

"No. I have something I need to do."

Icy air chilled Felix's hands as he swung the door shut behind him. He was ready for his final act.

### 12:39 AM ET

Felix knelt on the asphalt, next to a garbage dumpster. His head spun, and the smell of liquor was in his throat, his nose, it was everywhere. Over his shoulder, he could spot the Sonic and McDonald's across the street on Wilson Avenue. Above him, a sign above the Uptown Baptist Church screamed CHRIST DIED FOR OUR SINS in white neon.

He released the catch for the safety.

He tried putting the barrel into his mouth, but the taste of metal and oil made him gag. Tears flowed down his face, but he made no moans, no cries. Just streams of salty water sliding down his cheeks like rivers going into the heart of a canyon.

"Come on," he said. "Come on, you shit."

Finally, he slid the steel tip through his open lips.

Felix was partially hidden by the dumpsters, but the pedestrians walking on Wilson would be able to see him fairly well, just ten feet away. In fact, two or three people walked by at this hour, but none of them took any interest in him. To them, he was just a hunched-over shadow, poor, vagrant, just part of the pockets of poverty and homeless people in this mosaic of a neighborhood.

The empty feeling in his stomach only widened, and he remembered the ocean, which he had visited a few times in his life. It roared, and he had liked that sound.

Thirty-two years on this planet, and most of them numb, empty, full of this hollowness he couldn't solve. He made fifteen dollars an hour, he had $380,000 of student debt, $78,000 in credit card debt, and a certainty that he would never get a teaching job.

He finally flicked off the safety and put his right hand on the trigger.

He howled and gritted his teeth.

"Fuck!" Felix screamed.

He tried squeezing the trigger, but he couldn't.

He punched the garbage dumpster and stood up. Screaming would help, but he couldn't, just like not being able to scream inside a dream.

He emptied the chamber of the gun, pocketed the bullets, and tossed the empty firearm into the dumpster.

By the time he got on the elevated train to go to his apartment, he was no longer crying. Instead, he carved deep grooves on his forearm using his house keys. He bit down on the long end of his mustache and bit the black hairs, and he didn't care if people stared at him. The grooves were deeper now, and he was going to cut into the skin pretty soon. A way to punish himself for what he could not yet do.

## QUEENS
## 3:00 AM ET

Nestor shut off his laptop. He needed to come back to the manuscript tomorrow and not lose any time. Tony Lam, his agent, was breathing down his neck for this book, but Nestor would deliver.

"Speak of the devil," Nestor said.

Tony had sent him a text around midnight *Dude, I gotta take you to this Ukranian joint in Sunset Park next week. Best food. We can talk about the new book, come up with a good title for it. You're massive, man, just massive! And this book's going to slay.*

"Jesus Christ, shut up," Nestor said out loud. Tony was one of the best agents in New York, but he was relentless in his phone calls, his need to be loved by the people around him. He was able to achieve great contracts for book authors, but with each new deal signed, he required more attention, more devotion to the cult he had built around himself. Nestor dreaded seeing his name come up on his phone. And yet Tony was Nestor's ticket into his new life. He owed a lot to the man.

"Call me this weekend," Nestor typed, and he scheduled the text to send at 11 AM. The last thing he wanted to do was to let Tony Lam think that he was available to talk to him in the middle of the night, because Tony was likely to show up right at his door with beers in hand.

Nestor stretched out his arms and took in a few breaths. He yanked out a yoga mat from under the sofa, slid it into the space between the sofa and the coffee table, and breathed through a few poses. His one-bedroom apartment was so small that he couldn't even move furniture out of the way to do yoga, but the rent was cheap, and he had a view of Manhattan. And even better yet, people left him the fuck alone.

When he finished, Nestor still felt too wired to sleep. He slid a USB stick into his laptop and copied the file for *9 Lords of Night* from the laptop to the stick. He popped the stick into his television, which woke from its sleep.

"Hi, Nestor. Would you like to watch a movie from your portable USB drive?" said the silky female voice from his television's agent.

"Uh-huh. Play *9 Lords of Night,* please."

The familiar opening credits from Warner Brothers swirled around the screen, and a few ragged lines and pixels slid across like melting icicles. Presumably, this copy had been copied over from VHS. Nestor grabbed a mineral water from his fridge, but he changed his mind. Instead, he poured a glass of horchata from a bottle he had purchased at the bodega on his street.

The title credits for the movie opened in a calligraphy script. *A film by Samuel Kahan* faded out, and a new title appeared: *9 Lords of Night.*

The film opened as a Catholic priest whispered into the ear of an aristocrat inside a palace from the sixteenth century. The priest twisted his black rosary beads in his hand, transferring a secret to the young man. In the background, a row of brown-skinned servants waited for instructions from the priest. After he finished speaking in the ear of the aristocrat, the priest snapped his fingers, and the servants followed him out of the palace. Sunlight drenched the priest's robes, turning them from black into bear brown. The camera followed the priest with precision, and the short man marched into a square. The Spanish architecture's understated gray colors stood in stark contrast to the massive Aztec pyramids on the right side of the square. Crews of several dozen men were demolishing the pyramids and erecting new buildings right over them. The new architecture, gray like stone, eclipsed the red, white, blue, and black paint of the former city.

"Holy shit," Nestor said, as the camera swept through the square. He recognized it immediately. It was El Zócalo in Mexico City, the very place where the empire of the Aztecs had been founded. When he was twenty five years old, fifteen years before he had transitioned, Nestor had asked his father to travel together as a family to Mexico City so they could visit that very square. His father had nodded and promised they would, but he had never come through. Nestor had pored over maps and globes all his life, and if there was one place he wanted to visit, it was this one.

The priest led the servants through the streets of the city, past horses and Spanish soldiers in metal armor and helmets curved like crescent moons. In the sky, an eagle swooped into a flock of doves, hunting for prey. The camera then zoomed in again on the hind legs of the powerful Spanish horses, as butterflies scattered into the breeze.

Nestor sipped from his horchata, and a fire truck screamed past on the street, its alarms blaring. When the siren had faded out into the distance, Nestor felt his eyelids grow heavy, and he caught a sound, far away yet also close.

Something, someone, was cooing nearby. It felt like it was right outside the window or coming from the apartment above. Nestor pressed hands on the windows and checked out the street. Mostly empty at this hour. The cooing grew louder, and then it faded away.

He'd be damned if it didn't sound like a mourning dove.

### 3:30 AM ET

Nestor took a seat back on the sofa and tried concentrating on the movie again. The camera tracked the priest slowly, over his shoulder, and it panned over Tenochtitlán, in New Spain, through his eyes. The music was baroque, authentic to the time period and true to the Spaniards who colonized; the sound of the lute, the harpsichord, and the guitar flooded the living room.

He took small sips of the horchata as he watched the film. The plot was utterly simple. An indigenous man and wife infiltrated the aristocracy of the capital of New Spain by disguising themselves as servants of the royal court. The wife dressed as a man to pose as a servant, while the husband used his oratory skills to fake his way as a visiting poet to impress the courts with his memorizations of Spanish poetry and the rapidity in which he had learned the language of his colonizers and slave masters.

The husband and wife devised a plot to murder La Malinche, the woman who had acted as translator for Hernán Cortés and aided him to infiltrate and claim victory over the Aztec Empire just eight years before. La Malinche had borne a son to Cortés, and the infant was half Aztec, half Spanish, and an additional target of the planned assassination.

The husband and wife met in secret, in the streets behind the cathedral, invoking their devotion to someone they called the Night Drinker, praying for renewal and fertility of the Aztecs in exchange for the murder of La Malinche and her baby.

Halfway through the film, Nestor took a small break to refill his glass with horchata.

The husband and wife finally consulted a small piece of deerskin to confirm the timing of their planned murder. The parchment showed intricate and colorful pictorial images depicting many birds, set into rectangular spaces on the page. The married couple spoke in Nahuatl, and the subtitles shed light on the secrets of the deerskin. According to the panels of that codex, they would appease the Night Drinker by delivering him a sacrifice.

Malinche, beautiful in her raven-black hair and voluptuous beauty, walked through the halls of the palace in Spanish clothes, her face distant and melancholy. She kissed her son good night and walked to the lower levels of the palace to a large pool. There, she bathed her naked skin under the blue light of the moon, and staring into the camera, she divined her own future, by singing a song in Nahuatl over the surface of the water in her bath. The baroque music from the soundtrack swelled, syncing up perfectly to the rhythms of her ancient song.

From the shadows, the husband and wife emerged, their eyes glinting like jewels in the dark. They were both clothed in their servant apparel, and each one of them held long knives. The husband's knife was made of limestone, and the woman's was obsidian, dark as night. They jumped onto Malinche and wrestled with her in the water, attempting to drown her at the same time that they tried to slice her chest open. The young woman promised in Nahuatl to kill Malinche, repeating the word *temactecahuani*, or "traitor", in a rhythmic chant.

Shots rang out. Through the shadows, Spanish soldiers emerged, holding muskets that they had shot just a moment before. The camera cut to the bodies of the husband and wife in the bloody pool. One of the Spanish soldiers, frenzied in rage, used the obsidian knife to stab the intruders. The soldier's blond hair shook and flailed as he jammed the knife into the woman's throat. As he did so, he prayed to the Virgin and to the Christ for the eradication of these filthy pagan savages. The camera tracked smoothly into the soldier's mouth to relish the ecstasy on his lips as he invoked the holy trinity and blood spattered his face. The soldier stepped away from the bodies, and the camera focused on the ragged wound in the husband's chest, exposed under the moonlight. Right there was the single frame of film that David Avila had shown Nestor. But in this video version, there was no spectral figure hovering over them. Instead, just naked violence.

He asked his TV to pause, and he moved through the scene frame by frame. After the camera cut back to a wide shot of the pool, he let the movie roll at normal speed again.

Nestor gasped. As the sounds of birds and of footsteps filled Nestor's ears, the movie drew to a close, with La Malinche's face pressed against the walls of the palace and tears sliding down her cheek. Her face remained stone-like, unmoving, showing not a single note of emotion, even as the tears cascaded down. Her baby was alive, and she had survived the attack. The room was lit only by candles, and the shadows that were cast onto the walls loomed gigantic, like colossal giants. The credits rolled.

Nestor took a sip from his drink, and he tasted something off, vile.

He looked down at the lip of his glass, and the creamy white horchata was gone. He was sipping blood, tangy and metallic from the mason jar he used as a glass. Nestor put a finger to his lips, and they came away bloody. He spat out horchata, blood, and very soon thereafter vomited into the kitchen sink.

## 4:17 AM ET

Nestor vomited one more time into the sink, spat and coughed. He looked down. There was no blood. Just white and gray liquid from the water and horchata he had drunk earlier.

He turned back toward the living room, armed with Windex and paper towels, and as the credits continued to roll, the same priest from the beginning of the film was walking at night now, toward a church whose windows glowed in gold.

He picked up the glass, disgusted, afraid, unable to shake his disbelief.

The glass only held horchata, white as snow. Not one drop of blood.

He dipped his finger into the milky liquid and put a drop on his tongue. Sweet and infused with the taste of rice. Nothing wrong with it. He wiped the table down.

He shook his head and moved on to wipe down the photos on the walls. Why not. He was already wired as hell. He stared at photos of his mother, father, sister, and below those photos, a tiny icon of the Lady of the Rosary of Chiquinquirá, which his mother had blessed in Medellín in person twenty years before. The virgin's face, creamy white, looked down on the crowned baby Jesus in her arms, and she was flanked by Saint Anthony of Padua and Saint Andrew.

Immediately, the four icons took Nestor back to a simpler time, when his mother cooked potato patties in a kitchen the size of a matchbox, and he, wearing a pleated skirt, twirled his braided pigtails while waiting for the hot cakes. His grandmother Paloma had lain in the living room, propped up by pillows and already succumbing to late-stage dementia, but the icon of the Virgin and her son brought him comfort in this memory. No pain.

Nestor genuflected and put his fingertips on the surface of the icon, at the foot of the Virgin's red robes. He went into his bedroom, stripped, brushed his teeth, rinsed with Listerine, and got into bed.

As he drifted into sleep, he heard the mourning dove cooing again, as if it were perched right along his windowsill. He thought about getting up to check it out, but soon, he was asleep.

His sleep was restless and his dreams full of sorrow. In dream, he listened to harpsichord sounds through silvery speakers shaped like satellite dishes, and his heart steeped in sadness.

# DAY 2
## TUESDAY OCTOBER 21, 2025

**MANHATTAN**
**9:58 AM ET**

Nestor pulled out Marlene's dresser drawers one by one. The warrant had come in quickly this morning, perhaps too quickly, because he wasn't exactly ready to go through the woman's belongings. This is one of the most humiliating parts for crime victims, and though he had desensitized himself to many parts of the job over the years, this was a ritual that he would never be comfortable with.

He started with the bottom drawers first. Expensive cashmere sweaters, in only two colors: black and gray. The middle drawers contained summer clothes, including shorts and tanks. Beneath the swimsuits he found a baggie of marijuana, tucked in next to bottles of oxycodone, Norco, and fentanyl. Toxicology had already confirmed that Grue had alcohol and Norco in her system, but he was surprised to see such an array of other painkillers.

Above the smooth surface of the dresser, Marlene Grue stared out into the camera in several photographs set in Barbados, Washington DC, and also from Prospect Park in Brooklyn. Her smile was radiant, magnetic. But away from the kiss of the smartphone lens, Marlene had consumed these candy-shaped opiates, softening the sharp edges of life. Nestor tucked the weed and the bottles into a ziplock and labeled them.

The second-to-last drawer was an absolute mess, a tangle of shoelaces, loose change, four dog-eared romance paperbacks by Paolo Midori, old receipts, and assorted watches and jewelry. In the back of the drawer he found a Polaroid photo of Marlene Grue outside a movie theater. It didn't look like any theater in New York City. Its marquee glowed gold with soft bulbs lining the border. In the photo, she hugged her sister Lilith and a tall man, presumably their father. Grue looked to be about twenty-four years old. She wore her hair in what was clearly the Rachel haircut, as worn by Jennifer Aniston.

In those days, Nestor too had asked his hairdressers for the Rachel. He got many compliments on it, but he had only been going through the motions then. The truth was, he hated getting his hair done, had hated makeup and lacquered nails. It seemed so long ago that it felt like a dream.

The top drawer contained neatly folded underwear of a brand Nestor had never seen. Perhaps custom, very expensive-looking. The ivory-colored pieces were extremely soft to the touch and still as a museum object. He ran his gloved fingers beneath the panties and the bras, and he felt underneath, finding some hard edges.

He pulled out Marlene's passport. Born May 12, 1973, just one day after he had been born.

He tucked the passport into the ziplock. He also withdrew a flat plastic container with handles. Inside he found a prescription for estrogen and progestin, part of Marlene Grue's hormone replacement therapy. Nestor had a similar plastic container in his house, but his was tucked into the shelves of his tiny bathroom. His container held tiny syringes and vials of testosterone, which he administered on a weekly basis, but which most people politely pretended to know nothing about. For Nestor, the hormones were not a replacement but an augmentation of who he had always known he was inside. He felt embarrassed for the dead woman as he jotted down the name of her doctor and the dosages of her hormones. The dosages had nothing to do with her murder, but curiosity forced him to scribble the milligrams nonetheless.

Marlene Grue was no longer on this earth to defend herself, to feel any embarrassment over a strange man going through her panties and her drugs, and her artificial hormones.

Nestor had read once in a magazine that though hearts were biologically very similar for men and women, the differences between the two genders were dependent on its sensitivity to the male and female hormones. He put his hand on his chest and felt the beats, mellow, like a tropical song, and glanced around the room.

So far, he could find not a single trace of anything amiss in Marlene Grue's life. It was as if she had been snatched very much at random, as if the universe were out to prove its horrors by creating a random signature.

He looked out the windows and noticed that the sun had come out for a moment. It burst into the room in harsh white light, creating shadows sharp as blades, and dark as tar. It didn't exactly feel good, or noble. It felt like an intrusion.

## 10:50 AM ET

Nestor sat in the reception of Morton & Morton, opposite Bryan Berger, who had come out to greet him with a handshake like a vise. Nestor was not permitted to step inside the offices of the law firm. Instead, each of the lawyers who he had interviewed had come out into the reception area to talk to *him*, one by one. Bryan Berger had been the last of the interviews. Berger took a seat directly opposite of Nestor, on a leather sofa. His skin glowed; his voice was soft, pleasant. By God, he was handsome.

"And how long had you known Marlene Grue?"

"Since I was hired at the firm three years ago. That was in 2022."

"What kind of manager was she to you?"

"One of the best. A strong decision-maker, extremely smart. I feel like I learned so much from her."

"What was she like when she was not in leader mode?"

"I couldn't answer that properly. She was always, always working."

"Was she a workaholic?"

"Yes. I don't think I could imagine what she would be like outside this office, because she was always here."

Berger's eyes lost their focus, and for a moment, they moistened. Then he came back to the present moment.

So far, everything checked out with Bryan Berger. He had an

alibi. He had been in meetings at Morton & Morton at the time of the murder. He seemed very vested in his life there at the firm.

"Mr. Berger, who has inspired you the most in your life?"

Berger frowned.

"Detective, I don't see what that question has to do with my coworker's death."

"Indulge me."

"You ask very strange questions for a policeman."

"Who inspired you the most?"

"Well, that would have to be my father. His work ethic, the way he stood up to adversity."

"What adversity?"

"My dad, everyone called him the Tin Man, worked two jobs as a cabinet maker, and at the same time, he fought hard for equality and social justice. If you were to ask him today to roll up his sleeves, he'd show you the third-degree burns he got on his forearms in a lynching when he was a kid, growing up in rural Indiana. He made a good life for himself and his children."

"Marlene was African-American, like you. Do you think she made many enemies at the firm?"

"Detective, are you saying this crime was racially motivated?"

"I am asking you if she made any enemies in this firm. I'm asking you if she was unliked. Did she have problems being black around here?"

Bryan Berger's lip quivered, and then an icy stare hardened his eyes.

"She was the first partner of color here at the firm. I think it's inevitable that would irk some people that think in old ways."

"What old ways are those, Mr. Berger?"

"You should know. You're Spanish, aren't you?"

"No. I am Mexican and Colombian."

Berger's lip quivered and he fidgeted in his seat.

"My apologies Detective. That wasn't very politically correct. I should know better than assume—"

"No apology needed. But Miss Grue—"

"She fought hard to get more black lawyers into this firm. She was relentless in driving diversity in hiring. I don't think anyone could match what she did."

"You didn't answer my question. Did she have any enemies?"

"She was well liked."

"Would you say she was…perfect?"

"Detective Buñuel, what are these questions all about?"

Nestor let his eyes soften, to let Berger believe that he too was bewitched by Bryan's collegiate good looks. Nestor smiled, letting the wrinkles in his eyes crease and fold. Flirtatious, without being overt. It didn't matter if Berger was cis and straight; he clearly liked attention from men.

"Just indulge me, Mr. Berger."

"Well, yes, I'd say she was like no other lawyer I ever met. Smart, beautiful, politically driven. A beacon of social justice."

"And besides enemies, do you think she had any romantic partners here at the firm?"

"None, Detective."

Berger leaned forward. There, a pull on the line, like casting a fishing line in the ocean.

"She was a bit of a loner, if you want my honest opinion."

"Can you explain?"

"She was untouchable. Perfect looks, with lots of money and power. But also black," Berger said. "That combination of traits doesn't bode well for a single woman — after all, most of the partners here, who are white, tend to marry white spouses, if you know what I mean."

"What are you trying to say?"

Berger cocked his head and scrutinized Nestor silently.

"Is there anything else you'd like to ask me, Detective? I have clients waiting for me in my office."

"Just one question. Are you the second black partner here at the firm?"

"Only my father was black. My mother is white."

"You didn't answer my question."

"Get out of this office, Detective Buñuel. Your line of interrogation is inappropriate. If you want to profile me and my blackness, I will take this up in a lawsuit against the NYPD."

Nestor buttoned his suit jacket and stood up. He offered his hand to Berger, but the young man kept his hand to himself.

"And yes, I am the second African-American partner in the history of this firm."

*Bingo.* Men with big egos love to talk about themselves, to showcase their accomplishments.

## 11 AM ET

He exited the elevator of Morton & Morton, and his phone throbbed inside his coat pocket.

"Ahhh, Mom, why are you calling now?" Nestor said.

"Excuse me?" said a woman working at the info desk. Nestor shook his head and waved.

"Parents," he said.

Nestor put the phone up to his ear and said "Mamá, hi."

"Nestor, I had an idea."

"What's that, Ma?"

"I have an idea. You, me, and a couple of your cousins — we go to Medellín next month. We leave before the snows come."

"I doubt I can do that, Ma. I have to deliver my books."

"But you will be finished at your job. You will have free time."

"And another job continues."

"You take a break from writing your book. You will need the break."

"Can't do that, Ma."

His mother hummed to herself for a moment. It was nothing more than a single high note. But when she made this sound, he knew that she disapproved of his answer, and that she would bide her time until she pushed back on him in a future conversation.

"Ma, what do you think of when people talk about La Malinche?"

"From Mexico?"

"That's the one."

"Ah, Doña Marina, La Traidora. According to your father, she's the one who sold Mexico out to the Spanish crown."

Nestor's ears rang for a moment, and he pulled the phone away from his face. Pain rang throughout his skull, and he winced. As his eyes turned upward into the modern atrium of the building, he spotted a smudge, nothing more than a stain, flittering above the revolving doors.

"Keep talking, Ma," Nestor said.

"You're distracted," she said. "Are you checking your email while we talk?"

"You are like a psychic, you know that?"

"I'm shaking my head."

The shadow shifted. Nestor broke out in goose bumps. The tiny smudge dove in lazy figure eights around the edge of the steel frame of the revolving door. He couldn't pull his eyes away from it. Nestor found a spot right off to the side of the doorway, where he wouldn't obstruct traffic.

The smudge was the most brilliant shades of blue and red, and it flittered and buzzed.

"How in the world?" said a security guard at the door. She was portly, solid. "Fucking moth."

"That's no moth," Nestor said. The security guard opened a set of service doors for people with disabilities. It slid open with smooth, controlled movement.

"It's a hummingbird," he said.

"Now shoo, shit."

The bird flew right toward Nestor's nose and hovered for a moment, starting at him with beaded eyes like black jewels. And as if on cue, it flittered out through the doorway.

"Ma, what would Dad say if he were alive, about La Malinche?"

"That we'll never really know the true story about her life."

"That's helpful, Ma. I'll call you soon."

"May the Virgin keep you blessed, Nestorcito."

He terminated the call and stepped through the doorway, nodding to the security guard, and as he walked through the rectangular opening, a thought came over him. Yes, the rectangle meant something, and the bird inside the rectangle, passing through it, reminded him of something he had seen. Something that was...important.

*Holy shit, man. The rectangles.* He remembered the movie he had watched the night before, and how the married couple from *9 Lords of Night* had pored over the deerskin, planning a murder that could have changed history, and the neat rows of rectangles painted with red borders, filling the space like a grid, showing them a story, panel by panel.

Each rectangle had a little bird in it.

And he had seen little symbols, neatly lined up like icons inside a grid, recently, carved right into Marlene Grue's skin. Icons, indecipherable, neatly lined up, unknowable.

But only unknowable until someone deciphered them.

Nestor turned his mouth again toward the mouthpiece of the mobile. "Ma, I'll have to call you back."

He needed to understand those symbols, and he needed to do it soon. As he walked out onto 42nd Street, he broke into a jog.

## CHICAGO
## 11:29 AM ET

"Shoshannah flows down the stairway because she's much too elegant to simply walk. But never mind her glamour; she's dead set on her mission, and the way the camera lens eats her up, the way it cherishes the sheen of her hair, her lips — that in itself is pure poetry."

Wes was almost out of breath. His words were machine-gun rounds, interrupted only by his break to inhale weed off the vaporizer.

Felix turned down the heat on the pan and cracked two eggs into it. Wes exhaled marijuana vapor. Felix suspended a pinch of salt in his pressed fingers above the eggs, and he let the crystals snow downward for even seasoning.

"Shoshannah sounds like a badass."

"Because she *is* a fucking badass. Just think Ripley."

"Who?"

"I forgot. Felix Andersen Calvo was way too *kewl* to see *Aliens* back in the day."

"Fuck off," Felix said. "Or you don't get any breakfast."

"It's good to see you up and about, doing something other than sleeping. Been worried about you."

"Is that so?"

"You never leave the house anymore. As in *never* leave the house anymore."

"Haven't felt great."

"And?"

"I went to Big Chicks last night. Doesn't that count?"

Wes Cravis chucked away his expensive Nikes and untucked his shirt. It was funny; he not only looked like an East-Coast boarding school poster boy, he had lived the life of one as if he could not escape his destiny to remain one. His aloof but astute alcoholic mother had placed him in boarding school when he was fourteen, and the trust fund had surely helped to make sure he stayed on track, heading for the law school of his destiny. But behind closed doors existed queer Wes, who had a thing for hairy tattooed men in seedy bars, and who preferred Coors Light over wine knowledge his father wanted him to master in order to "live up to expectations".

"If you've been asleep for the past ten years—and I'm going to tell you that you have been asleep, Felix—real talk—then you would have missed *Inglourious Basterds*. Why don't we watch it? I took a sick day today and it's in my library."

Felix hissed. "Do we have to?"

"You packed for New York already?"

"Yep."

"Then we have time to watch it."

"Man, you don't give up."

"What does the interview consist of, anyway, for one of these teaching jobs?"

"The first day is a tour of the campus, meeting some of the doctoral students. Then we go to dinner with other faculty."

"Dinner? Sounds like torture."

"It's not that bad."

"And then?"

"On the second day, I give a guest lecture."

"And in this lecture, you dazzle them like some sort of sissy Da Vinci Code Tom Hanks guy."

"Uhm, it's not at all like that, bitch, trust me."

"And then? How else do you make these professors stay shook?"

"Then there's the interview with the faculty committee who will make the decision to hire me. Or not."

Felix took another drag from Wes's vaporizer and began to plate the food. Felix couldn't help but arrange the links in a perfect arc, and he garnished it with a sprig of cilantro. It was a composition and not just a plate. Lessons from his mother's restaurant he was never going to give up.

"So, tell me more about this Nazi-killing badass," Felix said.

"Bowie begins to croon, and with each cross-fade, we come in closer to Tarantino's gorgeous blonde, his cinematic nymph. Quentin shares a similar obsession over his heroines as Hitchcock had over Tippi Hedren and Janet Leigh. For Hitchcock they were birds of paradise to be studied from afar, and for Tarantino his women are jungle cats, silent predators in a hellish world that doesn't understand them."

"One would almost think you want to fuck women."

"Ew, no, shush, girl. Just don't talk about Tarantino and Hitchcock's obsessions openly in a women's studies program, because they'll only tell you it's misogyny. But if feminists took just one second to see how much magic Tarantino imbues in Shoshannah... Well, fuck. But back to the scene. She applies eyeliner and rouge — the femme fatale with a secret mission. We cut to the cameraman and lover filming her in a hallway below, in flashback — it's a movie within the movie, you see?"

"Okay. I still don't know why I need to see it."

"Shut up. Shoshannah loads the reel, and the camera is still in love with her. On goes the pillbox hat, and she lowers its mesh like a war mask. It's all as primal as you can get and bigger than war. It's absolutely tribal, her war paint. She's the biggest force in the movie, the real hero."

"You should have skipped University of Chicago and gone to film school."

"Stop interrupting me. Picture it: Shoshannah inspects the decadent Nazis seated in the movie theater one last time, and then the chaos begins. She's going to make a lot of people suffer."

Wes's words stretched thanks to the cannabis, and soon, his retelling of *Inglourious Basterds* faded into a fog. Wes poured the last can of IPA in the fridge into clean coffee mugs. They always split the booze and the weed down the middle. Wes was a good roommate.

"Okay, let's watch your movie."

Felix tried to follow the plot of the film, but his mind was hazy. Violence exploded on the screen without warning, and he recoiled from seeing so much blood. When the characters spoke—and boy did they talk a lot—too much really—their words turned tinny, as if someone had put the TV speakers at the end of a long tunnel.

"Christopher Waltz's chin is fucking huge," Felix said.

"You're ruining the magic."

At the bottom of Felix's notification screen, a direct message from someone named Nestor Buñuel arrived. Felix read the message three times, unsure of what to make of the text. The profile photo showed a bearded man with a thick neck and eyes like charcoal.

"Check this out. Some cop just DMed me."

"Wow, you're really branching out in the dating pool. Cops,

eh?"

Wes grabbed Felix's phone. He squinted, forgetting about the Tarantino movie. He tapped a few times until he arrived at the profile of the sender.

"Oh my god, he's a fucking hot butch bear. You gonna say yes to a date?"

"Shut up. How strong is this weed, anyway? I can't even focus my eyes."

"So, what's he asking you? If you're a top or you bottom?"

"No, he wants me to call him."

"Call him Daddy?"

"No, he wants to talk about a police investigation."

## MANHATTAN
## 11:46 AM ET

Nestor knocked on the door, but no one answered. NYU students walked up and down the hallway behind him, alert only to their own problems. He might as well have been invisible, and he preferred it that way.

He knocked one more time, right below the plastic plate that read SHAZEB UMRANI, FILM STUDIES CHAIR.

No response. Nestor looked up the professor's name in his contacts app and tried texting. Couldn't hurt. Maybe Umrani was running late.

*I'm outside your office, let me know if we're still on for meeting,* Nestor wrote.

A metallic ping rang out from inside the office. Then he heard shuffling.

The door cracked open, and a short man in his early fifties peered at Nestor through eyes dark as coffee.

"Can I help you?"

"I'm looking for Professor Umrani," Nestor said.

"And you are..."

"Detective Nestor Buñuel, NYPD."

Umrani showed no surprise.

"Ah, of course, you're the policeman, Alexa's—"

"Ex-husband."

"Ah, yes, I miss Alexa a lot, I need to call her. Sadly, Detective, I'm afraid right now is not a good time."

"But in our phone call earlier, you agreed to see me at 11:45."

"At the time, I thought this might be for something *actually* important."

"This is related to a case I'm working on."

"You'll need to wish my best to Alexa; maybe we can just reschedule."

"Mr. Umrani, I need to talk to an expert in film, and Alexa said you two—"

"Not right now, Detective." Umrani started to shut the door, but Nestor caught a glimpse of another person inside. Without stepping through the threshold, he leaned forward, to suggest to the professor that he was about to come in. Umrani was unprepared for Nestor's sudden move, and he opened the door.

A handsome man about twenty years old sat on the sofa. He wore a gauze-thin hoodie and skinny jeans. His sandy hair was disheveled; the small office smelled of cologne and sweat.

"Come back this afternoon, Eli," Umrani said. "We'll resume our chat later."

The student smirked, and smoothed out the front of the hoodie. Nestor could see the young man was built like a varsity athlete.

"Since you insist on interrupting my office hours, what can I do for you, Officer…Buena?"

"It's Buñuel."

"Well, if you can be bothered to read a bit, you can read my book *Maps of Being*. It lays out all my theories about film. I'm not sure you and I need to actually meet."

The reedy professor inspected Nestor's face, his body. He was being sized up sexually, even though this man was about to kick Nestor out of this office. Sun broke through the slats of the window blinds, and for a moment, Nestor covered his eyes with one hand, and the professor faded into the room.

*Is this truly the best person Alexa could have thought of?* The man was a prick. Instead of nurturing the urge to squeeze the professor by the neck, Nestor chose to remain loyal to his ex-wife by remaining polite.

"Professor, do all your office hours include heavy petting?"

But not that polite. *Sorry, Alexa.*

Umrani blushed, and he flicked the nail of his middle finger onto his thumbnail, making a hard clicking sound.

"Excuse me?"

*Good, now I really have his attention.* Nestor removed his black jacket and draped it over his forearm. Umrani stared at the razor-thin tattoo that ran down Nestor's right forearm in Arabic, but he didn't ask about it. Instead, he kept his eyes focused on Nestor's big chest and bearded face.

"Mr. Umrani, what do you know about the films of Samuel Kahan?"

Umrani turned his head toward his computer, walked around the desk so he could shut it off, and put papers away, answering Nestor's question without looking at him directly.

"Samuel Kahan's films are precise as Swiss watches, cold and full of intelligence. Also, highly overrated."

"May I have a seat?"

"No, you may not. I'll need you to walk out with me. That's all the time I can give you."

*What. An. Asshole.* Nestor repeated the three words to himself mentally twice. Umrani collected his suit jacket and slipped into it. Nestor held the door open while the short man scurried through and locked up the office.

"You got a good glimpse of Eli, didn't you?"

Nestor nodded.

"The chiseled looks of Tab Hunter, and a cleft chin like Cary Grant's. Stunning."

Nestor shrugged as Umrani chuckled. This short man was probably sleeping with more than one of his male students. He had met men like this before, and they didn't operate on modesty or low volume.

"I did, yes."

"I'm a very lucky academic, Detective. Many men could only dream of having students such as that one, don't you think?"

"Professor, are you aware of any hidden messages inside the films of Samuel Kahan?"

"You must be kidding. I have been debunking that idea for thirty years. Each of his dozen or so films is disconnected from the next. His movies were nothing but the exercises of a control freak. Beautiful, yes, but not my favorite."

"Nine out of ten people seem to disagree with you. They say he is a master of film."

"Everyone today has an opinion, especially in the comments

section."

"His movie *Kino Ludovico* was banned in the UK after it incited vandals to break store windows in central London."

"Means nothing, detective. Kahan took an original idea from the novelist Anthony Burgess and turned it into vulgar, low-grade pornography."

This was getting Nestor nowhere.

"Professor Umrani, do I have to actually pay you a fee so that you'll help me?"

Umrani pressed the button on the elevator.

"Detective, you can't afford me. Just look at you."

"I'll ask you one more time. Beyond the *Kino Ludovico* incidents in the UK, have people been…inspired to commit crimes based on the movies by Kahan?"

The elevator hummed on the way down. The professor adjusted his tailored jacket and fixed his glossy black hair.

"The tenure system has been good to me, and I don't intend to bring the wrong kind of attention to my personal brand. Do you understand that, Detective?"

"What *is* your personal brand?"

"You are looking at it. I have three TED talks under my belt, five books, and a recurring spot on MSNBC on Tuesday nights. Currently negotiating a new show on Discovery. I don't have time for conspiracy theories. Shouldn't you be at customs at JFK Airport arresting Pakistanis like me for being terrorists anyway?"

"Do you talk this way to everyone?"

"No, just to those in blue uniforms. Or in your case, cheap T-shirts from The Gap."

Nestor and the professor stared at the LED readout. They reached the ground floor. Why had Alexa tipped him off to this asshole? He had wasted half a morning to get there and had nothing to show for it.

The doors opened, and they walked out into the lobby. "My next available appointment is in four weeks."

"I need answers sooner," Nestor said.

"I have an appointment across town. It was good meeting you, Detective."

As they exited the elevator, a hard body crashed into Nestor, and he felt sharp pain in his ribs. Long black hair flailed around his face. A young woman's face flashed in his vision and her backpack crashed on her floor. Her smartphone also hit the marble with a hollow cracking sound.

"Clara, what the hell is your problem?" Umrani screamed. The young woman turned her gaze toward the professor. What Nestor saw in her eyes was pure rage and defiance. If he didn't know any better, he thought she might punch the scholar with her fist.

"Detective Buñuel, this is Clara Montes."

## 12:02 PM ET

The young woman fidgeted with her phone and tucked it away. She cracked a thin smile, and he noticed one of her eyes was discolored, a watery gray that suggested she was blind in that eye.

"Professor Umrani is my doctoral advisor, yes. I'm Clara Montes, nice to meet you."

"I have to run, Detective, but it was so great talking to you," Umrani said. The professor was all smiles now that they were in a public space. He took a short bow and wandered off into the street.

"I hate him," Clara said.

"You're a candid one."

"And at this point, it's too late to request a change."

"Maybe you can help me."

"You are police?" she said. She crossed her arms and stiffened, her feet planted firm on the floor. Nestor showed her his badge.

"NYPD, yes. I'm investigating a case, and I wanted to know more about the films of Samuel Kahan."

"I'm the wrong person for that. PhD students tend to know an inordinate amount of things about a very narrow subject. That particular subject is not mine."

"And that means?"

"That I haven't watched most movies film buffs talk about. I don't care about the latest adventures of Darth Vader, Wonder Woman or Harry Potter's neurotic son. Much less Samuel Kahan's puzzle-box films."

"And your focus is on what then, Miss Montes?"

"The right-wing propaganda films of Clint Eastwood."

"That's very specific, for sure."

"He and Leni Riefenstahl were both a very specific kind of war criminal."

"That's what you think they were?"

Clara did not answer his question. Instead, she smiled, inviting more conversation to happen.

Nestor hadn't fallen in love since he had met Alexa, but he knew that if he were just a couple of decades younger, a woman like this could win his heart within seconds. Clara wore a plain black turtleneck and jeans, and she exuded a restless energy, as if molecules and atoms were vibrating all around her.

"If your scholarly focus is that tight, then you probably can't help me, you're right."

Nestor stared down at his hands, folded his smartphone into a tab the size of a stick of gum, and slid it into his jeans. Silence spread between him and Clara Montes, and he waited just a moment or two before she asked the next logical question.

"What's this crime you're investigating, Detective?"

"The murder of a woman."

"A white woman?"

"Black."

"Well, all right, then, you have my attention."

"Is it possible for someone to be inspired by the films of Samuel Kahan to commit a murder? I admit I only saw his vampire flick, *The Marsten House,* and the space movie, *Xenogenesis,* a long time ago."

He didn't mention seeing *9 Lords of Night.* He needed to keep that card close to his chest.

Clara turned her shoulders toward the street, and the muddy light of Manhattan lit up her large cheekbones.

"I suppose anyone can be inspired by any piece of art to commit murder. *The White Album, Kill Them All, Natural Born Killers, Watchmen.* It's all fair game."

"What about *ØIE?*"

Clara Montes started walking, and she put her hand on Nestor's shoulder.

"Come down to the bodega with me. I'll buy you a coffee."

"You don't seem keen on cops."

"I'm not. But I like seeking justice served, and besides, I have questions for *you.*"

"Oh, do you?"

"When I bumped into you, I was going to go upstairs to get some reading done, but I have a little bit of free time, and I haven't

106

had any coffee yet."

"Yes, I would definitely like a coffee."

"First question, then."

"Shoot."

"Are we being recorded? I need you to turn off your body cams and mics if it's so."

"I've been doing this job a long time. You have my promise."

Nestor showed her the airplane mode on his smartphone and also on his portable camera in his pocket. He also shut off his smartwatch completely. She nodded, though she narrowed her eyes with suspicion anyway.

"Second question."

"Okay."

"Is it true that the traffic drones at intersections can be armed with guns?"

"What gave you that idea?"

"It's not an idea. It's a type of certainty. No other city invests this much money on equipping the police with army-like tech."

"The drones use facial recognition technology, and cameras and speakers so they interact with people."

"You didn't answer my question."

"That's because I honestly don't know."

He really didn't know. It hadn't occurred to him that the flying traffic drones could be outfitted with weapons. What did this young woman think about?

"I'm telling you the truth," he said.

Clara's gray eye stared vacantly into space, and she nodded.

"I know," she said.

"And what do drones have to do with your doctoral thesis?"

"I am interested in the drones because they are everywhere nowadays. There's no public space that's free of their surveillance. And I worry."

They walked down 14th Street and turned onto smaller streets. The coffee in the shop was weak, but the privacy they had in the bodega was better than what they could get at Starbucks or out on the street.

"So, the film *ØIE*—"

"I saw it last weekend."

"You said you had no time for other movies."

"I have a life, too. And my friends wanted me to see it. I said yes because it won't be long before the movie theater as we know it dies like the dinosaurs."

"What do you mean?"

"Movie theaters lose money. A lot. People prefer to watch movies in their homes or on VR sets. Cinemas are becoming something else altogether. I go to the movies to hold on to the memories of how movies used to be."

"And so, tell me about *ØIE*."

"It's another movie that objectifies and oppresses women of color and Muslims."

"Is that so?"

"Just like the novelist who wrote the book."

"Is the film similar to the novel?"

"Mostly, yes. Though Kahan simplified a few things, and he made the film's themes more about womanhood than the novelist David Saba did."

"How does *ØIE* oppress women and Muslims?"

"It's a piece of garbage. Kahan appropriated every culture for entertainment purposes for decades."

"Not sure I follow."

"When Kahan bought the film rights to Octavia Butler's novel *Dawn* and made *Xenogenesis*, he had no idea what black women really go through, but he got his sci-fi film about a black woman made, didn't he? And now we have this new movie. He never set a foot in Iraq, he didn't consult Muslim women, but he sure felt like he could speak on their behalf in *ØIE*."

"I am not sure if I agree with you on this idea of appropriation."

"You don't have to. His films are objectifications of women, people of color, and Muslims. It's an objective truth at this point."

Nestor had so many responses in store for this woman, including his own struggles to write his novels, to inhabit the lives of fictional people, creatures, and things, as well as the fiction of his own identity, the challenges of a lifetime spent trying to understand what was true, what was borrowed, and what was simply an artistic act that he made up every day he got out of bed. He could see a rage building in the young woman, and he decided to change the subject before she grew more irate. Her anger seduced him further.

"Do you think that a viewing of *ØIE* could inspire someone..."

"Inspire them to do what? Murder a black woman?"

"Correct. I can only say that the case I am investigating is very violent. And there's a link to that film, possibly or maybe others."

"No, I don't think ØIE would be the one to trigger someone, to be honest. It's just premiered. And the murders in that film come from a terrorist bombing. The murders come out of an ideology, not a motive against a single person."

"You're smart. This is part of what we do when we develop a profile."

"A movie to inspire would have to be one that's been around for some time, a movie with a lot more of a legacy. A picture from when he was at the top of his game."

"I guess most people would say he was at his creative peak around the time he made *Kino Ludovico*, *The Marsten House* and *Hasford and the Body Count.*"

"I liked *Body Count,* actually. It's both grim, and a technical masterpiece."

"Matthew Modine used to be one of my favorites."

"What's your story?" Clara said to him. She was defiant, maybe even arrogant like her advisor Umrani, but there was a fire behind her eyes, and when she asked, she was listening intently, taking everything in. She had a real curiosity about the world.

"Been a cop for thirty years. I'm good at mining data and going through records. It helps me solve a lot of my caseload. I like the work, as long as other people don't interfere. I have worked a lot of beats. Narcotics, transnational crimes, cybercrime. Cop work is most of what I know."

"I get the sense you're not telling me the full story, Mr. Buñuel."

He felt uneasy, suddenly, as if the young woman could see through him, like an X-ray.

"Well, I write books, too."

"I thought I recognized your face," she said, smiling. "Buñuel...I read one of your novels in high school."

"You say it like it was a long time ago."

"High school was the last time I felt the innocence of childhood, so yes, it was a long time ago."

"Fair enough." This woman was tougher than she looked. He noticed she had scars running underneath her jawline and across the right side of her face, as if she had been mauled by some wild animal.

"In your books, it is the young characters who organize to take down the regime of interdimensional dictators."

"That's correct."

"I want to thank you for making those main characters brown and black people."

"I don't know who else to write about."

"However, you should know those characters didn't go far enough. They weren't *revolutionary* enough."

"Oh."

Nestor choked on his coffee. The young woman had found his Achilles heel. He did his best to hide his shock, and swallowed his pride. And yet he was amazed she knew his novels so well.

"Autograph my copy of your book sometime, Mr. Buñuel."

"Of course. Whenever you want."

He handed her his business card, and she broke their Internet silence as she checked her phone for texts and Facebook messages. He relished the cheap bitterness of the bodega coffee and the oily feel of cream on his tongue.

The brief silence between them felt very comfortable, very right. His mother always asked him why he wasn't more offended when young people checked their phones in the middle of a conversation, but the truth was, he did it too. He plucked out his phone, turned the wireless access back on, and checked his feeds.

"Tell me about Kahan's *9 Lords of Night*," Nestor said. He turned the airplane mode back on so the young woman could see their conversation was private again.

She also tucked her phone back into her jeans. She frowned, as if she had just tasted something bitter.

"There are myths around that film. That it's cursed, that it drives people mad, that the film itself will haunt the person who watches it. The urban legends that surround *9 Lords* inspired many other films — like the horror film *The Ring* — but Kahan's fans believe that *9 Lords of Night* is a real-world source of — what would you call it — evil?"

"And you— you have—"

"I have seen it, and I can attest, it's likely to inspire madness — if you are an unstable person."

"Why is that?"

"Because Samuel Kahan was a master of movie-making. His

visual compositions are so dense, and intellectually maze-like that many fans over the years have been seduced by the clues they find in all of his movies. Conspiracy theories. Notions of the Illuminati, which is ridiculous, and even mystical connections."

"So, what type of person is likeliest to have seen *9 Lords of Night?*"

"Film nerds and geeks who like bootlegs. It's not that hard to get a hold of it. Do you know what a torrent is?"

*I look so old to her*, Nestor thought.

"Boy, do I. I investigate cybercrimes from time to time."

"You can find the film there."

"Thanks."

"But rest assured, *9 Lords of Night* is also a film that has no shame about appropriation."

"Why do you say that?"

"Kahan appropriated Mexican culture and history to make his prophetic film. That film should have been made by a Mexican filmmaker instead of him. If you ask me, Kahan was a thief."

"So, no one can make a piece of art about an experience that they have not lived out in person?"

"Don't play innocent, Detective. You sound like a person with white privilege."

"That's something I do not or will ever have, Clara."

"Thought so."

"And why didn't *9 Lords of Night* ever get released?"

"Battles with the studio over the final cut. Excessive violence and gore. Insurance costs. There were many accidents on set, including two crew members who were decapitated by a lighting rig. Weird-ass rumors."

"Look, I should get back now, Clara. But it's been nice meeting you. I realize you are not keen on police, so I appreciate your time and attention."

"Sure thing."

Clara turned her face toward the windows, and despite the dim light of the sun behind the clouds, her eyes took on a bright quality, as if she were older and wiser than she was lettting on.

"The woman who was murdered — how did she die?"

"Most likely severe blood loss, but can't say for sure yet. We're still investigating."

"Murders of black women are always forgotten." Clara's

expression changed from deep anger into melancholy. She moved her eyes away from Nestor's.

"One last question—what did *9 Lords of Night* make you feel that time you saw it?"

Clara tossed her coffee into the trash, and she crossed her arms. She looked around from side to side, as if making sure she wanted no one to hear what she was about to say.

"I have lived things in my life you would never, ever believe, Detective. Do you believe in monsters?"

"No."

"Do you believe in God?"

"Despite it all, yes."

"So, if you believe in a being called God, or gods, then you must believe in monsters, too."

"What is your point?"

"I have seen the monsters up close. Smelled their rank breath. Heard the violence in their songs. They wear helmets and batons they wield like scepters."

"You sound like my mother with her stories of Colombian boogeymen."

"Kahan's movie is just a movie. It's absolutely different from the dark places I have actually descended into, and yet it does remind me of that place. But I do know people who have been forever disturbed after watching *9 Lords*."

"Miss Montes, thank you for your time."

"Anytime."

Clara Montes peeled off back toward 14th Street, and the crowds in the streets of Manhattan swallowed her up.

**1:37 PM ET**

Felix hopped into the yellow cab, and the world sped up outside the windows. They pulled away from JFK Airport, headed directly for Manhattan. On his phone, a new message from the policeman, Buñuel.

"For real? A question about a movie? I don't have time for this," Felix said out loud, and blocked him.

"Say something?" the taxi driver said. Felix shook his head and grunted.

Felix yanked a tie from his backpack and tied it around his neck, squeezing the air from his throat, and ran his hands through his hair. He tried to calm his mind down, to focus on what he was going to say about his dissertation, and his teaching experience, and his research, and how basically this was his very last chance at surviving in the world at all.

He daydreamed a tune, a soft melody, and as the song formed, he imagined the lyrics to it.

*I am the world's biggest fraud, being fraudulent, doing fraudulent things. And nobody knows it.*

*Only the rocks in the ocean know it.*

"Maybe I need a job as a songwriter."

"Excuse me?"

"Never mind. Talking to myself."

Manhattan grew in size as the taxi sped toward its labyrinth of streets.

## 3:10 PM

The interview was scheduled for 3:30, and Felix had a little extra time. He walked in the direction of the NYU humanities Center in Cooper Square. His heart pounded in his chest, and two stains of sweat already marred his suit. He tightened the knot on his tie. Slow down, he reminded himself.

His mother called on video. He accepted the call. She was in the kitchen of Masa, her restaurant.

"So what's shakin', Brother Bear?"

"You're never gonna give up on my nickname, eh?"

"Lighten up," she said.

"I loved the Berenstain Bear books Ma, but I'm over it."

"Well, I'm not."

His mother radiated a cold, distant beauty, even through the video conference. Today, she had tied her hair up in a ponytail, and he could see her kitchen staff running behind her, prepping for the day in her restaurant. He was surprised she had called at all. She had always been very hands-off with their communication.

"So…I'm back at NYU, for the second round of interviews."

"Neat," she said. She was doing something with her hands off camera, perhaps playing with her phone or evaluating produce from the market that morning. "Will it pay well?"

"That's not exactly the point. It's a tenure job."

"Pay is always the point. Plus, living in New York City — you know I won't be paying for any of that."

"I know."

"Yep."

"I need to get this job. Otherwise…"

"Felix, you need to hustle. Just look at how I made this restaurant come together out of nothing."

Indeed she had. His mother had earned one Michelin star and was one of the best Mexican restaurants in the Twin Cities, even if she didn't speak a lick of Spanish and had virtually no real connection to Mexico.

"Mom, teaching is different than opening a restaurant."

"Meh. It's the same. It's about the work you put into it," she said. In a lifetime, his mother had been brutal, unforgiving in her work ethic. She constantly denied herself any idle or down time, much less expenditures on what she called frivolities.

"I can't just be an adjunct," Felix said.

"And that's because…"

"I've told you. Being an adjunct marks you as obsolete, not fit for tenure. It's a sign of failure. Plus, it pays below minimum wage when you do the math."

"And you would rather keep packing boxes in a warehouse?"

"I don't think you're in touch with how bad the job markets have become in this decade."

"I pay some of my kitchen staff minimum wage. They make it work. An adjunct can make it work too."

"Mom, don't be such a —"

"Such a bitch?" As usual, her face remained flawless, unimpressed.

"Why can't you just be like other moms and just wish me well?"

"Look, Felix, if you're not pulling your weight to get the job you want, there's other options."

"Okay, let me mention one," he said. "How about fast food — because you won't hire me at your restaurant, ever."

"True, go on."

His cheeks burned with humiliation.

"And I could drive an Uber, I suppose, or become a data miner for Microsoft."

"Felix, when you turned eighteen, I told you, figure it out. Get a job, go to college, but you are on your own."

"I remember that, Ma."

"You will figure it out. Since you're on your own."

Felix clenched his toes through his dress shoes. One of his shoelaces popped. Fuck. He held the segment of shoelace in front of his face and tossed it in the trash.

"Can I talk to Dad?"

"He's upstairs in the office, reconciling the books for the restaurant. Why don't you try him tomorrow?"

"I guess," Felix said. His father was just the opposite of his mother, warm, effusive, interested in the details, but often overscheduled, and too busy to talk.

Felix checked his watch. It was time to go in. The committee of the anthropology department was waiting for him. He popped a mint into his mouth and walked through the mouth of the hallway.

"Look, I'll call you and Dad later today or tomorrow."

"Enjoy the city, Felix. Stop into Ivan Ramen in the Lower East Side and eat Ivan's noodles. You won't regret it."

"With what cash?"

"Look, Felix, I gotta go. Kisses."

He hit END on the screen, leaving his mother frozen as she blew a kiss toward the screen. Felix shivered. Just beyond, at the end of the long hallway, sat the hiring committee that would decide his fate.

### 3:29 PM

Nestor wiped his face with a towel, and it came away wet with sweat. His tank top was drenched. He slid his shorts down and flicked the tank into his locker. He grabbed a fresh towel and tied it around his waist.

Nestor's feet made wet taps on the tiled floor of the shower stall. He pulled the vinyl curtain closed, and only when it was closed did he remove the towel from his waist.

He washed his hair, and as the suds sluiced down his scalp and neck, he realized that it wouldn't be long until the media caught wind of Marlene Grue's murder. He scrubbed his neck and he let his mind drift to thoughts about the toxicology report.

It would take at least three weeks until he got the complete results, and in the meantime, he knew he needed to go deeper in his footwork with sources in the city. Berger at the law firm would not be enough. There were other connections to Marlene Grue that he needed to find.

He soaped up his hard body. At the age of fifty-two, it was packed with muscle, as if a mason had hauled slabs of stone, one on top of the other, onto a skeleton. He could thank his father's biology, and, to another extent, hormones, for his lean musculature. He was grateful for being able to hold on to his athleticism, even as the age of sixty peered down at him from around the corner. The thickness in his middle would one day be a belly. And perhaps he was okay with that.

When he finished rinsing, he tied the white towel back around his waist. When he peeled back the rubber curtain, he spotted three males in the locker room. They walked around fully naked. The first two, friends, chit-chatting, ignored him. Only one of them, a tall black man roughly his own size and build, stared Nestor down, evaluating him as a sexual object.

Nestor made eye contact, and he smiled from one of the corners of his mouth. The man nodded, his eyes scanning Nestor's torso and looking at his crotch.

Time moved faster as the steam in the locker room fogged up the air. These were moments that Nestor always had to consider carefully. Cruising in a locker room made his cheeks glow with heat and his neck sweat. This was the intersection of excitement, and, as always, a certain kind of danger.

Nestor considered approaching the man, making plans for a sex date outside the gym, but doing so would take too many steps, and it would require the usual explanations up front about his identity in order to ensure a good sexual encounter. It was honestly easier to do this on a dating app, where the potential partner could know up front who Nestor was.

*Maybe some other time,* Nestor thought. *Not today.*

And yet, it was nice simply to be *seen,* to be visually appreciated by another person in this way. Nestor had lived decades inside his own head, always wishing he could be truly visible to the world, and sometimes, a moment like this landed in his lap.

"Nice day out, huh?" Nestor said.

"Sure is. You live nearby?"

"Queens. I just work near here."

"May be worth taking a break."

There, the stranger had made his invitation. Nestor's mind

focused on the image of the man's muscled body, the sensuous lips, the eyes brown and handsome. But then it morphed into something else: the naked torso in front of him turned into the body of Marlene Grue, its cuts deep and red, like gills on a fish, and the smell of movie-theater popcorn slick and greasy. There was also something else, a sinister image of deep fog, like a swamp, and tiny orbs inside the muck, hundreds of spheres. Nestor tasted something bitter, like bile, on his tongue. He remembered Marlene's eyes rolled back into her head, and how he had arrived at the cinema, with his tiny Sony camera, trying to capture the poor woman's story. Tiptoe, tiptoe.

He snapped his focus back to the present, in the locker room.

He bit his lip and tightened the towel around his waist.

"Maybe some other time."

The other man nodded as he beamed with a smile, and went back to organizing clothes in his duffel bag.

Nestor got dressed and cinched his jacket tight on his body. He brushed his beard. How many times had he turned down encounters like this? How many times had he been turned down when they learned who he was beneath the police clothes, and a layer beneath that, who he was beneath the tank top and briefs? It had happened so many times, he couldn't count them anymore.

"Doesn't matter," he said to himself in the mirror.

He left the Manhattan Sports Club and walked toward the F train.

Nestor hurried into the police station through the side door. In the break room, he poured himself an Earl Grey tea, using a supply of tea bags he carried in his bag. At his desk, he placed his firearm in the drawer. He repeated this small ritual every time he was in the station and needed to focus on writing.

Nestor logged onto his computer, and he entered his credentials into Muninn. The system lit up and Nestor read through his inbox. The message's subject line matched the case of Marlene Grue's murder: MS 10-1-4. Every time a crime was registered, all requests for electronic surveillance were tracked through the software.

*Subject: Case MS 10-1-4*
*Mobile communications: 11*
*Phone communications: 2*
*Video captures: 3*
*Email intercepts: 5*
*Email intercepts (encrypted): 7*

The report only showed the digital communications that officers in the area that the Muninn software was able to link to the case. The software worked on its own, without the aid of human beings. In the two years since its rollout, it had a 99.3 percent accuracy rate. Nestor had a deep respect for the tech startup that had created the product. Muninn pretty much always got it right, and the engineers had paid attention to every single detail. They had really designed it with police in mind.

Nestor scanned the mobile communications first. Out of thousands of messages moving at the time of the murder, Muninn identified eleven that could be connected to the case. Nestor read through them. The majority were sent by David Avila, the cinema's manager. The messages were the typical panicked missives, and it embarrassed Nestor to read through people's personal anxieties like a fly on the wall.

The first messages were from David to his manager at the corporate offices of the theater chain. David Avila had made terrible errors of judgment in using his personal messaging app (tied to Facebook) to communicate with his superiors. Though encrypted, the app was the easiest fodder for Muninn, or anyone else who cared to decrypt the messages. Ward Johnson was David Avila's manager.

*David Avila: Ward we have a bad emergency*
*Ward Johnson: ?*
*David Avila: There's a dead body in the theater. I called 911, but it's really bad*
*Ward Johnson: A customer?*
*David Avila: Yes.*
*Ward Johnson: Did you already shut down the front doors?*
*David Avila: Just like the rulebook says, yes. But — what if the person who did this is still inside the building?*
*Ward Johnson: Can't help you with that. Just keep the phone handy while*

*you wait for the police.*

Nestor shook his head. *That asshole manager was willing to have his employee potentially shot over managing the brand's street presence in Times Square.*

"Brutal," Nestor said out loud to himself.

"You called?" Smith was right behind him, drinking from his usual Starbucks cup.

"Oh hey," Nestor said. "Just checking digital intercepts from yesterday."

"Anything good?"

"Just the theater chain looking out for its interests."

"Any word on a suspect? A name will help us look really good with the mayor."

"None."

Nestor hated talking to people while one person was seated and the other stood. He rose from his seat and took a seat on the edge of his desk. He was of average height at 5' 9", but Smith was taller, 6'2".

"Have we ruled out a husband or lover?"

"She had no love life to speak of. Or so it seems. But still working that angle."

"Any enemies?"

"She worked in corporate law, HR kind of stuff. Most enemies would have been corporate litigators and corrupt CEOs who can't keep their dick in their pants, not sadists with razors."

Smith put his arm on Nestor's shoulder.

"I've been able to hold off the media for a bit, but by today, they'll be running with the story. We've told them that a female attorney has been killed, but we are asking them to hold off on name and personal details."

"Did you disclose her race?"

"No," Smith said. "You know that's like a stick of dynamite in this city."

"I hear what you're saying, but…she was a prominent member of her community. Surely those who knew her will spread the word."

"Then let them, but I won't do it. In the meantime, I need to keep this as vague as possible. If the particulars get out, we will have protests in Times Square."

"But if you suppress her race, you will also get pandemonium," Nestor said.

"I seriously doubt that. Nowadays people focus too much on race. I mean, I don't constantly remind you that I'm white and that you're Hispanic, right?"

"You really want me to answer that?"

"Fine. But in the case of a murder victim, I don't see what the point of her race is, based on the details of the case."

"If she was a white woman, rich, successful, just like Grue, would you treat her murder like this?"

Smith stuffed his hands into his trouser pockets and ignored the question.

"Nestor, this looks like a serial killing so far. And you know that most serial killers select victims of their own race."

"What exactly are you saying?"

"Don't read into it too much if we're dealing with a psychopath."

"I've been working on building a profile, and there's elements of this case that don't seem like those of a serial killer."

"So?"

"Well, we can't say for certain yet if race was part of the motivation for the killer."

"Then you see, you do need me to keep this vague for the media."

*Fuck,* Nestor thought. I have backed myself into a corner with my own boss. *Fuck.*

"Just leave this to me," Smith said. "I am buying you time so you can find us a suspect."

Nestor bit his lip. Smith was right. Smith stepped out of the station, winking at Nestor as he strolled on.

# DAY 3
## WEDNESDAY OCTOBER 22, 2025

**MANHATTAN**
**5:00 PM ET**

Felix nodded and smiled at the anthropology department committee members with as much warmth as he could muster, but inside, he felt a sense of wrongness as cold as ice. He could barely keep their names straight. Abercrombie. Bailey. Grant. Rogers. Hansen. Faces blurred, and their genders melted away.

And then it was time to go. The rounds of questions about his dissertation were over. Mostly.

"I'm curious," said Professor Ana Radimachos, who led him toward the door. "Where did you get such a provocative idea from?"

"Me? Provocative?" Felix said.

Radimachos smiled and displayed age lines around her mouth, a ginger bob cut with razor-sharp precision, and smart glasses.

"Your theory — how did you come up with it?"

"My theory of political tributes?"

"Yes, exactly that."

Felix's dissertation posited the idea that Codex Tudela, a sixteenth-century book, was proof that the Aztec writing system had contributed to the political and military victory by the Spanish.

According to his dissertation, the Aztec had given key secrets away to their enemies pictorially. Through images, and not words.

"As you know, that's my area of focus as well," Radimachos said. "In all my years, I have never seen someone make put together such solid research as you."

"You serious?"

"Yes, congratulations. You're a good writer, a good researcher, you know how to tell a good joke."

"You liked my jokes, eh?"

"You had us rolling in there, yes."

*But,* he thought. *She is going to say "but."*

Instead, he beat her to the punch.

"But," he said. "the market for tenured teaching jobs is more than competitive."

Ana Radimachos pressed her lips together, unsure of how to respond. Despite her lovely smile, she was also an awkward person.

"Your body of work is provocative, and rigorous in its approach. I loved your dissertation."

*Aaaaaand now she's blowing smoke up my ass.*

"But as you know, the market for tenure jobs is not even big enough to call itself a market," Felix said.

"True. The position you're applying for probably won't be available for another thirty years."

"The classic dilemma of our age," he said. "Too many people graduating with PhDs, and all of them fighting over a job or two, like hyenas battling for a scrap of meat."

"You make it all sound so grim, Felix."

"Because it *is* grim."

"I am hoping for good outcomes," Radimachos said, but the words were flat, without any emotion behind them.

"I can't give up on teaching," Felix said, speaking out loud but mostly talking to himself. Her face remained serene, pretending she didn't hear what he had just said. This was normal in academic settings. If things get uncomfortable, just pretend they're not happening. *La la la,* Felix thought. *I can't hear you, la la la.*

He thought that if he could just get a teaching job that he could keep the tides away, the feeling of hopelessness that washed over him sometimes.

"When you all get back together and discuss, just know that I want this job with every fiber of my being."

"I'll keep that in mind," she said.

She shook his hand, reminded him that a decision would be made in the next few days, or even weeks, and ushered him out the door.

**5:10 PM ET**

Nestor scoured through the report from Muninn. The software's neural network had scanned video calls that had been generated from the movie theater (Avila's) and his manager at corporate. Muninn had decrypted the seven messages, but they were banal, mostly just chatter from the front-door attendant at the theater, communicating with his wife about the theater closing down for the day. The attendant had told his wife they had found a body, and that was potential for a bad leak, but considering that the theater was in Times Square and that at any given time, thousands of messages were being sent and received wirelessly through the area, that was pretty damn good.

Using a warrant, Nestor had accessed the contents of Marlene's smartphone. Clean as a whistle, except for two items that bothered him. First, the fact that her Signal app showed that she had used the encrypted messaging to contact her mother, her sister, and of all people, Bryan Berger. All the messages had self-destructed, per Grue's instructions, so there was no content to see. But the recipient list was still visible. Why was she messaging Berger on that app? The law firm used its own enterprise encryption software for its emails, and it made no sense to message offline.

From the front windows, he heard a familiar voice.

"Detective Buñuel!"

It was Devin. Nestor walked around the rows of desks and found Devin staring up at the flat screen TV on the northeast corner, set right next to the windows that looked out onto 35th Street. ABC7 Eyewitness News had a reporter outside the Patriot AMC Theater.

"Word is out, Detective."

On the screen, Smith spoke behind a podium, and captions on the TV showed his statement. *The victim's been identified as Marlene Grue, age 52. We have no suspect to speak of at this point, but it we encourage anyone with any information to come forward to help investigators.*

"Fuck," Nestor said.

**5:15 PM ET**

Nestor made the mistake of checking social media for reactions to the ABC Eyewitness News report. He couldn't help it.

*This takes us back to the good ol' days of Times Square before Giuliani when you could get a good murder to happen on 42nd Street. #nostalgicnewyork #bucolicbigapple*

*Girlfriend complained too much about the $25 movie ticket prices and look what happened.*

*They killing tourists now? smh*

Nestor didn't bother sighing. This black humor was always part of tragedy. He dug in a little further, skimming past the jokes and memes, and ignoring most of the other news reports, which basically just repeated the same info from the TV station.

*Yet another crime against women. Will the violence never end?*

*I just went and googled this lady. Just another 1 percenter in NYC. Meanwhile, we can't even get jobs up in Wal-Mart down in St. Louis.*

*Here's a mosaic showing the 300 black people that have been killed in the five boroughs in the past two years. Wonder if this lady too, was killed by police.*

*These fucking theater chains and their "predictive algorithms" can predict what flavor of soda I am going to drink, as well as the exact fucking time during the movie I will fart in my seat, but they couldn't predict that someone would get murdered???*

And then a few more messages that Nestor wished he hadn't read. These were the scum he wished to avoid.

*One less nigger, one less problem.*

*She had that same simian look as Michell Obama.*

*The far-left is going to run to town with this murder, screaming about this lawyer's intersectionality and diverting resources to New York, yet one more time. When will this propaganda and black martyrdom end?*

*She looked like a fucking black dyke to me. Good riddance.*

Nestor bit down on his lip, hard, until he drew blood. He looked at his calendar. His last day in the department would be November 28.

"Not soon enough."

**5:27 PM ET**

Felix set the credit card down on the puddle of beer. The edge of the plastic made a hard click.

"Leave the tab open?" the bartender asked.

Felix nodded. He was already on his fifth gin-and-tonic. This was sanctuary, the safe womb of beer, liquor, and stale air. The Rolling Stones filled his eardrums with static, and he stared out the window into Bleecker Street from the booth he sat in.

He wasn't sure how he had found this place, but he knew he liked the sound of it, Bleecker Street Bar. He had considered looking on Google for gay bars close by, but right now, he was in no mood to think about bears, Manhattan queens, or Beyoncé.

He took a smiling selfie, added a geo-filter for Manhattan, added text (*New York, you're everything*) and a cute emoji, and he posted it to Snap. As soon as he finished posting, he checked the number of views, to see how the snap had registered, to see if he was still alive and relevant. The views slowly crept up to about fifty, but they stopped there. Bored, he let his head sink beneath his shoulders, and he drew lazy circles on the scuffed surface of the table. Another four likes arrived, but Felix clicked the screen off. *Blech.*

That fucking bartender, he had pecs like a Greek god. And lips like gold.

"Can I ask you a favor?"

"Sure."

"Can I make a request on your playlist?"

"I don't see why not," the bartender said. His hair was long, tied in a ponytail, and his eyes were blue and bright, like sapphire.

"Can you play 'Plainsong' by Arkangel?"

The bartender nodded and turned toward the tablet that pumped out music into the sound system. 'Plainsong' had once felt like Felix's lifeline, when he had attended college and everything was bright and new, and every single anthem by Arkangel mattered. He had played the track in his dorm literally thousands of times, over and over, and the way in which the brother-and-sister-duo Arkangel sang on the track reminded him of ice that melts at the tips, and sunsets over the ocean.

"Plainsong" washed over Felix, and he started to feel a little better. Two minutes later, when the second chorus hit, that good feeling went to shit. The melancholy of the song, the way the lyrics lilted on certain words — because Arkangel were not native English speakers — gave him a sense of deja vu that he could not shake. The song took him to a place that hurt, a lot. That place was a laundry room, in a coach house behind the house he had grown up in with his mother and father, and his dead sister Georgina, whose face he often couldn't quite picture anymore.

He slammed the drink in front of him.

## 5:33 PM ET

"Your hair is so pretty," Felix said. "And I don't mean that ironically."

"Thanks, I guess," the bartender said.

"Can I get another gin-and-tonic?"

The bartender shrugged.

"Did anyone tell you that you have kind of a Ryan Gosling look?"

"Look, here's your drink. I gotta work, buddy."

Felix swiped the drink off the bar, and it slid out of his hand. It tumbled down his flat stomach and crashed on the floor. Liquor soaked the crotch of his trousers and dress shoes.

"Oh, shit."

"I got it, buddy, just step back, okay?"

The bartender mopped the spill with swiftness, unfazed.

"Are you hiring?" Felix said.

The bartender shook his head. "Have you ever worked at a bar before, bro?"

"No, but you know, I can learn."

"Okay, I'll make you your new drink in a sec. Just go back to your booth, okay? I'll play some more Arkangel for you."

"See how you are?"

The bartender chuckled, and his hard tits bounced in his perfectly weathered tee. He winked at Felix and shook his head again.

Felix stumbled back into the booth and swiped inside his dating apps, hoping the bartender might have a profile available to view. None. Dammit. Of course, Felix could try to actually just flirt and find out in person, but no, not today. Not now.

Within seconds, the new gin-and-tonic landed on the table.

"And that's your last one."

Felix nodded, and he let his smile curl while one of his eyes drooped shut. The bartender vanished, and Felix took a large swig.

He finished three fourths of the drink and counted the bills in his wallet. Three dollars in singles. He shuffled up to the bar.

"Gonna closhe up my tab," he said.

The bartender ran the card through the reader on the side of the tablet.

"Declined. Got another card?"

Felix had none. He knew this credit card was close to its max of $25,000 but not this close. His bank account was -$450 thanks to an overdraft fee for his airfare, and he had no cash in his wallet. Just an MTA card and his phone.

## 6:28 PM ET

"I don't care who you gotta call. Your tab's $113."

Nestor could only see the drunk's back. He was hunched over, swimming inside a suit too large for his frame. The bartender picked up the phone behind the bar.

"I'm calling the police."

"Don't bother," Nestor said. He flashed his badge. The bartender's eyes widened in surprise, and once he was satisfied verifying the badge, he deferred to Nestor.

The drunk in the suit perked up, and he tucked his chin into his neck. Early thirties, but he looked like a kid. He looked sideways at Nestor, held his gaze for a moment, then snorted into laughter.

"This guy runs up a tab, and now he's cashless," the bartender said.

"Pour me a glass of water," Nestor said.

The kid looked queer as hell, even in the suit he wore. His asymmetrical haircut, his Magnum PI mustache (Nestor couldn't believe this was a real trend now among young people), and the single earring dangling from the right ear were only veneers, but what was beneath there was young, handsome. He could have passed for a Mexican movie star from the twentieth century, the kind Nestor's mother adored.

"I got no cash. I'll text my parents."

"Your parents? How old are you anyway?"

"Thirty-two."

"Jesus Christ, man, don't text your parents. You're thirty-two," Nestor said. He wasn't sure why he had wandered in here again. He had made no plans with Alexa, and yet he was back at Bleecker's.

Must be the booze calling his name.

"You look like someone famous," the kid said, looking up at Nestor.

"Hardly."

"But you do. Maybe like someone in those Marvel movies. Or that guy who won the Oscar…"

"Just stop, okay?" Nestor hated this type of conversation. It always led to some racist typecasting of what he was and who he resembled.

*And yet you just typecast this fucking kid. Mexican movie star, eh?* Nestor shook his head at himself.

The kid hooked his right hand over Nestor's right shoulder and stared out the window into Bleecker Street, with a forlorn gaze that seemed bigger than New York City.

"Do you live in an apartment building?" the kid croaked.

"Twentieth floor."

"Good. Have you ever wanted to just…throw your stuff out the window?"

"Huh?" Nestor said.

"Yeah, like throw all your belongings from the window of your apartment, presuming, of course, that you live at least on the second floor."

"I don't think I have, no."

"Well, I have. I'd like to toss my laptop, my bedspread, alarm clock, and my dishes. Everything."

"Why?"

"To see how they break, how they crack open."

Nestor took a sip of the beer and shook his head. He motioned with two fingers to the bartender, whose long hair and mustache were also revolting. The bartender slid a beer before Nestor, and a seltzer water with lemon for the drunk.

"What's your name?"

"Felix Andersen Calvo."

Nestor extended his hand. The kid pumped his fist back with surprising force.

*Well whaddya know?*

This was impossible but also wonderful.

"I'm Nestor Buñuel."

They exchanged glances for a moment.

*Wait for it…* thought Nestor. *Wait for it…*

"Oh my god...you messaged me."

The realization sobered the kid up, at least for a moment. Nestor smiled and took a stool next to him.

"You—"

"Yeah, you muted me, remember? Or maybe you even blocked me."

"Holy shit."

"Felix, let me buy you another — what are you drinking?"

The bartender shook his head.

"I'm not pouring this guy anything else until he pays. What, are you going to pick up his tab?"

"So what if I do?" Nestor said. He slid cash over the counter. The bartender started pouring a new drink.

Nestor had closed many cases in his lifetime, but not because he was the smartest guy in the department. Sure, he had some brains, but the fact was, he knew how to develop and maintain sources and informants. He cast a wide net. And sometimes, all it took was a little favor.

Felix cocked his head, and smirked. "Yeah, make it a double."

"You like gin, eh?"

"What do you want, Officer?"

"I just took care of your debt, so let's go tit for tat. I need answers."

"Fine," Felix said. He smiled. The kid looked scared as a jackrabbit in the middle of a two-lane blacktop.

"Let's start with you. I read parts of your dissertation."

"Oh, that thing. I'm sick to death of that piece of shit."

"You wrote that certain elite social classes — priests, or what we might call politicians or executives today — used calendars to talk to the gods and mythical creatures on the other side..."

Felix shook his head, and a long strand of hair fell down over his eyes. Now he was alert, his eyes wide, and his mind racing. "Who the hell wants to know?"

"A dead black woman."

**6:48 PM ET**

Felix fished in his pocket for his phone. His battery was virtually dead, down to one sorry sliver. He didn't want to stare, but he was intrigued by the cop. Nestor Buñuel moved with a calculated gait that Felix had seen somewhere before, and the image suddenly appeared for him. The cop was like one of those jungle cats in National Geographic's YouTube videos. Constantly calculating, stalking on bunched-up haunches, ready to spring with power.

Felix wanted to text Wes, to give him an update, to feel like he wasn't spiraling out here in the city, but a screech and flashing lights snapped him out of his thoughts.

The cop yanked Felix hard, by the collar of his suit jacket, and he heard a few pops as the seams split around the shoulders. A taxi cab swerved around Felix, and honked, but the screech continued.

"STEP BACK ONTO THE SIDEWALK, PLEASE." The voice was soft and silky, without imperfections, but loud as a bullhorn.

A metal object shaped like a disc, painted white and royal blue, hovered five feet in the air above Nestor and Felix. Its six propellers and long flat shape were beetle-like, and it made a soft buzzing sound as it floated above them.

"Ah, come on, kid, work with me. You know this thing's footage goes back to my boss right?"

Felix staggered and held onto a light post for stability.

"Never seen those."

"I'm surprised you haven't. Chicago has poli-drones, too."

"Are these the new meter maids?"

"Hardly. The city's using neural networks to power these drones. Their job is to identify pedestrians and..."

"And what?"

"To predict."

Felix felt a twinge of dread in his belly. "So you mean to tell me that this thing thinks I'm about to cause a traffic accident?"

"The neural network is not that good yet, but it learns more every day."

"Is it artificial inte—"

"Shh, don't say that word. It will hear you."

Felix cocked his head. He got the queerest sensation that Detective Buñuel wanted the drone to give them both privacy.

"Okay, okay." Felix stayed quiet for a moment, and the cameras on the drone enlarged. Their red lenses felt like the eyes of a fly, compound and all-seeing.

"So, is it going to write me a ticket from the air?"

"Just shut up kid, or it will think you're worth arresting."

The drone flew lower to the ground, and its six camera eyes blinked in unison, revealing flashes of purple inside their shutters. It seemed satisfied, and then it flew off in a straight line, to another intersection.

"Did you just make that drone move on and fly away?"

"You read too many comic books. The poli-drones do what they want. They use machine learning. It does help that they can scan faces, so in a way, yes, maybe I pulled some strings. They defer to any officers on duty on site."

Detective Buñuel straightened out his black jacket and tucked his black tee into his pants. He was so jacked, like some sort of CrossFit monster. But was he family?

"Look, I gotta get back to work. If you want to talk, well, let's do it. But I'm not about to beg. There's no begging in police work."

Felix felt a pang of shame at the thought of letting this policeman pay his tab and clean up his mess. He wanted to say something like *thank you*, but even that was too difficult. His stomach tumbled, twisted into knots.

"Where you staying, Felix?"

"I fly back to Chicago today. This is just a short day trip, basically."

Nestor frowned, straightened out Felix's tie with a hard yank, and dusted lint off his shoulder.

"You better text your mom and dad, dude. Flights at LaGuardia and JFK are getting canceled."

Felix's head swam again. The sun was setting, swollen and fat like an egg yolk, and even its faint light made him feel sick.

"What do you mean?"

"Storm system is coming in from the ocean. A nor'easter is on its way."

"You're kidding me, right? It was like summer earlier today."

"It's Storm Tobe. Look."

The cop held his smart phone up and aimed the camera at the slice of yellow sky between the buildings on Bleecker. The augmented screen showed key information from several sources, the letters crawling like ants in rows. Red stats dotted the horizon, and a series of stickers and arrows moved to show the weather patterns in the clouds above. *Storm system scheduled to arrive by 6 PM in Tri-State area*, the phone announced.

Felix checked his notifications and—

"Aw shit, you're right. They canceled my flight."

"I told you," Nestor said.

Felix giggled.

"I'm a remix of Eeyore, Charlie Brown, and Barb, man. I mean, what else can explain my bad luck?"

He saw that the joke connected. Nestor laughed heartily.

"You always a comedian?" Nestor said.

"Only when the pay's good. I don't play clubs for free." Felix said as he stumbled toward Buñuel and promptly threw up orange-and-yellow vomit all over the detective's shirt, jeans, and shoes.

## 7:21 PM ET

The academic slumped over in the subway seat, a rag doll with a mustache. He was conscious despite the deep inebriation.

"You know, we could have taken a taxi if your tab hadn't been more than one hundred bucks," Nestor said.

"I'll pay you back, dude, relax," Felix said. Two women seated in front of them moved to the back of the car, holding their noses.

"You're making a really good first impression," Nestor said.

"Are you always this unpleasant?" Felix said.

"Yes, I am."

"Then stop being unpleasant."

"What did you just say to me?"

"Be nice, Detective."

"Where you getting off, Felix?"

"I'm not. Just gonna ride the subway as long as I can."

"No, I mean, where are you staying?"

"In the Palace of Nothing. AirBnZilch."

"No suitcase?"

"Left my backpack at the bar, shit."

Nestor dug through his leather bag, and shook his head. He handed Felix a couple of sticks of bubble gum. Felix popped the gum into his mouth with long hands and slid away from Nestor, leaving a full empty seat between them so their thighs wouldn't touch. The veins in his neck strained and stretched as he chewed on the cinnamon gum.

*Just look at him,* Nestor thought. *He's a fully grown man. He's not a kid. Gotta stop calling him that.*

The N train roared along the tracks, and several passengers shook their heads and clicked their tongues. Construction was causing delays again. Nestor had done his best to wipe off Felix's vomit from his clothes and shoes, but the scent of stomach acid and half-digested sandwich was undeniable. Luckily, almost everyone in the subway car had their head buried in their smartphones. A small benefit of a society that no longer paid as much attention to its surroundings as before.

The train rose above the city street onto its elevated track in Queens. Nestor's phone lit up with notifications.

"Shit, shit," Nestor said.

"Having problems?" Felix said.

"Just the case I'm working on."

"So, weren't you going to ask for my help?"

"Not the way you are right now. And certainly not in front of people in a subway car."

"Good point. You're sharp."

"Shut up."

Nestor cracked a smile and chuckled to himself.

"You can crash at my apartment. Rebook your flight, then get your ass back to Chicago."

Felix nodded and then dozed off into drunken sleep.

When the train arrived at the Astoria Boulevard station, Nestor lifted Felix out by the shoulder onto the platform. Snow struck their faces in fat clumps, and the wind howled like a loon in the woods.

The nor'easter was arriving.

## QUEENS
## 11:57 PM ET

Nestor was in the middle of typing up his notes on the Grue case when the apartment building lost power.

The laptop switched to its battery, and the living room glowed blue. The windows rattled as the wind current slapped the front of the building. Normally, Manhattan was visible through the glass, but tonight, it was just white drifts.

Felix lay across the sofa, shrunken, dehydrated by the booze. The radiator banged, but at least there was heat in the building. The

Somali family that lived in his building was outside building snowmen, and goddammit, those teenagers should get inside, but the street was otherwise empty.

The phone rang, and Nestor's mother's name popped up on the screen.

*Nestor,* she texted, *did you lose power?*

*Yes, Ma. You?*

*No, but I saw it on the news. You can come over if you like.*

*Too much snow out there.*

*But you can't stay out there all alone.*

*I sure can, Mom.*

Nestor closed his work laptop and flipped open his MacBook. He yanked the USB stick from his television set and slid it into the slot of the laptop. Felix groaned on the couch and mumbled, turned over, then fell back asleep.

Nestor loaded the file for *9 Lords of Night* and scrubbed to the first five minutes of the movie, past the credits and opening. He hit PLAY using the spacebar on the keyboard.

The movie came to life, and the camera followed one of indigenous servants who followed the priest. The young man walked through stone-cobbled streets as the sun began to set, and he hummed a song to himself. The camera traced his flat forehead, his aquiline nose, and his full lips. He walked for what seemed many miles, until he reached an alley. There, he entered through a red door. He walked into a small wood shop lit by candles. Inside the shop, the young man disrobed, untangling a bandage that crisscrossed his chest. Beneath the linen, breasts like apples shone under the light. This was the female main character, who had taken on the disguise to enter the royal palace. The priest drank in her naked flesh with his eyes, and behind him, a shadow grew into a terrifying shape. *How long have you been posing as a man?*, the priest asked. The young woman answered, *for as long as it takes to sacrifice a traitor, to slice her throat, to bathe her black hair in blood.* The priest reached out with his hand toward the naked woman when a thundering clap tore through the apartment.

"Holy fuck!" Nestor said. He hit the spacebar and ran to the front door of his apartment. Felix slept, oblivious to the sound. Nestor peered out into the hall, and dogs inside the units of the apartment building barked. His neighbors stayed inside their apartments, except for one: Damien, the dog-walker who lived on the opposite end of this floor.

"Was that noise coming from the street? Sounded like a truck splitting in two," Damien said.

"I don't think so. Sounds like it was from the first floor."

Nestor walked out into the hallway, looked around the gloom, and went back into his apartment. He grabbed a flashlight and slid into his gun holster. He threw on a hoodie.

"I'll come down with you," Damien said.

"No, you won't. Stay inside."

Nestor took the stairs, listening for the noise of the apartments. He heard a few voices, but the lower he went, the quieter the stairway became.

He reached the dirty foyer, caked with grime along its white-tiled walls, and the row of mailboxes along the eastern wall loomed like old high school lockers. Nestor pressed his hands up against the heavy metal door that led to the street and its pane of glass that acted like an eye. No cars traveled down the one-way street, and only the wind howled now. All other noise was gone.

Nestor remembered how the milk in his hand had turned bloody the last time he tried to watch Kahan's film. Could this be finally the midlife crisis that had never quite arrived?

"If so, I could use a sports car and some pussy," he said.

He laughed out loud, but the dark foyer before him swallowed the sound. He stepped outside.

The street was pristine. Whatever had made that cracking noise was nowhere to be seen out here. There were no collapsed buildings, no broken cars, no ambulances or fire engines. In fact, New York City looked utterly deserted at this moment, as if Nestor were the only man left.

As he glanced at the snow, Nestor got the sense that something out in the snow was watching him.

It was a thought that was simply irrational, founded on nothing more than intuition, but he could feel a thing peering at him from the farthest end of the street.

He shivered and turned around to climb up the stairs. The flashlight bobbed up and down. Every couple of flights, he would swing the flashlight down toward the first floor, as if expecting someone to be following him up the stairs, but the pale blue light only swept through dust motes.

Nestor's shoes clicked on the risers, and by the time he was up on his floor, he was sweating, though not out of breath.

"So, what was it?" Damien said, peeking out from his darkened apartment. Candlelight backlit his neighbor.

"Nothing at all. It must have been an engine in the street popping, or maybe a furnace in a neighboring building. With this storm, there's no one out there right now."

"Well, that's funny," Damien said. "I keep hearing shrieks coming from the street. As if someone were getting murdered out there. You don't hear them?"

"I don't hear a single thing. A patrol car will be out here shortly. I'm off duty."

Nestor waved to his neighbor and shut the door behind him. He locked it with two deadbolts and a security chain, and he put his back against it. He was panting now, terrified of something, or someone, of things that had never been there, and voices whose source no one could confirm.

# DAY 4
## THURSDAY OCTOBER 23, 2025

**QUEENS**
**5:00 AM ET**

Felix pressed his lips under the faucet and let the cool water wash out the taste of puke.

What a nice apartment Nestor lived in. Felix didn't know what he expected to find in the house of a cop, but this place was modern, comfortable, and...colorful. He peeked at sun-drenched photos of the detective's family. One in particular caught his attention. What looked to be his parents played with a tiny child at a playground. The child, a girl with pigtails, wore a pair of boy's overalls. Felix studied the face, the tiny eyebrows shaped like crescent moons, the full lips.

"You're wondering who that is," said a voice in the corner of the room.

"Fucking shit, you scared the shit out of me!" Felix said, stumbling into a side table. He turned to face the detective, and the room spun. Felix put his hand on the sofa next to him to keep his balance.

"Sorry about that."

"You think you're Batman or something?"

"I hate superheroes."

"No…everyone in America loves superheroes."

"I'm not everyone."

"Do you ever sleep?"

"I was watching a movie. Ever heard of *9 Lords of Night*?"

"You asked this before. I have heard of it. But I'm not keen on movies, really."

"Anyway, the little girl in the photo is me. Age five."

Felix took a moment to study the face of the man in the chair. He was like a goddamn sphinx, sitting there with his laptop on his big thighs. He had no idea what to say to the revelation. Sure, he had learned all the right words to use, adopted the recommended and required language at school to interact with trans people, but he never had to just sit in a room alone with someone like Nestor.

"Look, I'll get out of your apartment  as soon as the snow lets up a little."

"I doubt that. They're predicting a full eighteen inches when this is all said and done."

"Fuck my life."

"Just have a seat," Nestor said.

"Okay."

"I need your help."

"Try me."

"Tell me how the Aztec ruling class executed people to the gods."

"Oh, that sweet story. Full of joy and fuzzy teddy bears."

"Pink teddy bears holding up bloody knives."

"You talking about *Skulli Bear*? The TV show?"

"I love it. Makes me laugh so hard, my stomach hurts."

"I didn't think you'd be a fan of that kind of humor."

"I love comedy. I just can't tell my own jokes to save my life."

Nestor smiled and gave Felix a bowl full of Skulli Bears. The pink gelatin candies shimmered under the light, perfectly molded into the shape of a little bear holding up a butcher knife.

"These help fight nausea."

"My grandma said 7-Up does the trick."

"I have no soda, so these will do for now. You'll like them."

"Thanks." Felix chewed on the bears, and the artificial taste of strawberry and cherry did quell his nausea a bit.

"So, tell me how these sacrifices were done."

Felix felt a little sorry for the man. Despite the gorgeous

apartment, Nestor Buñuel reeked of loneliness. Indeed like a sphinx — untouchable, recessed into the hard angles of this apartment.

"I'll need a couple of things. Some paper to draw on, a large bottle of Gatorade, and four ibuprofen."

When Nestor procured all the items and Felix had swallowed the painkillers, he scribbled on the paper with fury.

"This is how you sacrifice humans on a regular schedule."

## 5:15 AM ET

Felix drew circles on the notebook and around the margins, then he sketched symbols in neat rows beneath the circles. Some resembled houses, others animals like birds and reptiles.

It occurred to Nestor that other than visits by his mother to drop off some of her home-cooked dishes every month or so, he hadn't had a guest of any gender in three years in his apartment. While Felix drew on the paper, Nestor dove into the cupboards and started to make toast. He set water to boil estafiate leaves, just like his mother made. Toast would help Felix with his hangover. The estafiate tea would settle his stomach further.

Felix bit into the toast without looking up from his drawing. He chewed with joy, and hunger. Nestor took a seat next to him.

"Not so close, okay?" Felix said.

Nestor, startled by the response, scooted down to the end of the sofa.

"Sorry. So, what have we got?"

"A calendaring system. It's called the tonalpohualli. Instead of 365 days like our Gregorian calendar, the tonalpohualli is only 260 days, and it's counted by rounds of thirteen days. If you repeat those thirteen-day-counts by twenty, you get the full calendar year."

"Okay, I follow. And the emoji there?"

"Oh!" Felix said, laughing. "Cute, real cute."

"You're being serious?"

"Yes, your observation's cute as hell. It's what I love about showing this to non-academics. You all actually have a sense of humor about what you're looking at. And emoji is in fact more appropriate than you know. The writing system uses pictographs and ideograms."

"Okay, so what do the emoji do?"

"They correspond to various sacred symbols, like the snake, reeds, the wind."

"And what are those glyphs over there?"

Felix had drawn two columns of symbols with unusual speed and detail. He was clearly in his element.

"So, these two columns correspond to different Aztec gods. So...."

Felix smiled, drawing out the suspense. Nestor couldn't help but smile back.

"So....Let me guess. If you combine these different astronomical time-measurement systems and their corresponding symbols—"

"You get a calendar. And of course, some days are very auspicious and are ruled by a particular god."

"How many gods are we talking about?"

"A lot. But only a few asked for sacrifice. In any case, this calendaring system would easily tell you when and how often you had to sacrifice someone as tribute to these many gods.

"Okay, I'm with you. What am I looking at here?"

Nestor reached into a locked drawer in his desk and brought out the Sony camera he used for work. He showed Felix images of the body of Marlene Grue.

Felix gasped, and he scooted farther away from Nestor.

"Holy fuck, that's horrible. What's your problem? You know I'm nauseous as hell."

The screen showed symbols carved into Grue's skin, in the rib area. Nestor sat right next to Felix again, ignoring his request for personal space. He zoomed out of the image so he could see Marlene's dead expression, the gaping hole in her chest, and the way the skin had been peeled away from the chest cavity like a cellophane wrapper off a candy.

"Drink the tea. It will help you fight the nausea." Felix followed orders and sipped the tea.

"Next time, give me a heads up."

"What do you see in these photos?"

Felix set the camera next to his drawing. The red flashing lights of an ambulance lit up the snow that swirled out in the street for a moment, then were gone. Felix pointed his finger at one of his pictographs that looked like a dog.

"If you asked me, that's a match."

"So…is that a dog god?"

"Nah, Nestor. Use your imagination. These are symbols. That's no dog. It's just a symbol representing the Night Drinker."

"Come again?"

"Yes the Night Drinker. One of the gods I just mentioned. Let me show you what he actually looks like."

Felix flipped through the screen on his mobile and showed Nestor.

The search result showed a photograph of a statue carved in stone. The figure looked human, though its vague shape hid any defining musculature and even gender. The head was enormous and his uniform or clothing loose, somehow too big for him. Tiny little appendages sprouted from his wrists and ankles, like an extra pair of hands and feet.

Suddenly, Nestor was the one who felt nauseous.

"That's the Night Drinker?"

"Yes, the carving on Marlene Grue's skin is invoking him. It's sending a message to The Night Drinker, for mercy, and to ask for his gifts."

Felix quickly sketched a figurine with arms and legs, a face with clumsy features, very mask-like, and unusual protrusions at its joints.

"What's with the tiny extra hands on the wrists?" Nestor said.

"I hope you're not easily grossed out. Here's why."

**5:55 AM ET**

"The Night Drinker wears the skins of human beings as a suit. Or costume. A war uniform."

"This is fucking disgusting," Buñuel said, as he stood up and paced around the room. Thankfully, he had now given Felix his personal space back.

"Told you it was gross."

"You did."

"But…not any sicker than Cronos eating his own children or Zeus having a fetus of his son sewn onto his skin."

"So, the Aztecs sacrificed people to this god?"

"Sometimes. Not as much as a couple of the other major gods, but you know, the Night Drinker needed his blood gifts."

"As a cop working on cases like this one, what I look for is a motive. What would be the reason why blood sacrifices would appease this god?"

"Because if he gets his human tribute, he'll bring renewal and fertility to their agricultural society. Good harvests, fertile soil."

"And the calendaring system, the tonalpohualli—"

"It's one timekeeping tool for this stuff. Kings, aristocrats, and priests scheduled these sacrifices. They had it down pat, like clockwork, in a manner of speaking."

"Ha-ha, but not very funny in this context."

"No, not if your theory is correct."

They drank tea and watched the snow pile on in silence. Felix had a lot more questions for the cop, but for now, he appreciated this quiet moment. Nestor went into the bathroom, and Felix listened to the rattling from outside the windows.

On the side table, Felix noticed a colorful hat, tiny, as if it belonged to a Ken doll, shaped like a cowboy hat but woven with the brightest colors and white stripes. So bright and colorful, it looked like candy. He recognized the hat as a sombrero vueltiao, a popular type of folk art from Colombia.

He listened to the detective shuffle around in the bathroom, and the hiss of the water faucet. Felix pocketed the hat in his hoodie.

Nestor returned, staring at his phone as he walked.

"I'm gonna had to head back into the office. You can't stay alone here, but if you'd like, you can come with me. I still want to talk about those calendars."

Felix smirked. *I don't have any fucking choice.* He would rather stay here and nap in this cush apartment, but he also didn't want to be alone right now. Otherwise, his thoughts would drift back to the images of the ocean, inescapable dread, and then about gin.

"All right. I just need a few minutes to get ready."

"There's towels and clean clothes laid out in the bathroom."

"Thanks."

"And one more thing. Why are you stealing from me?"

*Holy shit.*

The cop fished his hand into Felix's hoodie too fast for him to push him away. Nestor retrieved the tiny hat, and Felix's cheeks went hot to the touch. Suddenly, the detective loomed large. It wouldn't take much for a man like him to punch the shit out of someone. Felix glanced at his hands.

"Answer me. Why are you stealing from me?"

"I don't have an answer to that."

The truth is that it was a habit he had picked up since he was about four years old. He didn't know why, but he took things from people's houses. Especially in houses of people he liked.

The detective's response, however, was unlike the response of teachers and Felix's parents during previous incidents of theft. Nestor looked unfazed, and not surprised in any way. Instead, he looked at Felix with understanding in his eyes, forgiving him without judgement.

Nestor patted Felix on the shoulder as he put the hat back on the side table. "Come on. We have a lot of work to do today, and you're going to help me."

"Help you with what?" Felix said. Using his own hand as a spatula, he removed the detective's hand from his shoulder. "I don't like touching all that much."

"Fine. I want you to help me decipher the full message on Grue's skin."

"I can do it here, from the photos."

"That won't work. I want to show you more evidence. Put on these boots, they should fit you."

"We're going out into that mess?"

"Hurry up."

## 8:00 AM ET

Felix chewed a breakfast sandwich that Nestor had paid for. The gooey American cheese and egg were pressed between two halves of a bagel. The crust was crispy and the inside chewy and soft. He never wanted this feeling to stop. He ate standing up at a small counter that looked out into the streets of Queens.

Felix was wearing a down parka and boots that belonged to Nestor. The parka was a little too short for his lanky frame, but it felt good to stay warm.

"So, you'll help me?" Nestor said.

"Are you going to pay me for all my troubles?" Felix said.

"Are you always a smartass?"

"You didn't answer my question."

"What are your rates?"

"$150 an hour."

Nestor laughed, jotted down notes in his notebook and shook his head. He twirled the hairs on his mustache where it connected with his beard.

"I got you a roof over your head while flights return back to normal at JFK, and something to eat. I don't think you have leverage, bud."

"You make a good point."

"Just give me two days' worth of your expertise. Then we're done."

Felix took a sip of coffee from the white paper cup. This bodega, jammed with crap, edible and useful crap, was like nothing he had ever seen before. And it was just below Nestor's house, like some sort of fairy-tale marvel. He didn't want to trudge out through the snow again, he hated snow, but he liked the way that the detective talked about the investigation.

"Fine. I do owe you for letting me crash. Thanks for helping me."

"I assume NYU will rebook your flight once they become available again."

"Correct. Waiting to hear back from them."

Felix waved his mobile in front of Nestor.

"Do you always keep that thing on?"

"Sure, why?"

"Ever heard of privacy and security?"

"Meh, I'm not that important."

"Every single person in this country is important."

"Yeah?"

"Here, put this on."

Nestor handed Felix a thin slab of metal. It looked like an old-school cigarette case, but it fastened at the edges with a series of snaps. A single opening the size of a pea allowed the phone's camera to peer out. He folded it open in two halves.

"A phone case?"

"Of sorts. Razor-thin, made of aluminum, zinc, and and copper. While it's on your phone, it will completely block the radio signal that connects it to the internet."

"And you want me to put this on my phone...why?"

"Because you're going to help me out with some research, and I don't want anyone to know you're traveling with me."

"What do you call this thing?"

"The product is called Hadescap."

"These are illegal to own."

"Not for police they're not."

"You know, I don't think I like you very much. You're kind of…creepy."

"I haven't made up my mind about you yet. Not sure I like you much at all, either."

"We couldn't have just stayed in to watch your Netflix?"

"Come on. Let's get going."

Felix snapped the case over his mobile, swallowed the last of his sugary coffee, and followed Nestor out into the snowstorm.

## MANHATTAN
## 9:15 AM ET

Their boots barely made a dent in the snow drifts, and the sky pelted their eyes with snowflakes. Even through the gray haze of the nor'easter, the city dominated the landscape. The streets were for sure a little quieter in Manhattan today, but the smell of exhaust, halal food trucks undeterred by the storm, and corporate coffee shops fought the work ethic of the storm around them.

Felix struggled to keep up with Nestor, who had said he wanted to get into the morgue before the business day really ramped up. On their way from the train, they spotted about a half-dozen homeless people wandering without direction as the storm worsened. Those people would likely not survive this storm. Their black and brown faces didn't even bother to make eye contact at this time. They knew how things turn out during a blizzard.

Felix's neck craned in all directions, taking in the energy of the streets and the handfuls of people going to work on foot.

They finally slogged through the sheets of snow and the gray sludge on the sidewalks at the Office of Chief Medical Examiner. The wind screamed behind them as they pushed through the glass doors. Nestor dusted off the layers of snow from his parka.

Felix struggled to unzip his jacket. Nestor let the man take care of it himself, and yet there was a childlike quality to the way Felix bunched up his shoulders to exit the confines of the parka, his nose dripping with clear snot as he wriggled out of the coat.

A redheaded uniformed officer stepped between Nestor and the hallway that led to the morgue. Scars crisscrossed his forehead.

Though his features were boyish, his skin had the tough, weathered quality of shoe leather. Bags pulled downward on his eyes. He had been put through the paces of life.

*And haven't I, too*, thought Nestor. *Sometimes it feels as if Fred Astaire used my back as his rehearsal studio.*

"He can't come in here," the officer said, pointing to Felix, who huddled over forms that he was filling out with a ballpoint pen.

"Of course he can," Nestor said. "I just have to sign him in."

"Is he new?" the cop said.

"No, visiting. Subject-matter expert from Chicago."

"Have I met you before?" the policeman said.

"Don't know. Have you?"

Nestor examined the man's face, the ginger beard, the cleft chin, and the eyes the color of rain. Suddenly he remembered. *I went on a date with this fucker before I came out to the department.*

The year was 2009. The date itself had been mostly ordinary, a drink or two at one of the last dive bars in Hell's Kitchen, and later, cheap sushi. But what Nestor remembered was the fumbling afterward on a leather sofa in the cop's apartment, his collection of heavy metal records lining one of the walls in his cramped studio, the way he placed a bible on his coffee table next to the magazines, and how quickly he had ripped his shirt off to show off his 260-pound physique. Today, the redhead was closer to 310, and much fatter.

Nestor had never been petite, even before he transitioned, but on that night, he was no match for the advances of the cop, and after all, what was his name? They had tumbled on the bed, and despite the thrill of the redhead's kisses, the taste of passion fruit ice cream still on their tongues, the man's body had encroached on Nestor's, squeezing too hard on his breasts, threatening to choke Nestor while he started to straddle him.

Nestor had called off the sexual encounter. *Get off me.* The redhead cop had clicked his tongue, calling him a cocktease. Nestor had excused himself, ashamed and red-faced over the awkward way it ended. In the bathroom, he had washed his face several times, removing layers of makeup and revealing his brown, wide face to the mirror. *I want that silky Latin body, girl*, he heard the cop say through the closed bathroom door. *You're going to give it to me.* The pop of a fresh can of beer being opened on the other side.

At the time, Nestor was a uniformed police officer. In the

greasy bathroom, he had nothing to protect himself, and in fact, he was close to naked, wearing just a pair of teal panties and his firearm very much out of reach, tucked into his clothes, which were folded in the living room. His neck had burst into some sort of splotchy rash, and his heart pounded. He didn't know why he felt such a threat to his life, but it was real. Or so he thought at the time. Memories sometimes had a way of changing over the decades.

Nestor popped the door open so he could exit the apartment, but as brave as he wanted to be, shyness overpowered him. The cop lay spread-eagled on the bed, naked, his right hand cupping his erection. Images of Metallica, Mötörhead, and Judas Priest lined the upper parts of the wall like molding made of metal spikes, guitars and black paint. *Don't you get it?*, Nestor said. *I'm done here. I'm going home.* As Nestor passed the bed, the cop—and why couldn't he remember the name, why?—grabbed Nestor by the wrist, crushing it. *Next time, you let me choke the shit out of you, Martina. I know your type. You like that shit.* Nestor walked straight to his pile of clothes, which he knew would be more protective than his own firearm. He was dressed and out the door in less than sixty seconds.

Such things, such times. The Martina days.

Sixteen years had passed, and the redhead towered over Nestor again, completely unaware that they had once rolled naked together in a grimy studio in Hell's Kitchen above a massage parlor.

"I do know you. I just can't place it."

"You probably know me from the Internet," Nestor said.

"What's that supposed to mean?"

"I'm Detective Buñuel," he said. They shook hands. The uniformed officer wrinkled his nose, as if there was an aspect of Nestor's appearance he didn't like.

*He still doesn't recognize me*, Nestor thought.

Felix reappeared after his trip to the front desk, wearing a white badge that he could use to swipe into the main hall of the morgue. The cop's badge read DONOVAN. And then, in the blink of an eye, Nestor recalled the first name.

"You're Kevin, aren't you?"

"Who wants to know?"

"Just an old friend I don't really talk to anymore. She made a lot of bad choices."

Kevin Donovan nodded, unfazed. There were other problems, much bigger problems, that were visible in his weathered eyes. Nestor recalled that back around the time of their date, Kevin had a father with Alzheimer's, and lots of credit card debt. But it was old hat, and he honestly didn't give a shit anymore.

Nestor winked at Felix, who was right at his side.

"Who's that guy? He looked at you like you're an alien."

"I'll tell you some other time. Put your badge there."

Felix pressed the badge on the metal box, and the edges of the reader lit up in green. Nestor and Felix walked into the morgue.

## 10:00 AM ET

"Is it always this cold up in these places?" Felix said.

"No, not this cold," Nestor said. "Miriam, you joining us today?"

"Sure thing," she said, pulling up a stool next to the table on which the body of Marlene Grue lay. "Can I go get my coat? I'm freezing."

"No," Nestor said.

"Oh, come on, Nestor," Miriam said.

"We don't have time."

"Fine," Felix said. "But can you move to the other side of the table? You're standing too close to me."

Nestor walked around the body. Miriam giggled.

"No one's ever been able to move that ox," she said, winking at Felix.

Nestor shook his head and peered into the chest cavity of the body. Felix cupped his hand over his nose.

"So, what do you see?" Nestor said.

"Looks like a carved side of beef."

"Look harder."

Felix pressed his lips together and pulled the magnifying glass from the stand next to him. "This okay?"

Miriam nodded. "Just don't touch anything, and you're fine."

"Well, the heart's surely gone, and shit, this is gross. But I see carvings around it. Just a sec, takin' a look."

And there they were. Pictograms, carved in detail. Felix traced lines in the air above the flayed skin of the black woman on the table.

"Looks like the person who carved these ran out of time. The message is only half complete. But sure enough, this is some type of storytelling."

Nestor sat back on his stool and took off his gloves, and crossed his arms.

"So, what does it say?"

"Lyricisms."

"Huh?"

"It's poetry. The Aztecs and Maya wrote poetry. It was an essential part of who they were."

"And what does it say?"

"Well, it mentions flowers."

"Why?"

"The Aztecs believed it was flowers where poetry sprang from. As if the flowers had minds of their own. As it the flowers could actually *sing*."

"Can you read it out loud?"

"*Where thou walkest, o dark woman, let it stand among beautiful feathers and a palace made of flowers.*"

Miriam McGuire leaned into the body, as if peering into the crater of a volcano. She flicked a tear away from the corner of her eye, to keep her mascara from running.

"Shit, what's wrong with me?"

Felix frowned. "Excuse me?"

"That bit of poetry, I don't know. I had a sister once, and it makes me remember how I regret the things I—"

Miriam let out a single sob, sharp like a a gun shot. She looked confused, but morose.

"Don't you hear it?" she said.

"Hear what?" Felix said.

"The rain and the birds. I hear birds crying."

Nestor turned to Felix and shrugged. "Miriam, you okay?"

"But don't you hear them?"

Felix cocked his head, but his ears only picked up the hum of the refrigerators that held bodies.

"I don't hear anything, honest," Felix said.

A sharp trill burst into the room. For a moment, Felix thought it really was a bird, but it wasn't. It was Nestor's phone.

"Fuck me," he said, standing up to pace along the length of the room. "A group of teenagers just found another body carved up in

Harlem."

## 10:40 AM ET

"We're going to need to go Uptown," Nestor said. "But we're still not done here."

"We are most certainly not," Felix said. "I'm only halfway done reading this writing, dude."

A tingle crept up Felix's neck. He hadn't felt anything like it since the early days of his dissertation. It was that tingle that let him know there was an idea he had to investigate. The tingle that kept him up at night, his brain overstimulated as he problem-solved.

"Okay, you got my ear." Nestor pulled up a stool and sat across the cadaver from Felix, with Miriam seated by the head.

Felix read the symbols, and he spoke the syllables out loud. He scribbled notes on a notepad Miriam had given him. Almost there. As he pressed the pen onto the paper, his ears plugged up, and he felt a twinge in his stomach. He wasn't sure how much time had passed when he looked up. Nestor had his hands in his lap, waiting. Miriam had turned over to the desktop computer at her desk just a few feet away. Felix remembered that just a few days before, he had tried sticking the barrel of a gun in his mouth, and now, he was here, in a morgue, and how strange was the world, how unusual to be here now, far away from Chicago, actually doing something useful instead of stuffing meal kits for avocado toast into boxes in an assembly line in a West Loop warehouse.

"So, I am pretty sure I got something here," he said. "I mean, it's gonna be rough, but something to start from. Something."

Nestor bit his lip. Chewed on his black mustache.

"And?"

"Well, it's a warning. A prophecy, in fact."

"Spit it out," Miriam said from the back of the room.

"It says: *There comes from the Coil an omen. He is the Night Drinker, our Lord. He embraces us in his folds, the mutilated flesh.*"

Felix moaned under his breath. The buzz in his ears was unbearable, but he needed to get this last bit out.

"*All praise the Night Drinker. He who was exiled. Behold, he returns to the dwelling of men soon.*"

## 11:00 AM ET

"So, unpack that for us, Felix," Nestor said. He was running out of patience.

"You're very pushy, you know?"

"Colombian momma, that's where I get it from."

"So politically incorrect to say."

"I don't give a fucking shit."

He could have smacked that silly mustache off his face. Maybe just punch it right off, make the skin bleed. Punch the gut, once, twice. Over and over—"

*Stop it. Just stop it.*

He had been down this path before. It always started this way, with some wiseguy, mouthing off and minutes later, a berserk-like anger that refused to die.

Captain Smith had made a joke once before at a Halloween party, turning to Nestor and announcing, *All that artificial testosterone must give you roid rage.* Smith stood tall, wearing a Spider-Man costume, while Nestor sipped from a red Solo cup, dressed as Charlie Chaplin. *No, you fuck,* Nestor thought, *I have felt rage from my earliest days, when I still had breasts and answered to my now-dead name of Martina. I have lived with that anger in the pit of my stomach, always. And that night at that party, I would have smacked that red cup off your fucking snout and broken your goddamn nose. But I didn't. I ignored the comment, the party carried on, and I understood then, you will never be able to ever understand fully what life was outside of your own little bubble.*

Felix cracked a smile at Nestor, and it was clear that he was nothing at all like Smith. Naive, yes, rude and bit strange. The smile was meant to defuse the tension between them, and dammit, it worked. Nestor relaxed his shoulders.

Antagonizing Felix wasn't going to get him answers. Nestor turned on the the coffee maker and brewed two cups of creamy brew. He poured one for Felix, and one for Miriam.

"Our killer has no high regard for human beings," Nestor said. "In this killing, he never covered up Marlene's body. He didn't cover her face. Covering the face or the body will sometimes reveal some remorse on the killer's part, but instead, she was displayed as widely and visibly as possible."

"Three days have passed since the killing, and there has also been zero sexual trauma," Miriam said. "The focus to me seems on killing and I don't know—creating some type of art piece?"

"Exactly," Nestor said. "This feels like an art installation, like it's meant to be seen, but by whom?"

"I can help a bit there," Felix said. "She was found face up, palms up. That suggests that she was meant to be seen by a higher being."

"Such as a god," Miriam said.

"Such as a god," Nestor repeated to himself. He jotted down more notes.

"A stabbing and the carving of the chest would need to be executed quickly. We estimated that the killer had roughly twenty to thirty minutes to perform these acts, but—"

"*But*, indeed," Felix said. "There's no way in hell these intricate cuts could be performed in such detail on the skin in that time. No way."

Nestor looked at Miriam in the eye, and he nodded. Felix was right.

"And who is the ideal reader of these carvings?" Nestor said.

"Well, I would say that it's a modern audience," Felix said. "Audiences who have cameras."

"I don't follow," Miriam said. She leaned over, studying Felix up close. Nestor could see that she was trying to figure out how he could know so much.

"Well, we don't have any archeological record of Aztec sacrifices that featured skin-cutting or tattoos during the sacrifice itself. Surely, there was a lot of bloodletting, but usually, it involved sticking a needle or stingray barb in one's tongue or in one's penis."

"And we have no such evidence in this case here," Miriam said.

"Correct. This decision to write on the body using such a fine blade says to me that perhaps whoever did it was aware that the body would be photographed. He wants to show off, and he knows the body will be photographed."

"Yes, but we still have the problem of time," Nestor said. "Not enough time to do such detailed work."

"True," Miriam said. "So, this man hates women, but not enough to rape them."

"We also don't know that, Miriam," Nestor said. "It's possible he had plans to have sex with the corpse, and again, he was out of time."

Felix tossed back the last of his coffee.

"Can I have another?" he said.

"If you think I'm going to be your maid, you're dead wrong," Miriam said. "Coffeemaker's right there."

Felix worked the machine and spoke to Miriam and Nestor from across the room.

"Aztec society was built on prophecies. The return of the Night Drinker would fit right in with the times we are living in. Ultraviolent times for the return of an ultraviolent god."

Felix's face had gone flat as he returned to the table with his coffee. Nestor could see that he was uneasy about something.

"But there's an issue," Nestor said.

"Yes, Detective, there's an issue. As far as I know, there are no written prophecies about the return of the Xipe Totec. There surely was a prophecy about Quetzalcoatl returning, but no such stories about his brother Xipe, the Night Drinker."

"So, we have a hallucinating killer?"

"Well, not so fast. Keep in mind that the Spaniards destroyed virtually all the records of the Aztec Empire, including their books. Just because we don't know of such myths doesn't mean that they didn't exist. Hell, they could have been passed down orally as well."

"Tell me more about this Night Drinker."

"That's just one of his many names. He is one of the four brothers born to the original parent gods who created the universe. The four children they bore were messy, heroic, bloody. It's those four brothers who became the major deities. The Night Drinker is the most misunderstood of the four brothers. Also the deadliest."

"Sounds to me like our movie-theater killer has himself a new name," Miriam said. "Night Drinker fits."

"Aw, Miriam, don't do this," Nestor said. "You know I hate naming these pieces of shit."

"Look, I'm not going to the press with this, but if Calvo here is right, this murderer took an infatuation with this Night Drinker very far."

Nestor's phone rang again. *Dammit, will the calls never end today?* On the screen, Smith's avatar.

"Gotta take this. You all chill, okay?" Nestor said.

"'Chill?' You sound old," Felix said. "Like an old lady."

Nestor gripped the plastic chair so hard, the plastic squeaked. He felt his blood boil and his chest tighten. The rage again.

"I'll be back. Miriam, don't let him touch a fucking thing."

**11:10 AM ET**

"What does he mean don't let me touch a fucking thing? I'm not a toddler."

"You really pissed him off," Miriam said.

"Why? Because I called him pushy? It's always big butch queens like him — they just piss me off and they think that just because they got muscles—"

"Oh, no honey. You pissed him off with the *old lady* comment. He hates feeling old."

"Oh, fuck him," Felix said. "I'm gonna catch my flight back to Chicago." He put his notebook back into his backpack.

Nestor strolled back into the room, his face calm and serene. All the anger he had shown was gone. His eyes sparkled with intensity.

"Glad you're getting your coat on. It's time to go Uptown."

Felix flicked his index fingernail against his thumb, hoping to slowly rip it off if he just repeated the motion enough times. *I hate you, and yet I want to go see this through.*

"I really should check in on my flight, but oh, wait, you won't let me use my phone in here."

"There's no flights in or out of JFK and LaGuardia, still. I looked it up for you just now."

"Shouldn't we stay inside? It's not safe to be out in this blizzard."

"It's not a day off for me. You can wait in my apartment if you really don't want to come with me."

"Really?"

Felix studied Nestor's face up close. Rugged and handsome, full lips, and a thick neck like a bull. He searched for answers in and around the brown eyes, looking for clues of a former life, of Nestor's former body or his life living as a woman. Though Felix knew it wasn't polite, his eyes searched and searched. He couldn't help it.

"But—"

"Ah, yes, I knew there would be a *but*."

"I need your help. You haven't even told me who that 'prophet' might be, and I need answers."

*I don't even have ten dollars to get my ass on the train back to the airport,* Felix thought. *Do I really have a choice?*

Underneath the smell of disinfectant, Felix detected the scents of spoiled cabbage, rotten fruit, French cheese, and something worse. All of it was a bouquet of dead people in this metal-and-ceramic garden on the east end of Manhattan.

"As long as you pay for all my dinners, beers included." He couldn't help but try to squeeze some jokes in there.

"Done."

"Oh, I was joking."

"I'm not. You're a legitimate subject-matter expert. We're going for a ride, and you're going to help me."

## 12:30 PM ET

Delia Douglas could not, for the life of her, open up the lid on the goddamn cup of coffee. Snow pelted her face, eyelashes, and eyebrows, and there was no way in all hell she was going to take off her gloves to risk more of a chill in this storm.

"Come on, work with me," she said. Her walkie-talkie gave off a couple of beeps but was quieter than usual today. The one good thing about snowstorms was that it slowed down the reporting of crimes. It didn't *actually* minimize the actual crimes. It just took a while longer for people to call them in.

But not in the case of the body beneath her. Forensics had put up a semi-transparent tent around the crime scene to keep out the heavy layers of snow that kept on coming down. They should have used an opaque tent, but this transparent one was all that was available at the time.

The tent occupied an area of about a hundred square feet along the sidewalk at 235 West 139th street. The brick townhouses in this part of town gave Delia a sense of order, like things were just in the place they should be. But she knew she was holding on to dreams. Even as she flipped off the plastic tab on the coffee cup, she could see the changes in the neighborhood that crept in. New cars parked along the street, an expensive coffee shop at the end of the block, and lots of white babies in buggies. Of course, no white babies were to be found on this street today. Those white babies were safely tucked away inside. Just snowplows and those people who could not afford to take a snow day.

Delia knew this stretch of 139th well, because this was the very block where she had thought she could buy her first home, back in 2020.

She had done all the right things. She had maintained impeccable credit, saved for a hefty down payment, proven her job stability with the department as a violent crime unit investigator made her the right candidate to buy a one-bedroom unit in a co-op. But the truth was, Harlem, the place of her father's jazz dreams and the birthplace of her mother and her grandmother, would never be within her reach. Delia was black and middle class, but real estate in Harlem was a place that didn't really have room for her anymore.

She sat on the stoop of the building, only partially shielded from the relentless snow. She was happy now, sipping. Forensics technicians worked with multiple LED lights inside the tent, and Delia remembered seeing a VHS tape of *ET* a long time ago, where men in masks poked through transparent plastic in the same way, probing, investigating. But the victim under the tent was no alien.

He was as human as could be, with gorgeous white teeth and strong musculature; eyes hazel like a jar of honey seen through a sunset.

But all resemblances to normalcy ended there. He didn't exactly look human at the moment.

She had just spent a full hour on the crime scene, photographing, taking notes, lurid notes, that she would have to input into her report. How to explain what she was witnessing on this sidewalk?

No one would actually believe it.

*A sharp blade has been used to cut into the victim's skin. The murderer has peeled the skin off the body, except for the feet. All that remains is exposed fascia, muscle, and a very small amount of fat. The victim was lean. The skin of the feet looks intact.*

*And that's the rub,* Delia thought as she sipped her coffee and lit a Marlboro with gloved hands. *It's those feet which I am never going to be able to forget. Why leave just the skin of the foot behind? Did the killer run out of time? Was he trying to say something?*

She could see the legs now through the translucent tent, skinless, red as cherry, and the feet. Those feet were very black, and the soles cracked and dry. But the nails were in perfect shape and the top skin supple.

The residents of the apartment building where she sat poked out through the front door. Delia twisted around.

"Get the fuck back inside. We're not done here."

*I'm angry because I am disgusted, people. Sorry I have to take it out on you,* she thought.

"Get the fuck back in, I said!"

The teenagers, mothers, and fathers squeezed back into the building. Faces stared out at her from the brick townhouse, their eyes wide and curious. To them she probably looked like an alien, too.

## 12:40 PM ET

Nestor spotted Delia Douglas from two hundred feet away, even as wet snowflakes pelted his eyelashes. She wore a single blue braid woven into her hair, and under the reflective surface of so much snow, the sapphire strand vibrated with electricity. She favored jeans and crisp white blouses, and, in this weather, long coats that came down to her knees.

"Felix, I'd like you to meet Delia Douglas."

"Hey," Felix said, waving his hand and quickly tucking it back into his coat. Delia flicked a cigarette butt onto the snow and tipped her cup toward Nestor first, then Felix.

"Nice to meet you, Felix. You with the department?"

Felix snorted. "No, but that's a really hilarious idea. I'm just…providing some consulting, LOL."

Nestor shook his head. He had always thought that people speaking in emoticons was urban legend, but here it was, real, and depressing as hell. "What Felix means to say is that he's a subject matter-expert in anthropology for our forensics work. He's helping me with the case."

"I'm intrigued. Expert in what, exactly?"

"Old texts. Ancient, really," Felix said. His eyes darted around the street, up the stairway of the townhouses, and up at the tree branches, as if expecting some celebrity to show up. His lips opened into a smile made of his own amusement. If Nestor didn't know any better, he would say Felix was starting to fall in love with the city.

"Nestor, can I talk to you for a moment?" Delia said.

"Stay here, please," Nestor said. Felix nodded, but he was

already walking around the tent, trying to peer at the technicians and investigators inside.

"Who the hell is this white boy you brought with you?" Delia stared at him with the very same intensity and directness that made her great at her job but also a threat to her superiors.

"He's not exactly a white boy."

"Okay, fine. But he is here because…"

"You'll see it in my report, but would you mind keeping this info hush? I don't want the rest of the department to think I'm back in some Bowery Murders kind-of-shit."

"Bowery? Are you serious?"

Nestor felt uneasy as soon as he said the word *Bowery* out loud. His stomach twisted, and Delia adjusted her glasses so she could get a better look at him.

Nestor had known Delia for more than two decades, and she had stood by him before, during, and after his transition. She had been the only person to consistently use his new first name, Nestor, in those awkward first two years in which most other officers squirmed uncomfortably or snickered when they took a seat next to him. She had been the first person in the department to refer to Nestor as "he." She was the officer who peeled off the Post-it that said TRANNY FAG off his locker and reported it to her superiors.

*You've been alone up in your apartment in Queens too long, old boy*, he told himself. *You're forgetting how to trust your people. Come on, spit it out.*

He leaned in close to Delia. Despite the emptiness of the street, he whispered in her ear, his heart paranoid. How eyes darted around to see who might be watching them.

"I think we have a ritualized murder on our hands. You saw my notes on the Grue case."

"I read them. Definitely agree it's probably a ritual act. But what's eating at you, Nestor?"

"I am…unsure of things. There's aspects about this case that are making me uneasy, almost sick—"

"Okay, this is why I can't deal with you Catholics half the time."

"This isn't Catholic guilt."

"You sure?"

"Very. Fucking."

He shook his head.

"Then what is it about, then?" Delia said.

"It's about seeing horrible things done to people. Rapes, child murders, stabbings, gunshot wounds. It's all starting to wear me down."

"You're spooked by her missing heart? Is that it?"

"No. I think that part was probably quick, though violent. It's the carvings on Grue's skin that bother me. Who would take the time to do such a horrible thing to a body? Such torture?"

"Okay, big man, take a step back with me, lean into the Delia office."

He did as she asked. She put her hands on his elbows, like an aunt consoling her frightened nephew. He had to admit that he was thankful for the human touch.

"This isn't the Bowery case again, okay? It's different. And, my friend, you're retiring. In one month. You can assign this case to *me* before you go. Got it? You don't have to take this on."

"Captain Smith assigned this to me, and I feel like I am running out of time."

"You don't know how long a case will take to close. You need to be letting go of this already, because it may not wrap up neatly."

"I know that. The Bowery case was in the courts for almost eight years. I know that."

"But you say you're out of time, Nestor. Why?"

"It's a feeling, the kind you get in a nightmare. This feeling reminds me that I will never have time. I will never have enough time to save anyone, including, murder victims, friends, and much less family, like my mother or my nephews. I feel like a shadow is sweeping across the sky in this country, and I don't have enough time to find shelter."

"Where's all this coming from?"

"Don't know, it's what I feel lately. Maybe I always felt it but it's getting worse with this case."

"You think you're going to die?"

"No, I don't know how to explain it. It's like an alarm clock is going to go off, right here, inside my heart or my brain. Or maybe it's going to go off in the city, the subway. But not like a physical thing. Metaphorically. It's bad."

"This is really unlike you. Are you on any medications?"

"None. I only take T."

"And what's the hipster with the mustache doing here?"

"He doesn't seem to give a shit about time. And it looks like he understands some of the connections in this case that I myself don't have the time to research. He can help me compress my time on working this case."

"Okay, but he's basically just a professor, right?"

"Sort of. He's looking for a teaching job, but he works for Amazon at the moment."

"I'm gonna pretend I didn't just hear that."

"But he's talented."

"But he knows *nothing* about police work."

"I looked him up, and he checks out. He's got radical but well-supported ideas in his field."

"He's weird as all hell."

"Delia Douglas never holds back."

"I don't think I like him."

"What are you saying?"

"You should be working with me on this. Been waiting for you a long-ass time out in this cold."

She was right. While he was nursing Felix's hangover, he could have been here, on site, with Delia. Nestor felt very drawn to Delia, and she was a fine-looking woman, too. If he would allow himself, hell, he would even ask her out to dinner one day, though he really knew nothing about her personal life. And yet his mind clicked right back onto the investigation, and he ignored the notion.

"If Felix is not white, what is he?"

"He's half. Mexican on his mother's side."

"Huh."

"Something tells me I need Felix around to work on this case."

"Okay, you're really worrying me now, Nestor. You're not an 'intuition' kind of guy, and you don't always play well with others. You're a lone workhorse, in fact. This is very unlike you."

"It's been a hard year," he said. "Maybe you're right, I should just dump the professor and move on to closing this case on my own."

"Well, I hate to alarm you, but you better hurry. We have a problem. Look."

Nestor looked over his shoulder. Felix was already inside the translucent tent, squatting to touch the cadaver.

**12:53 PM ET**

Felix pushed down on the flesh of the dead man's thigh with his bare finger. The tissue sprang back with firmness, like a medium-rare steak.

The skin was absolutely gone. All that was left was the flesh and bone, red and slick like strawberry Jell-O. Even though there wasn't a single drop of blood body near the body, a bouquet with the scent of blood floated inside the tent.

The body was propped up next to the hood of a Toyota Prius in a lotus position, with the skull rolled back, touching the fender of the vehicle. His arms hung slack at his sides, and his long and thick penis, skinless, dangled onto the floor like a melted gumdrop.

Felix had grown up around sous chefs and line cooks, always under the militarized command of his mother's restaurants. The smell of raw meat had never bothered him. In fact, this smelled no different from a raw side of beef, with the only difference being a few single notes of sweetness.

Something strong and hard yanked Felix back by the collar of his parka, and he heard a few of the seams pop.

"Get the fuck away from the body!"

Felix got whisked around, and suddenly he was face to face with Detective Buñuel and those scary brown eyes of his.

"This can cost me my job, and it can send you straight to prison, you fuck."

Nestor had gone red as a cherry, and for a moment, Felix thought he might start delivering punches. Nestor took long breaths in and out, and in a flash, his anger dimmed, though it was still there, behind the eyes. Felix pulled away from his grip.

"Aren't you going to apologize for your outburst and for assaulting me?" Felix said.

"Oh, you little entitled bitch," Nestor said. "You follow the rules I give you. Or you're back in the street."

"Oh, good point. That."

"Now come on, tell me what you see. Since you were so eager to touch the body."

Delia Douglas stood off to the side, taking notes on an iPad. Felix didn't like the way she stared at him.

"Can I have some of those cute gloves you got?" Felix said.

Nestor handed him a pair of blue nitrile gloves.

"Just don't fucking touch a thing."

"This person has been butchered with care," Felix said. "To strip an animal of its skin, you have to do it with a high level of respect."

Felix pointed toward the smooth muscle fibers of the pecs, the abdominals, and the white tendons and fascia, and the way they had been stripped without marring the grain of the muscle fibers.

"This couldn't have been done out here in the street. The killer's hands would have been too cold, even with gloves. To really strip the skin off well, you need at least room temperature."

"Why's that?" Nestor said.

"Well, you need a strong person to do it. First of all, because you cut a flap, sometimes at the neck, sometimes from the feet, depends on the animal, and then you have to peel it with your bare hands. It's really one of the best ways to do it."

"Always with bare hands?" Nestor said.

"No, you should always wear gloves. Protect yourself against cuts, or bacteria from the animal."

*Well, this is strange. Isn't this man a professional police investigator? Shouldn't he already know this?* At that moment, Felix realized then that the detective was testing him. *I think he knows this already. He just wants to see how I think.*

His heart speed up a little. He liked the thrill of this kind of game. He too, pretended like Nestor Buñuel didn't know all that much about the murders of human beings.

"As you peel the skin downward, you can use a blade to separate the skin from the flesh. It must be sharp as fuck."

"Why move downward?"

"Because the easiest way is to handle the carcass is either by the feet or by the neck. It also helps to drain the blood from the carcass first. Looks like that was done here. Not a single pool of blood."

"Why are you trying to get behind the body?"

"I'm trying to see if there's a puncture or cut in the back of the head."

"How do you know all this? They don't teach butchery to doctoral students at the University of Chicago."

"I grew up in the kitchens of my mom's restaurants. Trust me, I've seen this done many times. On lambs and pigs."

"Okay, big boy, then tell me what you see. Don't touch the

body, but take a closer look at the collarbone, the neck, the base of the skull."

Felix crept around the side, careful to not touch anything, not the parked Prius, not the body, not even the pool of motor oil mixing in with the snow.

"No puncture mark in the back of the neck, Nestor."

"Look closer, Felix."

Now Felix could see something, a thin line beneath the jaw, and signs of softness around the red meat in the throat.

"Holy shit, how did you see that?" Felix said.

"See what?"

*Oh, he's really testing me now.*

"He wasn't hung on a hook. He was hanged from a rope around his neck."

"The longer you work this job, the sooner you spot some patterns."

"Some fucking job."

"This does fit your idea of how he was skinned. Much easier to skin a man if he's hanging. But *where* was this done?"

"In a place called fucking hell, ha-ha," Felix said.

No one, neither Delia, nor Nestor, nor the forensics technicians inside the tent, laughed at his joke.

"What's that in his fist?" Felix said.

The victim's left hand was balled up. One of the forensics technicians moved in, and using several steel instruments, they pried open the hand, which was starting to stiffen and did not want to give. Felix took several steps back before Nestor could chide him.

After a few minutes, the technicians held up an object with tweezers.

"Unfold it, please," Nestor said.

The team placed a flat sheet of plastic on the ground and slowly unfolded the leathery pack. Its red-and-chocolate folds came undone, and the object had bloomed into a square that measured about six by six inches.

"Holy mother of god," Nestor said.

It was a square of skin. Whoever had done this had used skin as their canvas. Drawings of tiny glyphs had been carved in neat rows, forming a grid on the black skin. The cuts were precise and the images rich in detail.

"We can't assume it came from this body," Felix said.

"Very good," Delia said. "Forensics can help confirm if it's a match."

"But what does it say, Felix?" Nestor said.

"This one's a easier to read than the glyphs on Grue's body. Gimme a second."

Felix focused on the images, and he got lost inside the writing. He needed a few reference materials, but even without them, he could get the main gist of what was being said in the square of skin. Felix stood back up and pursed his lips. All the cops stared at him with caution but also curiosity.

"It says, *The Night Drinker is returning soon. Purification is at hand.*"

"So, the prophecy, part two," Nestor said.

"Or, if we're looking at the killer's perspective, another threat," Felix said. "More death is coming."

"Good point."

"And there's one more line right here which I don't yet understand."

"Go on," Delia and Nestor said at the same time.

"*Beware the 9 Lords of Night.*"

### 1:15 PM ET

No matter how hard he tried, Felix could not keep up with Nestor, who trudged through the snow like some sort of mythical snow beast, his muscular legs pistoning up and down  and his boots leaving behind flat imprints. Felix was sweating buckets inside the parka, working out his legs with such intensity that his calves and thigh muscles burned, and no matter how hard he pushed, he seemed to make no progress through the snowdrifts.

*What am I even doing here? I was supposed to be on a job interview, and now I'm in a snowstorm, with a creepy cop, and shouldn't I be having a beer instead?*

"Hold up, man," Felix said, out of breath, barely making any progress in the snow drifts.

"Hurry up," Nestor said, holding open the passenger door to an NYPD police car. Inside, Nestor greeted two police officers, who sat in front. The three cops made small talk as they drove back downtown. The snow had thickened into a wall of white ice, and bits of hail hit the top of the vehicle, making tinny metal sounds as they drove south. After a while, the two officers in the front resumed their own chats with each other.

"The writings are encoded, would you agree?" Nestor said.

"On the victims' skins? Yes," Felix said. "Don't forget that the Aztecs did not have an advanced writing system like the Maya. What I'm interpreting from evidence is like figuring out the meaning from sequential pictorial art, like reading a comic book."

"If that's the case, I need you to put all this prophecy stuff in terms I can understand. I don't have time to get a PhD in archeology."

"Anthropology, actually."

"Well, you just distill this for me, okay?"

"That's ironic, man. You write stories about gene-editing and nanotech in all of your books."

"Not here, okay?"

"What, you don't like people talking about YOUR MUTIE BOOKS, MISS JK ROWLING?"

The two officers in the front giggled.

"Shut up, okay?" Nestor whispered to him.

"Why? You must be a celebrity around here with your book series, handing out autographs and being mister badass."

Felix's arm went blisteringly hot with pain.

"Holy shit, what's your problem? Did you just pinch me?"

"Stop talking about my books, okay?" Nestor whispered in his ear.

Felix's breathing sped up. He didn't think the detective would violate his space, but here he was, with his fucking horse thighs pressed against him, jamming him against the passenger door like a sardine, and pinching his arm, just like—

A knot formed in Felix's throat, and his stomach turned. The hail from the storm was growing stronger, and the balls of ice, the size of grapes, rattled the windshield. Thunder cracked in the sky.

"This is worse than Hurricane Sandy," said the cop in the passenger side, staring out the window, as if the city and the storm were lyrical.

Felix wanted to bat away Nestor's hand, to get him to stop twisting his forearm like taffy, but in fact, he could not.

He wanted to scream.

Because when Felix had been pinched like this before, he hadn't been able to get away.

There had been a day, back in Minnesota around 2003, when he had gone into his mother's closet while his babysitter fell asleep. Using his ability to run free throughout the house, he tried on his mother's clothes, like many children often did. Felix had stepped into a pair of her pantyhose, thrown a dress over his head, and wobbled in heels in front of her mirror.

He never heard his mother pull up to the driveway, having forgotten her cell phone in the house.

She had walked in and gasped. Her tall and thin shape, the angular crook of her long arms — all of her body stiffened, as if she were turning to stone. Her face grew white as she examined Felix's homemade fashion show.

She hadn't said a single word. Instead, she pinched Felix by the arm, with her left hand, and with her right, she dug her nails and fingers into his clavicle so hard, he felt she might break the bone. The babysitter was still asleep as she had dragged him all the way down the stairs, past the first floor of their house, through the kitchen and into the basement. There, with just a flashlight to light the way, she had sat him down on the mildewy concrete, and pinched, and twisted her hand in his collarbone some more, and he had cried, screamed, barely catching glimpses of her face from the flashlight.

While Felix whimpered and rubbed and tears snot and tears off his face, his mother leaned in close so he could see her face up close.

"Never again, do you understand?" is all she had said. The flashlight fell off the bench on which they sat, and the cellar went dark. Felix screamed, and his mother stifled him, cupping her hand to his face. Only after he calmed down did she let him come back up to the kitchen. She pinched his arms all the way back up the stairs and into the kitchen.

He had only been seven years old that day, and not the only time his mother had left black-and-blue marks on his forearms from pinching. However, it was the instance he remembered with the most detail.

Felix's lip quivered, and he felt the hot sting of Nestor's fingers on his flesh, and shadows wrapped in memories filled his heart. He wanted to shout at the cop, *Please stop hurting me, please. PLEASE.*

Nestor shifted, as if he had heard Felix's thoughts, and he cocked his head so they could make eye contact. Suddenly, the cop eased up on his arm, and he pressed his lips together. He did not apologize, but he seemed to understand something about how bad the pain was making Felix feel.

The big man scooted a few inches farther away, giving Felix some room, but his eyes never stopped staring into Felix's. Felix was about to say *I'm sorry*, when Nestor held his index finger up to his lips.

"Save it until we get to the department. Not here."

## 2:30 PM ET

The tiny office kitchen was deserted at this hour. On its walls, photos of merit badges and officers posing with the mayor and the president for excellence in service lined the walls. Felix studied the faces of the police officers, squinting to catch the details of what lay behind their eyes. While he browsed his way down the framed photos, Nestor dove into the contents of a massive refrigerator.

The detective withdrew several plastic containers from the fridge. All of them were neatly labeled to an obsessive degree: turkey breast, chicken breast, spinach, quinoa, roast beef, cottage cheese. It was a full assortment of meats, vegetables, and food so healthy, Felix felt a certain kind of envy.

"Have a seat," Nestor said. He toasted slices of sprouted wheat bread and tore pieces of lettuce in his small hands. He applied a healthy layer of mayonnaise on the sandwich for Felix, and on his own he only squirted mustard. By the time he was done, two gigantic sandwiches, better than anything Felix could get in a deli, waited in front of them. Felix bit into his sandwich, and he felt such warmth in his belly, and such satisfaction in a place beyond his body, that he shut his eyes as he chewed. He took sips off a Mountain Dew from the vending machine. It was like champagne.

Nestor took a seat across from Felix and ate slowly, more slowly than Felix had ever seen someone eat. He spoke to Felix without looking up from the precise methods of his eating.

"We don't have to talk about what happened in the car," Nestor said. "Just want you to know that getting too touchy-feely, too *emotional* — can backfire if you do it in front of cops like the uniformed men in the vehicle."

"Do they know you're trans?"

"Not sure. NYPD employs about 45,000 officers, but word

travels fast. I have stopped managing the thoughts about who might know about me or not. I don't give a shit."

"And yet."

"And yet. You're right."

Felix nodded. Nestor shepherded a rogue leaf of spinach back into the sandwich.

"I still have to play by some rules, especially the rules of men. Besides, too many conversations about me take focus away from conversations about the actual cases I am handling at any given time. I want to be known by my work, not my genitals. You understand me?"

"Yeah. They'll think you're soft if you're babying me in the car." Nestor nodded.

"I feel that same way in places with a lot of straight dudes," Felix said. "Like, I have to veil myself in some kind of way."

"*Veil* is a really interesting metaphor. You very religious, Felix?"

"Avowed atheist. My rational mind won't let me operate on a concept like religion or any such trash. And you?"

"I don't know how to be anything other than a Catholic."

"I should have guessed."

"What does that mean?"

"You just have a look about you. Kind of like a goody-goody."

Nestor giggled for a moment and looked up. *He looks both strong, and sad,* Felix thought. Like some old jungle animal forgotten in a cave.

"A goody-goody, really?"

"The worst kind of goody-goody."

"You'd be very wrong about that."

"Well, you look very Catholic to me."

"Not sure if that's an insult or not. Thanks, buddy, ha."

"Why don't you like to talk about your books with the other police?"

Nestor shifted in his seat, and he scratched his beard, twisting one end of his mustache.

"We can pick this up some other time. I have some of my other cases to tend to."

"Other cases?"

"My cop life is not like the movies or TV. Besides the Grue case, I have two gang crimes, three identity thefts, and two cybercrimes with databases so large, it would make your brain hemorrhage. And more. This means I'm going to have to tend to those cases, and with this winter storm raging—"

"I'm in New York. I somehow don't think boredom is in my future."

"I'm not giving you cash to drink. And I don't want you wandering outside in whatever mega storm is trampling the city."

"Why's that, Daddy?"

"Do *not* call me Daddy. I'm not one of your *besties* at the gay bar."

"Okay, detective Nestor Antonio Buñuel del Consuelo Miranda."

"You looked me up?"

"You're not the only guy that's curious and meticulous. That makes us just a little similar to each other."

Nestor's face turned bright red, and a large vein in his neck pulsed. Then the big man dropped his shoulders and sighed.

"You're such a little shit, you know that?" Nestor said, smiling and truly enjoying himself. He scooped up their empty plates and stood up. He clapped Felix on the back. Felix let the body contact slide this time.

"Give me about three hours. I would prefer if you stayed here, where I can find you if I need you."

"Can I get a computer, or at least Wi-Fi, to log onto the Internet? I can access some academic papers and digital archives from here and help you."

"I can arrange that."

"And then, after the three hours?"

"We're going to go over some of the evidence, you and I. Then you can take your flight back to Chicago. But first, I want you to help me put a sketch together."

"Eh?"

"A figurative one. A profile of our killer."

"How so?"

"I think we have a single killer, but we need to know what's motivating him or her."

"I can do that with ya."

"And one more thing. I need you to work hard, and fast, with your research. Three hours is not a lot. While we were eating, I got an email with a break in the case."

"*A break in the case*...So, you actually use that phrase?"

"Shut up."

"Make me."

"You don't want that. Trust me."

Nestor glanced at his mobile, raised an eyebrow as he evaluated Felix.

"It looks like they found Marlene Grue's missing heart."

## 3:00 PM ET

Delia Douglas walked past the front desk at the police station, and officer Chris Stuart flagged her down.

"Delia, Delia, hold on."

Chris was an odd bird. He was a reformed meth addict, gaunt yet meaty, and abrasive as hell.

"You gonna see Buñuel later on?"

"Yep, why?"

"Package arrived for him, looks like something from Amazon. Who knows what kind of weird shit he'd order."

"Why do you care?"

"I don't. But you know, that Buñuel is a fucking creeper sometimes."

Delia had always suspected that Chris was the person who had scrawled TRANNY FAG in the locker room back in the days when Nestor had first transitioned, but no hard proof had ever surfaced. What she did know is that Chris avoided Nestor at all costs, and he never passed up the chance to toss some tranny jokes to whoever might listen.

Chris handed Delia a mustard-yellow package, indeed from Amazon services. She tucked it into her bag and made a note to herself to give it to Nestor.

## 4:08 PM ET

Nestor sucked down multiple cups of tea, reviewing records, making phone calls, until he was interrupted by a tap on his monitor. He looked up, and saw Miriam McGuire looming over him, with assistant coroner Carson J. Mitchum at her side. No matter where he went, Carson Mitchum eclipsed the men and women he stood next to. At 5'11", and with the build of a pro bodybuilder, he moved with grace and delicate movements. He peered down at Nestor through rimless glasses and a beard that was once sandy brown but now mostly gray.

Carson Mitchum never, ever left his office on the other end of town. Seeing him now was like seeing a lion out of its den.

"What's shakin', Buñuel?" Carson said, and he tapped a fist with Nestor. Despite the friendly tone of his voice, Carson hardly ever smiled. It took a lot to make that happen. Miriam crossed her arms and rolled her eyes at Carson. She fished Jelly Belly beans out of a ziplock, evaluating each flavor before popping it in her mouth.

"You got any Skulli Bears in there?" Nestor said.

"No, just eat one of these."

"Not the same."

"Oh my god, your obsession with those Skulli Bears, Nestor."

"Miriam, it's called good taste. They're the best candies."

"I call it a sweet tooth that will kill ya."

"They make me laugh."

Nestor took a jelly bean out of the bag and rolled it around in his mouth.

"I had to call up my associate Santa Claus here today to give me a hand," Miriam said. She never stopped giving Mitchum shit for his snowy beard.

Carson clicked his tongue at Miriam and brushed his whiskers with sensual strokes. "You don't like it?"

"I'll buy you the razors to cut it off myself."

"You only treat me like this because you know I voted Democrat," Carson said.

"Why are you so damn liberal, anyway?" Miriam said.

Carson shook his head, and broke into a wide smile, showing perfect white teeth. "She busts my balls, that's why we don't hang out that often."

"You're just a bleeding-heart liberal."

"And I bring a sense of common sense to ya, Miriam."

Miriam's smile faded as she pulled up emails and notes on her smartphone.

"The human heart was found on Houston Street, near 2nd Avenue," Miriam said. "On a fucking park bench, of all places."

"That's a long way from Times Square," Nestor said.

"It looks like it's a match," she said. "We're both sure of it. Blood analysis should also confirm it within the next twenty-four hours or so."

"We went over it together, and looked at the body most of this morning," Carson said. "It looks like the organ was removed after time of death."

"This means the stab wounds and incisions were meant to kill the victim. She was conscious as she bled to death," Nestor said.

"Yep," Miriam and Carson said.

Nestor shook his head and scribbled a note for himself.

"He wanted Grue to witness," Nestor said.

"Witness what, exactly?" Carson said.

"Her own death, or perhaps the movie on the screen, or the killer's face, or…maybe all three."

"But then, why remove her heart? A trophy?" Miriam said. Carson shook his head.

"So, why are you here, Carson? Let's cut through the shit."

"I came down here with Miriam because A, we have some depositions to review, and B, because I want to give you a heads-up about what's likely to happen next, Nestor. And you know that I never use email or smartphones for that kind of shit."

"Spit it out, Carson," Nestor said.

"If the heart's been carved out like that, and if you have a legitimate link between the two murders, you're going to be taking a backseat to the FBI sooner than you know. They will deploy their behavioral analysis unit. Then they'll take over this case."

"Maybe that's not such a bad thing," Nestor said.

Carson frowned, and his voice took on a gravel-like texture.

"What kind of weak bullshit is that, Nestor?"

"What do you mean?"

"Just because you're retiring, you're just gonna pass the buck? You have never, ever passed the buck."

*How can I tell Carson that something isn't right? That it's getting fucking weirder by the minute to do this job, and that I feel like ground-up shit the more I think about the mutilated body of Marlene Grue?*

But Carson was right. It was very much unlike Nestor to defer to the Feds. For a moment, he pushed through the dark spot. He looked Carson and Miriam in the eye.

"Carson, remember that time you spotted me on the bench?"

"No, not at all."

Miriam laughed, and Carson beamed an impish grin.

"Well, I do. The bar came within inches of my throat, and I couldn't raise it back up. You stepped in and shouted at me, telling me I could push through to get the bar back up."

Carson's barrel chest shifted in his shirt and tie, and his icy blue eyes went soft, sentimental.

"And what did you do then, buddy?"

"I pushed it way the fuck up. And I even burst all the capillaries in my eyes."

"You looked like a tweaker for about a week."

Nestor nodded, twisting the end of his mustache with his right hand, and cleared his throat.

"I'll get you and Miriam some updates later this week, as soon as I have them. I plan to close this case. Fuck the FBI. This one is mine."

"Big promise, bro," Carson said.

"Big case."

A shadow flickered across the ceiling. It was very faint, and it fluttered, as if it had wings.

"D'yall see that?" Nestor said.

Miriam walked around the room, tested the light switch. "Brownout, probably from the storm."

"Storm Tobe," Nestor said, "is really here."

"I didn't see anything," Carson said.

"You didn't?" Nestor said.

"Not at all. Just these big, bright lights and your ugly, hairy face."

Nestor appreciated Carson's joke, one which he would only make to other males he was comfortable with in the department. Nestor shrugged, and Miriam shook her head. "I felt it, I saw it. It was like a bat passing over a lightbulb, just a flicker."

"Man, fuck this day," Nestor said, and Carson and Miriam walked toward the back of the office, away from the cubicles.

"Miss me?" said a reedy voice behind Nestor. He jerked around, spooked.

"What the hell are you doing there?" he said. Felix was in the cubicle next to his.

"I wanted to change spots."

"Did you just listen in on that whole conversation? I told you to work in the office I set aside for you."

"Gotta say, that Carson guy is hot as hell. Porn-star looks."

"Fucking A," Nestor said as he stood up. He was about to spit a round of obscenities when he saw what Felix was working on in the laptop Nestor had loaned him.

"That can't be possible," Nestor said.

"What?"

"That photo you pulled up there. Looks just like our murder. Body draped over movie theater seats. Carvings on the sides of the chest and—"

"And a big cut in the rib cage to get the heart out."

## 4:12 PM ET

The person in the photograph lay face up, arms at their sides, draped over a row of movie theater seats. The light from the projector distorted some of the details, but sure enough, there was a big gaping hole in the chest. The gender was impossible to determine from the compressed JPG.

"Where is that from?"

"4chan. It's been photoshopped, so don't get too excited. It's fake."

"Even if so, it looks incredibly accurate. Coincidence?"

"I don't operate on coincidences in my academic work. I just work with the evidence."

"Good point. Same here."

"But the coincidence is not the interesting part," Felix said, zooming into the composition. "Here's the thing: the author claims to have *dreamed* this image back in 2001. And that's his reason for posting the image."

"That's almost 25 years ago, shit."

"Okay, go on."

"Well, it's 4chan, so you have to assume it's been posted by scum. But he says that in his dream, a tall man with wings showed him this image."

"That would never hold up as evidence in a court."

"Well, it's not the content of the image, or the silliness of the dream, but the metadata that matters here," Felix said.

"What metadata?" Nestor said. This kid was suddenly talking in his language.

"We know this image was published almost a quarter-century ago, but we can use metadata from Twitter, Facebook, and other places to see who else might have been talking about the image, or for that matter, keywords associated with the Night Drinker or the

9 Lords of Night."

"The movie?"

"Excuse me?"

"The movie *9 Lords of Night?*"

"You are still talking about that fucking movie, Nestor? Told you I don't get into movies."

"Then what *9 Lords of Night* are YOU talking about?"

"Relax, dude. Have a seat. It's really just about metadata first, then a theory second."

Felix flipped up the rows of data stored in his database queries, and sure enough, there were some patterns there. People on Twitter, blogs, even YouTube channels, who commented and posted using words related to the investigation.

Working with metadata was Nestor's specialty, one which other cops in the department didn't always understand. And here was this rake of a man, young enough to be his son, going down the right path to sniff out evidence, moving very, very fast. Maybe faster than Nestor ever had or would.

"We don't have a lot of time, man," Nestor thought. "Join me in this empty office over on this side."

Suddenly, Nestor's anxieties about the case vanished, and he felt regret about letting Carson down, even if it had been for just a moment.

Now Nestor was sweating under his collar as adrenaline pumped blood through his body and electricity made his scalp tingle. As they crossed the carpeted hallways, the snow outside turned the windows bright white. It was impossible to see out into the street.

### 4:15 PM ET

Devin tapped on the dashboard in the patrol car, as if knocking would somehow bring the gas gauge up past the letter E. *Come on, man,* he thought. *Just six blocks to go.*

He just needed to get back, do some paperwork, and call it a night, but his patrol car was going to surely prevent it. He should have filled up the tank when he had the chance, and now this. Boy, was he going to get so much shit from folks. The radio blared, the volume way up. He liked the way the voices kept him company and cast out the silence from the car. Devin didn't like silence of any kind.

"We'll be brining you live coverage of Storm Tobe, while we track George, a secondary storm that is on its heels and may cause further damage to the tri-state area. Authorities are warning residents in the five boroughs to stay indoors, particularly because of the large hail that has already caused severe damage to several buildings. Meteorologists recorded accumulation in Manhattan and Brooklyn in the past hour at ten and twelve inches respectively, and we're expected to get at least twelve more overnight."

If he stranded himself with an empty gas tank, what would his fellow officers think of him? His own father would laugh when he heard the anecdote. *Typical*, he might text. And after all, it was important to meet expectations, and Devin knew it. Things had to be done the right way in life. And if he had to radio in a call for a tow truck so he could take the patrol car to a gas station, he would be the laughing stock of the place. Just a sissy who couldn't take care of his own responsibilities. But right now, it wasn't very likely that he would make it to a gas station.

The *ping-pong* of ice pellets on the windshield grew sharper, faster. The hail that landed on the glass cracked, drowning out the radio. The stoplight ahead went blurry and became just a smudge of red against the gray sheets of ice.

"Jesus," Devin said, and the hail grew bigger, the size of golf balls. Up in the corners of the windshield he spotted a single tiny crack, no bigger than a hair. He looked around, as if the sidewalks would offer some sort of safety. For the first time in all the years he had lived in New York City, they were deserted. This really was a bad storm, and goddamn, so early in the season. Halloween hadn't even arrived.

The red traffic light blinked.

"Oh, fuck me," Devin said. The car sputtered, and gave its last cough. The tank must be fully empty now.

Snow engulfed the buildings, the pavement, and parked cars. Though it was only early afternoon, darkness spread out, as if night had already arrived.

A FedEx truck cleared the intersection, and suddenly he was all alone. Devin had an urge to call his partner Dave and check on the kids, to make sure they too were safe during this snowstorm, and he fumbled inside his coat pocket for his phone.

The red lights of the traffic poles lit the snow in shades of pink and crimson, and there, in the snow, Devin saw it.

A tall shape walked west across the intersection. It moved slowly but with certainty, slicing through snow drifts. Devin couldn't tell if it was male or female, because it was wearing a flowing navy-blue coat that touched the ground, like a cape. It was at least twelve feet tall. The giant was lit blood-red by the streetlights, and hooded by the navy cloak. The figure reached the intersection and stopped for a moment.

The giant craned its neck, and its eyes, each one the diameter of a softball, glowed from within with blue light.

Devin wiped condensation off the glass, and he panted, afraid, unreasonably afraid. He should have drawn his weapon already, but he could not. He had forgotten about finding his cell phone, too. Instead, his hands were hooked around the steering wheel, the knuckles white.

The giant shook its body and opened its mouth, which bristled with metal, as if there were thousands of sewing needles inside.

"Shit."

And then Devin saw its feet poking out from under its cloak.

"Oh my god," Devin said. "What in all mercy is that?"

The figure walked on a pair of naked human hands instead of feet.

The skin of the hands was white, almost as pale as the snow, and each one of its five fingers had a long nails. *Fuck, more like a talon,* Devin thought. The claws were the color of seafoam, three inches long, and sharp as a butcher knife.

Thunder broke out in the distance, and lightning lit the giant for a brief moment. It opened its mouth and let out a howl from another world. The sound it made was a throb of bass tones, combined notes that seemed to sizzle, like a steak on a hot pan.

The giant had its back to him now as it moved through the intersection.

The figure twisted its neck to stare Devin in the eye, and it craned its shoulders around at an impossible angle, twisting almost 180 degrees. All he could think was, *Oh, fucking shit, I have seen that, I have seen that, the little girl turned her neck like that when she was on the bed, and oh fuck, it was so wrong. The exorcist, this thing turned its head like the girl in* The Exorcist. *And her name was Regan.*

Lightning burst from the sky, and white light filled the street. As the flash of lightning passed, the figure disappeared, and the streetlight flicked from red to green. Beneath his feet, the patrol car roared to life again, as if it had been given a last gush of gasoline. The radio came back on, and a commercial for debt-consolidation services screamed for Devin's attention.

He shut the radio off, and the hail softened again into thick snow. He pressed on the gas pedal and drove through the intersection, looking for footprints of the giant he had just seen. *Well,* handprints *would be more correct, wouldn't it,* he reminded himself.

Suddenly, Devin felt very afraid, very anguished, and a sadness like the kind he had felt when his mother died in the home, moved through him. He wept, drove past the streetlight and hurried to make it to the gas station.

By the time he got out of the car at the gas station, Devin realized he had wet his pants, and tears crystallized on his face as fat snowflakes fell from the sky.

## 5:00 PM ET

Felix tapped on the screen so hard that the display burst into rainbow splotches.

"Here, here, and here, and here," he said, moving his fingers on Google Maps and tapping some more. "It's like veins."

The kid was incredible, and his proficiency with databases pretty great, considering he worked in the humanities. In just a few hours, he had pulled up the rough geographic locations of mentions of Nine Lords of Night and the Night Drinker over the past twenty-five years. The map showed lines, ragged like scratches or, yes, veins, concentrated in various cities around the North American continent.

A heavy red slash emanated from Mexico City. Another one spilled out from the waterfront of Chicago toward the northwest side of the city. This one was fatter, more like cluster of dots. The third was thick and black, and moved out 150 miles away from Manhattan and into upper New York State.

"So, you see it too," Felix said.

"Of course," Nestor said. "This line, it's right where we are. Looks like it maps right onto the turnpike. But we have to be careful with analyzing this, Felix. These are only *mentions* of Nine Lords of Night and the Night Drinker. They're nothing but Facebook posts, tweets, and Instagrams. What you're showing me here is nothing more than a map of where modern American folklore gets talked about."

"I get what you're saying, but you're wrong."

"Excuse me?"

"Yeah, you're wrong."

"You gonna tell me how to my job? I've been using databases longer than you, okay?"

"Yeah, but you haven't used *all* the data."

"I can feel my blood pressure rising already."

"Here's the deal. I tied those mentions of the Nine Lords of Night, and yes, I am accounting for the fact that those mentions are probably about the movie *9 Lords of Night*. But I also looked at the very brief instances when Samuel Kahan used social media in his lifetime."

"I thought he was a recluse."

"He was. But toward the end of his years, he started live-streaming the view from outside the black car that always drove him around. Used an iPhone and YouTube. He didn't know it at the time, but all that video was geo-tagged. Ten years out, and we can mine that metadata, just like I did here."

Nestor could not have come to that conclusion as fast as Felix. He felt a certain kind of awe and an excitement come back again.

"And here, where his live-streams end, well, that's where we have to go," Felix said.

"That's the Catskills. We're never going to be able to get up there. There's a nor'easter, remember?"

"Would you rather we have cocktails at your place?"

"Actually, no."

"So, we go up to the Catskills. We go see him."

"Who?"

"The man at the end of this data set."

"Kahan?"

"No, you goofball. Kahan is dead. Someone even better."

"Who would that be?"

"Gregory Meyers, Kahan's personal assistant of thirty years."

Nestor didn't like the sound of this. Suddenly, he realized that he really had veered away from established protocols. *This hipster with a mustache is driving the car, buddy.* He was supposed to be looking at evidence, reviewing the data, leaning on forensics to do the heavy lifting, and—

*But you know you want to go,* he thought.

"The name Gregory Meyers hasn't come up at all for me so far. Why him?"

"When Kahan died, he left his art collection, his books, and film archives to Meyers. He lives, in fact, in the house he inherited from Kahan."

"I'm gonna get my shit, and you should too. Calling it a day."

"What the hell?"

"I'm not going down this rabbit hole with you, Felix."

"But you have to."

"Oh, I have to?"

"Yes."

"Look, I'm going to be off duty for the next three days. I need to take some time off from this. I think you should get ready to head back to Chicago. Our time together is over."

"*But you have to.*"

"I don't have to do shit, okay? Why do you think I'd do what you say?"

"Because we already got an invite by Gregory Meyers himself to see Kahan's house."

"What are you talking about?"

"I called him up. Said I was with the PD."

Nestor jammed his phone, camera, and notepad into his briefcase so hard that the bottom of the bag rattled. "That's a fucking felony."

"Well, I was careful in how I phrased it. Didn't actually say that I was PD, you know? He said he would never want to talk to cops, but he was intrigued by my work as an anthropologist."

"Oh, jeez," Nestor said. He caught himself snarling from the corner of his mouth in a small mirror set into the wall behind his desk. That tiny snarl reminded him of his days before he transitioned, of days of discontent with how he looked and how his body forever betrayed him. It was funny; he would have expected his legs or his arms to be the ones to take him back to that time, but it was that snarl, that snarl of Martina, that was always going to be there. He slid out of view from the mirror.

"Meyers said, in fact, we can stay there a couple of days, if we can make it through the turnpike."

"No."

"It's not that far."

"No."

"Meyers claims he knows about our two murders."

"Two? Only Grue's murder has been reported, and it's already dying in obscurity."

"Meyers says he knows about the two killings."

"If those are his claims, he could be a suspect, but he could just be another nut case. They pop up all the time with murders like this."

Nestor let out a deep sigh. This time, he really did need a drink. He felt no option but to try to close this case, and Felix Calvo seemed like the only person willing to go to the end of the story with him.

"I own a car," Nestor said.

"I'll pay for gas."

"Shut up; you're writing checks you can't cash. Come on, let's go get a bite to eat. I am done with this place for tonight."

They put on their coats and gloves, and walked down the rows of offices, past the kitchen, and through the door that led to the holding cells. They took the stairs down to the first floor, where a man tapped on the elevator button with fury.

The door to the stairway slammed behind Nestor, and the person by the elevator spun around as he let out a howl.

"Jesus! You scared the crap out of me."

Officer Devin's eyes were wide as saucers, and he was sweating buckets. A dark stain spread out over the crotch of his pants.

"Devin, did something happen?"

### 5:15 PM ET

Devin spotted them coming down the stairs, but it was too late to run away from the elevator bank. The young man was incredibly handsome, dark-skinned and youthful. Behind him, Nestor loomed like a shadow.

He couldn't let anyone know.

Because no one would ever believe him.

Devin was sopping wet with cold sweat, and the stink of urine made him want to vomit.

"Devin did something happen?" Nestor said to him.

*How the hell am I supposed to answer that, you fucking tranny?* he wanted to scream, and shout, but that thought tumbled in his mind, fell into a dark place, and soon, another sentence, covered it up, to save face, to not let anyone know about that first thought.

"I'm okay, don't mind me. I'm fine, guys."

He didn't hate trans people, but he despised how much praise Buñuel got, how it seemed like good things were always coming his way, and others, who didn't get any of the breaks, got left behind.

And there it was, that sentence, that thought he was trying to suppress, came raging back. Devin's heart was thumping so fast, and his scalp felt like electric current was scorching it. Nothing made sense anymore. Winter storms in October. Black folks, including one of his cousins, beat to death in Millennium Park. Clouds of red pollution turning the sky crimson and pink. His two kids on medications for ADD already at the age of eight and ten. And demons, fucking demons walking through the city. Demons that only Devin could see. And now, this no-neck tranny had the nerve to check in on him, to catch him at his weakest, to just sit there so smug.

"Just had a little accident out there, couldn't hold it in the car. Hilarious, I know."

Buñuel put his paw on Devin's shoulder.

"You're cold as ice."

"You have quite a grip," Devin said.

Where was this rage coming from?

*I've been here forever, Devin. Inside you.*

For a fraction of a second, he thought about telling the detective about the hooded figure with the hands for feet.

But he didn't. "I gotta go clean up. Gentlemen, good to see you," Devin said, then headed for the locker room.

# DAY 5
## FRIDAY OCTOBER 24, 2025

**UPSTATE NEW YORK**
**10:00 AM ET**

The car fishtailed and the blue light from the snow spun.

"Holy shit," Felix shouted. The snow was relentless.

"I'm not turning this car around, though," Nestor said.

"No, me neither, so you better drive more carefully. I'm precious cargo."

They laughed together. The windshield was a single white eye, with the wipers snapping like eyelashes over its surface.

"What's the name of the town we're going to?" Felix said.

"Deposit."

"Seriously?"

"There's stranger things than a name."

**10:23 AM ET**

Carson Mitchum walked through the threshold into Smith's office, interrupting him as he drafted an email. What the hell was he doing here? He never showed his face around here.

"This is the second time in a week you come down here."

"You know I am not going to email you. Ever."

"Talk to me."

"I'm worried about Nestor."

"Me too. He doesn't know moderation."

"This very job is a temptation for him," Carson said. "I should know; I know the grind too. Two heart attacks and I still won't retire. Ever."

"Nestor takes things very personally," Smith said. "The identity of the Grue victim. He's treating her as if she were one of these transsexuals or LGBT social justice warriors."

Carson wrinkled his nose. "That's not what I think the issue is. I think Nestor's not equipped to handle this case. There's so much complexity. I warned him the FBI will be here before we know it."

"Indeed, they are forming a task force. It's already in motion."

"And have you told Nestor yet?"

"No."

"Why the hell not, Smith?"

"I'm trying to protect him. He's just days away from retirement."

Carson shifted from foot to foot. Despite his gargantuan size, he fidgeted like a kid when he got worked up. Smith decided to be careful. The last thing he wanted was an outburst from this potentially loose cannon.

"No one's known Nestor longer than I have, Carson."

"With all due respect, knowing him a long time doesn't mean you know what's best for him."

"Are you calling my decisions into question?"

"You take it wherever way you want. Nestor works harder in a day than most people ever do here in a lifetime."

"I know that very well."

"Well, you give him a farewell whatever way you like," Carson said.

*No one understands how fucking shitty my job is,* Smith thought. *Can never please anyone. On the other hand, I can't wait for the FBI to take this case off my hands.*

### 10:23 AM ET

"Have another sandwich, really," Nestor said.

"Are you trying to fatten me up?"

*No, I enjoy seeing you eat. Calms me the fuck down.*

"No, not at all," Nestor said. "We're going to need our energy."

They sat in a booth in a Subway like any other. The sandwiches tasted like any other sandwich they had ever eaten before at the chain, but the blankets of snow outside the shop inside the gas station made this meal feel special. Felix pulled out his smartphone out of the Hadescap and looked for his likes, his notifications, but since he hadn't posted anything since meeting the detective, his friends and followers had nothing to show him love for. He was becoming invisible.

"Gonna grab us a few sandwiches to go. Some cookies, too," Nestor said, and he left the booth to order at the counter. He left his parka and sports coat behind. His firearm poked out from the harness strapped around his arms and back.

It was strange as hell for Nestor to forget to keep the gun invisible, but then again, the Subway was empty. Nestor couldn't keep his eyes off the gun, and suddenly he wanted it in his hands, with his thumb resting on the safety again, just to see if he would feel the urge to pull the trigger again.

What was even stranger was that Nestor came back to the table with the sandwiches, doing the oddest thing: smiling.

"Something funny?" Felix said.

"Nothing at all," the detective said. The smile never faltered. "Just remembered a time like this, in a snow storm, with my father, when he was still alive. He drove us in the sludge, to a movie theater. We saw *Beetlejuice* at an old theater in one these tiny towns. That movie makes me laugh something fierce."

"You look like that fucking shrunken-headed dude in the waiting room from that movie."

"Yup. Dead as fuck and shriveled up."

They cackled until their stomachs hurt.

Nestor slid back into the booth, and he tucked his arms back into his coat and parka, and the gun disappeared.

**12:55 PM ET**

Delia Douglas sat in the chair, as she got her hair done. Rebraiding her hair took a few hours, and this was a good time to catch up with her mother.

"I like the sound of your voice lately, Delia," her mom said.

"Taking it in stride, you know, fighting the fight, and mostly glad to have a day off."

"How's the love life?"

"I keep swiping, Mom."

"What?"

"Yeah, you have to swipe."

"And okay, are they good men?"

"Somewhat. I'm managing."

She sure was. At the age of fifty, Delia Douglas felt good about being self-sufficient enough to live without a man or a family. And it was these connections, to her mother, her one sister who was not fucking insane over Christ, and her college friends, that kept the glue in place for her to be all right.

"I'm grateful for what I got, Mom."

"Speaking of being grateful, can you send me that photo of your father I asked you for?"

Delia's mother was building a scrapbook.

"I got it right here in my purse. Mom, mind if I just send you a pic?"

"Yeah, that's fine."

"Jennifer, can you hand me my bag?"

Jennifer paused the braiding and put the large bag in Delia's lap. The braiding resumed.

"Got it right here, Mom."

She was about to pull out her wallet, when her hand grazed a crunchy object. She pulled it out.

"Aw, shit!"

"Honey, what's wrong?" asked her mother over the Bluetooth connection.

The Amazon envelope lay in Delia's lap. He was already gone for the weekend.

"Ma, I gotta let you go. Will send you dad's photo in a bit."

She texted Nestor. *You got a package from Amazon.*

*I didn't order any packages sent to the station,* he texted back. *Open it.*

Delia's hands tore into the paper, and her sense of danger didn't go off until she was halfway through the interior of the envelope. She should not be opening up such a package like this at her hair salon, much less off the clock. She had fucked up.

But it was much too late.

She only found a piece of paper inside. It was white, and cut into a perfect square, about six by six inches.

It was printed in plain sans serif type. The text occupied two rows.

12.7.19.14.11
NO LONGER INVISIBLE

Delia shivered, and it took her a full two minutes before she could text the information back to Nestor.

Whoever had printed this message had punctuated this note with a maroon dot right beneath the rows of text. Delia knew that maroon color well. She had a feeling that it was not printer ink but most likely blood.

**1:10 PM ET**

"You know, you shouldn't text and drive," Felix said.

"You're right."

"Here, I can read it for you. Delia says that you got a package," Felix said, but Nestor snatched his phone back.

"No, not yet. I'd rather look at it when we get to Deposit."

"Come on. We've been talking about the case all day. We're on a roll."

"No," Nestor said, and turned up the radio.

**3:55 PM ET**

The car got stuck outside of Harriman. The snow was too thick to push through, and Nestor and Felix listened to the radio while they waited for the snowplows to come through the turnpike. They idled on the shoulder. Nestor got hungry and pulled out one of the Subway sandwiches.

"Want some?" he said.

"I'm good," Felix said.

"Tell me about the Nine Lords of Night."

"They're real."

"What do you mean?"

"Well, real literary and mythical figures. I haven't seen the movie, but the reason Kahan used the Nine Lords of Night is because of the book it was based on."

"Okay," Nestor said. He felt more comfortable around Felix. He could trust him to be open about his ideas about the investigation, and often, they were quite good.

"According to what I read, the book is a little different than the movie. The married couple, the two Aztecs, who plot their murder against La Malinche, they visit a shaman. Do you know what a nagual is?"

"No."

"It's a type of Mexican shaman. In any case, he sings them a song as a warning to the couple. The song tells an old story about the gods. You see, the gods have their own problems and conflicts. And according to the old song, the gods needed to decide who would rule over the day and who would rule over the night."

Nestor lamented not ever learning about his own history. Felix had so much knowledge about this stuff, and here he was, writing about nanobots and futuristic mutants, but it had never occurred to him to write a novel about his own cultural past, both from Colombia and Mexico. He took a sip of iced tea from the plastic Subway cup.

"So, nine, huh."

"Yes. Mostly forgotten in time, though just as iconic as Zeus, Apollo, Thor or Loki."

"And you know them all?"

"That's all I've ever done as an adult. Welcome to my PhD."

"And who are they?"

"Do you really want to hear all their names?"

"Names are very important to me. As a novelist, I hope you will humor me. And as a trans man, I want to know what names they bore. I really must hear you speak them out loud."

"The nine are, Tlaloc, the rain god. There is also Tepeyollotl, Heart of the Mountain. He's The Lord of the Echo, and Bringer of Earthquakes."

"These names are beautiful," Nestor said.

"There's seven more, don't interrupt."

"Sorry."

"Chalchiuhtlicue, Goddess with Jade Skirt. The fourth is Mictlantecuhtli, Lord of—"

"Lord of Death. I know that one."

"Powerful, and ruler of the realm of Mictlán, a world of shadows and death. Number five is Centeotl, the God of Maize.

Six is Piltzintecuhtli, Prince Lord."

"Ha ha, like Purple Rain."

"Okay, I'm going to pretend like you're not interrupting me all the time. You get one point for the Prince references. And yes, Piltzintecuhtli is a young prince, but also the god of hallucinogens and of solar energy."

Felix turned on the radio, and the soft electronic chants of Arkangel seeped into the car through the XM signal. "The seventh is Tlazolteotl, the fifth goddess. She's the goddess of medicine, healing plants, and even lunar energy. The eighth is Xiuhtecutli, a very old god, older than most, and keeper of the fire at the center of the universe where thins are born from. He's old enough to be everyone's dad in this group of the Nine Lords."

"And who's the last one?"

"Perhaps the most powerful of them all. Tezcatlipoca, the one they call The Smoking Mirror. He's the true trickster, chaotic, benevolent, and malicious all the same time."

The car shook and wind gusts screeched as the windshield turned white. Nestor grunted a few times as he thought about what Felix had just shared.

"Xipe Totec, the Night Drinker, is missing from that list."

"Yes. He's as powerful as Quetzalcoatl, Tezcatlipoca, but he doesn't get invited to rule over the hours of the night, like his brothers did."

"Is he on the other list? The Nine Lords of Day?"

"Nope."

The music took on a soft and silky texture, as Karyn Andersson crooned about a tunnel made of water and butterfly wings. The song ended, Felix flicked off the radio. Silence thickened around them. Nestor felt the hairs on the back of his neck bristle, and a twinge of dread made his hands shake for a moment.

"Anyway," Felix said, breaking the silence, "the shaman said that once the gods organized themselves into the nine lords of day, and the nine lords of night, terrible things happened. Death, disease, and evil."

"How, exactly?"

"They caused a rift in time, according to them. Like a seam on a suit coming undone. Or like your skin becoming infected and filled with pus. And bursting."

"But of course, this is just a story within the story of that novel."

"Yes, and I have no idea if it's in the movie. Kahan's movie seems to be about something else altogether."

"That's how most novels that are adapted into movies end up."

"Not a huge movie guy, so that's good to know."

The snow plow roared past, and they trailed after it. The wheels crackled beneath them as they rolled over the road salt.

### 9:00 PM ET

Delia Douglas checked her phone as the credits were coming up. Nothing good. *It's a Friday night, and here I am, alone in a movie theater, hoping that something interesting might happen. This is what happens every damn week. I gotta get out there on some dates!*

She checked the phone again. No response at all from Nestor. She was worried as hell about him.

The three women who sat behind Delia exited the theater, and that left her alone with a man at the end of her row. He wore a hoodie and stared at the screen with intensity, as if every credit of the production mattered.

Delia felt a twinge in her stomach and a tingle up the back of her neck. The man broke his gaze from the screen and checked his phone, just like she did. He was plain, handsome even, clean shaven.

Delia didn't like the darkness of the movie theater suddenly, and even though she was about ten seats away, she wanted out from this theater and to be away from the man in the hoodie, at all costs. She banged her shin on the seat in front of her as she stood up, and she left her popcorn and drink behind. By the time she walked out onto Houston Avenue, she felt uneasy and out of breath.

### 9:01 PM ET

The car slid down a service road, but Nestor handled the skids with ease and care. The harsh lights from the turnpike had now faded away, and the serenity of the snow and darkness deepened. They passed the sign for Deposit, New York, population 1,712.

"How many people do you think have seen the movie *9 Lords of Night*?" Nestor said.

"I don't know, Kahan was pretty famous. But it was canned for a long time, yeah?"

"Yes."

"Maybe a few million around the world. Hard to say. It's very obscure."

"It certainly not one of his big movies, like *Xenogenesis* or *The Marsten House*."

"Has a movie ever scared you?" Felix said.

"*You've Got Mail* did. That kind of life-affirming garbage scares the shit out of me."

They laughed and finished what was left of a bag of Skulli Bears.

"We've arrived."

They inched their way along the icy road, and they crested a hill. A sign on their right read

THRACIAN WOODS

"Meyers said we'd see the sign for Thracian Woods and we would know we're here," Felix said.

As they drove down toward the shore of a small lake, they saw a massive house, three stories tall and shaped like an L, jutting out from the snowdrifts. Its windows were lit, but the darkness of Storm Tobe devoured the air around the building.

Felix grunted, tapped on the dashboard, and kicked out his feet.

"I don't want to go there anymore."

"What? You got us the invite, Felix."

"I don't like this. Turn the car around."

"We are almost out of gas, and the next station is more than twenty-five miles away. Plus, deadly storm out here, remember?"

"Nestor, listen to me. We have to turn around," Felix said.

Nestor framed the house ahead in his mind like a photograph, with the mass of Thracian Woods house at the corner, and the lake filling in the rest of the frame. Just like he had done with Marlene's crime scene, he would start from that wide angle and work his way in, toward smaller details, and dammit, he was going to get the knowledge he wanted.

"No."

"Nestor, please."

"We can only go down the road from here. The car won't make

it back up through all this ice."

The house grew in size, and the wind shrieked every few seconds or so, as if trying to get in through the windshield. They had arrived.

**9:22 PM ET**

Felix hopped from foot to foot, but the wind whipped right through him. The snow had gathered into several blue snowdrifts, and thin sheets spun off the top of the mounds, dispersing into the wind like silver dust.

"He's not gonna answer the door. It's been fucking ten minutes!" Felix said.

"Relax, his lights are on, and the steam on the side of the house shows the heat is on."

Nestor didn't budge an inch, despite the rocking motion of the wind and its howls.

"This is one motherfucker of a storm," Nestor said. Ice had already covered his mustache and beard. "Thanks for making me come, then changing your mind, Felix."

"Get off my case."

Orange light flooded the front steps of the house as the front door opened.

"My apologies, come in, come in!"

An athletic man with blond-and-gray stubble opened the door. The light from inside the house drew chalky shadows on his square jaw, but his eyes glinted like opals. They were set into a deep brow, weathered, but free of worry lines.

"Come inside, it's brutal out there, guys!"

Gregory Meyers stepped through the threshold and ushered Felix and Nestor in, scooping them into the warmth of the house by the shoulder. Felix smiled as warmth brushed his face. The front door led into a massive den surrounded by large windows. On the west side of the house, a fireplace roared before an arrangement of rustic furniture. On the north side, a massive stairway led up into a loft space that enclosed the den below in endless shelves of books. On each side of the staircase, doors opened into the rest of the house. Gregory was already pouring giant mugs of hot tea, which he jammed into Felix and Nestor's hands. He wore a three-piece suit, despite the casual air of the house.

"You need to warm up first. Once you come up to room temperature, we'll have a cocktail."

"What's that smell?" Felix said.

"Shabu shabu. You know it?"

"No."

"Japanese hotpot."

"You did all this just for us?"

"Of course. Does it look like I get many visitors here? I make it count when I do."

Gregory rushed into the back of the house, and for a moment, the only two sounds in the room were the shrieking winds and the soft notes of a Phillip Glass album playing through speakers built into the walls.

"There's not a single movie poster in this place," Felix said.

"Why would you expect that?" Nestor said.

"I don't know, big Hollywood director. I would think his house is full of ego-boosting posters and Oscars."

"It's a giant estate. I am sure there's more to see. Relax."

"I will, once I get a little pick-me-up in this mug."

## BROOKLYN
## 9:30 PM ET

Devin put the kids to bed, and watched TV for a while with Rob, and for a few moments, he enjoyed the numbing effect of the mindless thriller they watched in serial form. The murders on the screen were completely unlike those from real life, and Devin smirked as the killer was shot dead during the climax. *They don't just drop dead from gunshots. It takes whole minutes to die from bullet wounds.* Rob slid up beneath Devin's arm, and wouldn't you know it, there was a new Skulli Bear movie coming out this year. The kids loved Skulli Bear. He often wondered if they were too young to watch a cartoon about a murderous gelatin bear, but the addiction had already set in. As the rest of the cop procedural on TV unfolded, Devin's mind wandered, and he thought he heard sounds, like coos and a rustling, like a sack of feathers. He was drifting off. It was time to call it a night, he announced. Rob nodded.

After brushing his teeth, Devin considered sliding into bed, but instead he wasted time on his phone, standing at the foot of the queen mattress. He spun his thumb on his Facebook and

Instagram feeds, like a seasoned gambler at a Vegas slot machine, waiting for the novelty to drop each time the quarter slid into the slot.

"Something wrong? How was work?" Rob said.

"Fine."

This was the same canned response Devin had given to Rob for the past ten years, and he thought nothing wrong of it. Rob would never understand the job, and besides, Devin had no way of explaining what each day was like, the way the clock spun hour after hour, robbery after rape, after break-in, and the monotony of paperwork, the physical exhaustion, and the insomnia.

"Okay, suit yourself," Rob said as he turned over and cocooned himself int the sheets.

Devin set the phone down, adjusted himself in his boxers, and went into the hallway, where blue light spilled onto the wall from a tiny window that let him get a glimpse at the storm.

Windsor Terrace in Brooklyn had a few streets that were quiet as this one, almost suburban in their serenity. Though the snow kept on falling, the snowplows had already cut through the accumulation. What was left was yellow light bursting from the windows of the other apartments on this street.

Devin put his hands up to the glass, the way he used to when he was a boy. Steam curled in shapes around this palmprint, and he blew on the glass to reinforce the steam effect.

He turned his head toward the corners of the street. He expected that monster with hands instead of feet to come slogging through the snow again. How could he explain such a thing to anyone and not expect to be put on medication, or worse?

Devin had been very good at wishing as a boy, because wishing was something he could keep to himself. Wishing could be kept secret, and safe. When he was nine years old, he had visited Macy's on 34th Street with his mother. As they exited the elevator, an old man with a cane tapped Devin on the head, tousling his hair. *What a precious little boy*, the man had said. The man had looked a lot like Devin's own grandfather, whose black skin had wrinkled around his sad eyes like lava flows frozen in time. Devin had hated the stranger's touch, the way his palms were scratchy and his breath stank. *Get off me!* Devin had said, and batted the man's hand away. Devin's mother had grabbed him by the wrist and shaken Devin, once, twice. *You put that anger away, you hear, Devin?* she had said. *You put it away, and show some respect. I don't care*, Devin had responded, but his mother's grip shook him a third and fourth time. Devin broke into tears as she hauled him into the ladies' department.

What had made Devin think about that day in Manhattan? His mother had been dead for two years, and he couldn't fault her for what she did. She was a young mother at the time, and she tried to teach him good manners, just like Devin was trying to teach his own little ones nowadays. And yet, the more detail that reappeared from the memory — the smell of Clinique and Dior perfumes, the sound of Mariah Carey pumping through the speakers as background music, the mustard -yellow corduroy of the old man's jacket—the more that Devin's heart fell sideways into the past.

He felt that frustration again from his nine-year-old self. He wanted to not be shut off from his own anger, and he wanted to twist his face into a frown, to stomp on the floor in a tantrum, to maybe even push the old man over and see what happens when you mess with Devin, age nine, thank you very much. That rage came back now, twisting inside his 34-year-old body.

Devin realized, as he stared out into the streets of Brooklyn, that tears were spilling down his face, clear as air, but salty as they reached his lips. His legs shook, and he didn't understand how a single memory could feel so painful. He let out soft cries that had lain hidden for a long time, and because he was so focused on the way in which his memories looped like some prophetic animated GIF, he never noticed that a gigantic figure had drifted down from the sky, and had perched itself right before him, on the other side of the glass.

It was only when Devin looked up from this sobs that he realized that the hooded figure he had run into before was here now, and it was staring right into his face.

**9:44 PM ET**

Gregory Meyers wore a three-piece suit tailored to an impossible degree of elegance. He caught Felix eyeing the lapels and sleeves, and smiled.

"Don't mind me. I just can't break habits from when I used to work with Sam."

"Kahan made you wear the suit?"

Meyers laughed. "No, not at all, but good question. He usually just wore a white button-down with rolled-up sleeves, and he left my own styling choices up to me. He gave me advice early on when we started working together. *Make whatever you like to wear for work a uniform,* he said, *and you'll be stepping aside so your best work can come through.* For me, it was tailored wool suits from Hong Kong."

Nestor enjoyed watching Felix take things in like a sponge. Felix made eye contact at all times, and wouldn't you know it, he was jotting down notes. Where had the notebook come from?

"There's so many ways in which we can start, but I guess I'd like to you ask you about some of the most basic things about your employer, Mr. Kahan. And I would be honored if we could get a tour of the house."

Meyers had eased into a recliner, and despite the hard angles of his suit, he appeared relaxed. The man's receding hairline gave him a dignified air, and Nestor was reminded of the photographs of Ian Fleming on the back of the book jackets. His icy blue eyes were full of curiosity, and his casual stubble planted him more squarely in the twenty-first century. The man was in his seventies now, but he moved with the energy of a man forty years his junior.

"Felix—may I call you Felix? Wonderful, wonderful—I will answer everything I can, though I am subject to silence on a few topics. Blame the nondisclosure agreements we have signed in our lives. We can start tonight, and tomorrow morning I can give you a proper tour of the estate. I can also show you the archives and you can ask anything you want. I just ask for one favor."

"Sure. Shoot."

"No cameras, and no microphones. I trust you to not use them, so you don't need to check them in, but I would be grateful if you voluntarily keep them only in this foyer in the metal box near the windows. I would prefer only bio eyes view the rest of the house."

"I am fine with that. Nestor?"

"Yes, of course."

Nestor made a mental note. *What an odd phrase to use: bio eyes.*

Meyers unbuttoned his jacket, revealing a lining that looked more expensive than all of Nestor's wardrobe put together.

"Why live in the Catskills?" Nestor said.

"Great question, detective. By the time Samuel hired me, he had already backed away from the corruption of Hollywood, and this estate, as well as his estate in the UK, became his main workspaces. You see, he wanted nothing to do with Hollywood. Working near the town of Deposit, New York would mean that even most folks around here wouldn't know who he was."

"And why did he hire you?"

"I auditioned for a role in *9 Lords of Night,* and to my surprise, I was cast as a Spanish soldier in the viceroy's palace. Sam didn't speak a single word to me during that shoot, until the last day of filming. That day, he asked me to do the most peculiar of favors for him. Could I please travel to UNAM, the prestigious university in Mexico City, and retrieve a book on calculus for him?"

"Why calculus?" Felix said.

"That answer is the very essence of my employer of more than thirty years. Sam never explained why he wanted things done, but he had such a friendly way of asking for tasks that one simply couldn't say no. It's taken me almost forty years to understand why a book on calculus would have any relevance for a shoot for a movie about the fall of the Aztec empire."

## 9:45 PM ET

To stare into the eyes of something that was not human but whose eyes were full of an infinite consciousness took Devin's breath away.

The being blinked its eyes, and multiple membranes flickered over their convex surface, shimmering in shades of blue and purple. No pupil was visible in those eyes, only an ocean of dark space. Up close, Devin could finally understand the enormity of the creature. What he had thought had been a cloak was nothing of the sort. They were feathers. They looked smooth to the touch and a deep blue, like the color of the summer sky at night. Pink and gold glints reflected off the surface in long vertical streaks that seemed to have a life all their own.

What he had mistaken for a hood were feathers that created symmetrical coverage around a round skull. He knew this shape, because he had seen it many times before in books, movies, classrooms and at the zoo.

This thing before him was an owl, the largest owl he had ever seen in his life. It held onto the side of the building by grasping the fire escape. It was easily six foot four. The eyes stared into Devin's, and its sharp-looking beak was closed, though it was evident that it was sharp, and deadly.

Devin leaned closer to the window so he could see the creature's feet. It was missing claws and talons. Instead, it moved about on human hands, both of them a golden brown with claws the color of noon sky. They curled around the iron of the fire escape, the skin impervious to the subzero temperatures.

Though fear bubbled in Devin's throat, the monster's eyes only softened. Between them, the glass shook and vibrated, as if music were passing through it from one side to the other.

Without knowing how his thoughts drifted into a new place, Devin's memory took him to the places of his youth. The images from the past solidified, and he was transported to the smells and the sounds of those times. In these images, he recalled his shame at being born gay, the confusion over his grandmother's sudden death when he was twenty years old, the rage he felt when he first heard the word *nigger* being spat out at his family during a trip to a Fourth of July parade in Ohio. The longer he stared into the eyes of the creature, the more he spun into a place of remembrance. Inside those eyes Devin floated in a weightless sea of memory.

Pretty soon, he was no longer afraid. He only felt love, hot to the touch, as if his own heart had turned into molten metal. The emotions from his youth had no category, no name, but he felt them in his body and in his heart, all the same.

"Why are you here?" Devin asked the thing behind the glass.

The animal opened its beak, and music made of thousands of simultaneous notes punched through the glass and into his heart. The tongue of the animal was metallic and filled with three cone-like structures that swelled up like balloons. The creature shifted its weight onto its left hand and it cocked its head. What stared back through those eyes had no humanity, yet it showed a curiosity that Devin had only ever seen in the wide eyes of his adopted children.

The bird unfurled its wings in a fluid movement that resembled silk ribbons shooting out toward the sky. Their wingspan was incredible, almost fifty feet across from wing to wing. The navy blue feathers shimmered with sparkles of silver and green, and for a moment, the creature blotted out the sky.

Devin's fear fell away, and his heart rose in his chest. Suddenly, he was smiling and warmth filled his belly. Night was arriving, and this iridescent wonder before him was trying to communicate further with him, to reach his heart. He put a finger up to his cheek. The digit came away dripping wet with tears of joy.

## 10:00 PM ET

"I returned to the set with copies of *Intégrale, Longueur, Aire* by Henri Léon Lebesgue, a partial translation of *Yuktibhāṣā*., an early calculus text from India, and *Anatomy of a Differential*, a lesser known work by the mathematician Elsa Carmona, who had published her work on calculus in both English and Spanish, but who remained virtually unknown to most scholars because of her gender.

"Sam took the books from me, inspected them, smiled, and said, *Would you mind coming over for dinner tonight?* I showed up that night at his house with a bottle of wine and an ill-fitting tie. To be honest, I don't know what I expected to happen at his house. I expected Sam to have an aloof demeanor, like on set, but instead, he brought me into the kitchen to show me how he and his wife Marina cooked pipián, a delicacy of Mexican cuisine.

"After dinner, Sam brought me into a large study, where grotesque piles of papers, books, old newspapers, and magazines threatened to bury one under an avalanche of pulp. *I need help around here*, Sam said. *Are you good at organizing archives?* I was so broke in those days that I of course lied. *Sure*, I said. That night, Sam hired me, and what started out as a small errand to retrieve a set of books became a lifetime of service, and I guess, now that he's passed away, I can say that it was also decades of friendship."

"But the books," Felix said. "Why calculus?"

"You don't know Sam's movies, do you?"

Felix shook his head. Nestor kept his mouth shut. Though he had seen *9 Lords*, he preferred for Meyers to reveal as much about himself and Kahan on his own.

"If there are any of Sam's films you would like to see this weekend, I can certainly spool them up in the projection room."

"Spool?" Felix said.

Meyers laughed. "We are of different generations, aren't we?"

"Not sure what you mean, but if that's an insult, I feel very uncomfortable right now."

"Relax, Felix. Tell me, how does Sam figure into your research?"

Felix fidgeted, bit down on the long hairs of his mustache, and took a long swallow. Nestor could see his elaborate set of lies coming apart at the seams. He couldn't help but intervene and give him a hand.

"Mr. Meyers, Felix—if you let me interject for a moment—I'd like to say first that I am glad we can all come together like this in one room."

"Why is that, Mr. Buñuel?"

"Well, it starts with my own love affair with the movies, you see. I only discovered *9 Lords* recently because of a case I am investigating in Manhattan, and it led me down a strange path. It's the reason I contacted Felix. You see, he's the expert on Aztec religion. He's got quite the brain on him, better than mine. But this urge to find you, it started with me."

Meyers frowned, and set his drink down.

"I don't like vagueness. What exactly are you trying to say?"

"Samuel Kahan's followers revere his movie. And that reverence could almost inspire crimes. It's why we are here."

Meyers wrinkled his nose. "Felix, you said this was for work for an article for an academic journal."

"Of course," Felix said, though he couldn't find any other words.

"But it's me that you want, Gregory. Here's my badge."

Nestor handed over his badge, and Gregory took it in both hands.

"You have incredibly graceful hands, mister Buñuel."

"*Detective*, actually."

Meyers handed the badge back.

"This weather is brutal, and I can't send you back out there in it until the snowfall slows down. But if I could, I would send you back to the city right now. Am I being charged with a crime?"

"Not at all. We just need your help in understanding the archives of your former employer."

"This no longer feels academic to me, gentlemen."

Felix walked over to the windows and shuffled around in a loop, with his hands in his pockets.

"Gregory, I am no film buff," Felix said, "but I do know about the backdrop of Kahan's movie."

"You sure do. I looked you up. Your dissertation looked interesting."

"We're not here to investigate you," Felix said. "And we are not here for movie industry gossip."

"You expect me to believe you?" Meyers decanted a bottle of red wine, and his face took on a distant expression.

Felix took a seat opposite of Meyers. His lanky body moved with new confidence, like a fox squatting in its burrow.

"How deep did Kahan go in developing his film projects?"

Meyers chuckled, and he fished out a cigarette case from a case in his jacket. Then he chuckled again, mocking Felix and Nestor with his throaty laugh. He shook his head.

"No one understands the depths of Sam's obsessions. He completed thirteen films, but each picture contained multiple lifetimes of work. Would you believe me if I told you that we have six thousand boxes of archival materials in storage?"

Meyers fired up the cigarette. The smoke curled, turning blue, then purple, and back to white, under the refraction of light from the snow and the lights inside the house.

"I do believe you," Nestor said. "If we can earn your trust, perhaps you can show us."

"I don't doubt it at all either," Felix said. "I wish I had the drive that your boss had."

"I'd be careful what you wish you for, Felix. Sam made all of us who worked for him cry on a regular basis. He was more exacting than any man I have ever met. And yet, there was real respect and love there. But that's neither here nor there. I don't think you would be prepared to peek into the horrors and wonders of Sam's work ethic on each film. What you want is something more specific and more…lurid."

Nestor slid a hand into his button down. This was a gesture he had tried getting rid of a long time before, but one which resurfaced from time to time. He explored the soft ridges of his top-surgery scars. The grooves and embossed lines gave him a sort of comfort, while at the same time, his touch intensified his own focus. If Kahan had poured all his life, all his energy and soul into each movie, then Nestor could understand him on some level. With each pass of his index and middle finger over the soft horizontal grooves of the scars, he could see Marlene Grue's face in detail, the shadows draped over her face, and her chest carved open.

Nestor's thoughts about solving her murder moved in his head, not as sentences made of words but instead as an image. And that image looked like Marlene's bedroom, wealthy and neatly ordered, with sunlight entering at an almost horizontal angle. He would get to that place, that sanctuary, that location where her murder was solved, he knew it. Neither Gregory nor Felix had noticed his hand slip into his shirt. He withdrew it and curled his fingers around the wine glass next to him.

"Sam read the three calculus books over the next seven days as the movie went into post-production. He wasted no time. On the eighth day, he put the books in my hands at start of day at 5 AM. *Take these back, and can you get me copies of each for my own library? How would I do that?* I said. Sam just smiled and said, *have them mailed to Thracian House. That's my place in New York State.*"

Meyers pulled down three volumes from a side table. The three calculus texts lay inert, but maybe it was the warmth of the house, or the wine, but Nestor felt as if the books radiated with their own heat.

"Getting those three books nearly cost me my life. And yet I would do it all over again."

Felix flipped through the Elsa Carmona book, stopping every few pages or so to focus on certain passages.

"And this dense little brick informed the movie?"

Meyers took a sip of his wine but remained silent. He stared out the window, reminiscing. Sharp screeches burst from the snow.

"It's during the storms when the animals howl like that."

"Howl?' Felix said.

"It's the best word I have to describe it. It doesn't sound like the sounds they usually make. But in winter, they howl, almost like wolves."

"It's getting late for me, after all this driving," Nestor said. "Perhaps you can treat us to that tour and a matinee tomorrow?"

Meyers smiled and nodded. "Of course, friend."

"Okay, but—" Felix said.

"But?" Meyers said.

"But one more question. Before I brush my teeth."

"Okay."

"Would Samuel Kahan have the foresight to try to invoke an ancient god to come back into the world?" Felix said.

"Excuse me?" Meyers said. He crossed his arms and frowned, as if he had been insulted.

*Felix, Felix,* Nestor thought. *Slow the fuck down, boy.*

"This is something that maybe we can talk about when I see the archive, but the question remains. Did your employer have the urge to revive an ancient god, to give him new life, to help him enter the twentieth century?"

Meyers stood up and buttoned up the to button of his jacket. "I am not sure if I feel a certain repulsion or absolute admiration for you, Mr. Calvo."

"Why?"

"It's best we sleep. Your linens are already set out in your respective bedrooms. We can talk more tomorrow."

"But—" Felix said.

"And please don't mind the howls out in the storm. The creatures that are out there are harmless, no matter what you may see through your windows at night. Understand?"

## 11:50 PM ET

Felix flipped through screen after screen of pornography on his phone. He couldn't produce an erection, and yet he flipped through images of naked bears, gymnasts, men in cop uniforms and one of his favorite images, men in business suits. He fondled himself with his free hand, but his body only returned boredom and indifference. He sighed. This lack of sexual vigor happened sometimes, when the tide came in, and he knew for sure now that it was here again.

His mind turned over and replayed the scenes from the NYU job interview, and he recalled passages of his dissertation with absolute regret and shame. Nothing was ever going to be good enough. And after all, there was no sense in trying, was there? Even this side jaunt with the cop at his side felt like a waste.

Felix let out a long burp, and the ghosts of all the liquor he drank from Meyers' cabinet came forth. He wanted more. If he could just get himself drunk enough, he could pass out. And fuck the next day; he would just deal with the hangover. By his count, he had drunk about six drinks, but he knew he had room for plenty more.

Felix threw the blankets aside and slid into a tank top. He padded barefoot up to the doorway and cracked the door open. All he could hear was the howling of the wind outside. He walked down a long hallway and past a small den, until he reached the stairway that led back down to the liquor cabinet in the living room. He paused at the top for a moment, to take in the massive proportions of the house, which felt more like a shrine than a mansion.

Above Felix, a snap broke the silence. He turned his head, but the wood-paneled wall behind him lay inert. He looked over his shoulder and inspected the snow outside. Perhaps a large tree branch had collapsed under the weight of all the snow. But the window only offered a smooth white surface of the roof of the house.

And suddenly, another snapping sound, and the sound of laughter — no, more like a giggle, a child's giggle — from the very wall he had just looked at a moment ago. A chill ran down from the back of Felix's skull, all the way down to his legs. He suddenly forgot about the liquor, and instinct told him to step away from the wall, to retrace his steps back toward the bedroom. As he did so, the windows at the top of the staircase shimmered with snowflakes. Felix refused to turn his back to the wall, and he didn't want to knock over a side table, so he took steady steps backward. The wall only became blacker as more distance expanded between them.

He saw something that shouldn't be possible. The wall blinked. Not in one, or two places, but in hundreds of them. The whole wooden surface came to life as tiny red eyes blinked open. The ruby-red eyes shut and opened in unison, like a machine, and in each pupil, Felix could see an incredible depth, as if the center of each eye offered a glimpse into a place thousands of miles deep.

"What the hell did that old fag give me to drink?" he said out loud. The wall emitted one more giggle, young, like that of a teen, and the eyes stopped blinking. They inspected Felix, like the tiny red cameras that lived in every street corner, business and private space in Manhattan.

Felix had backed away far enough that he could reach out with his right hand and feel the wall for the door handle of his bedroom. There it was, solid, made of hardwood, and a form of safety. He tucked himself into the doorway, just as the eyes blinked once, twice, three and four times. They then closed and vanished.

Felix darted into the room, closed the door and slide under the blankets. His father would have had him pray to that Protestant God of his, but Felix couldn't feel that, couldn't want that. He went face down on the bed and jammed the pillow over the back of his head. And wouldn't you know it, despite the mad pace of his heartbeat, the warmth of the room calmed him down, and soon, he dozed into a liquor-soaked sleep.

## 11:55 PM ET

Nestor's mother had texted him while they had met Gregory Meyers. He stared at her text, unsure of what to reply.

*We lost power in the building, but the heat is still on. Son, how is your trip?*

By now she would be asleep, and he knew that texting her might wake her up, and then he would progress into a text exchange with her that could last for up to two hours. He knew she was scared by the storm, but in the part of Queens where she lived, she was going to be all right. She had survived Hurricane Sandy in 2012, but after that event, she had never been the same.

And for that matter, Nestor had never been the same either.

He texted back, *You'll be all right, ma. I am praying to the Virgin tonight. I'll check in on your in the morning. Save your phone battery.*

And then Nestor powered off the phone. He wasn't ready to talk now. His mind spun in many directions, and he felt a sense of excitement and anxiety that made his acid reflux come right back up his belly and chest.

Nestor turned over in bed, and he heard footsteps in the hallway. Probably Felix getting up to piss. As Nestor curled deep into the duvet, he caught a glimpse of a figure in the windows, which overlooked the driveway and the sloped road that led there. The figure was delicate, and strangely lit, as if she was impervious to the cover of night. She was draped in a blanket or a cape of the most iridescent ocean green color, like a jewel. A snowdrift cut through the image, and then she was gone.

Nestor prayed three Hail Marys in Spanish, and because his mind had memorized each word over a lifetime, his thoughts cross cut into the memorized words, and his voice and lips recited the prayer out loud.

"Dios te salve, María."

*My mother still believes in the apparition of the Virgin of Guadalupe.*

"Llena eres de gracia,"

*And I do too.*

"El Señor es contigo"

*But what did I just see?*

"Bendita tu eres entre todas las mujeres."
*Does the Virgin still appear to people?*
"Y bendito es el fruto de tu vientre Jesús"
*And why couldn't the Virgin appear to Marlene Grue instead of a monster?*
"Santa María, madre de Dios,"
*Why did she have to die…*
"Ruega por nosotros pecadores,"
*Bleak, bleak as shit, this is—*
"Ahora y en la hora de nuestra muerte,"
*I just want to sleep, just a few hours*
"Amén."
*Because when I sleep, things don't hurt like they do during the day.*

# DAY 8
## SATURDAY OCTOBER 25, 2025

**UPSTATE NEW YORK**
**6:01 AM ET**

Felix tossed and turned. He needed to piss. He stood up from the bed, and the storm screeched against the windows. Fat snowflakes struck the glass in clumps.

He walked down a short hallway to the bathroom. He caught a splash of yellow light coming from the room adjacent to it. Something was chattering its teeth, and it was coming from Nestor's room.

Felix softened his steps, using only the balls of his feet to make contact with the hardwood floors. The chattering sped up in short bursts, sharp and crisp. He peered in.

Nestor sat in a chair, writing, with his back ramrod straight, and his bearded face looking out into the storm. A portion of the lake was visible from this bedroom, and the surface lay frozen, inert, like terrain from another planet. Nestor bit his lower lip as he worked, completely oblivious to his surroundings.

The detective was naked, except for pair of white briefs, and Felix couldn't help but stare. The brown body before him was bathed in blue light from the large windows, and the soft glow brought out every detail of its surface. The skin was taut, smooth, and muscular in a way that Felix could not relate to. Were bodies like that even real? He certainly didn't have one like that. And there, just beneath the pecs and nipples, tiny pink slashes, the scars he recognized from other friend's stories about top surgery, but real in a way that no story could accomplish. Felix caught himself staring at those pecs, and the muscular lower body. His eyes focused on the crotch of those white briefs, and suddenly, he felt embarrassed, ashamed for intruding.

Felix darted into the bathroom to piss. He considered washing his hands, but he didn't. Instead, he got the hell out of there as fast as he could. On his way out, he glanced sideways into he bedroom, expecting Nestor to scowl at his gaze, but the man was still typing, lost in a mental zone that seemed very far away from this house in the woods of upper New York State.

He slid under the covers, and sleep soon took over.

## 8:30 AM ET

Felix wandered into the kitchen, running his hand through his disheveled hair. Wow, was he a mess.

"Good morning, sunshine," Nestor said. He was already showered. He had picked out a black polo shirt and jeans. He had successfully slept a handful of hours, but the thoughts about *The Neural Network,* his latest novel, had shaken him out of bed. His eyes had flown open, and the sapphire-blue snow outside the windows had jump started his urge to write. He had fished his laptop out of his duffel bag, and he began to write in a way that he hadn't written in years. The words just poured out, and he did not have to put thoughts about the body of Marlene Grue aside, because they simply weren't there. Instead, he wrote his fiction, in a world where a technological utopia really had arrived on Earth, and artificial intelligence had brought back nutrients to the eroded crops of the Earth and prevented the deaths of billions of people.

"I never heard the howls, by the way," Felix said, as he slurped hot coffee from a white mug. "Did you?"

"Nothing," Nestor said. He omitted mentioning the green figure in the robe he had glimpsed at the driveway.

Miles Davis played softly through the house, and the hard clicks of expensive shoes on hardwood echoed in the hallways.

"Gentlemen, good morning," Meyers said. He was no less

formal than before, but at least today he wore a maroon sweater and an open-collared button down instead of his three piece suit. "You found the breakfast I left you, yes?"

"It's delicious," Felix said, tearing into pieces of French bread and cutting quiche with his fork.

Nestor shook his head.

"We have today and tomorrow for you to get your work done, and I thought we could see the house in two parts. Today, I could show you the archives. You will need to dress warmly, because some areas are not well heated, and that's on purpose. Many materials need the right temperature and humidity for preservation purposes. Later tonight, I would like to show you the screening room. Then tomorrow, we can tour the aviary."

"There's an aviary?" Felix said.

"Yes, but it no longer houses birds. I think you will enjoy its transformation."

Nestor stirred sugar into his coffee. "You gonna shower first, Felix?"

"Nah, I'm good like this. I'll just throw on a T-shirt."

Nestor could feel his cheeks flush and his stomach twist into knots. *I am going to wring your neck, you bum,* he thought. Felix wore a threadbare T-shirt, grease-stained skinny jeans, and his hair reeked. It hadn't been washed in days. Even though Felix Calvo was just a traveling companion, Nestor felt as if he reflected badly onto Nestor's work as a cop.

"You sure you don't want to shower first?"

"Nope."

Nestor clenched his fists so hard that he left half moon marks in the palm of his hand.

"Come on gentlemen," Meyers said. "We're off to the archives."

**8:37 AM ET**

"The estate is easy to navigate," Meyers said, as they traveled down a long hallway toward the back of the house. "This is the original building, which Sam remodeled and expanded many times. It consists of 65,000 square feet with eight bedrooms. The house is part of a U-Shape. If you continue down this hallway, you'll see it forms an artery that leads straight back to an exit in the back. The curve of the U-shape is where the archive is found. Sam built that in the last fifteen years before his death. Another set of parlors and bedrooms lead back out into the aviary, completing the U."

"You know, the long hallways of this mansion remind me of the scenes inside the Discovery One spaceship in *Xenogenesis*," Nestor said,

"A fine observation. You would make Samuel chuckle if he were here." Meyers' eyes creased at the corners as his smile expanded.

"Do you miss working on movies?" Felix said.

"Not at all. I gave my heart and soul to Sam's films. But at a certain age, you move on. Other things besides career become important."

Felix ran ahead to keep up with Meyers. He nodded his head and made eye contact. *This kid's got some skills in making a source comfortable,* Nestor thought. *At just any moment now, Meyers will share his next thought without prompting...*

"I met Carolyn just a few months ago. She lives in the town of Deposit just a few minutes away. She was a CPA in Manhattan for decades, but she retired out here after her son Oskar went off to college. And wouldn't you know it, getting to know each other has put the tasks of Thracian House on the back burner. Of course, I expect you will keep that in confidence. I don't want anyone to think I am slacking in keeping up with Sam's affairs, but you see, now that my youth is gone, and so much of myself was invested in Sam, I realize that some things are more important than work."

"Last night you wanted to kick us out. What made you change your mind?"

Nestor shook his head. *Felix is bold. He's gonna lose the confidence of this source, or win it forever.*

"Good question, Felix," Meyers said. "I chatted with Carolyn this morning, and she advised I relax, to improve my blood pressure numbers. But to answer your question, I don't know exactly. You have been the least annoying of the Samuel Kahan aficionados who want to enter the archive. In fact, it's your ignorance of my employer's movies that charmed me. You're like a person who has never been seduced by cinema."

"I am not a movie guy," Felix said, and nodded.

They reached a set of heavy oak doors that were unlocked. Up above the doorframe, twin red eyes blinked. *The place is full of cameras,* Nestor thought.

"I still don't know why Sam obsessed such over *9 Lords of Night,* but that obsession is found in here."

They pushed through the doors, and the air whooshed around the three men as they left behind the airy lightness of the house and its gigantic windows, and entered a vast, enclosed darkness.

## 9:01 AM ET

Felix tripped as he walked through the doorway.

"Easy, there," Meyers said. "You'll need to look down as you step through."

"I had expected something a little tidier," Felix said. He had stumbled on a small cooler, the kind families take to picnics on Lake Michigan in Chicago. Further up ahead in the shadows, he spotted cardboard boxes, stacks of newspapers, and other objects blocking the way.

As the three men walked into the room, automatic lights detected their movement and snapped on with robotic precision. They passed through several aisles and rows of vertical file cabinets, metal shelving, and wooden cases that reached the ceiling. But it was only the tall structures for storage shelves that had any sense of orderliness.

The automatic lights had an unsettling effect on Felix. As soon as one entered a new aisle of storage, the bluish LEDs burned brightly, washing the messy shelves with harsh shadows and transforming all colors into icy grays. But as soon as one walked a little farther, those lights would turn off, leaving the trail behind in utter darkness. It was like driving on a highway in fog and only being able to see a few feet ahead.

*This mess of boxes feels like my own life. A hot, hot mess,* Felix thought.

Tiny red dots flickered in the upper right corners of the shelving units. The cameras were here, too. There seemed to be no place in Kahan's estate that wasn't monitored by a camera.

And down a the farthest end of the archives, a pile of trash loomed, threatening to spill over. It was stacked high with papers, old posters, movie props, and camera equipment. It was heartbreaking to see a hoard like that.

"Ever try to hire help to organize this stuff, Meyers?" Nestor said.

"Oh I have tried, many times, but Kahan's son Orlando refuses. He's the most frustrating, egocentric paranoid I have ever met in my life. Though I am the owner of the estate, Orlando has a majority ownership of the actual archive. And he refuses to cooperate with any museum or film institute to organize this — excuse my language — bloody mess. I tidy things up when he's not looking, but as you can see, the full job would take a lifetime."

"Does Orlando know we are here?" Nestor said.

Meyers only grinned and winked.

They made a sharp turn and walked into a set of wooden shelves that gave off a distinct smell of pine sap. The blue lights flashed on, and Meyers slipped on a pair of nitrile gloves.

"These shelves, from numbers 39 to 52, are all from the film *9 Lords of Night*. It's one of the few sections that has any semblance of tidiness."

A gust of warm air brushed up agains the back of Felix's neck. He turned around and saw nothing but the dark corridor they had walked in from. He looked up at the shelves and spotted several items housed in clear acrylic boxes. Most of them were no taller than twelve inches, but they were carved in beautiful, curving shapes, and some still shone in their original colors.

"This makes no sense," Felix said. "Are these replicas?"

Gregory Meyers laughed, but when Felix looked for him, the man was nowhere to be seen. He had already reached another aisle. His laughter rumbled, and Felix recalled that the rock musician Shirley Manson laughed that way. Impish, with soul, but also with an edge of danger.

"I suppose I should have made you sign the nondisclosure agreement before we came in, but what's the point? You have a big burly cop with you here, and it's such a shame to keep Sam's genius behind lock and key. Nevertheless…I have to trust that you'll just keep certain things…to yourselves, gentlemen."

"I am not burly!" Nestor whispered in Felix's ear. "*Burly's* just another word for *fat.*"

"Relax, Adonis. Hold on."

Felix picked up a ceramic figurine. It was molded into the shape of a man, a youthful man. And the expression on the face was strange, bloated, but it wasn't a mistake by the artist. Felix pulled the item down and showed Nestor.

"This looks so legit," he said. "Every detail is there. The mask made of human flesh, and the bodysuit."

"What bodysuit?" Nestor said. He also touched the statuette, tracing his hands over the torso, which seemed to have little scales.

"He's wearing the skin of a sacrificial victim," Felix said.

"Oh," Nestor said and pulled his hand away.

"How many artifacts like these are in these shelves?"

"About two dozen," Meyers said. He reappeared under the harsh lights, and he took a pull off an electronic cigarette.

"And these are not replicas?"

"When I said my employer was obsessive, I don't think I was emphatic enough."

"That would make these evidence in a criminal investigation," Nestor said. "To steal artifacts from archeological sites is an international crime."

"I know, Mr. Buñuel. But no one gives a shit once men achieve a certain position of power. I never saw Sam abuse his status, except when it came to his obsessive collection of Mesoamerican artifacts."

"We will need all of our two days here to go through these shelves," Felix said. "This is unreal."

"Take as long as you like. But be careful with that statuette. Samuel always warned me about that one."

"Why is that?"

"He said to mishandle it would be to anger the deity it represents."

Felix put the statuette back on the shelf.

"It was only a joke, Felix," Meyers said.

Nestor put a hand on Felix's shoulder.

"What is that thing?" Nestor said.

"It's Xipe Totec, the Flayed One," Felix said.

"The Night Drinker," Nestor said.

"Indeed," Meyers interrupted. "Sam's movie starts and ends with this deity."

"I have seen the movie," Nestor said. "There is no mention in the dialogue, and certainly no image of Xipe Totec in the film."

"Detective," Meyers, said, "must you be so literal?"

"No, I get it," Nestor said. "I'm a novelist, and I don't spoon feed my readers. But you have to remember, I work *only* with words. Kahan used sound and moving images, and decoding such a combination is not exactly my forte. But maybe it's yours."

"I think you two need a few hours in here. You will have more questions besides that one. I can answer them all after lunch. If you need me, just text. All the lights are automatic, as you know. And please, don't take anything. Because I will know if you did."

## 11:47 AM ET

Nestor knelt by the cardboard box and yanked as hard as he could. The lid would not pry away. Felix held on to the base, and he was also working up a sweat trying to get it open.

"It's been glued shut," Felix said.

"Come on, man, you reek of booze. How much did you have last night?"

"Do you want to open this thing or not? Because I can go back up to the den and make myself a cocktail right now."

"Good point."

"I thought so."

"But seriously, you have gin coming off your pores."

"Thanks, DAD."

"Got a question for ya."

"Shoot."

"Do you think these Aztec gods belong only to Mexicans?"

"No, not at all, but I am afraid to express that opinion."

"Well, because some people don't see me as fully Mexican. White dad, after all."

"But you are fluent in Spanish, and you know this stuff better than many Mexicans themselves."

"Doesn't matter. I don't meet the criteria for authenticity."

"Have you ever gotten pushback from Mexican academics about your work?"

"No. But I have gotten it from American academics many times."

"Really?"

"Yep."

"Yep. It's really a thing in this country of ours."

Nestor heard a rip, and the lid gave way. Decades-old glue came undone.

"It has to be in here," Felix said. At Felix's feet, a pile of manila folders, books and old magazines spread out around him like a skirt. For the past three hours, they had scoured the shelves, looking for anything that might lead somewhere. Nestor had been absolutely overwhelmed, but Felix had caught started to see patterns. His makeshift collection of artifacts were mostly written notes by Samuel Kahan, and in several of them, he had referenced Box No. 26, which was supposed to contain his original notes for the script of *9 Lords of Night.*

In just a handful of hours, Nestor had seen Felix Calvo truly in his element, collecting materials, taking notes, cataloguing each artifact using his own system, and walking Nestor through the process as well. Samuel Kahan, as it turned out, was more mysterious than fog. The deeper they went into the archive of the film, the more...disparate the evidence became.

They had unearthed boxes of dirt from Tlatelolco in Mexico City. They had also found desiccated butterflies, dozens of books on lights and optics, several dissertations on linguistics, and a very detailed set of notes in the margins that Kahan had scrawled on a copy of Darwin's *On the Origin of the Species.* Besides that, they had also found several cookbooks from France, an old flatiron, and a treatise on robotics from the 1950s from MIT. As far as Nestor could tell, none of these objects made a direct connection to the film, if at all.

As they pored through the contents of box number 26, Nestor revisited scenes from the movie in his mind. The vast and epic opening in which the Catholic Church set its presence in the city of Tenochitlán; the husband and wife making a pact to avenge their people; the various disguises the wife wore to pass as a man and act as a spy inside the National Palace; the moral uncertainty of La Malinche, who had given away her people to Hernán Cortés by acting as translator; and the bloody final scenes of the movie, cast in a harsh reddish light of sunset and the way in which the camera showed the people of Mexico as if they were inside a living painting. *What a bleak movie,* Nestor thought.

"Felix, what do you see in all this evidence you collected?"

"I can almost articulate it. Here, help me with this box."

They pulled out the object together. It had a circular shape, like the tin boxes that grandmas like to reuse to give away home made cookies. The paint on the sides had given way to orange rust. Felix pried the lid open, and an explosion of scent sent both men reeling back. There were notes of poppy flower, black pepper and wilted roses in there. And beneath the three notes, a single, deeper scent of water, the smell of lakes, mangroves and swamps.

Felix retrieved a sheaf of papers held together by string. There must have been about one hundred pages, and acid had turned all the sheets a mustard-yellow color. Nestor knew that a single bend on that paper would make it crumble away and break.

Nestor's knees hurt, and he had a headache from smelling so much dust, but he realized in that moment that for the past hours, he had been having a very good time, playing Watson to Felix's Holmes in this strange cavern of old things.

Felix whispered to himself as he read the notes to himself. He flipped to the middle, and his breath sped up.

"This is not right," he said.

"Can I see?" Nestor said.

"Of course. Look. Here, and here."

Several scribbles in Kahan's longhand scrawled across several drawings he had made. The sketches suggested giant beings made of cartilage, fish gills and eyes that pointed in many directions, as numerous as pores. And throughout the pages, the story of the film emerged. Scribbled again in the margins, several observations written by Samuel Kahan:

*Copycats emerge, circa 1983.*

*Film institute will restore my film in the 90s'.*

*Computer technology to compress celluloid into digital wireless tech — approx. 2004.*

"These are no actual notes about the movie script," Felix said. "I mean, they could be, and I am not a biographer, but they are odd. And look at this one."

*October 2025: Unsure of where I might be, but a sacrifice will be made in the name of The Night Drinker. And the numbering sequence will be restarted. Rift begins here. Day 10, 1-Ollin, Year 13.*

A thin line in pen traced from that note to another note in the margin, connected as if by umbilical cord.

*She will be black, beautiful, and she will live in a high tower. Gruiform, number 476.*

Nestor turned the pages over and over, as if the back of the paper might offer some clue that this was all one big practical joke.

"These notes all seem like predictions, far as I can tell."

Felix wrinkled his nose. "Don't look at me. I study anthropology, not the Tarot."

"What do you make of these, then?"

"Sounds like an artist just making up things for his fictional movie to me," Felix said. He was putting the papers away in the box. "I'm not inclined that way, so you tell me, mister writer."

"Kahan predicts the year of the killing correctly. And Gruiform 476. It's fucked up."

"Try me."

"476 is the case number for Marlene's murder investigation," Nestor said.

"Okay, sheer coincidence from the police computer system, but then there's gruiform—"

"Which for biologists is another way of saying Grue."

## 4:45 PM ET

They found Meyers on the treadmill in the gym. He wore a navy blue tracksuit with white stripes, the kind that had been popular in the 1980s. For a man in his 70's, he held on to an incredible amount of hard muscle, which roiled beneath the nylon pants. Felix would love to get an outfit like that and wear it out. It was the kind of retro fashion that made him love dressing up.

"You all done, gentlemen?" Meyers said. He kept his eyes locked onto Felix. Outside, the wind howled again, and the windows shook as ice pelted their surface.

"We left everything more or less how it was," Nestor said. "The place does need more organization."

"Why Mexico?" Felix said.

"Excuse me?"

"Why did your boss make a movie like that about Mexico? I mean, where did the idea come from?"

"Where all new ideas come from," Meyers said. "A place beyond consciousness."

"What do you mean?"

"Sam considered *9 Lords* one of his biggest failures. It was canned by the studio, shredded apart by the few critics who reviewed it, and it inspired strange crimes, if you believe the rumors of the internet. And trust me, Sam did read internet sewage like 4chan and Reddit, even if he always denied it. And yet he came back to that film, time and time again. He would show me so, about once a year, right around this time, in the gray window of time between Halloween and Thanksgiving. *Greg, I'm off to hunt,* he used to say, and he would spend a week in the archives, reliving old memories from that period in our lives when he made the movie. At the end of that week, he would watch the film by himself in the screening room. And then I wouldn't hear or see him for another three days after that. He would come back to this very gym on the fourth day, gaunt, and thin as a heroin addict. And all those years, I never asked him why he revisited *9 Lords* in such a cyclical manner."

"Why didn't you?" Felix said.

"Because I know how to do my job. I was there to support Sam's work, not judge it."

"He sounds sort of awful."

"He found a lifetime of success in nurturing his obsessions, Mr. Calvo. Can you say that for yourself?"

Felix felt his insides wilt and his heart weaken when he heard those words. How could he argue with Meyers? That question said everything. The old man knew Felix was a fucking fraud, a failure. Felix lowered his eyes and left the room.

### 4:52 PM ET

Nestor hadn't seen Felix that sad, ever. And it was very likely that his next steps would be the liquor cabinet. But he wasn't his babysitter. Felix would cool off when he was ready to cool off.

"Since your assistant is so direct, Detective Buñuel, I'll break out of my own British tradition and ask you: why did you choose such a sensitive young man to help you with such somber and gritty work?"

Nestor was going to explain that this arrangement was nothing but temporary, and that Felix was not his assistant in any way, and then he dropped his shoulders and fiddled with his T-shirt, smoothing out the hem. He crossed his arms.

"You leave him be, okay? Felix is very good at what he does."

"I am still not sure *what* he does, exactly, Detective. Though he has a certain charm, he broods and feels entitled to a certain level of attention I will not give."

"Look, we can help each other out," Nestor said. "You let us finish our research, and I will owe you a favor; you cash it in whenever you need it."

Meyers draped a white towel around his neck and drank from

bottled water.

"What's your age, detective?" he said.

"Fifty-two."

"And what kind of favors would you propose to offer a man like myself?"

The question hung in the air. Meyers' chest rose and fell, unusually virile for someone his age. Meyers took one step toward Nestor but didn't touch him. Instead, Meyers draped his meaty forearm over the treadmill. His eyes zeroed in on Nestor.

"Look, Gregory, I don't do favors like those."

"I am sure you don't. That's why I am asking. Makes the promise of such a favor even more delicious."

"You don't know me."

"But I do know an attractive trans man when I see one."

Nestor felt the hairs on the back of his neck go erect. He wanted to be angry at this direct reading from one man to another, and yet, he was stunned and caught off guard.

"You thought I didn't pick up on it when you walked in?" Meyers said.

"Get the fuck out of here," Nestor said. His Queens accent crept into his voice.

"No, I don't think I will. There's a nor'easter out there."

"What gave me away?"

"Certainly not your face or body, Detective. It was something else. The essence of you, the face behind the mask."

"What mask?"

"You clearly never read Octavio Paz's *El Laberinto de la Soledad.* Mexicans are the best at wearing them, but in the end, all humans wear a mask."

"You stay right where you are, motherfucker. Not one more step forward."

"Relax, Detective. I'm only making you a proposition, not sexually assaulting you. I am in love with the shape of you. And it's been a long time since I have been with a man."

Nestor felt all his cool fade away. He had been buried so deep in his police work and his writing, that he had forgotten that erotic exchanges like this happened often between people. He was absolutely unprepared for the barrage of feelings he was experiencing in his belly right now. Embarrassment, arousal, anger, and even fear churned and bubbled in a thick sludge in his gut.

"I can't do that," Nestor said. "I am here to work."

"My sexual tastes are on the esoteric side," Meyers said.

"You know how insulting what you just said is?"

Meyers shook his head. "Detective, you still think I am exoticizing you, don't you? A pity."

"Fuck off."

"If you must know, I have no limitations on who my partners would, should, or can be. I don't care for labels, and all forms of female and male bodies are stunning for me."

"Then what do you mean by *esoteric*?"

"I am turned on by men who have lost their way to loneliness. They make great lovers."

"You don't know me, Meyers."

"In any case," Meyers said. "I retract my proposition, though my ears remain open. But rest assured, I am still willing to help you in your anthropological police project. It's just a shame that you have your mind, and your own eros, in such a sorry and dark place."

Meyers walked to the back of the room and turned off the fans. "I'd like to screen *9 Lords of Night* for you two after dinner."

Nestor clicked his tongue and punched a stack of towels as Meyers left the room.

## 7:01 PM ET

Droplets of water from Felix's wet hair fell onto his open notebook. He still couldn't believe the artifacts he and Nestor had found in the store room. They could be forgeries, of course, because even the major museums of the world sometimes acquired forgeries, but that's not what Felix had felt when he put his hands on the figurines in the series. Each and every one had been made to resemble the god Xipe Totec, and his rough guess was that whoever curated these statues wanted to sample the various epochs of Mesoamerican art from Mexico. There were Toltec styles, which were the oldest, as well as Chichimec and Aztec. And each time he turned the idols in his hands, he felt that same uneasy sensation he had felt in the hallway with the red cameras: a sense of being stared at, of eyes tracking him.

And yet, he was not afraid. Instead, he scribbled notes madly into his notebook.

He was still in his underwear, and he was due downstairs for dinner. He jammed his legs into jeans and yanked a tee over his head. As he took the stairs down into the first level of the house, he passed the windows, which revealed nothing but snow and darkness. Felix fingered the deck of cards in his pocket. He pulled out the pack and drew a card. He glanced at the card. The ace of clubs.

*"Again?"* Felix said out loud. Just beyond the white borders of the playing card, something moved in the snow, outside of Thracian house. Felix put the card away and pressed his hands up against the glass.

"Shit."

Through the trees, just about twenty-five yards away, a set of eyes blinked open and shut in unison. They looked just like the red eyes he had witnessed inside this hallway, but these were much more iridescent and beautiful. Each orb was a perfect circular shape, and the pupil and iris the most dazzling shade of green. It was that very emerald color that shone bright in the darkness of the nor'easter, and Felix estimated there were at least three dozen of them, as if someone had constructed a wall of eyeballs behind the trees and strung up lights along its surface.

The eyes blinked again, and then they were gone.

Felix was about to mention the phenomenon to Nestor, who waited at the bottom of the stairs, reading in a leather chair.

"*Laberinto de la Soledad,* eh?" Felix said.

"Samuel Kahan's collection is vast."

"Good book, maybe a little dated. The globalized, internet-connected world is something Paz didn't really anticipate. It was his blind spot."

"You're in a cheery mood again, angel."

"Don't call me angel, *Nestor.*"

"Fine."

"What's that smell? Reminds me of something back from the Midwest..."

"Meyers is cooking chiles rellenos en nogada."

"That's it. My mother makes those in her restaurant."

"She's a chef?"

"Has a Michelin star."

"Interesting."

"Hardly."

Nestor didn't ever wear anything but that black T-shirt and black jeans, did he? The detective stood up and put an arm over Felix's shoulder, the way an uncle would. "Come on, let's go enjoy the food."

For a moment, Felix forgot what it was like to feel like the tide was out, and to know that despair was just around the corner.

### 8:45 PM ET

They finished every single chile relleno, as well as two dozen homemade tortillas, a salad of nopales, and flan that Meyers had prepared. The more they ate, the more the storm outside faded away, like a bad dream.

"But you see," Felix said, "it makes absolutely no sense to think of these Aztec gods in modern terms. They were appreciated in their time by people who saw the world in a much different way than we did."

"Spoken like a true academic," Meyers noted. He lit a cigar and offered some to Felix and Nestor, who declined.

"To me, these old deities seem savage, scary even," Nestor said. He felt woozy from the beer and the mezcal, but he could sit with that feeling all night. It had been a while since he felt his body relax like this.

"The deity itself is not what's scary," Felix said. "It's the blood tribute that earlier peoples thought they owed them that makes it savage."

"So…Xipe Totec—" Nestor said.

"Required a sacrifice, yes," Felix said, slurping up the last golden sliver of flan into his mouth. "Just like many other deities did. But not only did Xipe need blood, he needed human skins."

"So, humor me, then, both you, Gregory and Felix —" Nestor said. "If someone wanted to appease this god, and they wanted to select a victim, why would they choose someone like our victim?"

"I would pick someone beautiful, powerful, smart and healthy," Felix said. "I would basically offer up the best specimen to the god, to receive good fortune."

"That would fit the profile of our first victim. Wealthy, gorgeous, and powerful. But the second?"

"There's a second?" Meyers said.

"Hypothetical, Meyers."

"The second victim," Nestor continued, "was poor, destitute, addicted to crystal meth and alcohol, and known to prostitute himself to make ends meet for another fix. He was a nobody, by New York standards."

"That's the very problem with that sentence," Meyers said. "The standard set by New York. Does affluence and class need to validate a human being?"

"Of course not, I am just telling you how most New Yorkers see a gay black homeless man."

"But," Felix said, "what if our murderer saw some other sort of value in this homeless guy that we could not surmise?"

"That's the very reason why this line of logic doesn't work," Nestor said. "So far, these killings, if connected, would point to an opportunistic serial killer, rather than someone who was planning the selection of his prey much more in advance."

Felix shook his head, poured another shot glass of mezcal, and cleared away the dessert plates and spoons so he could rest his index fingers on the table, as if he had discovered some unique idea there.

"The second one is the *real* sacrifice, you see," Felix continued. "If you ask me, the first victim is simply a way of invoking the god, to help him come back to this world. And the second is the actual tribute of human skin, to keep him happy and bring fertility back to the land."

"We don't live in an agrarian society anymore, Mr. Calvo," Meyers said. "This is the age of cities."

"I know that. But these are the old beliefs about Xipe Totec. It's why he's called The Night Drinker. Because he brings torrential rains back in Spring, and with them, the fertility of the earth."

"This scenario doesn't work for me," Nestor said. "Such elaborate ritual sounds like the kind of thing that a cult would do, not a lone serial killer."

"But, Detective," Meyers said, "how can you say that? You were the very policeman who caught the man behind the Bowery Murders. Weren't those..."

Nestor nodded. "They were. It just...I just would prefer to not encounter such a thing again."

"Gentlemen, more flan?"

"I'll take one more slice," Felix said.

"It still doesn't make sense. Who would take the time to do

such elaborate crimes?"

"That's what I think I have almost figured out," Felix said.

"Go on," Meyers said. He leaned forward, with his hands hooked under his chin.

"The novel *9 Lords of Night* showed us a glimpse of the god Xipe Totec gone mad, although Samuel Kahan cut those scenes from the movie script," Felix said. "In the book, Xipe Totec was left out of the fellowships of the Nine Lords of Day, *and* the Nine Lords of Night, yet he was a key figure venerated by the Aztecs in actual history. He is a god who rages, but soon is forgotten by the passage of time."

"But wouldn't you agree that he got folded into elements of the Catholic faith in Mexico?" Nestor said. "Maybe he's remained there all along, waiting to come back stronger than ever."

Felix folded his arms and cocked his head "Perhaps," he said, "The Night Drinker is the most fitting metaphor for these chaotic times we live in the 21st century. But he's just not needed by modern man."

"You see," Felix continued, "this god, venerated as the bringer of spring and fertility for crops, is not so much needed anymore, in our age of science, genetically modified plants, lab-grown meat, and our ability to harness the natural world through man-made technology. We can now perform the wonders that the gods used to, but in a more efficient and terrifying way."

"On this point Sam would agree with you," Meyers said. "He mentioned to me in private more than a few times, that there were no real needs for these gods in the Western world. And that of course, that would lead to the very downfall of modern society."

"Xipe represents the true essence of what nature is like," Felix said. "Savage, violent, blood-drenched. He is a mega storm, an active volcano, an earthquake, and also an epidemic, such as the flu. Each of those natural disasters bring the earth back to stillness, so new life can emerge."

"You make him sound all too noble," Meyers said.

"Well, that's the problem with religion, isn't it? How man interprets what he thinks the god wants? If Xipe demands blood sacrifice and human flesh, well, we have also given him that. We are more technologically advanced in the 21st century, but we are still so primitive and unwise that we murder each other without abandon. You could make the argument that we have been sending

Xipe gifts—blood and skins— very often."

"But does Xipe demand *actual* human skin and blood? I mean, we're talking about a myth, not an actual being," Nestor said.

"True," Felix said. "Xipe is just as fictional as Harry Potter or Alice. But it would seem someone in New York thinks he's pretty real."

"But weren't other Aztec gods just as demanding for sacrifice?" Nestor said.

"They were," Felix said, eating the last bite of flan. "Tlaloc, Huitzilopochtli, Tezcatlipoca demanded tribute. According to Aztec religion."

"And why does this killer invoke Xipe, then? Why now," Gregory said.

"Because he's *the most chaotic,*" Felix said. "And we live in an age where chaos rules. He who can harness chaos can control the masses."

Felix helped stack plates of dirty dishes. "But let me just make this clear. This is just myth. Technically, there are no more Aztec gods to appease. They just don't exist anymore."

"How so?" Nestor said.

"You see, by 2012, the five ages of the Aztecs are over," Felix said. "In essence, all the gods had died by then, just as the Aztecs predicted. As of today, they should all be dead and gone."

The room filled with silence, and Meyers scratched his chin.

"Unless," Felix said, "we are not thinking correctly about how time works. We can't confirm some of our most interesting theories, such as string theory, dark matter, quantum physics, but if we could, we could make the argument that the five epochs of the Aztecs weren't just linear time."

"You're losing me," Meyers said.

Felix took a long sip from his drink. He was slurring his words, but he was also invigorated by this conversation.

"If time is not linear, it can exist as a circles, as wheels," Felix said. "It can even defy the Newtonian laws of physics. If we choose to believe that the Aztec gods didn't die according to the myths, then time is rebooted, and those gods can return *beyond* the five ages and into our world. If physicists theorize that wormholes could exist, why wouldn't gods be able to pass through them into another dimension of time and space?"

"I'm afraid this is getting to be too Dungeons and Dragonsish for me," Nestor said. "This is a projection of occultism and metaphysics that I don't care for."

"It's just ideas, man," Felix said. "Just science and ideas, and—"

"Imagination," Meyers said, nodding.

Felix smiled and continued. "Well, if we just had proof that such a gate in space and time could let these ancient gods through—"

"We would have a terrific science fiction saga," Meyers said. "And detective Buñuel here would write it down for us and become the next Frank Herbert."

"I would definitely not do that," Nestor said. "My science fiction worlds are governed by science, and worsened by politics. There are no gods or religions left in those worlds I create. They are secular worlds of materialism. The characters in my books are much too smart to believe in deities."

"So says the devout Catholic," Felix said.

Nestor's face went stone-still, and unreadable. He took a sip of water without making a rebuttal, but also without breaking eye contact with Felix.

"It's fiction, Felix. The day you write a novel, you call me up."

"Regardless of what you think, Nestor," Felix said, "Marlene Grue's killer could use the resurrection of Xipe Totec, as a valid reason to kill."

"What's the point here?" Nestor said. "Sure, Xipe Totec is misaligned, he's not needed in an age of cloud computing and neural networks, but now a serial killer wants to bring him back by selecting black people?"

"Well yeah, more or less," Felix said. Meyers giggled.

"I'm not laughing about killing black people," Meyers said. "I didn't mean to make it seem like I'm some sort of racist—"

"I know that," Felix said. "I got you. This Grue murder is surreal."

"So Felix, you surmised all of this from the archival material from my boss?" Meyers asked. "Are you suggesting that Sam was trying to appease this deity?"

"Not at all."

"Then what?"

"Kahan's notes are super cryptic, but I can see why he dedicated his film to the god Xipe Totec. He is obsessed with The Night Drinker. He made that piece of art not as invocation for that god, but rather, as a warning for us in later generations."

"What kind of warning?"

"To not repeat the downfall of the previous five ages of the Aztecs."

"I don't get what you mean."

"Well, I haven't yet seen the movie, but I get the sense that Kahan didn't think very highly of human nature. If you ask me, I would guess he thought man was deplorable."

Meyers smiled and remained quiet. He tipped his drink toward the two men and rinsed the dishes. As he did so, he stared wistfully out the window, as if he had remembered something tragic, hurtful, and perhaps also beautiful in the corners of his mind.

### 9:11 PM ET

The screening room was paneled in oak, and a fragrance of pine, wood lacquer and old cigarette smoke gave the small movie theater a worn-in feel. Meyers spooled the film onto the projector in a small alcove beyond the room.

"You know that the projectionist is now a thing of the past, right Meyers?" Nestor said.

"What do you mean?"

"It's all robots that do the projection now."

"Didn't know that, but not surprised. I mostly just watch Sam's collection when I come here. Ingrid Bergman, Andrei Tarkovsky, the American greats, too."

Felix burped next to Nestor, and a pallor washed out his facial features.

"You okay?"

"I'm fine," Felix said. "Just not a movie guy."

"Something else is bothering you."

"Oh you know me that well?"

"I'm starting to."

"You're correct then. It's something else."

"Go ahead."

"I've been seeing strange things in this place. Maybe it's just my depression playing tricks on me; dunno."

"Are you on meds?"

"Hell, no. The most I can tolerate is weed, but if it was up to my mom, whose second career is being a domestic pharmacologist, she would put me back on all the antianxiety meds she and my father take."

"What is your depression like?" Nestor said.

"It's a daily thing, is what it's like."

"And you feel it now?"

"Maybe. I feel empty, but also, I have a feeling I can't shake. You're going to think what I'm going to say is weird."

"Try me."

"I don't think I should watch this movie. It feels wrong."

"You don't have to."

"That's just it. I don't think I have a choice. I still have too many questions about that amazing archive, and the movie will help me get that last piece of the puzzle."

"You talk like a detective. Seeing things through, even when they are going to get ugly."

"I never want to be a cop. They're fucking up everything for marginalized people."

Nestor took a sip from his cocktail and rested the back of his head on the headrest. His pride in his work was hard as metal but somewhere deep inside, he also felt like he needed to listen to what Felix was saying.

"Ready, gents?" Meyers said. He sat next to them with a bowl of popcorn, a packet of Mexican tamarind candy, and a remote control for the projector.

Nestor leaned in close so only Felix could hear him. "You really don't have to—"

"It's okay, Nestor. Curiosity killed the cat."

The room went pitch black, and for a half second, no sound was heard. Then, the bright white eye of the projector exploded with light and motion before them.

**10:11 PM ET**

Halfway through the film Felix craned his head to get his bearings. For the past hour, he had forgotten that he was tucked away inside a palatial house in the Catskills, next to two old dudes in the middle of a snowstorm.

The movie forced the viewer to watch it, to go deep into its world, like a planet with so much physical mass that its gravity was inescapable.

At this point in *9 Lords of Night*, the sense of loss, humiliation and horror felt by the indigenous husband and wife in the film was too much for them to bear. And it was in that inflection point, in which they stood under an orange sunset, that the married couple made a pact to avenge their people by committing an assassination that was needed now more than ever, if they were ever going to take down and usurp the white men who were taking their world away from them. Three birds flew past the sky and perched before them. One was a white dove, the second a gorgeous quetzal, and the third, a wild turkey, whose feathers were as brilliantly blue and red as the most precious gems from deep inside the earth.

Felix refilled his drink, took a large swig, and he felt a strange sense of relief in the dark cocoon of the screening room. He leaned back in his seat and returned to the world Kahan had created. For the next seventy minutes, Felix fell back into the world of *9 Lords of Night*. His awareness of his body, his skin, and even his drunkenness, vanished, and the movie swallowed him whole.

## 11:21 PM ET

"I am not sure what I have just seen," Felix said, "but I can say I have never experienced a movie like that."

"That's the kind of comment many have said about Sam's works," Meyers said.

"It can only really be appreciated on the big screen like this," Nestor said. He was still tipsy, and he needed to piss, then hit the sack. Felix sat in his seat, unmoving. He looked ill. Was he sensitive toward everything, even movies? He was pale as milk, as if the movie had stunned him.

"I need to think about what I just experienced," Felix said.

"Just don't overthink it," Nestor said. "What I'd like from you are some general ideas on what this film could mean for the investigation. We can check out the archive again tomorrow, and then we both go back to our merry little worlds."

"*Merry*," Felix said. He tugged at the collar of his shirt and stumbled out of the screening room. "See y'all tomorrow."

"Good night," Meyers said. "And good night, Nestor. You can make yourselves breakfast at whatever time you wish to get up tomorrow. I'll be driving into town for a few errands."

Nestor took his shoes off and padded through the hallways and up the large staircase up to the second floor. Even after he had brushed his teeth and drunk a few glasses of water, he still felt the swoon of the liquor. He tossed and turned on top of the comforter, and outside, the snow had slowed down. The snowfall had stopped, and now the smooth drifts remained still as a modern sculpture, white and vast.

# DAY 7
## SUNDAY OCTOBER 26, 2025

**UPSTATE NEW YORK**
**12:11 AM ET**

Nestor should have texted or called his mother, to check on her, but every hour that passed in this mansion seemed to yank the world of New York and its boroughs far away from him.

Nestor recalled scenes from *9 Lords of Night* as the husband and wife wore disguises to infiltrate the royal court of the Spaniards. Nestor relived the quick glances as they prepared to stab La Malinche, the traitor, to death, and then the terrifying sounds of wings, flutes, and the shards of light that burst into the courtyard as the crime was foiled by the Spanish guards. It was that flapping of wings, the musical melody of the Aztec flutes, and something else, rhythmic and hard, yes drums, the drums of the Mexica, that turned over and over in his ears, and suddenly, Nestor was sweating, his body face up on the bed, with his arms at his sides, almost paralyzed by the memories of the movie soundtrack, and he felt a chill move down his spine, as if a demon were whispering in his ear.

Nestor rubbed his arms to warm himself up. He couldn't shake the chill away, even though the central heat of the house was as warm as a down duvet. It was the kind of cold that ate away at your bones, and which made you shiver uncontrollably.

He pulled on a tank top and a pair of briefs, and unsure of why he was doing so, he walked down the hallway, to the very end of the wing. The house offered no sounds at this hour. He tiptoed in the dark, shivering, down the long hallways on hardwood floors.

When he reached Meyers' bedroom, he found the door ajar.

"You can come in," Meyers said. Nestor stepped into the room, which was just as dark as the night sky. He slid into the bed, and he discovered a body under the blankets that despite its advanced age, was still firm and brimming with life.

Nestor hugged, caressed, straddled and thrust, and Meyers returned his touches with kisses, hard grabs, and deep embraces that Nestor had not felt in many years. No one spoke. Perhaps Meyers had been right. Maybe it was the loneliest of souls that offered the most erotic pleasures, but neither of the two men discussed the matter. They made love in the womb of the bed, and when it was over, they embraced in silence again, until it was time for Nestor to return to his own bed.

When Nestor's head hit the pillow, he fell into a vast, dreamless sleep ruled only by the color green, and all his fears and bodily chills vanished.

In all the years that Nestor lived, he never told anyone about what he did that night in the Thracian house with Meyers, the keeper of Samuel Kahan's secrets.

### 3:00 AM ET

Felix rummaged through the cabinets in the living room, searching for a trinket to keep, a memento to take. He was barely aware of what he was doing, but he knew that collecting an item, stealing something, would help take his mind off the tide, because he could feel it moving, taking along with it vast gallons of water, and it was that tide that would take him to the place he did not want to go.

He dug through books, old playbills from Broadway musicals in Manhattan, a autographed photos of Rock Hudson, Jack Nicholson and Vincent D'Onofrio, old lighters, and a vintage chess set made of onyx, but his hands couldn't decide on anything to keep. He sighed, and he walked up to the large windows. From there, he could see very far across the lake, and the deep valley in which the house sat.

"Please blink," he said, fogging the glass, but whatever being had made its dozens of eyes glow bright before, was not in the woods tonight.

*Even the monsters outside don't want me,* he thought. How could anyone understand what it was really like to feel this way for a major portion of the year? He thought about getting the good news next week that yes, he would get the teaching job at NYU, and wouldn't that be great? Wouldn't that job, that new life, keep the tide away, where it should remain?

But despite arriving at that dream scenario, he still felt a nagging emptiness, a sadness that dispersed itself through him in multiple layers and waves, always mocking him, reminding him, that others would always have it better than he did and that he was missing something at his very core, like the Tin Man without his heart.

His hands fumbled in the dark, open and shutting drawers. And then he spotted it. The liquor cabinet. He opened it and drank half a bottle of vodka in just a handful of swigs, right from the bottle. He felt the burn of the liquor move down his throat, both repugnant and delicious.

He took one last glance at the tranquil lake and its rim of snow-covered hills. The stillness of the woods brought out grief from deep in his belly, up into his chest, and right out into his throat, as he heard his own cries.

As he put the bottle back into the cabinet and closed the doors, he made himself weep quietly so he wouldn't wake anyone up. He stepped on the balls of his feet to prevent the hardwood from creaking, but it was his soft cries that would give him away.

"Just shut up," he said to himself, "shut the fuck up you fucking piece of shit." But his whisper only made more tears roll down his face. He slapped himself, and he only cried harder, as if a fountain of pain had surged from his center. By the time he slid into his bed, nausuea twisted his guts into knots, but before he could vomit, he passed out face down in the bed.

### 4:50 PM ET

"You need to slow down," Nestor said, but Felix only dug further into the archives. As he scoured the contents of the boxes, he had skipped lunch, taking breaks to vomit, but he carried on through the hangover.

"I don't think the world was ready for the movie *9 Lords of Night*," Felix said, with his hands inside a manila folder, and his eyes lowered as he inspected Kahan's old receipts for camera equipment.

"What makes you say that?"

"Well, it's a movie that would have been more appropriate today. It would have empowered many people, especially young people of color, to fight for more social justice and overthrow their oppressors."

"Because the two main characters try to assassinate the person they claim sold them out?"

"Yes. Those eight years we endured under one authoritarian US President—remember how we all thought it was going to get better when he was out of the White House?"

"I do remember," Nestor said. He felt a chill run down his spine.

"Well, it got worse, didn't it?"

"Yeah, our country elected someone even worse after him. This is the hell we live in now."

"Statements like the ones being made in this old movie by Kahan could have mobilized more of us brown and oppressed people."

"You really think so, Felix? I don't want you to think I am jaded, but I write novels for a living, and the more I do this, the more I feel that people just want an hour or two inside these fantasy worlds of movies, TV, video games and books to get their rocks off, to numb themselves to the shitty grimness of what the world is actually like."

"Dunno, dude; I feel like *9 Lords* could have been a very cool success, at least with certain people."

"I don't think I agree with you, but I think now I understand a little more about how you think."

"There's a second reason this movie could have slayed in this current decade."

"*Slayed?*"

"Shut up. The reason is that for once, Hollywood made a movie that took the splendor and the beauty of the Aztec empire seriously. All of the good things, and also its bad things, are gorgeously laid out on display in Kahan's movie. It breaks down the stereotypes people have of what they think Mexico and its traditions are supposed to be like."

"I would agree on that."

"Yeah."

Felix's last word echoed inside the chilly air of the archives.

"You have a white father and a Mexican mother. What's your connection to Mexico?"

Felix stared into the gloom of the archive before speaking. "I really don't know what I am. If I try to be more Mexican, I feel like I am appropriating something. And yet, I don't want to be just white, knowing what those ancestors did in this continent and this country."

"Have you ever talked to your parents about how you feel?"

"Of course not. We don't talk about these topics. We only talk about following rules, being frugal, and becoming a successful professor."

"But those are not topics that you seem to want to talk about. If you asked me, you're more interested in architecture, art, and going down odd rabbit holes."

"No one's ever said that about me. Most people just want to talk to me about my PhD."

"I don't care about PhDs."

"But my mother does."

"She knows everything about you, doesn't she?"

"Sort of. It's like she's got eyes or cameras everywhere."

"Does she know you're here?"

"Yes, I told her."

"Well, you've sold yourself out, friend. Parents don't have to know everything. And trust me, this is from a man whose mother and father know virtually everything about me, too."

"Do they know…"

"Yes, of course."

"Then I don't get it. You're suggesting I just cut off my mother?"

"I'm not suggesting anything. All I can tell you is that you have been strangled so hard that you can no longer tell that you're running out of air and a coil is wrapped around your neck."

Felix stuffed his hands into his pockets and took a deep breath as he looked around the cavernous storage space. Nestor felt awkward too, so he changed the subject.

"You know, there's rumors that Kahan used his artistry in filmmaking to stage NASA's landing on the moon and fool the American public."

"I just don't get the sense that Kahan was interested in hoaxes, Nestor."

"Then if not hoaxes, what?"

"I think Kahan didn't think highly of human nature. That is evident."

"I don't see it," Felix said.

"That's because you haven't seen the rest of his movies."

"He didn't have much faith in us evolving into something better. But I got a sense from watching his movie that he felt that there was something beyond us, that was worth touching. Something divine, perhaps."

"Did you see his movie *Xenogenesis*?"

"No, *9 Lords* is the first of his movies I have seen," Felix said.

"You might want to see *Xenogenisis* sometime soon. You almost quoted word for word one of the most famous lines of dialog by Lilith Iyapo, the main character."

"Well that's fucking weird."

"No, *you* are fucking weird, buddy," Nestor said, laughing and smiling. "Come on, we gotta meet Meyers at five thirty. He's going to show us the aviary. And then we have to get ready to drive back tomorrow before dawn."

This time, Felix didn't flinch when Nestor patted him on the back as they made their way out of the archive.

### 5:31 PM ET

"Right this way, gentlemen," Meyers said, buttoning up his three piece suit. "It's been a few weeks since I've visited this part of the house, but most things are likely to be in their place. Watch your step."

The three men walked down four risers to a recessed landing. Before them, a double set of doors made of oak and inlaid with stone loomed over them. The designs on the doors were both familiar and foreign. Nestor had seen these repeating patterns of hooks and vegetal forms on architecture of the great pyramids of the Maya and the Aztec empires, but these were not exactly such. These were leaner, stronger, more simplified, and at the same time

236

more stylized. They coursed up the height of the doors into curving arcs, like tree branches. Seen from afar, those tiny patterns resembled computer circuitry.

"This is the Aviary," Meyers said. "I will ask that you leave your wallets, belts, and of course, your notebook, Felix, out in this hallway. And you do indeed need to sign these nondisclosure agreements. You cannot talk about what you will see."

Nestor and Felix laid their accessories on a side table, and Meyers slid keys into two locks over the door. They signed the documents, and Meyers put the papers into a folder. He pulled back the massive doors without any effort, as if the mechanism was made to make things easy for humans.

Nestor took two steps into the room, and the first thing he noticed was the blue light that permeated the space. It was like seeing into the depths of the ocean and the sky at the same time. Around Nestor, various shapes and objects of metal and glass glistened, but he had a hard time making out what he was seeing, because there was a very distinct sound demanding his attention. It was a low warble, almost like a hum but more organic, that pierced his ears. Felix gasped next to him.

"I was expecting... real birds," Felix said. "What the fuck is this?"

"These are birds of a sort," Meyers said. "You just have to let go of your preconceived definitions of avians as you make this journey."

Various contraptions stood like sculptures, or perhaps, Nestor thought, like men that had been turned to stone by Medusa in the old myths. The blue light grew deeper as they stepped into the room, and the low warble shifted as new musical tones began to emerge from the various metal arms, arcs, and orbs before them. The way in which the metal arms and torso-like trunks of glass were constructed gave the figures a human-like appearance.

Nestor counted nine of them. He approached one in the center of the room, shaped like a female torso, with orbs of milky glass that resembled breasts, and a skirt that fanned out with hundreds of snaking rods of what seemed to be made of stainless steel and whose tiny mouths and eyes at the ends indeed resembled rattlesnakes. As he approached the sculpture, it generated music from its bosom. The music added harmony to the warble that still permeated the space, and suddenly, a melody was forming. The sculpture had a head that was humanoid but which had no eyes mouth, or nose.

"Is this an art installation?" Felix said.

"Not in any way, shape or form," Meyers said. He was standing along the wall at the very end of the room, fiddling with a laptop that was set atop a white ceramic podium. "Please be sure not to touch any of the Volatiles, unless they ask you to touch them first. Consent is very important here."

"Excuse me?" Nestor said, and that's when the towering skirted figure before him lit up. Her metal skin glowed with thousands of tiny green diodes, giving the appearance of movement, even though the sculpture did not move. She spoke with a gentle voice, smooth around the edges, and deeply female.

"Please share an interesting adjective to describe yourself," she said. Nestor looked around, and Felix, who was just six feet away, shrugged.

"Nocturnal?" Nestor said.

The sculpture repeated the word *nocturnal*, once, twice, and then over and over, elongating Nestor's sampled voice over and over like taffy, until it became a series of pleasant notes. The sculpture dropped these notes into the rhythm of the sounds around her, and suddenly the melody generated by the room became a deeper, more complex composition. Her body emitted music, as if every part of her skin were a high-end sampler, synthesizer and stereo speaker.

"Do you have a name?" Nestor said.

"My name is Atl, which translates roughly to *water*. I am named after a symbolic representation of Xiuhtehcutli, the god of fire. Nice to meet you."

"Nestor. My name is Nestor."

Atl emitted a series of musical clicks and chirps. Her skin faded from neon green to dark brown, and then she fell silent. Nestor was still holding in his breath; this machine was sublime, like a sunset.

Meyers reappeared before Nestor and Felix.

"The Aviary," Meyers said, "was Sam's last project before he passed away. He and Steven Spielberg collaborated on these animatronic AIs you just met for an upcoming film. Eventualy, the release of the film would have given way to a very ambitious video game and a theme park expansion at Disney World. But Steven knew that Sam's cancer was advancing, and at some point, they both abandoned the project."

"These are AIs?" Nestor asked. "You can't call them AIs."

"Eh?" Nestor said.

"It's true," Meyers continued. "Now that Congress has started regulating speech, AI is not to be uttered or written, unless it's one of several copyrighted products sanctioned by federal authorities as such. But since this project never saw the light of day, we can call these AIs, can't we?"

One of the sculptures, stocky and round, with thick arms that resembled those of a circus strongman, nodded. Its movements were fluid, not robotic in any way, and its eyeless face twitched, then cocked itself at an angle, as if evaluating Nestor.

"It's all very primitive technology, but Sam had gone so deep into the science of artificial intelligence that he could have given a PhD at MIT and Tsinghua University a run for their money."

"Are their computer brains running all the time?" Nestor said.

"Yes and no. They need sensory input for their brains to be stimulated, and as far as I can tell, they do not interact with each other when there are no humans around to create music for. This room is kept dark and soundproof, to prevent new input."

"Where are their brains?" Felix said.

"Not in their heads, if that's where you are looking. They are on their skin. Which is why you should not touch them ever, unless you are asked."

"And what is the purpose of these AIs?" Nestor said.

"To do what Sam could never do with his friends, family, and associates. Make people happy."

"Define *happiness*," Nestor said.

"To create beautiful things, and to share them with others."

"And what do these have to do at all with our project on the movie *9 Lords*?"

"I thought they would simply be an extravagant yet inspiring curiosity for you, Detective. Each of these Volatiles is dedicated to one of of the Nine Lords of Night, you see."

Nestor's heart skipped a beat, and he broke out on gooseflesh. Felix scurried past the sculptures so he could listen more closely to Meyers. "How?" he said.

"There are Nine Lords of Day, who rule over the daytime and the business affairs of the solar time, and then, there are Nine

Lords of Night, who rule over the nighttime, which is not only lunar and governed by darkness, but also plugged directly into the darkness of the realm of dreams. Sam envisioned these animatronics as new composers of the twenty-first century. In the AI film he was developing, these nine volatiles would have each contributed music to endless symphonies that would bring men together instead of apart. Sam said that in the twenty-first century, it was the lunar and nocturnal energy of the collective psyche of men that would bring peace and a sense of unity."

"But why are these things called Volatiles?" Nestor said. "I don't get the name."

"Mr. Buñuel, I thought your Mexican mother would have filled you in on some of this older lore."

"It gets lost a little more with each generation, but actually, I'm going to pretend you did not just insult my family, so please go on, Mr. Meyers."

"Each Aztec god and goddess enjoys the power of transformation, and when they transform, they take the shapes of various animals, but in particular, some gods thrive on the shape of birds. In Nahuatl, this type of supernatural familiar is called a *tonal*. There are nine gods represented here by these nine AI animatronics, and each one is named after their corresponding bird. Don't mind their humanoid shape; Sam designed them conceptually as  songbirds, even if they are anthropomorphic. It's one of the pleasures that working on robotics gave him."

"And the movie with Spielberg was going to be about those Aztec gods?"

"Of course not, Felix. Sam was much too clever for that. He was going to let that bit of information recede into the subconscious of the viewer. Sam was never so obvious. He would think it vulgar. The movie was to be called *The Neural Network*, and its ideas were more about humanity evolving into something new."

Nestor's book was called *The Neural Network*. Had he perhaps read about this project in the internet rumor mill and subconsciously used the phrase as the title of his new book? He could not be sure, but he kept his mouth shut.

The nine sculptures shifted in unison, leaning and bending, as if they too were trying to hear this conversation better.

"They are not very good AIs, you see. No one has developed their code much further than what was available back in 2018.

They are also missing a key component of a good AI: massive data sets. In the isolation of this estate, they are languishing without data that we can feed them. You see, there is no internet of any kind in this room. That means they have no access to social media, cryptocurrency trades, or satellite data. But the Volatiles make for gorgeous art, so maybe you are right, Felix. This is an art installation after all."

The nine sculptures heard the words *gorgeous art*, and they instantly took the sounds apart, creating percussion, wind instruments, synth waves, and whistling sounds to make a song that felt bold, intrepid, and also dangerous. The lullaby they generated lasted only two minutes, and when it was done, the sculptures returned to their static poses. The nine figures turned their skin a bright teal color, and they held it there, like a note on a musical instrument.

Meyers flipped a switch along the wall, and the light turned white and warm again. The sculptures looked even more alien under this light. Their bodies were the colors of minerals, blue and purple, and their limbs a vision from a nightmare.

"Why did you really want to show us this room?" Nestor said.

"Your directness is refreshing. I dit it so you could get a better understanding of Sam. What you read in the magazines about him is not accurate."

"Go on."

"While it is true that I spent all my best years working for that man and struggling under his whims, I can say I enjoyed every minute of them. These Volatiles help me remember him, and they are a hint of how much more he could have done if he had reached a fourteenth film."

"Did you ever think you hated him?" Felix said.

"Yes, many times. He controlled everything I did. He told me I was no good at my job more than once, and his silent rage was worse than any curse word he could have spat out at me. I also cannot mention how many mind games he played not just with me but with actors on his sets. No man, other than my own father, ever made me cry as much as he did."

"And yet you are still here," Felix said. "Bewitched by the things he made."

"Somehow. There are days I wonder if I have become nothing more than a ghost, chained to the legacy of my boss in this mansion. But Sam would not like for me to say that."

"Why?"

"Sam didn't believe in the supernatural in any way. The very word *ghost* made him want to vomit."

"I have seen enough," Nestor said. He didn't like this room, or the Volatiles, or the music they made. In fact, he wanted to get the hell out of there. The nine figures shifted at the sound of his voice, and the one with the serpent-like skirt turned bright blue along her metal arms. She craned her neck forward, searching for him. Nestor was reminded of the queen Jadis in CS Lewis' *The Magician's Nephew*. It was that hateful queen that governed an empty castle inhabited only by statues, who themselves were once kings and queens. That story had sent shivers down Nestor's spine when he read it as a kid, and as he examined the quiet figures of these Volatiles, queens whose LED skin glowed with a life of its own, he imagined Marlene Grue as one of them, forever pinned into a standing position like a butterfly that has been collected, propped up and forced to sing an endless electronic song as an eternal curse.

Nestor brushed the image away from his mind and shook his head, hoping to free himself from it.

*I never want to have this much money*, he thought. *Building something like this is…wrong.*

As the three men neared the door, Felix leaned in close to Nestor. "I will never make anything as interesting as this stuff."

"How can you say that? You're a brilliant academic."

"Just look at how many hours went into making this. It's the most stunning thing I have ever seen."

"Look, you'll be a brilliant professor, and you'll write several books in your field. Won't you?"

Felix stared at Nestor but he did not answer.

Behind them, the nine Volatiles emitted a forlorn song. Their voices sang in a language that sounded like English but wasn't, and though it lasted only a few bars, the catchy and raspy hooks of the music lingered in the mind for a much longer time.

### 9:02 PM ET

Dinner was a quiet affair. Steaks on the grill and roasted root vegetables. They drank a cabernet that Felix enjoyed so much, Meyers opened a second bottle just for him. They didn't talk much about Kahan or the archive. In fact, the whole dinner had a sad air about it, but no one commented on its solemnity.

Felix caught Nestor checking his messages on his phone. He hovered over his shoulder to take a better look.

Nestor bunched up his shoulders and cursed under his breath. He let the phone fold itself back into a square shape. He turned around.

"Were you fucking looking over my shoulder?"

"Yes. So sue me."

"It's police business," Nestor said, but his voice quivered. Something was wrong.

"I didn't really anything, but it can't be good."

"It's. Delia. She's good people, keeps me informed. What I feared would happen is definitely going to happen. FBI's taking over, and my boss is taking the case from my hands."

"You can now just retire in peace, yeah?"

"It's bullshit."

"Nestor, what are you trying to prove exactly? That you can do it all?"

The detective puffed up his chest and ran a hand through his black hair. "Fuck off," he said.

"I'm sorry, I didn't mean to—"

"Relax, it's fine."

"Your face doesn't seem fine."

"I always thought I would make not just a good cop but a *great* cop. My father was delighted when I went to the academy. Twice as excited when I got promoted to detective. But in all that time, all those years, I am not sure I accomplished what I should have."

"And what would that *should have* been?

"A better rate at closing cases. More justice on the behalf of the victims. There is so little compassion sometimes for the victims of violent crime, did you know that? And maybe I should have fought harder to protect trans people. Sometimes I feel as if by becoming a cop, I somehow sold them out."

"How so?"

"By perpetuating the notion that trans people, the good trans people look and talk in one particular way. You see, when a trans person doesn't pass, they set off alarms of fear and hatred for cis people. I wish that it were different, but many people in the police think that trans men like me are more valid, only because we pass more readily to cis people as men, according to their definitions."

"But you really think that solving Grue's murder would help you feel better about these things?"

Felix had never seen the detective look as exhausted or confused as he looked now.

"You make a good point, Felix, but it really hurts to have this snatched away from me. It stings, with retirement just four weeks down the road."

## 11:10 PM ET

Meyers collected the last of the wineglasses and the cheese plate he had laid out after dinner.

"It will be a pity to see you go," he said. "Visitors here are few, even in summer, when the folks from the city get away to the Catskills."

"If I ever needed to revisit the archive, would you let me?" Felix said.

"As long as Orlando doesn't know, it's fine by me. And incidentally, the figurine you pocketed from the archive earlier, you may give it back now."

Felix turned a bright shade of red. Nestor felt his own face go flush with embarrassment.

"You did not, Felix," he said.

Felix nodded and pulled out a tiny representation of the god Xipe Totec. He set it on the tiles of the kitchen table as if he were starting a game of chess.

"How did you know?"

"I told you that I can see everything in this house, didn't I?"

"You have eyes in the back of your head?"

"There are cameras in every single room. That includes the archive. And if you must know, every object, including the messy sheaves of papers in boxes, have RFID tags. Nothing escaped Sam's obsessions over detail."

"How the hell did you get RFID into paper?" Nestor said.

"It's a single fiber that gets thrust into the paper. And who do you think Sam asked to place those fibers when items entered the archive?"

Felix tapped his fingers on the table and took a long swig of wine.

"My apologies," Felix said.

"Accepted, Mr. Calvo. But tell me, if you are a professor of anthropology, why would you commit such a theft?"

"I don't actually know. Can't your cameras tell you that?"

Gregory Meyers adjusted the buttons on his three-piece suit and sliced off the tip of a cigar, which he smoked by opening up the window above the kitchen sink. Frigid air screamed as it rushed into the room. Meyers did not seem concerned over the loss of heat.

"I don't think we can ever go back to a time when cameras are not present everywhere," Meyers said. "Before Sam could install video technology throughout this compound, he was already wishing for such a future."

"It's creepy," Felix said.

"You own a smartphone, don't you?" Meyers said.

"Of course."

"Well, you are being surveilled in a deeper way than me, then. I have allowed internet access in this house in many ways, but one thing I will not do is carry a smartphone with me."

"The man has a point," Nestor said. "I don't think we ever get to go back."

"But what kind of life is that, then? Yes, I know, I am the one snapping and texting the most here, but do we ever have privacy?"

"That's the irony, Mr. Calvo," Meyers said. "For those who believe in the Christian god, He is ever-present, watching men's every move. He is the first pervasive surveillance camera of the universe. Do you agree, Nestor? You are the one Catholic in this room besides a young atheist and this former Baptist."

"Well, yes, God can see everything."

"And tell me, Felix," Meyers said. "Can those gods you study, those Aztec gods, see everything, too?"

"That's a question that's impossible to answer. We will never know how the ancient people of the Americas thought about those gods in that way."

"Sure, but what do you think? What's *your* theory?"

"Well, if we go by the myths and stories of those gods, no. They couldn't be everywhere and see everything. Just like the Greek gods. They did not have so much power."

"But yet they find out what men do. How?" Meyers said. He was looking his most radiant now, amused by the remnants of the cigar smoke in the room, and the quality of his company on a cold October evening.

"Can I interject here?" Nestor asked. Both Meyers and Felix nodded. "In the Bible, it's the angels that help God see further. It happens more than once."

"True, and though the Aztec myths had no angels, each god had its servants in nature," Felix said. "And of course, each god had a *tonal.*"

Nestor scratched his beard. In this moment, he wanted time to stop. This room, and this moment, were basically just good enough for him to be satisfied. While a storm raged outside much too early for the season, he had a belly full of steak, wine in his hand, and the warmth of this house. He had no pets, no wife, no children, but this moment, was just as good as any moments in those fictional lives that had never quite come to be. He wanted to reach out over the table and put his hand on Felix's arm and say, *Hey, I'm really glad you're here, even though I have thought you were a little shit from the moment I met you.* And he also wanted to shake Meyers' hand, to say *thank you for the strangest encounters in this remote part of New York State.* But Nestor fell back into his old ways. He stayed quiet, and refrained from reaching out to these two men. The moment was too good, to precious, to put a fine point on it.

"Felix," Nestor said. "Who do you think killed Marlene Grue?"

The kid straightened out his shirt collar, and he took a long sip of wine. His eyes were bloodshot, turned down at the corners, and yet he was deep inside a sort of celebration. "An amateur."

"How so?" Meyers said.

"The victim selection emulates tribute selection, so I'll give him that. He's at least done his homework. But the execution feels sloppy. It's lacking…elegance and pomp. And it's lacking a true taste of darkness."

"But the murders themselves are as dark as can be. A woman gets her heart removed, and a man is skinned and left in the cold."

"That's just it. I can't express it quite yet, but it's as if the murders are a kind of nostalgia. Cheap. Lacking elegance."

"Are you advocating for human sacrifice and skinning of victims?" Nestor said.

"Not at all. Not at all. What I mean is that if this person is meaning to send a message to the world in the name of Xipe Totec, it's going to land on deaf ears. What modern people really care about now are rogue lone killers, like the shooter in Vegas, or the monthly school shooters who really grab headlines. This person is trying to revive a past vision of sacrificial killings that seems, I don't know—"

"Like schlock and satanic cult paranoia from the 1970s?" Meyers said.

"Exactly. This person seems very well versed in information, such as rituals and customs of ancient sacrifice, but it's as if there is no…what's the word — wisdom— to put it together in a better way?"

"This is suddenly very grim," Nestor said. "I don't like to speculate on what makes an elegant murder. It's offensive."

"No, no, no" Felix said. "You are missing my point. Catholicism was able to take a figure like Jesus and turn his sacrifices, his gruesome death, and the cannibalistic eating of his flesh — into symbol. If this killer understood that symbolic representation better, well, maybe he would have no need to kill actual people in order to appease Xipe."

"You are way off on profiling a killer," Nestor said. "This would never fly in an actual investigation."

"That's why I don't work for the police," Felix said.

"Good point. And with that being said, I need to go to sleep. If we're going to get up at 4 AM and see if the roads are plowed enough to get out, I need to grab a handful of hours at least."

"It's been a pleasure, gentlemen. Get to sleep and I'll clean up in the morning.

Nestor made his way up to the bedroom, and suddenly, he missed Alexa. It was a strange feeling, but he knew that she always had his back. Maybe she was thinking about him at this very moment, but he doubted it. From down the hall, he heard Felix shuffling around, but by the time the footsteps faded, Nestor was deep asleep.

# DAY 8
## MONDAY OCTOBER 27, 2025

### UPSTATE NEW YORK
### 1:15 AM ET

Felix paced outside Nestor's door for exactly fifty-five minutes. He had counted them on his phone. Each time he was ready to knock, he pulled back his hand, because he knew he was a chicken shit.

*What am I doing?* he thought. *But I do know what I'm doing, it's what I know I should be doing.*

He tried knocking again, but instead, he pressed his fingertips onto the cool surface of the door.

*Hey good chap, mister detective, can I just sit down on the side of your bed and chat for a couple of hours? Well yes, it's because I am lonely, and you're the only person around here who actually listens to me. You won't mind, would ya? I mean, it's not like I am asking you to tuck me into bed, I mean, that would be just so gay, such a sissy thing to do, such a faggoty thing to do. And after all, I wouldn't ever internalize the word faggot, no no no, I am an educated person, a man that has a PhD from University of Chicago, my mind is calculating, empirical, and I don't need any kind of help. I don't need anyone, except that in the middle of the night, when there is a blizzard outside and I feel the loneliness of my bed, I just want someone to be there in the dark to answer my question, "Are you awake?" And of course, Nestor, you won't be awake, because you don't think of me as much more than a nuisance, some eccentric parasite that just latched itself to your back so he could get a free trip to the Catskills, but yes, I know what you really think of me, and how silly everything is about me, and you too, you too probably know that I am just a fraud out here. For god's sake, I box groceries for rich people in an Amazon warehouse, and I teach adjunct classes when I can get them, but really, who the fuck am I? Not much, not much, just a grease stain on a runway where the real vehicles—heavily built cars and elegant taxi cabs—run right over me. Nestor, do you know about the tide, the way it feels like a real tide in my heart, and how it lasts many weeks? No, of course not. You have everything you need, and you have your own problems of course, you probably deal with a bunch of bullshit for being trans, but you don't seem to show any frailty, any weakness, and that's why I am hoping you will just let me chat with you for a bit, because otherwise I will never be able to get even just five minutes of sleep tonight. You can listen to me, and then I will be out of your life forever.*

Felix raised his hand again to knock, and the door slid open on its own as a draft of warm air pushed it open. He stepped inside.

## 1:19 AM ET

Nestor snored as his body rose and fell beneath the thick comforter. Felix took three more steps into the room.

All the courage he had felt earlier to wake up the cop had vanished. Felix bit down on his lip until he broke the skin. That sick, oily feeling, the tide, the depression he knew so well, flowed stronger than ever. If he could cry, he would do that, but as he stood over the sleeping detective, his mind only repeated the same thoughts, rendering him unable to take any action.

His paralysis broke when he caught a glint of metal at the foot of the bed.

Nestor's holster was draped over the chair, and the light from the windows reflected off its metal snap buttons.

An idea grew in his mind, and he slowed down his breathing in order to make even less noise than he was already making.

He moved instinctively, and with smooth, controlled movements, he slid open the drawer in the nightstand. Inside, he found what he was looking for. On the left side, he felt the round leathery curves of Nestor's wallet, and on the right, his pistol. He had guessed, and he got lucky on the first try.

Felix's hand reached in, closed around the steel, slid out of the drawer, and he retraced his steps, taking his time, knowing that rushing would only bring on mistakes.

He left the door ajar. He walked back down to his room, and he zipped himself up into his parka and walked back down the stairs, with his pair of boots clutched in one arm. When he reached the back doors in the kitchen, he laced up his boots.

The window overlooked the back of the property. The snowfall had stopped some time before, and the white drifts it had left behind rose to dissing heights.

The moon shone dimly, but there she was, nothing but a weak blue sliver in the sky as a waxing crescent.

Felix's heart beat like a drum, and he had to admit, he was a little excited. This was the end of a long and painful road, and though he could not feel any emotions as he trudged up the hill, he nonetheless hoped that he could find a sort of peace when it was all said and done.

The air stung his cheeks, but there was no wind tonight, just an empty black hole in the sky and an ocean of white powder beneath his boots.

He didn't expect the entrance to the woods to be so dense. In his haste, he hadn't thought of bringing a flashlight or his smartphone, and out here, the gray wash of moonlight made the snow glow, while it turned the woods into a deep curtain of black.

*I have to go in there*, Felix thought.

And so he did. This was his chance. He made sure the firearm was loaded and that the safety was on. Once he entered the depths of the woods, he would flip the safety off.

**1:27 AM ET**

He would leave no note. Any explanation about this act would never fully unpack what Felix felt inside. Words could never represent what he experienced. This state of being wasn't new, and in fact, it was as well worn and familiar as his name. Starting from the age of thirteen, he had felt this ache, this sense of not knowing exactly how he added up, and now, he hummed a song to himself, as he found a clearing, about a hundred feet inside the woods.

He switched the safety off, and the metallic click echoed.

There was a small opening in the canopy above him, and here on the ground, the snow crunched under his feet. There were no rocks, just flat grass that was somehow free of snow, and the whispering wind above his head.

Felix brought the firearm up to his face, and he wrapped his lips around the barrel. Not knowing why, he pulled it out of his mouth, and he tasted the gun oil that Nestor used to clean it. He licked his lips to dissolve the taste.

He placed the barrel on his right temple, and now things felt right.

*No need to wait, let's go.*

As Felix squeezed the trigger, a screeching voice, loud as a thunderstorm, tore through the night.

A powerful sound detonated around him, sending sharp pain inside his ears, and the clearing light up in green light. The world spun, went upside down, and the snatches of white snow swirled with the darkness like oil, as Felix's vision went out completely.

## 1:45 AM ET

Nestor dreamt that he was in an old movie house, the very old kind, like the Beacon Theater in Manhattan, with gilded balconies unfolding around the red curtain of an endless stage, and hundreds of people attuned to the projection of light and sound in the dark. Flanking the stage, statues with large breasts and snake heads instead of human heads writhed, like an infernal cabaret. Someone was making popcorn with coconut oil, which he preferred over butter. He heard a soft crunch of the pepper grinder, as Nestor cracked pepper into a little dish of ground pepper to sprinkle over the popcorn when it was ready. Nestor turned sideways, and he spotted an old woman fanning a tiny coal grill on her lap. The aisles were empty, except for the spot she had staked out with her tiny coal grill on the carpeted floor. She stirred a tiny pot with her right hand. The pot was cherry red, as red as blood, and he was waiting for that first pop, that first kernel, to let him know he could pour the full cup of kernels in to make his favorite treat.

*POP*, he heard in dream.

Nestor turned over, and the arthritic ache in his knees brought him back from the dream and into waking life. The room was very still but the house cozy as could be. He checked his watch on the nightstand. Still a few more hours. He was craving that dream popcorn now, and goddammit, what a great dream.

Suddenly, a wave of nausea crawled from Nestor's belly into his throat. The darkness of the room before him spread out, as if it had wings, and he felt a leathery touch on the back of his neck. Not understanding why, he got out of bed and looked out the window. He rubbed the sleep out of his eyes and saw tracks in the snow, leading from the woods and into the back of Thracian House.

Adrenaline shot through his body. He had dealt with break-ins and intruders before, and the shit had never, ever been pleasant. He slipped on a T-shirt and his jeans, and he yanked his holster over his back. When he reached into the nighstand, he pulled out his wallet, but his firearm was gone.

"Motherfuck," he spat. A churning heat crept up his chest.

Nestor tiptoed down the stairs, and when he reached the kitchen, he could see that the tracks in the snow were not coming into the house but instead going away from it. "Shit!" he spat, and he rummaged in the drawers until he found a pair of flashlights. He burst through the open glass doors of the kitchen and ran up the hill and toward the woods.

### 1:56 AM ET

Nestor ran over dead logs and rocks, and he prayed he heard anything, a moan, a shout, but the night only gave him silence.

He realized then that this was very foolish, to be out here in the cold, with no coat, with the doors of the house left wide open. Maybe he should have grabbed a weapon after all.

Nestor slowed down his pace, and snow crept into his socks where his jeans pulled up and the snow spilled in from the large drifts he cut through. About twenty feet ahead, he caught a snatch of something blue, or maybe gray. It lay still.

Nestor prayed under his breath, wishing for God to give him courage, because right now, he felt like he had none.

He stepped over a clump of rocks, dodged a thick branch, and walked around a tree trunk. When he stepped through the opening, he found himself in a clearing.

Felix lay inert, face up, and blood sprayed everywhere around his head, like a fountain. Nestor gasped and took three clumsy big steps forward.

And that's when the green creature that was stalking him in the branches lowered itself and hissed.

## 2:01 AM ET

The shape was hard to make out, and it had to be very big, because it blocked out the meager light from the moonlight up above, but Nestor didn't give a fuck. He shone both flashlights up toward the shadow to get a good look.

It was draped from tree to tree, and its long limbs were latched into the branches. Nestor swept the lightbeams in the dark, and the surface that they uncovered was slick, metallic, and dotted with thousands of green eyes, which blinked according to their own rhythm. And just about eight feet above Nestor's head, a thick head on a muscular neck twitched, like an old VHS tape stuttering while playing on a cathode television. It opened its mouth, and millions of metal clicking sounds rained down on Nestor, making pain bloom in his ears.

"Fuck," he said, and fell on his knees. He did not let go of the flashlights. He shone them up again at the thing, which hung like a circus tent above the clearing. He tried shining it on the face, hoping to scare the creature. But what he saw turned his blood cold.

The creature's face was most definitely that of a bird, one that was easily fifteen or twenty times bigger than any bird in the natural world, and it stared at Nestor with four eyes which glowed with the rich sweetness of honey, but whose irises felt distant, as if from a place that was not of this Earth.

The animal opened its beak and emitted more clicks, and this time, their texture became gooey, like taffy, like the fat bass sounds in a hip-hop track.

Nestor had no time to lose. He tucked the flashlights in his back pockets and crawled as fast as he could toward Felix. Nestor's firearm lay next to the young man, and blood poured out of his right temple.

This was all Nestor's fault, and suddenly, everything was much too confusing.

*It's a demon above you. Kill it,* he thought.

He held onto the back of Felix's neck, and he was about to check his pulse, when the being above him croaked words that sounded just like English yet had a rough copycat quality them.

"It's a demon above you. Kill itttttttttttt," it said, turning that last consonant into a harsh sound, echoing and unforgiving, like a cathedral bell.

Nestor fumbled with his hand until he could place it on Felix's throat. Holy shit, there was a pulse, a real pulse. He could almost taste the adrenaline on his tongue, and though he was happy to find life in Felix's body, he had to get him away from this situation.

Nestor dragged Felix away, and Felix grunted. As he propped him up to a sitting position, a new gush of blood burst from his head.

"No, goddammit, no," Nestor said, and as he put his hand up to Felix's forehead to look for the wound, the sound of giant wings roared around him. The trees lit up in neon shades of teal and red, and the thing above him landed, shaking its two impossibly long wings, knocking tree branches out of the way. It stood at least twelve feet tall, maybe fourteen. It took two steps on sickeningly sharp talons and leaned down into the clearing. It opened its curved beak, and screamed at Nestor, as its body turned into green smoke and its eyes roared with violence.

The animal used its strong neck to knock Nestor over, and he hit the trunk of a tree with his face and shoulder.

He turned around as fast as he could, but the animal was already sitting on top of Felix and trying to bite his face.

**2:15 AM ET**

Now that Nestor could see the full clearing, he recognized the shape of the being. It was an owl, but it was unlike any owl he had ever seen in his life. Its feathers vanished and curled into the air as they turned into wisps of smoke, and the clicks it emitted bounced through the woods, as if the animal could make sound disperse in whatever direction it wanted.

It turned its neck and glanced at him, as its sleek body roiled with smoke.

"SHHHHHHHHHHHHHH," it said, and it looked at Nestor directly with its double pairs of circular eyes. When he heard that sound, he felt a tiny flicker of tension drop in his belly, and he looked down at his jeans. He had wet himself.

The being opened its beak, and two protuberances emerged. At first, they looked tongue shaped, but soon they glowed orange like hot coals, and Nestor could see little eyes on their tips and a small forked tongue jutting from their tiny jaws. They were two snakes, and they slid over Felix's forehead and temples, lapping up the blood that gushed from the wound.

The owl creature then emitted four bell sounds, forlorn and melancholy, and Nestor felt a sadness sweep over him like a breeze, just like on the day when his grandmother had died. Then the two snakes turned to Felix.

Before him, one of snake tongues kissed Felix's eyelids. The other felt around his temple, rubbing its jaw on his skin. The serpent pulled its head away from Felix. In its jaws it held a round shape, flattened but definitely a bullet from Nestor's firearm. The snake slid the tiny nugget of metal around in the air, as if playing with it, while the other snake made coils in the air with its body. They both retreated into the mouth of the owl creature, and the monster stepped off Felix's body. It shut its four eyes for a moment, and then it spat out the bullet over at Nestor's feet. The nugget hissed in the snow, melting the ice around it.

Felix groaned, and he put a hand up to his forehead. His eyes were still shut, but life was coming back into his body, giving him movement. Nestor cried at the sight of his friend shifting in the snow.

The owl unfurled one wing, and suddenly, the smell of decay— a mix of rotted fish, bacterial infection, rancid organs and wilted fruit—came off in waves from the animal. The wing extended like a giant sheet of rain, and inside its folds, the hundreds of green eyes blinked. The tip stopped before Nestor's right pec. The owl bowed its head.

*It wants permission to touch me?* he thought.

"Touch," The creature said in its copycat voice, which now took on the quality of a thunderstorm.

Nestor genuflected and despite his confusion, fear, and a creeping wave of guilt, moved his arms away from his body, to move into a submissive position so that the monster could touch him.

### 2:34 AM ET

Nestor's vision flickered in waves of emerald and black, and he lost the connection to his skin, his ears and eyes. The world blew out, and he was left empty.

A sensation swelled at his center. Now he could feel his heart, the muscular organ which pumped blood. Nestor could see into the chambers of his heart, and he rejoiced in its beauty. The walls were strong, unmarred, and the blood itself was salty, almost translucent, sweet as ambrosia—and yet he understood this without his senses. He had no body inside this vast ocean of blood, and yet he recognized his own heartbeat with as much certainty as when he recognized his own voice.

The heartbeat slowed down, and suddenly, the blood around him washed away, like seawater leaving a peninsula. Before him, a vast galaxy began to appear, and as the crimson color receded into the vast vacuum, the lights of the stars began to radiate harder, faster, and Nestor marveled at the dazzling colors that burst from dead suns, newborn nebulas and mineral-rich planets.

Nestor began to travel backward in time, and as much as he tried to look down, up, or sideways, he could see no body or physical shape correspond to what he felt was his presence in this place.

He zoomed backward past a vast galaxy shaped like a cathedral door, crossed the threshold, and inside, he fell down and sideways at the same time, into a black hole in which no light existed. He came close enough to its surface, as if he were peering into a window or mirror, and it was then that the owl creature from the woods screeched in a series of polyphonic shrieks. Nestor laughed with no throat or voice as he felt the high-pitched cries rattle him, because he felt them *inside* of his consciousness, but not in physical form. After all, no sound carries in a vacuum. Yet the song of the owl flowed, dripped, and poured into his being.

Nestor's thoughts no longer formed in sentences. Instead, it was images and sounds that filled his being. As he stared into the nothingness that black hole, he pulled back, and the rim of the circle became solid, as yellow as golden corn, and soon, he pulled back further, and he could see he was no longer staring at a galaxy but at the face of the owl creature and its four eyes. The beak was hard and shone like metal. The animal's body grew, and Nestor felt an immense joy in seeing the way in which the monster's feathered body defied all laws of physics. Nestor's consciousness was all at once macroscopic, the size of a planet, and microscopic, as small as a single cell, and he could now see the creature with clarity, precision, sharper than anything human eyes could show him. Just as soon as he could glimpse the diagonal lines of the feathers on the animal's body, the feathers would vanish into thick smoke, and the sounds of something akin to a stringed instrument, like a violin, swelled deep inside the animal.

Nestor's vision pulled back, faster than was possible for human eyes, yet slow enough to appreciate the journey. Before he could realize it, he was back inside his body, and the animal was just two feet away from him, towering like a mountain, and still touching Nestor's pec with its feathered wingtip. Now that Nestor had his body back, the smell of burning coal, like the smell of a campfire, rolled off in waves from the creature.

The clicks and shrieks were no longer bursting from the owl's beak, and instead, Nestor could feel the words that the creature emitted, crisp and clean in English, even though the animal did not utter a single sound.

"You have to continue to save him," it said. "He is Felix, the Collector."

Nestor nodded. "Who are you?"

"I am she, and he, together. I am the daughter and son of my parents, whom I miss very much. This is my name."

The creature said its name and the sound it made tore through the night like a symphony, lasting a full thirty seconds. The name sounded like the mellow gurgle of water in a mountain stream, as well as the hiss of a caldera, full of hot steam and deadly fumes.

"Sounds like Tecolote," Nestor said, invoking the Spanish word for *owl* that he had learned from his mom and dad.

"A long time ago, people on this continent called me Tecolotl, yes, and you may call me that. My other name is 1-Knife."

"What did you do to my friend?"

"I removed the metal postcard from his head."

"Metal postcard?"

"That's what your weapons remind me of. Missives made of metal, meant to invoke my mother and father, but corruptions borne of human hubris."

"Who are your parents?"

"The Lords of Death," the creatures said, and the ground shook. "Mictlántecuhtl and Mictecacihuatl. They rule the realm of Mictlán, which my siblings and I also call The Coil."

When Nestor felt those two names, his chest rumbled and his

skin tingled. He was afraid, and his heart beat like a jackrabbit's dash through the snow before being snatched by a predator.

Nestor looked around the clearing. The air had taken on a bluish appearance, and the temperature was suddenly comfortable, even though the winter freeze of the nor'easter hadn't risen in any way.

"I have been trying to communicate with your friend, to tell him it's not his time yet," the bird said. It licked its lips with its lava-bright snake tongues, and its four irises flickered open and shut in a spiral motion. *Jesus Christ, its eyes are like camera shutters,* Nestor realized.

"But…why?" Nestor said, as he hooked his right hand over the wing which touched his body. His hand held onto a firm yet vanishing body, and smoke danced in the air, tinting the air with the colors of seafoam and blood.

"I have been traveling in time through the Wheels," the Tecolotl said, "and you have an important part to play. You see, the world I am from emptied out, and now the flow of the Wheels has a rift in it."

"Tell me about this rift."

"The rift will tear through time, distorting, bathing all in chaos. The rift must be stopped."

"I don't understand."

"You don't understand rifts, nor Wheels, because your species is living under a deception of its own senses. But that doesn't mean it precludes you from achieving that someday."

The Tecolotl brought its face inches before Nestor's. Its eyes spun like galaxies, and he understood that he was looking at something that was old, perhaps as old as the sun, the moon, and stars in the sky. Although Nestor didn't feel afraid, he also did not like staring into its face. It was like staring at the sun.

"So, how did you find us?"

"She sent me to you," the Tecolotl said. "In your world she has been called Xochiquetzal. She is another being like my mother and father, and yet she is different."

"How different?"

"She is not one of the Lords of Night. She…" the Tecolotl said, twisting his head 180 degrees so he could look behind him at Felix, "she is one of the Lords of the Day. And she said the gates of time and space are opening. She too wants to help stop the Rift."

"Help me, please; I don't understand," Nestor said.

"The gates can't be stopped from opening, but we need to prepare living things for the event. My brothers and sisters are coming through the gates. And someone on this side of the gates, one of your brothers and sisters, has invoked Xipe Totec, very dangerous member of our family."

The way in which the Tecolotl said *Xipe Totec* sent vibrations through air, as if the very atmosphere were shimmering.

"So, you know him?"

"I have never seen Xipe Totec's face," Tecolotl said. "To do so would mean instant death for me."

"And what happens if Xipe arrives here on Earth?"

"That I do not know, Nestor. What I know is that your species has decided to harm its kin instead of helping each other, like an immune system attacking itself."

"And you? Why are you here?"

"I told you. I had to help your companion Felix. This was not his time to die. If it were, I would have collected him myself to take him back to Mictlán."

"Mictlán from the old stories?"

"Yes. We who live there also call it the Coil, but Mictlán will do."

Mictlán was a place of death, rot and darkness, according to the stories Nestor had learned from his mother and grandmother.

The monster opened its beak and the snakes emerged, hissing and spitting sparks. "I have called forth the Volatiles to help you and the others, Nestor."

"Volatiles?"

"More children of the gods. Children of the Nine Lords of Night and even a few who are children of the Nine Lords of Day. There are some right here with us right now."

The trees shifted and undulated, as if made of taffy. They parted in gray waves, and behind their solid trunks, Nestor saw new figures. A macaw red as ruby with a tongue full of needles, staring at him from four eyes. And behind that animal, more bird shapes, each one larger than the next, terrifying in their size and non-terrestrial presence. The trees undulated and closed again, sealing the space of the clearing again.

"Please, just tell me this is a dream, and that you are just a hallucination."

"No such thing, Nestor Buñuel. I know your name, and thus, you are no longer inaccessible to me."

The Tecolotl rose, unfurled its wings, and the thousands of eyes of their interior stared at him. So many of them, each one as threatening as the eyes of a predator. He wanted this nightmare to end, and if was dead, he wanted peace and the hope of seeing a heaven.

"I see you, many times and over," Tecolotl said. "I may not be as clever as my mother and father, but I have inherited many of their powers. I see you, Martina, I see you Nestor, and I see you, Collider."

"Collider is one of my names?"

"It's a pity it took you this long to learn it."

"What is your gender?" Nestor said, as his legs turned to jelly.

The beast answered with a musical cry full of whistles, shrieks, drumbeats and a lone howl. Though Nestor couldn't fully process this sound, he felt satisfied with the answer. "You may use *he* in your tongue for now, but don't forget that time is as thin as water slipping through your fingers. Everything vanishes, and all of this— becomes just an image."

The Tecolotl took three steps back, tore a branch from a tree, and ate it. As he swallowed the bark, the wood burst into fire in his gullet and belly, and the body glowed orange, as if hot coals resided inside its breast. The insects living in the wood that escaped through the Tecolotl's beak grew to the size of doves and buzzed off into the woods.

"You worship killing in this world, and trust me, more death is coming, Nestor. Whatever you do, don't stop listening to what I am trying to tell you. Because I am loyal."

The Tecolotl leapt into the air and flew straight up into the sky, knocking over branches, and igniting into a ball of flame. Burning embers rained around Nestor, and the creature flew upward, until it was nothing more than a green pinpoint of smoke against the pale sliver of moon.

**2:50 AM ET**

Nestor slung Felix over his shoulder and heaved. His legs carried him out of the clearing, and into the snow drifts. The moonlight cast a glow over the woods, the lake and Thracian house.

Trudging through the snow was more difficult on the way back than on the way there. He prayed Hail Marys under his breath, and he could only think of getting medical attention for his friend.

He slid on the threshold as he entered the kitchen of Thracian house. Not understanding why, he carried Felix back to his sleeping quarters.

He set the man down on the bed, and the moon washed his skin blue. He was still breathing.

Nestor put his hand up to the rivulets of blood at Felix's temple. The blood had caked itself into a brown crust, and the skin beneath lay smooth, untouched.

"Where is the bullet hole?" Nestor said out loud. Felix groaned, and turned over, as if he were dreaming.

The shadows of the house thickened, and Nestor felt a deep dread, unlike any he had known in his life. He looked for signs of movement through the windows, but the woods were as still as a mountain now. He sat next to Felix, praying hail Marys until he lost count. Shortly before dawn, Felix began to stir awake. Nestor slipped out of the room before Felix could see him. The last thing Nestor wanted was to discuss what he had witnessed out in the clearing. As he slipped into his own bed, his skin burst into gooseflesh, and he was sure that someone, something, was staring at him through the darkness. He was still whispering Haily Marys to himself even as he dozed off to sleep.

### 9:11 AM ET

Nestor tossed the last bag into the trunk and blew air into his hands. Goddammit, he should have put his gloves on. The air was so cold, it burned. He glanced at the house, and the sun's rays blinded him for a moment. The thermometer in the car read negative five degrees Fahrenheit.

Felix sipped a cup of coffee from a travel mug as he exited the front of the house. Meyers followed behind.

"Detective," Meyers said, "you are quite the early riser. You somehow got showered and ready unbeknownst to me."

Nestor smiled out of the corner of his mouth and nodded. "Got lots of work to get back to." The truth was, he wanted out of this infernal mansion in the woods as fast as he could. It didn't seem as if Meyers had noticed any of the horrors from the night. The snowfall had picked back up, and the wind helped smooth out a bit of the trail Felix and Nestor had left in the snow in the back of the house.

Meyers played with the cuffs of his heavy parka, straightened out his back, and tapped Felix on the shoulder.

"Truly, come back whenever you want to access the archive," he said.

"Good thing," Felix said and straightened the knitted cap on his head. Felix looked about twenty pounds lighter than his previously rakish frame.

Nestor was not afraid of Meyers, but as he approached the driver's side of the car, he looked away from Meyer's stare. Felix was already seated on the passenger side and shut his door.

"Nestor," Meyers said, as the sun washed out his fair skin and drew a hard shadow across the right side of his face. "Now you know why I told you not to mind the creatures that howl in the woods."

Nestor felt a knot tighten in his throat.

"Come again?"

"It's all right, Detective. I am not alarmed about what you did last night. As long as what you saw in those woods did not alarm *you*."

"I don't know what you're talking about."

"I seriously don't mind whatever you and Felix did in the woods. If it's love, it's love."

"We are not lovers, Gregory. That's not what went down."

"None of my business. But I am curious— what does the creature in the woods look like?"

Nestor didn't know exactly why he felt like pretending innocence, but he continued. "What creature?"

"Oh, Sam used to rave about a tall creature in the woods that he said haunted one of the meadows just beyond the big hill. Sam said the thing's utterances kept him up late at night. He claimed it howled and screeched at night. I think that's what drove him to enter the horror genre and direct *The Marsten House*."

Nestor shook his head. "Look, we have to get going."

"If you want to play it that way, that's fine, Nestor. Just don't remain a stranger, okay?"

"This thing Kahan said he saw, did it have a name?"

"Not that I recall. Sam only described how it sounded, like music from another world, like an odyssey in space."

Nestor shut the door and pulled out of the driveway, which, thank God, was clean enough to drive through. His hands shook as he turned the steering wheel. Inside his parka, he was sweating and wishing he would never see Thracian House ever again in his life.

## 10:11 AM ET

They had just driven past the town of Monticello on I-84, amidst a sonic barrage of Felix's favorite death metal bands, when Felix's slender hands flicked the stereo off. They drove in silence for a few minutes as Felix fingered his smartphone in his pocket. He wanted to check it out of habit, but it wasn't time yet. Not yet.

"Thank you for coming to get me," he said. They hadn't yet talked at all about what happened the night before.

"Anytime," Nestor rumbled. The detective drove with his tongue poking out of the right side of his mouth, as if he were working out a math problem. "But do you remember what happened, Felix. What you did?" When Nestor said this, he kept his eyes fixed on the road, as if he was afraid to look at Felix.

"I don't know exactly what you want me to tell you."

"I think you do."

"No, I really don't. If you want to know why I took your gun—"

"No, I got that. And if you ever do it again, I will kill you myself."

"I don't like the aggression in your words. That in itself is an act of violence against me."

"Felix shut the fuck up and just level with me, SHIT!" Nestor said. His eyes never strayed from the blacktop and the car's dashboard.

"Got it," Felix said.

"I already know why you took my gun. If that's what you were going to do to yourself last night, I can't judge you."

"Isn't suicide a sin for you Catholics?"

"Look, I don't want to talk about theology. I want to know, why last night? Why the woods out behind Thracian House?"

"I don't have answers to those things. It was my time."

"Clearly, it wasn't. Because you failed at the task," Nestor said.

The cop said this without any reproach. He simply sounded factual.

"I no longer cry tears when I think about the word *suicide*," Felix said.

"I don't either. I have collected a lot of Laments and other suicides in the city. Kinda numb to it except when it's someone that matters to me."

Another stretch of silence spread throughout the interior of the car. Felix bit his lip and tapped his knuckles on the passenger-side window.

"Just seemed like a beautiful place to do it. That's all."

"That's all."

"Yeah, you happy with that, *Detective*?"

"Call me Nestor. Okay?"

"Yes, Nestor, it seemed peaceful out there."

"And did you see something, or someone, when you reached the clearing?"

"You're fucking strange, you know that?"

"Did you see *something or someone?*"

"I saw NOTHING. I walked alone into the clearing and after one failed try, I pulled the trigger. Just a lot of color black and green. Next thing I know, I wake up back in my bed, with a crazy scratch on my head that somehow healed up already." Felix yanked his cap off his head and looked in the mirror set into the visor. There wasn't even a scar.

"And so you grabbed my gun, pulled the trigger, and you saw nothing, heard nothing."

"What the hell do you want me to say, Nestor?"

Felix snapped his head around to yell into Nestor's ear, but he stopped when he saw what Nestor was doing. The detective was crying. He made no sounds, but tears rolled down his face, which had now gone wet and sullen, as if the deepest despair in the world had taken over his whole being.

"I saw something," Nestor said, his voice broken, and his shoulders losing all their shape as he sagged into the driver's seat. Felix understood then that this was not just a travel buddy; this was someone who had crossed a threshold into the category of friend. *If I only I was good at listening to him, at saying the right thing*, Felix thought, but then he tossed the thought aside.

"Tell me what you saw."

Nestor explained his experience, the way in which the wings of the creature spread across the open canopy like a mantle, and the way in which it flew down onto his body. Nestor described a bizarre out of body experience, and Felix had no words to say when Nestor described planets living inside the creature's four eyes on its face, or the unbelievable tale of snakes made of molten lava emerging from the thing's beak. But he did his best just to listen.

When the cop was done, all Felix could think was *He has lost his mind more than I have.*

### 11:01 AM ET

"I can't help you with what you saw," Felix said. "I honestly don't remember anything. I shot myself, and I expected to never come back again."

"I think that creature, the Tecolotl, prevented you from offing yourself."

"You said he was the child of the gods of death?"

"That's what he told me. He smelled of death: burning hair, rotting wood, decayed flesh."

"Very clearly you must have had a hallucination. There's no accounts of such *children* in the mythology of the Aztecs."

"The visions—what I experienced inside its eyes—felt just as real as this world."

"I don't know what to say."

"Just listen to me, please. Only listen."

"Okay."

"It said another goddess wanted to help. Xochiquetz—"

"Xochiquetzal. The maiden. Goddess of female power, fertility and beauty."

"The Tecolotl said she called forth the birds to help us."

Felix shook his head and drew circles on the condensation on the windows. Fuck, he needed to think. The endless highway, the noise from the engine, the growling in his belly and the slight waves of nausea from the hangover — they distracted him, and he needed to think about what Nestor was saying. The weird bullshit he was spewing.

"You and I have been steeped for two days in a lot of lore around the old gods and their stories," Felix said. "I don't want to discount what you saw, but maybe it's good for you to just…take a break."

"You might be right," Nestor said.

Nestor's phone rang, and he picked up using the hands-free assistant in the vehicle. He put his finger up to his lips to make sure Felix remained quiet during the call.

"Nestor, you coming in soon?" The voice that came through boomed. It had the air of authority that made Felix think, *That's one of the bosses.*

"Roads are fairly clean, will be there in about two hours."

"Good. I think you'll be glad to know that there's going to be a handoff at 2 PM."

Nestor pressed his lips and squeezed the steering wheel so hard the plastic squealed.

"And?"

"And I think all of this makes you look good Detective, and it makes me look good. Two things. One, FBI is the right team to handle the case, and two, we now have a suspect in custody."

"What?"

"He turned himself in today. He claims to be the Night Drinker."

"Fuck me," Nestor said, smacking the sides of the steering wheel. "Smith, we'll talk when I get to the station."

"Whatever you wish, Buñuel."

## MANHATTAN
## 1:03 PM ET

The rest of the car ride became a certain kind of torture. The road back into the city was so gray it looked black, and Felix never bothered to turn the radio back on. Instead, they drove in silence through traffic jams and irate drivers on the road.

When they reentered the city, Felix whipped out his smartphone and tapped on the glass with fury.

"Oh, come on," he said. "Come on…"

The phone beeped, and then it went silent, folding itself back up into a flat shape. Felix hummed to himself.

"What are you so happy about?" Nestor said.

Felix snorted. "Flights have resumed out of JFK. Okay, so I have two fun choices. Stop at a bar right now and get hammered before my flight back home to Chicago, or say fuck it, get an Uber, and use my credit card to get hammered at the terminal before my flight back to Chicago."

"But that's why your fucking smiling? I think not," Nestor said Felix's smartphone lay inert, lightless, and the smile was now falling apart.

"I didn't get the job at NYU," he said. "I just got the awkward email turning me down."

"Let me at least drive you to JFK."

"You have a serial killer waiting for you at the station."

"A suspect. He hasn't even been charged, okay?"

"Whatever. Now you can have that glorious moment of a career high to yourself when I shuffle off to the icy Midwest tundra. Oh, wait, you're stuck in the icy tundra now, too."

Neither of them laughed.

"You can just drop me off at a subway station."

"Of course. Whatever you like."

Nestor didn't want their last exchanges to be so dry and businesslike, but the truth was, he was kind of speechless. He really thought Felix would get that teaching job. He was a brilliant man, and a sharp, creative thinker.

"If your suspect confesses," Felix said, "be sure to ask him how he carved those pictographs on Marlene Grue's skin in such a short amount of time. And find out what sort of tools he used."

"I will do that."

"And also ask him how he learned about Xipe Totec. Though the crimes are a bit off in terms of historical accuracy, this person knew his stuff."

"I'll only ask if I get access to him. FBI's got this one, it looks like. I have to worry about 401Ks, my going-away parties and the hangovers I will need to avoid, and whether I will be too poor to live in Queens once my pension kicks in."

"You have your stressful book deadlines too; don't forget those."

"Ah, okay, yeah."

This time, they did laugh together.

"Felix, do you think that Kahan's movie…really does inspire people to…"

"To question themselves?"

"No, I was going to say *to kill other people.*"

"I'll have to get back to ya on that. Did I ever tell you about my mother and our Roku box?"

"No."

"It must have been around 2009, and I was fourteen years old. I was watching *The Dark Knight,* and I asked her if we could rent a few other movies on streaming. She was in the middle of her daily scheduling ritual in a large notebook she kept by the kitchen table. I thought she didn't hear me, so I shouted pretty loudly, *Hey ma, I want to rent some more movies.* After a couple of minutes of silence, she walked into the living room, unplugged the Roku, and tossed it in the trash. *There's no value in movies,* she told me."

"That's fucking harsh."

"The sad part is that I was too meek to say anything back to her. I stayed quiet, pretended like what she did was not a big deal. But I lived under her shadow for a long time. I divorced myself from movies that day, mostly because I didn't want such a thing to happen to me again."

"What did you think of *9 Lords* when we watched it in Kahan's estate?"

"It made me wonder for the first time how movies could be so profound, and also so beautiful."

"We're here."

Felix gave Nestor a brief hug. "If you need any more obscure trivia about the cult of Xipe during the Classic and the Post-Classic period of the Aztec—"

"I will do that, bud."

Felix bounced out of the car and scurried down the subway entrance, and with each fleeting moment, Nestor prayed to the Virgin Mary that Felix Calvo would not try again to kill himself.

## JFK AIRPORT
## 2:45 PM ET

The martini glass cast reflections in double rainbows as the sunlight from the skylight in the JetBlue terminal bounced off the bar. Felix looked at his smartphone, and he felt a pull toward its screen, a burning need to check notifications, to validate time by seeing what was new, and at that moment, he could only think of one person to text. Wes, his roommate, would probably like to know he was coming back home, but then again, he hadn't texted at all since Felix had gotten stranded by Storm Tobe.

*It's preferable that way, actually. Wes is a good friend, but I like that he doesn't hover.*

On the screen, four texts from Felix's mother awaited response. And what was worse, his father had also texted, which meant that his mother had prompted him to check up on Felix's whereabouts.

Felix clicked his tongue and took three savory swallows of the cocktail before him.

He was due back at work tomorrow at 6 AM, in the West Loop Amazon distribution center. At this moment, that was the last place Felix could envision himself.

He glanced up at the skylight, and he saw the most peculiar happening. A plane flew in the sky, headed east, nothing more than a tiny shape. And there, across the lower part of the circular skylight, a shadow darted. It was most definitely something akin to a bird, though its head looked cartoonish, much too large. Felix squinted and saw not just two eyes but four. The eyes blinked, and then in a fraction of a second, the head in the skylight blew away, as if it was made of nothing but vapor.

"Hell to the no," he said, shaking his head and laughing.

He burned through another twenty dollars on his credit card as he nodded to the waitress for another martini.

Felix tried to recall again what he had seen in the clearing in the Thracian Woods, and he still only came up with a curtain of darkness. He supposed it was just as well, because the whole point of taking Nestor's gun to kill himself was to create exactly that, a snuffing-out of light. But, as he sat in the terminal, watching parents care for their toddlers as they left their flights, seeing business travelers gnash their teeth as flights got canceled, and airport staff clean the floors with a lonely kind of resignation, that an idea arrived. It was an idea clear, simple and true, and Felix did not comprehend how it got there, all he knew is that is was a good one.

"Siri, shut off ALL notifications, please," Felix said, and Siri gave off a sad trombone sound.

"Are you sure, Felix?" the agent asked. Siri did not like it when notifications got turned off.

"Yes, Siri. Fuck it."

Siri stayed silent every time Felix used profanity. Its disapproval was obvious, and so passive aggressive.

Once he was sure the phone would not blow up with notifications, he went into his movies app and downloaded three films: *Miedo y Deseo, Kiss at the End of the Universe,* and *Shinigami.* Felix cringed at what the charges would be on his credit card, but he didn't care. The idea was driving him suddenly, and he didn't give a shit about stopping.

His flight would start to board in five minutes. He slammed the second martini, and without looking up from his phone screen, he walked to the gate. The first film, *Miedo y Deseo,* was the first of the thirteen films by Samuel Kahan.

He glanced at a Wikipedia at the full list:

*MIEDO Y DESEO (1966)*

*KISS AT THE END OF THE UNIVERSE (1968)*

*SHINIGAMI (1969)*

*ROAD TO TROY (1970)*

*THE THRACIAN (1973)*

*LEPIDOPTERA (1975)*

*MOMMA DO YOU THINK THEY'LL BREAK MY BALLS? (1981)*

*XENOGENESIS: HER BROOD (1981)*

*KINO LUDOVICO (1984)*

*9 LORDS OF NIGHT (1987)*

*THE MARSTEN HOUSE (1993)*

*HASFORD AND THE BODY COUNT (2000)*

*ØIE (2025)*

Felix's feet carried him as if he were walking on an airy cloud, and for a second, he felt as if time had actually reset, as if it had undergone a hard reboot, and things were starting afresh.

## MANHATTAN
## 3:15 PM ET

Nestor closed his fist around his smartphone so tight that he felt a pop as the glass on its flexible surface cracked.

"Goddammit," he spat under his breath.

Captain Smith passed around copies of the file that had been drawn up so far on the Night Drinker. Three FBI agents, two white and one Hispanic, read the information. None looked up at Nestor, but it was the Hispanic agent that caught his attention. He was almost a foot taller than Nestor, but he had an uncanny resemblance to him. Broad forehead, big brown eyes, and a beard as black as crow feathers. Except for one big difference, of course, and that was that the FBI agent, Marlo Ruiz, was cisgendered. The man was a little leaner than Nestor, but they could have passed for brothers. Nestor studied his movements, the slow twitch in the eye, the small hands, and he got lost in a wave of jealousy and resentment. No, of course it was absolutely irrational that they were replacing him with an agent who resembled him. But he couldn't help his own thoughts.

*They went and got a real man to do the job, you tranny faggot*, Nestor thought, wondering whose voice he heard in his head.

It was absolute stupidity to think it. But the way Smith fawned over the trio of agents, the way in which he dismissed Nestor, it felt like a slap in the face. This should have been his case, especially if a suspect had already come forward.

And yet here they were. This was the end of a long and winding road, and Nestor's final act of his career did not have a particularly heroic or happy ending.

"Nestor, your notes and profile on the crime are impeccable, thank you again," Smith said. "I think agents Piazzo, O'Donnel and Ruiz will take it from here."

"Don't mention it," Nestor said. He was too fucking pissed to speak out. If he did, he might regret his words and actions, and he knew it. The three agents smiled, and Nestor slipped into his sports jacket. He needed to get home and just say *fuck it* to all this shit.

He shook hands, and Ruiz was last. The agent smiled a broad grin.

*What is so fucking amusing, you shit?* Nestor thought.

"I know you're winding down on things, Buñuel," Ruiz said,

"But would you mind joining us later tomorrow in interrogating the suspect?"

"Sure." Nestor was shocked to hear this.

"Having a local cop with us will provide the right balance of people in the room. Trust me, your expertise is much needed."

"What time?"

"10 AM."

"See you then."

Nestor walked out of the station, and looked down at the spiderweb of cracks on his screen. "Fuck shit, fuck, fuck!"

## CHICAGO
## 5:00 PM ET

Felix had consumed *Miedo y Deseo,* released in 1966, like a piece of candy, while he sat next to a man who trimmed and lacquered his nails during the flight. As he watched soldiers try to reach their batallion in an unidentified war, Felix shook his head. He had expected a crime thriller perhaps, but not a love story. As he watched, he stayed alert for the strangeness and the grotesque beauty he had witnessed inside *9 Lords of Night,* but it eluded him. Felix got up to go to the bathroom, and he waited in line behind a short man about his own age, sporting two large earrings and wearing a baseball cap. As he waited, Felix couldn't help but stare at the guy. The bearded face, the masculine features were hot, but he felt something familiar in them. And then he realized that the man was probably a female-to-male trans man, like Nestor. The man in the cap caught Felix staring from the corner of his eyes, and he looked away. Felix felt embarrassment flush his cheeks. When the man exited the bathroom, Felix slid past the door. He pissed fast, and within seconds, he was back at his seat, watching Kahan's second film, *Kiss at the End of the Universe.*

Kahan had released *Kiss* in 1968, amidst student protests, the threat of war, and the imminent arrival of man on the moon, and yet he had chosen to go down the route of noir, with a crime thriller that was far more interesting in its use of shadows and light than in story itself.

*Maybe I overestimated Kahan. Maybe what I saw in 9 Lords was nothing but a lucky break.*

The man sitting next to Felix was done with a first coat of clear nail polish.

"Excuse me for bothering you," Felix said.

"No problem at all."

"Are you a movie guy?"

"Big time. My favorite movie of all time is *Aliens*, and *Jurassic Park* and anything Guillermo Del Toro are up there too."

"I'm not a fan of any of those kinds of movies," Felix said, recalling how Wes had tried to make him watch those blockbusters.

"Are you a religious guy?" The man said, as he put away the bottle of clear polish and pulled out a new one, colored cobalt blue.

"Atheist," Felix said, as he ate Popchips the attendant had just handed to him.

"Then I don't know if you would really be a movie guy like I am," the man said. "It's like they take me somewhere better than this. It's not cool to compare *Jurassic Park* with Heaven, I know, but that's just how I feel.

"Thank you," Felix said, and he continued watching *Kiss*.

## CHICAGO
## 8:00 PM ET

Chicago grew in size as the skyline approached and the CTA Blue Line made its journey southeast into the city. Felix's neck hurt from looking down at his smartphone, but he didn't care.

## QUEENS
## 9:00 PM ET

Nestor forgot to eat that night, and instead of writing, he lay down to sleep. Every muscle ached, and even his joints felt hot to the touch. Maybe he was coming down with something, but before he could speculate further, he plunged into a deep sleep where he dreamt of howling sounds and endless corridors of colored light.

## CHICAGO
## 11:00 PM ET

Felix brought back the whole pizza into his dilapidated bedroom. He shoved aside piles of dirty laundry, books from the University of Chicago library, and mounds of unopened mail.

"Felix, you home?"

Wes' voice echoed out through the tall ceilings of their apartment.

Not too long before, Felix might have felt a sort of shame about how he had holed himself up in his room like this, and yet tonight, despite wanting to ask Wes a million questions about the history of cinema and Samuel Kahan, he slid the pizza box under his bed, ripped off his shirt, dimmed all the lights in the room and he slid into the bed, making sure to lie down on his side so Wes could see his face as he peeked in the room.

Ten seconds later, he heard Wes push the door open.

"Fucking A," Wes said, and laughed. And what a welcome, warm laugh. Felix heard him shut the door, and he waited, like a feline in a cubby hole, until he was sure Wes had moved into the back of the apartment, where the kitchen led into his bedroom. Once it was safe enough to do so, Felix flicked on his laptop, slid the pizza back out, and pressed Play on *Shinigami*, Samuel Kahan's third film, which had been released in 1969. It was based on a novel called *Shinigami* by Yukio Shiroihana, in which the Japanese writer had imagined a version of America in which crime was romanticized even more than by American filmmakers like Orson Welles or Scorsese. In it, a group of criminals tried to steal four million dollars from a California bank, which resulted in bloodshed. As Felix watched the film and the headphones pumped the scratchy sounds of its old dialogue and soundtrack, he wondered what people saw in these old movies. *They feel so fake*, he thought. *The dialogue is so artificial, and by god, the camera never moves!* And just as he was thinking about how boring these old movies could get, he sat up in his bed, with a slice of sausage pizza in his hand.

There it was, an eerie tracking of the camera that felt different from what he had seen in the previous two movies by Kahan. The camera glided, no, it stalked was more like it — the main characters, and how odd, there was a skylight in the bank, creating a shape like a terrifying Art Deco eye. A new silhouette appeared in the skylight.

Was that a bird head? He recalled the shape he had seen at the airport terminal, and he wrinkled his nose. Whatever Nestor had caught in the woods of Thracian House must be sticking to Felix, because that shit looked…identical. He paused on the frames that showed the details, and after staring at it for five minutes, he couldn't be sure. Was it the head of a parrot? Or an owl? Or was it just a shadow, something more abstract and nothing more than series of Art Deco geometries.

Felix sighed and pressed Play again. He watched all the way until the very end of the movie, and when the credits rolled, he fell into deep sleep.

# DAY 9
## TUESDAY OCTOBER 28, 2025

Felix checked the value on his CTA card to see if he could get on the bus. His smartphone lit up and said, "You have negative value of fifty cents on the card."

He could still get to work on time if he could load the card, but he had maxed out his credit card the night before. On the screen, eight notifications from his mother and father had arrived overnight. He could ask them for money, but instead, he flipped the phone screen-side down, so he could think.

"Stop looking at me," Felix said to the smartphone, even though its camera sat inert, like a tiny belly button, looking up at him. He grabbed a kitchen towel and tossed it over the phone.

"Okay, okay, let's think," Felix said. "Now we hunt in the sofa for change."

He scoured every nook and cranny, as well as under his bed, and he only came up with seventy five cents. And Wes was already gone for the day. He fished out his Amazon ID from his pocket at stared at his own photo: the skinny face, the sullen eyes, the thick mustache.

"I look like a goddamn ghost," he said.

He walked back to the kitchen and picked up the phone.

"Hey, Terese, just wanted to let you know I'm not coming into work today."

"You're putting me in a bad position, here," Terese said. "Is there any way you can come in at all? You're gonna make me look so bad if you don't."

Felix relished the tension and anguish he heard on the other side from his manager. She wasn't a bad guy; she was just trying to do her job. But at the same time, fuck her, and the whole place.

"Actually, I quit," he said. "You can send me a check in the mail. Oh, right, corporate policy to only do direct deposit. Oh, you can't? Well, in that case, you all can go fuck yourselves."

He hung up, tossed his ID in the trash, and he headed out of the house on foot.

## MANHATTAN
## 10:10 AM ET

The last person Nestor expected to see was Delia Douglas. She exited the ladies' bathroom and rubbed her hands with lotion she fished out of her purse.

"You look as if you just saw a ghost," she said.

"Delia," Nestor said, and it felt good to say her name. As he approached her, he wanted to open up his arms and put them around her. She was a kind of anchor for him in this madhouse, and yet she felt very far away. Far away enough that he did not attempt the hug. "I was hoping we could—"

"Get lunch? Yep, the Halal Brothers truck is here on Tuesdays now. We can go after you finish with the suspect. You all right? I mean, you look pale."

"I think I need a vacation."

"You want me to make some crack about your retirement, but I'm not gonna."

"I was away during the weekend. Did you catch wind of anything interesting about this guy who turned himself in?"

"I was here when the patrolmen brought him in. Apparently he had uploaded a video of himself to Facebook, wanting to be picked up at his home and brought here. Strange as hell."

"I saw the video. Steve Puttock, from the Bronx. His eyes looked like they were bleeding in the video."

"He burst all his capillaries. We still don't know how."

"Delia, did Smith mention anything about the case, or about my handling of it, while I was out?"

"Nestor, relax. You're doing fine. I have never seen you like this paranoid."

"We definitely need to get that lunch."

"They're waiting for you, Nestor," she said and nodded toward the three FBI agents, who were holding the door to the interrogation room open.

"It's just gonna be you and Ruiz," Piazzo said. "Have at it, gentlemen."

Nestor turned to Ruiz, and nodded. *What do I have to lose?* Nestor thought. *I am down to just a handful of days here, and talking to this suspect is mostly just a case of entertainment. Case will soon be out of my life, out of sight, out of mind.*

Neither Ruiz nor the other agents had prepped Nestor for this interrogation, and it was just as well. He would listen and just observe. The room was bare except for three glasses of water, each one placed precisely before each man. Ruiz and Nestor took their seats, and across from them, Steve Puttock sat upright, with both hands on the table, as if he was ready to lean forward and shake their hands. Puttock had no record to speak of. He had been born in Anaheim, California, and he had worked as a mail carrier, as well as a tech hand for FedEx. He was a writer of sorts, and he had written extensively about his dissatisfaction with America, but otherwise, he had no previous history of violence.

Puttock's long brown hair was streaked with gray, and his beard was completely white. His knuckles were tattooed in a series of bars and dots that had no discernible origin that Nestor could see.

"State your name," Ruiz said.

"Steven Evelyn Puttock."

"This is Detective Nestor Buñuel."

Puttock flashed a smile at Nestor. He was missing several teeth, and his eyes shone bright red, like pools of blood.

"Can you recount what you told us in your Facebook confession?"

"Sure, if you want to put a fine point on it. But I said my piece already in it. I selected a person in the AMC theater on 42nd Street, and I processed her."

"Can you explain what you mean by *process*?"

"I relieved her of the burdens she carried. And I offered her up to someone who could redeem her."

"Let's take that in steps. What burdens did she carry?"

"Take a look around, Agent Ruiz. This is New York City in 2025. That lady had *burden* written all over her face. What can be worse than to be born female and black in this country?"

"You tell me, Mr. Puttock."

"Not much. In any case, I relieved her, and a couple days later, I also relieved a man named Jonas up in Harlem."

"And this man, Jonas, why did you choose him?"

"Similar reasons. To ease his troubles. To elevate him."

"Elevate what?" Ruiz said.

"To elevate his beauty. He had the most gorgeous skin, which I planned to wear as a mantle after I offered it up as tribute."

Nestor had the sudden urge to make sure his mother and niece were okay, and though the heating system of the station blew hot air from the vents at his sides, he felt a chill that struck deep in his heart. This investigation was not supposed to go like this. He was supposed to have solved this on his own, and the suspect was not supposed to be...this.

Puttock winked at Nestor.

"Your buddy here is uncomfortable. Is he going to say anything?"

Ruiz snickered. "We ask the questions here, and Detective Buñuel will address you when he's ready. Understand?"

"Yes, sir" Puttock said, though his smile remained.

Nestor didn't move a single muscle in his face. He appreciated the respect he got from Agent Ruiz, but nothing could shake the sensation he felt of being watched by Puttock, as if the man could somehow see into Nestor's insides, like a CAT scan.

Nestor coughed, adjusted the watch on his wrist, and nodded at Ruiz. He then turned his eyes to lock in on Puttock's.

"You committed these two crimes. Was this your first time?"

"Yes, these were part of my debut."

"Did you intend to do more?"

"Of course."

"Why?"

"You should know better than anyone else, Detective. Because of transformations. You understand transformations, yeah?"

Nestor pressed his tongue up against his palate, reminding himself to keep his face as still as stone. *Goddammit, is he calling me out for being trans?* But he couldn't be sure. He only knew that Puttock was seeing *something* in him.

"Explain what you mean by *transformations*," Nestor said. His voice was nothing but a rumble now. He put aside his fear and let the commanding aspect of his personality guide him. Puttock shifted in his seat.

"Just look at who's in front of me. A Ruiz and a Buñuel. Brownies, beaners, greasers, and spics. You see, what's transforming is America is you, *batos*."

Ruiz frowned but also kept his cool. Nestor simply nodded. "Go on," he said.

"It's not the America we wanted, nor the one we deserved. It's something worse."

"Are you referring to my race, Mr. Puttock?" Nestor said.

"Of course. We are headed to place much worse than we ever could have imagined. A society seen *only* through the lens of race. And full of immigrants, too."

"Are you trying to say that you would like America to be racially segregated?"

"Aw fuck this, you two feds have no imagination. You see, I have been writing for years about this."

"What is *this*?"

"The Millennium Riots, Ferguson, the Chicago Vigilantes. The NRA arming every toothless piece of white trash, and the way those fucks in Washington turn a blind eye to the drug war. I knew this was all coming. And I have been telling the world that we need to go back in time. To a time when these divisions mattered less."

"And what time would that be?" Nestor said. "Because I don't know of any such time."

"Precolonial time, motherfuckers. Oh, excuse my French."

Nestor was doing his best not to let his anger fly off the handle and engage in a historical and political discussion. He did as he learned from the best: instead of being reactive, he let Puttock open up as he spoke further.

"I was there, for the best and the worst of the culture that thrived in the '90s in California. I dated Black women, white women, Chinese chicks too, man. You can't tell me I don't know my shit, and you can't call me a racist, because I have been with them all. But through and through, the same fucking illness, the same societal parasite came coming back: racial oppression. Don't you think people were better off on this continent *before* the Europeans came?"

Ruiz and Nestor remained silent. Puttock took a pause to drink water and continued.

"You see, people forgot that there's some powerful fucking shit back in time. I made an appeal to one of the old gods to make things right. To roll us back in time. We are going to travel into the past, man. It's gonna be freakin' sweet."

Nestor couldn't take it. "Excuse me, but who are you to do this? Are you a person of color?"

"Of course not. Look at me. But, after trying out this American Dream shit, the great melting pot experiment, I think we have to say that it just didn't work out to anyone's benefit in America. Other than a select few who just own all of us. And yeah, those one-percenters all happen to look like me, but fuck them too."

"The mesoamerican civilizations that were here before the Spanish arrived were not utopias," Nestor said. Fuck, he couldn't just stay quiet.

"Sure they were," Puttock said. "They had a connection to nature, they had shamans, fuck, their food was not a fucking poison!"

"But inequality and injustice had to be part of their empires. What makes you think the Mayas, Aztecs, and the other peoples didn't fall prey to the same human fallacies we do?"

Puttock snarled and clicked his tongue at Nestor. He sneered for a moment and mouthed the words *Fuck you* back to Nestor and Ruiz. Clearly Puttock was smart enough to shut his trap once the conversation didn't go his way.

Ruiz checked his watch out of sheer boredom. Nestor could tell things were not looking good. "Tell us about your appeal to this 'god'," Ruiz said.

"I ain't addressing you when I say this," Puttock said, pointing at Ruiz, "because you don't get it. It's your buddy Buñuel here who does. I called upon divinity to guide these tributes I made."

"Tributes?"

"Yes, fucking tributes. And the thing is, I think it's working. You see, I am trying to awaken something that is so old, it has no comprehensible name. Except the people of this continent did have a name for it, a long time ago."

"And what name is that?" Ruiz said.

"The Night Drinker. He's gone berserk, and he's going to help me and a lot of other people."

Nestor picked up a smell like pennies, and when he looked down at his water glass, he saw it was filled with blood, thick and syrupy, just as he had seen in his apartment a few days before. He did not panic. He glanced at the two men to see if they noticed anything. Neither of them did.

"The Night Drinker is coming at us through orthogonal time, and I will be glad to welcome him."

"Orthogonal time?"

"Yeah, man, it's how the beam of dark light comes at me, and it's how it tells me things, feeds me information. And the Night Drinker's gonna travel through that highway of quantum physics to get to me."

"You're not making a lot of sense," Ruiz said. "Let me bring us back to the point here. Why did you kill those two people?"

"Because I am sick of our world, full of niggers, spics, towel heads and chinks and faggots. I have been pushed into this little corner, and I need to breathe. I didn't kill them  because I am not a progressive; it's because there is a fucking tension in my head, an anxiety that feels like it's eating away at me, like rats in the walls. Something tells me we have to put an end to this society, to cleanse it. And we also have to put an end to you, you fucking militarized police pigs, you fucking pieces of Nazi SS excrement. You know what a fractal is, Agent Ruiz?"

"A mathematical concept. A pattern that emanates into macro and micro scales. Looks like the waves in the ocean."

"Exactly. And we are living inside a country full of fractal anxiety, man. We are fucking diseased, all of us in this planet. TV, social media, our addiction to screens and fucking fatty foods, it's killing us without an ounce of dignity. That's why I did this. Because you can't eradicate disease unless you are willing to kill that fucking parasite once and for all."

"You think people of color are parasites?" Ruiz said.

"Ah, fuck this," Puttock said. "You two sissies don't get it. *Everyone* is infected."

Ruiz motioned to Nestor with a nod over his shoulder. He was about to wrap things up. "We are done here, Mr. Puttock."

"I'm still talking, shit," Puttock said, but Ruiz was already standing and buttoning up his coat. Puttock reached out and put his hand over Nestor's forearm. Puttock's touch felt like a lobe of raw liver. "They tried to stop me, man."

"Who tried to stop you?" Nestor said.

"The three fucking birds. One is a fucking giant macaw with metal needles in its gullet man. He tried to warn *her.*"

"Who?"

"Marlene Grue. The bird tried to warn her, to tell her I was coming."

Nestor couldn't believe what he was hearing. He didn't have much time, and he knew it.

"And the other two birds? How did they try to stop you?"

"Same deal. One showed up here in the city, walking on hands instead of talons, man, I saw it myself inside an LSD trip, and I have seen it too, up in these skyscrapers. Like a barn owl with hands. You see, I can hear it talking, even if I am far away, I hear it in my dreams, and I hear it when the beam of light enters my eye. The owl told me it has a brother who's green and made of smoke. Infernal, motherfucker, it was so fucking infernal and demonic. I mean, you're going to stop them, right?"

Nestor got up and ignored Puttock's question. This would be the last time he saw him, if he could help it.

"I am also done here," Nestor said.

"Detective! Tell them you have seen them! Tell the world that you have seen those things. They are trying to stop Xipe from rising, and you have to put an end to it, like I do! TELL THEM!"

Nestor exited the room, behind Ruiz. He felt an ache going down his arm, and he hoped he was not having a heart attack.

Ruiz shut the door and laughed. "Can I buy you a beer?"

"No, not today."

"I mean, that was some Unabomber, Charlie Manson kind of shit. You know he calls his writings his Exegesis?"

"No, I didn't know that."

"We found thousands five-hundred-thousand pages of his writing in his apartment, all of them in longhand."

"Fuck."

"He says a beam of light came down and instructed him to purify the world," Ruiz said.

"By killing people, huh."

"Well, not much different the right-wingers in this great country of hours, but that's a conversation better left for a beer. O'Donnel and Piazzo would agree."

"I'll let you three get to his case. I don't think I am that useful to you at his point."

Ruiz looked at Nestor, appraising something about him. "Early DNA tests already show a match. It's him."

"Good."

"And we found him in the security cameras in the theater. In the halls anyway. Wore a hoodie, passed off as a teenage kid, thanks to that scarecrow frame."

"Sounds like something from a horror movie."

"Funny you should say that, Buñuel. Take a look at this." Ruiz unfolded his iPhone, which unfurled from his palm into a wide screen. Ruiz nodded toward the glass, and the iPhone took that as his command to play a YouTube clip. "Ever seen the movie *Cube?*"

"Can't say I have."

The clip showed a bald man peering into a vast chamber lit in white and black geometric shapes. As he enterd the chamber, his anxiety twisted his face into a frown. Once he entered a trapdoor int he chamber, he found himself in a new room lit in orange. Suddenly, a whooshing sound filled the soundtrack, and an unseen attacker sliced the man neatly and cleanly into grid-like chunks, as an invisible blade mutilated him to death. Ruiz stood close to Nestor, and his bad breath and aftershave filled his nose with repulsion. But Nestor could not pull himself away from the clip on the screen. Because there was something familiar yet terrifying about what he had just seen.

"Now take a look at this," Ruiz said. He showed Nestor a photo of long slabs of plastic with tiny little markings on their surface, small as pores. The plastic was red and shiny, and the slabs reminded Nestor of the tile holders from the game of Scrabble that his mother liked to play so much.

"These are what Puttock used to carve the symbols into the body."

Nestor felt heat under his polo shirt, and he broke out in a sour sweat, the kind that often signals the arrival of a flu virus. How had he forgotten to ask about the markings? He must be in the real shitter, because even these small details were escaping him.

"I'm sorry, I'm not feeling great," Nestor said,"mind if I touch your screen to zoom in on these?"

"Of course not. Siri, I have a guest coming. His name is Nestor."

"Hi, Nestor," Siri said, and Nestor zoomed in by pinching his fingers, without having to unlock the screen.

"I realize you had this case pulled from you," Ruiz said. "But I think your opinion matters a lot on this. These plastic tools are called Cube-Its. Anyone can buy them off Amazon."

"Eh?" Nestor said.

"You don't cook much, do you?"

"Humor me."

"Three years ago, a startup launched a Kickstarter that combined a 3-D printer and an AI—excuse me, a neural network—to develop a cutting tool that could carve and etch into meats."

"I don't follow."

"It's tech-nerd stuff, but these developers gave the computer clips from the movie *Cube* and gave it the goal of making cutting tools to etch designs into meat."

"And the computer came up with these."

"Exaclty. The Kickstarter prototypes were used in a Food Network cooking show, and they are now more popular than ever. Sharper than Japanese chef knives, and only a tenth of the price. Delivered right to your door by Amazon. And customizable. You can use them to write your name into a steak or to draw little dicks on a chicken breast. Once you grill it the right way, you have the equivalent of a kid's name written on a birthday cake."

"I looked at the photos of the body for dozens of hours. If these tools are pressed firmly into the skin, they would make very precise cuts, with the fidelity of a master surgeon, but much more painful, of course."

"Which leads me to my question, Detective. What do these symbols mean? You brought in a field expert to look at them, didn't ya?"

The hallway suddenly went from stuffy to damp and cold, and Nestor brooded in silence for a moment, noticing how his own dread expanded inside his chest, the way it made him want to sink into the floors of the police station. This was a sense of dread worse than any he had ever known. Ruiz could indeed be a spitting image of himself, and yet, Nestor felt like his own intuition was failing him now, too. He couldn't read the man. He couldn't make a decision quickly enough on whether he could trust him, or not. If he told him what he knew, he could finally let go of this case, and pass it off to this FBI agent like some sort of eternal haunted-house curse.

"We looked at the symbols many times over, and all the evidence came up inconclusive."

Nestor couldn't let yet go. He had never lied to another investigator like this. But before he could think about the consequences, Nestor pumnped Ruiz's hand.

"It's been a pleasure, Agent Ruiz."

"Yep. Look, stay in touch, will ya?"

"You bet."

As Nestor walked back to his desk, he wondered if the taste of copper in his mouth was real or imagined. He put his fingers to his lips and they came away clean, even though he had expected blood to stain the tips.

## CHICAGO
## 12:00 PM ET

Felix lurked inside the aisles of the library, and he occasionally saw the lone patron, wandering, walking past the open spaces. Halloween was just a few days away, and two stands of books called out for his attention, but he slide past the garish orange cardboard cutouts and dove into the DVD section. He loaded his arms with discs, and wouldn't you know it, they had every single item on his list, except one. He scanned his list on his phone and checked each one off.

"*The Marsten House*," the librarian said, keeping her eyes on the discs as she scanned each item.

"You've seen it?"

"Once. And never again. Too scary for me. But you—" she said and peered at Felix through here eyes. "Maybe you don't get scared by movies like this."

"Maybe. Maybe not," he said.

Once the librarian scanned all of the discs, Felix let out a sigh of relief. He stopped at Chipotle to get some food and took it to go. He had a lot of movie watching to do in his room.

## MANHATTAN
## 1:15 PM ET

Nestor took a seat in the break room facing Delia. He took one bite of his sandwich, and he fell into a deep state of bliss, in which the silky fats of the meat, the savory taste of the flat bread, and the fragrance of the herbs and spices took him to another place. He needed the escape now more than ever.

"Wow, is this what it takes to get away from your Tupperware lunches?" Delia asked.

Nestor could only nod. The flavors of the food left him speechless.

"Something happened to you," Delia said.

"Life happened to me."

"Carson Mitchum was sniffing around here last week. He thought you might be in some midlife crisis."

"All I can say is that before this weekend, I felt as if the city has been draining me."

"We all feel that Nestor. I've known you a long time, and you love this city."

"It's true."

"But you look like shit. What's happening?"

"I'm never going to fit in with the average cop in this place, and I have been okay with that for a long time. It's strange–it's not cops that have me worn out; it's everything. My mother, my notifications on my phone, my worries about being broke by age fifty-five, it's just —"

"Okay, you need to take five," Delia said, and she put a hand up to Nestor's pec. She touched the same spot where the Tecolotl monster had fused its consciousness to him, except Delia's touch was welcome, loving even. He felt his heartbeat slow down, and she pulled her hand away.

"I really thought I would just keep the momentum on this case, Delia, but it's as if rather than seeing the world around me as a projection of what I wanted it to be, I saw it for how it actually is."

"And how is it?"

"An ocean of chaos."

Delia smiled, wiped her mouth with a paper napkin, and winked at him. "I think maybe Carson was right. No offense."

"No, it's not like that. I have seen things that are hard to explain, things no one would believe."

"Trust me, I have too. Is it because of the two victims?"

"No, just Marlene Grue. Every time I see her lifeless face, I keep thinking, why? Who can commit such atrocities against another human being?"

"Well we know who. What was he like?"

"Absolutely deranged. Paranoid. A mix of alt-right and deep-left insanity. I keep wanting for someone else to be the killer, not him. Because he doesn't make any sense as a killer."

"Nestor, this is what you just mentioned. You are trying to project your wishes onto the world. What if Puttock really is the killer?"

"In that case, he's also a madman. He's written half a million words on what he calls a message from another place."

"You need to let him go. And I hate to say this, but you need to let Marlene go, too."

Nestor felt very far away from his friend Delia Douglas in that moment, even though he wanted to be close to her. He thought that maybe, if she were open to the idea of dating a trans man, it would be nice if she agreed to have dinner with him sometime, but with each passing minute, he felt as if the room was closing in on him. Of course she wouldn't want to date a retired cop with nothing in his bank account other than the residuals from novels that didn't pay the rent. Of course not.

But he couldn't be sure that was what she was thinking, either. It was as if this very place, this police station, was marring his thoughts. He remembered how certain spots in the city would sometimes create interference with radio signals, and he felt it now.

And just as he wallowed in these thoughts, another idea arrived.

"I think I'm going to use the rest of my vacation days to just play hooky," Nestor said.

Delia smiled a grin more beautiful than any sunset. "This, I like, my brother."

## CHICAGO
## 4:00 PM ET

Felix fingered the golden top of a bottle of Cuervo. Though he was craving a drink, he could not bring himsefl to open the bottle.

The credits rolled on *Road to Troy*. Felix googled images of Kirk

Douglas, and he fondled himself at the faded scans of black-and-white photos in Google Images search results. Man, he had been hot. How had he never thought of looking up these old movies?

Felix texted Wes.

*You've been holding back.*

*Oh, what do you want now? LOL.*

*Why didn't you tell me about* Road to Troy? *It's good.*

*Oh, now the brand-new film studies queen rises. Thought you might be dead, bitch.*

*Maybe I was.*

*Whatever. If you liked* Road to Troy, *you will love the next one.*

The Thracian.

*Yep. Flawed, corrupted by the Hollywood Studio system, and yet a fucking hot take on Spartacus.*

*I have a few of these movies here. Let's catch one tomorrow?*

*Can't. Going out of town. Get the job at NYU?*

*Nah.*

Wes punched through a GIF of a puppy dog with eyes so sad they shimmered with tears.

The buzzer rang. Felix checked his phone, and his dating app confirmed that Henrik, age 24, had arrived.

They greeted each other on the steps of the apartment, and Felix swept the DVD cases off the mattress before he and Henrik lay down to fuck.

Henrik's face and body were beautiful, and tattoos covered his chest, biceps, and even his knees. They fell into a heap of skin, hair and sweat. Their cum, when it arrived, was voluminous, wetter than the ocean, and free of guilt.

When Henrik washed up and left, Felix threw on a sweatshirt and shuffled back into his bedroom. The tequila bottle stared at him again, and he felt a strange buzzing, like an alarm clock in a dream, go off throughout the house. And yet there was no source for it. He checked his phone, thinking the noise might be a phantom vibration. As he held the expensive gadget in his hand, it occurred to Felix that of all the friends in the world whom he wanted to text, it was Nestor, who rose to the top of his mind. Henrik, who had just left, was the first trans man that Felix had ever slept with, and he wanted to share the news with Nestor, to share a certain kind of joy in disclosing his sensual escapade.

And yet, he knew that it was a very bad idea to do so. What

would he be trying to prove, that he was a very well-educated academic who just had to prove his liberal tendencies to the one trans person whom he actually knew well? Nestor would laugh in his face, before telling him to get the fuck out. Felix wouldn't be special; he would just be showing the way in which he exoticized marginalized people.

"Stop it," he said out loud. "There you go, imagining every fucking scenario. STOP IT."

Felix wandered out into the hallway, stomping in figure eights through the vintage apartment. He soon caught himself falling back into those thoughts of guilt and worthlessness, and he said out loud once more, "Okay, stop it. Just do what you would do, not what you think you should do."

He picked up the phone and instead of texting, he called Nestor, who picked up on the third ring.

"What you got for me?" the detective said.

Felix felt so stunned that someone would actually pick up the phone, but after all, Nestor could be old enough to be his dad, and it was that generation that still liked talking on the phones.

"I'm still working on some ideas about why Kahan was so obsessed with Xipe Totec, and why he surrounded himself with the images of the Nine Lords of Night."

It was better to just start talking business, and to not mention what had just happened. He still wanted to share something deeper with Nestor, but this was not the time.

"I like that. You will need to pass that on to the FBI."

"What gives? You're a hundred percent off this case?"

"By choice."

"Bullshit."

Nestor's silence came through the wireless phone line in deep waves. Finally, the detective laughed on the other end. "JAY KAY!"

"What?"

"That's the phrase you say, right? *JK*?"

"Ha ha yes, but…why are you saying it? You don't talk like that."

"It's good to hear your voice," Nestor said, but the detective's voice cracked, as if he were about to break into tears. Odd.

"You too," Felix said, and that tiny exchange of two sentences, that was just good enough for now.

"So, what's the theory?"

"I am still going through all the Kahan films, but in each one, I have spotted one of the nine birds that are correlated with each of the Nine Lords of Night."

"Oh, really?"

"Yes. They are a pair of hummingbirds, one blue and one green. A dove, a quail, a raven, a turkey, an eagle, and get this: a butterfly. The Aztecs lumped it in as a Volatile."

"That's only seven."

"That's because there are two special ones; hold on, don't rush me. There's also a barn owl, you know the kind with the spooky black eyes?"

"They all have spooky eyes, Felix. Birds are freakin' weird."

"Fine. And a great horned owl."

"And you think Kahan started including these all the way back to his first film?"

"Fuck, yes."

"Why?"

"Because I think he was preparing for an event that would arrive in the twenty-first century. Something that couldn't have been prophesized by any Aztec codex."

"It couldn't?"

"Impossible. The Aztecs prophesized the end of their own five great eras. By 2012, they are all done."

"And then what?"

"And then nothing. There was no more story to tell. Unless."

"Unless…"

"I don't know; I need to finish Kahan's full oeuvre. He was kind of harsh, wasn't he?"

"I would describe his movies more as intellectual and cold, actually."

"I want to keep working on your case. The Marlene Grue woman."

"It's probably closing soon. Can't say more than that, but don't bother."

"What is wrong with you, Nestor?"

"Nothing."

"You keep acting fucked up like this, I'm going to come personally to Queens and barf on your doorstep."

"You go ahead and try that," Nestor said. Felix considered

saying something else, something more, one more time, but instead, he let silence fill the space. And then he giggled out of nervousness. His laughter echoed; they said goodbye to each other.

Felix set the smartphone down and moved on to *The Thracian.*

## CHICAGO
## 7:00 PM ET

Goddammit, he had forgotten to eat. Felix considered ordering something from a delivery app, but he honestly couldn't really think about food. He had just taken in *The Thracian.* How had Kahan made such an ambitious movie at the fucking age of thirty-two? That was his own age.

"Thirty fucking two," Felix said, and he wrote down notes in his laptop. The words came fast and furious, and he did what he was always told not to do in his doctoral program: he began to combine other things he knew, using outside disciplines, including his occasional interest in agricultural anthropology, database theory, a touch of Marxist theory, and even his love of punk rock music from the mid '90s, to create a collage of ideas that was merely arriving like a colossal melt from a glacier.

Kahan had just been thirty two. And he made that behemoth of a movie. He had to share this insight with Wes.

*And oooo gurl, he had made two flicks in a row with Kirk Douglas.* "I am obsessed," he wrote into a snap of Kirk Douglas that he googled. He loaded the post with half a dozen ridiculous emoji and sent it to Wes.

Felix remembered that it was that very realization about Kahan's genius which had sent him into a deep state of depression and a feeling of inferiority. But today, as the Fall wind whipped and screeched against the window panes of the apartment, the thought no longer bothered Felix.

Instead, he was now just absorbed by his own curiosity, and the way in which joy flowed through his fingertips as he typed idea after idea in his laptop.

## 11:11 PM ET

The phone screen lit up in a bright shade of blue, and Felix shook his head.

"SHIT!" he spat.

He waited a moment, and he was connected.

"Felix," his mother said.

"Hi, Mom."

"I got your dad on speakerphone here," and a male grunt that sounded like "hiya" burst into the call.

Felix's stomach tightened. He had been waiting for this call for a long time. His right hand shook as he tossed the last Dorito from an open bag into his mouth.

"Mom, you know I hate speakerphone."

"You've never mentioned that before."

"I did. You just weren't listening."

His mother made a sniffing noise that he did not recognize, as if she had just smelled something funny coming from a trash can.

"You want to turn on your screen?" she said.

"No, I'm not into cameras at the moment. I mean, I am, but not these kind of cameras."

"What?"

"Never mind. I got something to tell ya, mom."

He had used those same words when he came out to her, more than a decade earlier. And he still felt breathless with fear, like he did back then.

"Okay, go on," she said.

"I don't want to teach."

"Did you get into some sort of tiff with the NYU people?"

"No, I mean I don't want to teach at all. Not anymore. And by the way, I didn't get the job."

"But all that time you invested in the PhD."

"You're contradicting yourself now. Just last week you said I could do something else, have another career."

"But what will your grandparents think?" she said.

*I have had enough of this bitch*, Felix thought. Just as soon as he heard those words in his own internal voice, he regretted it. He shouldn't think things like that about his own mother. But something inside him salvaged the words instead of erasing them. He went as far as visualizing the sentence. He saw it clearly spelled out in black ink on a white background. *I have had enough of this bitch.*

"I will not be a trophy for you anymore, until you see me fully."

"Felix, what is wrong with you?"

Though Felix had dug deep for bravery, he didn't have the

courage to keep up this fight. Because he knew there was more coming. And he wanted to focus on one thing at this moment.

"I am fully adult, and you always said you kept things frugal so I would learn how to do things on my own."

The silence on the line really hurt, but Felix had to say that. He knew his mother was crying, even if he couldn't hear sobs.

"And in any case, I'm going to take care of myself now."

"You have no sense of propriety, Felix," his mother said, and there it was, the beast that lived inside of her, the woman who never really had wanted to have children, but who felt she had a lot to prove to the world.

"I'm just as upset as you are, Mom."

"Don't tell me how I am."

"And Dad, I love you too. But I need to take some time to myself."

*Dad's gonna stay quiet again, like a coward.*

"I am listening to you, son," his dad said, and Felix felt a wave of shock. . He may not be standing up for Felix with ferocity, but his father's statement also contradicted the strict tone his mother usually set in these types of conversations.

This was good enough for now. Felix said goodbye, and hung up the phone. When the texts arrived from his mother afterward, he deleted all of them without reading them.

He was shaking all over, but he pressed Play on *The Thracian,* and he watched the last ten minutes. When he was done, he laughed, googled a dozen or so articles about what he had just seen, and began to open the next disc in his queue. At that moment he decided he wanted to ration the movies out of a bit, so instead of playing the film, he went to bed and slept.

# DAY 10
# THURSDAY OCTOBER 30, 2025

## MANHATTAN
## 1:15 PM ET

Nestor sat on a bench for hours in Central Park, waiting for some type of inspiration, but the truth was the he didn't know how to his spend free time. He bit his nails. He realized that he had forgotten to give himself his weekly shot of testosterone. His mother rang several times on the phone, and he saw fifteen notifications from work on his email account. He blew out a gush of air through his lips.

"Fuck," he said.

He hated this expanse of time, the way it crawled.

## CHICAGO
## 6:45 PM ET

Felix had watched *Lepidoptera* while he skimmed a copy of the novel *Lolita* from his days as undergrad at University of Chicago. He had been enthralled not by the script or the actors but instead, by the camera work of Samuel Kahan's direction, which was just as perverse and brilliant as Nabokov's book had been.

Once the driver delivered his pizza, Felix had moved on to

*Momma Do You Think They'll Break My Balls?*, a satire about a dictator with a loose nuke finger, who was basically the same as the dictator who called himself President in the White House in 2025. Felix laughed with heart, even through the tragic ending of the film, and he wondered how Kahan had managed to switch to comedy after such serious films as *Lepidoptera* and *The Road to Troy*.

Police sirens screamed through the neighborhood, and Felix checked his phone for local updates. Several people had been injured in a robbery on Ashland, and later that day, a massive protest would take place in Millennium Park. It would be the first time the city allowed a protest in the park since the Millennium Riot. Halloween was just two days away, and Felix looked out the slats of his apartment across the street. The Mexican families in the courtyard apartment directly across the street had decorated the windows full of orange pumpkins and witches. Propped up in the middle, he spotted an odd decoration: A giant papier-mâché macaw, decorated with red and blue feathers so brilliant, they looked as if they were made of metal. Its beak was closed, but its eyes were open, bedazzled like a nightmarish drag queen creation. The five-foot figure was probably a piñata, but wow, was it sculpted. It stared across the way at Felix, still as stone.

He returned to the mattress, masturbated, ate some more pizza, and dove into *Xenogenesis: Her Brood*.

## MANHATTAN
## 7:00 PM ET

The cathedral swallowed Nestor, and he took a pew near the front. Nestor hadn't attended mass at St. Patrick's in more than ten years. He took communion, and as he waited for the rest of the congregation to do the same, he pulled out a kneeler and reflected.

He looked up at the gothic splendor of the interior of the cathedral, and he marveled at the kaleidoscopic effect of the colored glass. Behind him, above the organ, the glass radiated out farther, like a star going super nova. As Nestor took in the prisms of colored light from the windows, he felt a distinct presence behind their surface, as if something was watching him.

Each of the the panes of glass—colored blue, red, indigo and gold,—were like eyes. And if he counted all of them, there were literally hundreds of them, staring at him, as if someting on the other side were trying to come through.

He did not panic. Instead, he turned around, genuflected, and went back to thoughts about good health for his mother and a wish to not be broke for himself. And in that last fraction of a second before he finished meditating on life, he also wished for God to give Felix some peace. He hadn't thought much about Felix, except for when he had called to talk, and boy, had he felt lucky to get the call. If God was out there, he wished for him to take care of Felix Calvo.

The priest concluded mass, and the congregation of New Yorkers, plus a handful of tourists, exited the church.

When Nestor turned around in the pew to exit, he gasped.

Up above the organ, set into a giant wheel of artistry and decadence, the stained-glass panes blinked in unison, as if some entity from another place had taken a pause to examine him better. He heard a series of clicking sounds, and he glanced to see if the other church goers heard them, but it seemed no one did. The windowpanes blinked again, and the colors in the glass changed in hue and luminosity in freakish, garish colors. They blinked again, and Nestor remembered exactly where he had seen those hundreds of eyes before.

When he walked out of the church and took the wide steps to reach the street level, Nestor turned his face up toward the sky, expecting to see a smoke owl, somewhere up above.

All he saw were a few threads of pale clouds, and the lights of the city.

## CHICAGO
## 11:48 PM ET

Felix wept at the end of *Xenogenesis*.

He glanced at the tiny eyelet of the camera on his smartphone, and he wondered how such a tiny thing could make a film so grandiose, so much like a universe into itself. He had never read Octavia Butler's novel, so he downloaded it from a torrent, and he started to read. Every once in a while he would replay the film to match scenes from the book, and he marveled at how different the movie and the book were from each other.

# DAY 11
# FRIDAY OCTOBER 31, 2025

## QUEENS
## 4:22 PM ET

Nestor threw up in the toilet for the fourth time, and he noticed there were traces of blood in his vomit. He had never been this hungover, but for the first time last night, the alcohol had masked the sense of despair that shook him to the very core.

He wiped his mouth, and without washing his hands, he injected himself with testosterone. Who cared if he got infected? Not him. The face that stared back at him in the mirror was hollowed out, gray.

He took a swig off a bottle of beer. Goddammit, he reeked of piss and puke. What a sad cliché, he tought. All detectives ended up being the same, at the end of the day.

He had sworn he would never drink like this again. He belched and downed the bottle.

He picked up the phone, and he called her. He knew it was a bad idea, but the fact that he had nursed his hangover with more liquor let Nestor's impulses take over.

"Hello?"

"Clara."

"Who is this?"

"Miss Montes, I am not sure if you remember me. I am Detective Buñuel."

"Of course. I don't forget."

He was nervous suddenly, at a loss for words.

"I have a colleague who's also an academic — who posed a

provocative idea to me recently."

"Okay, go on."

"That appropriation can't really happen."

"Well, he's wrong," she said.

"But Clara, what if a person who, let's say, wasn't of Mexican origin could invoke something sublime but also terrifying out of the cultural past of Mexico?"

"That person would be a damn thief, unless he was Mexican."

"What if he was half-Mexican?"

"Are you trolling me, Detective?"

"I'm sorry; I digress."

"What else, Detective?"

"Would you go out to dinner with me?" Nestor slurred.

The line stayed silent.

"I would *never* date a cop," she said.

He hung up the phone, and he went back into the toilet to vomit again.

## CHICAGO
## 6:45 PM ET

Felix showered, and he wrote more notes, retracing his steps from the day.

He had watched Kino Ludovico and cringed through every scene of rape, torture, and government-induced conditioning. When he was done with the film, he had decided that though things looked different in terms of fashion and technology, the world he was living in was not all that different from the horrors of *Kino Ludovico*.

He had also re-watched *9 Lords of Night*, and this time, he saw even more birds in the frames of the movie, hidden in tree branches, or woven into tapestries on the walls. He even saw a bird in the dripping white wax from the candles.

He had watched *The Marsten House* next, and he had to pause several times because he was simply too afraid. No one, not even Wes, had warned him that a vampire movie could scare him so badly. But he made it through the movie, and when he was done, he wrote more notes. His hands hurt from typing at the keyboard, but he did not care.

He loaded *Hasford and the Body Count* next, and he fell into a fictional Vietnam—into emotions from the characters that seemed hard and as painful as anything from the real world.

## CHICAGO
## 10:45 PM ET

Felix arrived at the Music Box Theater and bought a ticket for *ØIE*.

He took a seat in the middle of the cinema, trying to approximate the place where Marlene Grue had sat before she was killed, but he felt frustrated. He really needed to do this in Manhattan and not in Chicago.

The lights went down and the film started.

# DAY 12
## SATURDAY NOVEMBER 1, 2025

**QUEENS**
**3:00 PM ET**

Nestor tried writing, but he failed miserably. The words were gone.

He did accomplish, however, a significant task. He logged into the police database and pulled up the cloned copy of Marlene Grue's phone. Using MUNINN, he finally got into her camera roll.

He didn't think he would find anything, and at first, he didn't. There were just lots of photos of nieces, food selfies, and the occasional photo of Marlene Grue in department-store mirrors, trying on skirts and bras, her face a beauty worthy of a master painter's brush, the eyes distant, and isolated.

He recovered images that she had trashed. He sorted through 300 of them, and there, near the end, a single photo caught his attention.

Marlene Grue and Bryan Berger, in love, posing for the camera, and a look of infatuation and levity turning Marlene's gorgeous face from just pretty into the face of a true natural beauty, a splendid image of womanhood.

So, they had been lovers.

Nestor knew he should let the FBI team know right away, but instead, he walked down to the hipster bar down the street and ordered a beer and a chaser. He could always send that info on Monday. The police had their killer, after all. Marlene's other life, her secret life, was something that he wanted to respect and honor at this moment.

Nestor's smartphone bulged and beeped. Smith's photo appeared on the glass, announcing his phone call.

"Nestor, it's me." Smith said.

"I know."

"What have you been doing with yourself?"

"Things. Keeping busy."

"Don't bullshit me."

"What do you want?" Nestor said. It hurt to talk to his captain this way, but he was in no position to talk about the Grue case, or his retirement. Nestor wished he could punch a wall, rake his hands on glass, spit fire and get some sleep, all at once.

"I am calling with good news. The Valadez court ruled in your favor. You're cleared."

Nestor pressed his lips together and stared out into the valley of ice that had formed on his streets. "Fuck," he said, and he let a long breath out.

"We have all been there, Nestor. We use force on suspects. It's part of our jobs."

"I know," Nestor said. "But nothing is ever that simple."

"You sound as if you actually wanted to be liable for millions of dollars, Nestor."

"Fuck off."

"Take it easy on the drama. It's behind you. We owe nothing to the family now. He was a criminal."

Nestor wanted to reach through the wireless connection and choke Smith and his politics, his maneuvering, his silky voice. But he didn't.

"I gotta go, okay?"

"I'll reach out soon."

Nestor shut off the connection and walked out of his apartment and into the street without putting on his coat and gloves. He punched a mound of ice until his knuckles bled and his forearms went pink from the cold.

## QUEENS
## 11:59 PM ET

Nestor lay in bed, and darkness filled the room.

He opened his eyes, and he felt the air vibrate for a moment. The door to the room was shut. He heard a soft noise, and the door creaked open.

A human figure, hunched over and shrouded in black shadows, entered the room. Nestor tried to move, but he was frozen as he lay in bed. He tried to scream, but no words came out.

The figure moved slowly, as if it knew this house, and as if it knew Nestor very, very well. It pulled back a hood from its head, and an old face, toothless, stared at him. It hummed a soft tune to himself and approached the bed.

Nestor tried to scream again, but nothing came from his throat and lips.

The figure's white face melted into a blood-red mask, and the black robe that the figure was wearing squeaked. Nestor recognized the material of the black hood. It was skin, black as ebony. The robes were made of human skin.

The old man leaned in close and put his arms around Nestor's neck. He squeezed with the strength of a thousand men.

Nestor bolted upright on his queen mattress, and he shook his body violently. This time, he could scream.

"No!" he shouted over and over, and when he looked around, he realized he had only dreamed the figure clothed in a robe of black skin.

# DAY 13
## SUNDAY NOVEMBER 2, 2025

**QUEENS**
**6:00 PM ET**

Nestor showered and shaved his beard off. The face before him was still Nestor, but it felt good for a change to be a little different.

He glanced at the calendar on his wall. Today was the second day of Día de Los Muertos, and he probably should have put together an offering for his loved ones, but lately, all he could think about was work and how to finish out his last days at the station with some dignity.

From the front of the apartment, a hard *clank* rang out, as if someone had dropped an appliance in the hallways of the apartment building. He suddenly got a very bad feeling in his stomach, and he remembered the nightmare that he had last night.

He grabbed his holster and pulled out his gun. He turned off the safety, and holding the grip with both hands, he pointed the firearm forward, letting the barrel of the gun follow his sightline. If there was an intruder in the apartment, Nestor was going to show no mercy.

He crept along the wall and hid himself around the corner from the door. Someone was turning the key in the lock.

When the door creaked open, Nestor turned on his heels and faced the doorway. "Police!" he shouted, and prepared to fire.

The figure in the doorway fell to the ground and screamed. Nestor recognized the hoodie and the hands right away.

"Nice fucking greeting!" Felix shouted. He was breathing hard but smiling from ear to ear. "Wanted to give you a belated trick or treat."

"Motherfucker, I almost killed you!" Nestor said and yanked Felix up by the collar. "How the hell did you get in?"

Felix held up a pair of keys. "I like to take things from houses of people I like."

Nestor gritted this teeth, dropped his shoulders, and gave Felix a long hug.

"You're a good friend," Felix said casually, and Nestor only hugged him harder.

"Okay, now I am uncomfortable, Uncle Nestor," Felix said, and let out wild laughter. Nestor pulled away and brought his friend into his apartment.

"Why are you here?"

"I want you to give me a job. Any job. Organizing your book stuff, or painting your house, or running errands. At least until I get a job here in the city."

"That's a big ask."

"You're a big man."

"Okay, you want to butter me up with compliments, I get it. Appeal to my vanity."

"What is this?" Felix said, flipping over a card he picked up from the counter.

"Put that back."

"12.7.19.14.11, NO LONGER INVISIBLE," said Felix as he read aloud from the card.

"Puttock sent that to me at the station."

"Get the fuck out. Really?"

"Really."

"This means he was trailing you, watching you as he did the killings."

Nestor coughed and leaned over the kitchen counter, letting his muscular arms support him. "I think that he was actually watching me a long time ago. Maybe as far back as the Bowery murders."

"What makes you say that?"

"Felix, I got the chills when I looked into his eyes. He was both intelligent, deranged, and something else."

"Why would he follow you for such a long time?"

Nestor shrugged, and a chill ran down his spine. He honestly didn't know how, or why Puttock would track him, but Delia and Agent Ruiz had confirmed it: Puttock's writings, his exegesis, mentioned Nestor by name several times among its thousands of printed pages. Nestor could taste something worse than fear now. He could taste dread.

Felix shook his head and smiled.

"Well that only confirms it, Nestor. You and I have a job to do."

"Oh, do we?" Nestor said.

"We have to discover what the hell a Rift is, and what these gates are all about. And we find out why Puttock was crushing on you for years."

"And you think I'm just going to say yes to your proposal?"

"I actually think you might say no, to be honest. But according to those two, you're going to say yes. They say it's already flowing in time."

Felix pulled up the blinds that looked out into Nestors' street. Night and darkness had already fallen onto Queens, but two massive birds clung to the rooftop across the street from them. The largest one measured about 12 feet in height, and it stared out through empty black eyes, while clinging to the roof with brown human hands tipped with claws. The other was about half its height, but its four star-filled eyes shimmered and fluttered with impossible swirls of light. They seemed oblivious to the activity below on the street.

"They say only we can see them. For now," Felix said.

"This can't be," Nestor said."

"Don't know, you actually seem happy to see them."

"They are terrifying."

"I know."

"But where is the third?"

"That's your favorite, isn't it?"

"Shut up. Is Tecolotl here?" Nestor said.

"No. It went to find someone else in the city who he said is going to help us. Someone named the Wanderer, Collider."

"How do you know that name? It's what the Tecolotl called me."

"I was just about fifty miles away from the city when I lost control of the car on the ice. Slid into a ditch. The two creatures outside pulled me out, and they gave me a debriefing. And you see, I am supposed to be here, in this city, after all. They said I am The Collector."

The two creatures took flight into the night, dissolving into the air.

"And who is this Wanderer we are supposed to find?"

"Someone who can help. So, you're in, right, Nestor?"

Nestor thought about what Felix was asking; at the same time, he took out leftovers from the fridge and bottles of beer. When he looked at the sad, stale ingredients, he put them back in the fridge.

"Come on; you can tell me over ramen. You like ramen?" Nestor said as he slipped on his coat.

Felix nodded, and it was in that moment in which the last purple ray of dusk filled the tiny apartment in Queens and turned the room into a bright sanctuary. Nestor had never seen such a color in his life before. It was richer than the color of berries, and more lush than the purple back of an Amazonian scarab. It was in that moment in which time felt as if it had not just suspended itself, but it started moving in new directions. Nestor savored the brief and temporary burst of joy.

## ABOUT THE AUTHOR

Cesar is the author of the The Coil book series, including *13 Secret Cities*. He is also the author of the *How to Kill a Superhero*, which he writes under the pen name Pablo Greene. He is the director of the short film *Beyond Built*.

# THE COIL SERIES CONTINUES

The third volume in the Coil Series will release in 2020 from Solar Six Books. For more information and to sign up for updates, visit CesarTorres.me. You can also get exclusive previews of the new books in the series by becoming a subscriber at Patreon.com/CesarTorres.